André Romijn

Hidden Harmonies: the Secret Life of Antonio Vivaldi

Dedicated to Marieke

First published 2008 by Roman House Publishers Ltd.

Original title: Het geheim van Antonio Vivaldi
                 Translated by Kate Ashton

Cover: Portrait of an unknown lady,
                 by Maurice Quentin de La Tour

Coverdesign: Martijn Brinks, APR Group BV -
                 Amersfoort, The Netherlands

www.antoniovivaldi.co.uk

ISBN 978-0-9554100-1-7

Music, when soft voices die,
Vibrates in the memory,
Odours, when sweet violets sicken,
Live within the sense they quicken.

Rose leaves, when the rose is dead,
Are heaped for the beloved's bed;
And so thy thoughts, when thou art gone,
Love itself shall slumber on.

Percy Bysshe Shelley, 1792–1822

The Republic of Venice of the eighteenth century still employed a calendar other than the "modern" version introduced by Pope Gregory XIII in 1582. The Venetian New Year began on 1st March. For example, according to the original Venetian calendar (*more veneto*) 1st February 1710 is 1st February 1709 *more veneto*. For the benefit of today's reader the modern calendar has been used throughout.

Prologue

Turin, February 1929

'Who in the name of heaven is Vivaldo?' inquires Filippo Giordano with slight impatience in his voice.

'Vivaldi,' corrects the man in a smart, perhaps slightly old-fashioned but still respectable tweed suit. He shifts rather uncomfortably on the chair that stands a shade too low before the impressive mahogany desk of Signor Giordano, adding, 'Antonio Vivaldi was an extremely gifted Venetian composer who lived during the first half of the eighteenth century.' He detects a spark of interest in the body language of the industrialist who had earlier declared himself to have only five minutes free to talk to Professor Alberto Gentili from the National Library of Turin.

Filippo takes a long pull on his cigarette and looks the musicologist astutely straight in the eye. He cannot remember ever having met the professor before but he seems a pleasant enough fellow. Rather naively dressed, but then what would one expect of an academic?

'How come then, Professor Gentili, that I have never heard of this VIVALDI?' Filippo makes sure to pronounce the name correctly this time.

Alberto Gentili knows Filippo to be a lover of classical music. The professor has encountered Giordano and his wife often enough at the Opera House. Not that Gentili knows the couple personally, for the Giordanos have their own box. A successful businessman and director of a factory, Filippo Giordano can afford the very best, whilst Gentili has to make do with a seat in the auditorium. Not that he minds. On the contrary! As a musicologist, Alberto most appreciates a performance from where he can best hear the music. He is sometimes invited through his work to listen to a performance from one of the galleries accommodating the richly decorated private boxes. But then he finds himself irritated beyond measure by the behaviour of the people up there, more interested in the latest gossip or the quality of the champagne – always, of course, flowing copiously – than the performance itself. The Giordanos are an exception. Although he has never shared a box with them, he can usually observe them from whichever one he is in and they are always listening attentively. The talk in the corridors is that they regularly host concerts in their sumptuous mansion far from the busy city centre of Turin, and that Signora Giordano in particular lends financial support to musicians whenever she can. Given all this, Professor Gentili cherishes high hopes of the present conversation. Clearing his throat softly, he takes a sip of water. He has politely declined the offer of coffee; over recent years it has given him heartburn.

He resumes his story. 'Well now, this Antonio Vivaldi has preoccupied me intensely over recent years. I will spare you the details, for you are a busy man. Suffice it to say I guarantee my words will be of interest to you!'

Filippo glances quickly at his watch, a stylishly designed Patek Philippe given him by his wife years before, and nods to Professor Gentili to proceed. As is his habit, the factory director plucks a cigarette from his silver cigarette case, then offers one to the professor.

'No, thank you. I don't smoke.'

Filippo frowns coldly, drawing together heavy eyebrows in which the first grey hairs are just becoming visible. He lights his cigarette, filling the room with the sharp aroma of Lebanese tobacco. With his first deep draw, fragile wreaths of smoke begin slowly to spiral up towards the high ceiling. Giordano leans back relaxed in his chair and gestures with his hand that Gentili should recommence his story.

'No one would blame you for never having heard of this composer. The name Antonio Vivaldi is long lost in the mists of time. Today only one or two people are familiar with his name and

6

some of his works. We still do not know exactly what and how much Vivaldi composed, but in recent years we have realised that his oeuvre must have been extremely extensive.'

'How did you reach this conclusion?' interrupts Signor Giordano. There is already more interest in his voice than at the outset of their interview.

'Ah. Call it luck, call it God's will,' smiles the professor. 'It all began a couple of years ago, in the autumn of 1926 to be precise, when our library received a request to value a collection of manuscripts and books. It concerned a collection from an old monastery in Monferrato; the order wanted to sell the documents to fund some renovation work. It immediately became clear that the portfolio largely comprised musical scores, so it was of the greatest interest to me. I have, in fact, for years been searching for the lost music archives of the Orchestra of the Court of Savoy, once resident here in Turin. As you are probably aware, the Court of Savoy at one time withdrew to Sardinia so as to stay out of the hands of Napoleon. According to tradition, the music archive was too bulky to take with them and it was thus decided to hide it somewhere secure. This was so thoroughly achieved that the archive has, alas, never since been found. You may imagine how excited both the director of the library, Luigi Torri, and myself were about the collection now offered us. Might this be part of the Savoy archive? What I discovered were indeed all musical compositions. Much work by another composer, Alessandro Stradella, but also fourteen volumes consisting of original work by Antonio Vivaldi. This last was most extraordinary, for all the manuscripts were original and annotated by Vivaldi himself. An absolute treasure-trove, and completely beyond the financial reach of our library. In the meanwhile there were other sharks in the ocean and we had to negotiate swiftly to ensure that the collection remained intact and did not become disseminated amongst hundreds of antique-dealers. That would only increase the risk of this music once more being lost, buried in the dark and dusty depths of private collections.'

'But what's so special about this collection, or about the music of Vivaldi?' Filippo once more breaks in upon the professor.

'Ah, it is a pity you missed the concert last year in January. Then I wouldn't have to use all these inadequate words. You'd have experienced for yourself what I mean.'

The manufacturer stubs his cigarette out in the ashtray, stands up and walks over to one of the high windows overlooking the valley; just visible in the distance is the spire of the *Mole Antonelliana* that for decades has dominated the centre of Turin. The chill February wind sends sheets of rain rattling against the panes. Filippo recalls all too well the reason for his absence; how about a year ago he and his wife fled the cold winter months for weeks aboard a luxurious cruise ship on the Nile. He remembers the languorous upstream voyaging, the slightly faster glide back downstream.

This had not been a flight merely from winter weather. It had also been to forget. To vanquish the joyful little voice of Renzo that had seemed always to fill every corner of the house. Renzo, their beautiful son; so mischievous and adventurous, and taken from them so cruelly. Yes, their home is quiet these days, deathly quiet. The fever had been prolonged and, despite the ministrations of the best doctors, still held the child in its murderous grip; until his tiny body could hold out no longer and, with a barely audible sigh, one almost of relief, succumbed. Renzo's life, hardly begun, was over.

It was the most dramatic event of his life so far and Filippo had at the time not known, and still cannot imagine, how to cope with his wife's grief. A long holiday abroad had not had the desired effect. Once back, the house was as silent as ever and still forlornly haunted by bittersweet memories.

Filippo takes a deep breath and turns his back on the rain. 'I'm sorry,' he says, 'I was away at the time. It seems I missed something quite special. Tell me, Professor Gentili, what sort of music did this Vivaldi compose?'

'It might be better to ask what sort he didn't!' retorts Alberto, smiling broadly. 'Church music, concertos, operas, you name it. And, what is more, this man was an innovator, both in terms of composition and in the use of instruments.'

'Mm, interesting.' Filippo seats himself on the edge of his desk and elegantly helps himself once more from the silver case. Tapping his cigarette thoughtfully on his left hand, he looks for a moment as if he is considering the pros and cons of lighting it. 'Professor Gentili, I should like to come back to something you mentioned earlier. You said there were not enough funds available to your library for you to be able to purchase this collection. But may I deduce from the fact that a concert has taken place that you somehow managed to gather together enough resources to put on the table?'

'Yes and no,' responds Alberto, shifting himself into yet another position on the impossible chair. 'Thanks to the enormous financial support of the wealthy stockbroker Signor Foa, the library is now the rightful owner of this collection.'

'My congratulations!' offers Filippo with feeling. 'But what do you expect of me? It is good to hear your news, but you must have some other reason for this appointment? The door opens suddenly and Alberto Gentili recognises the director's rather sombre secretary.

'Francesco?' Giordano exclaims, as if amazed at the interruption.

'Your next appointment has been waiting for some time,' Francesco announces officiously. His tone is almost a snarl. He gives Professor Gentili a disparaging glance, as though he were some sort of intruder in his sanctuary. Filippo quickly surveys the agenda placed on his desk for him earlier this morning, as every day, by his secretary.

'Five more minutes, Francesco,' he orders. The gloomy apparition is already nodding in assent. 'Of course.' Before closing the door soundlessly behind him he casts a final withering glance at the professor responsible for disrupting his diary.

'You heard, Professor, five more minutes. But my next appointment is someone from the government, and he can wait. How can I be of service to you?' Filippo has in the meantime resumed his formal place behind the desk. Professor Gentili attempts to shift his chair nearer the desk and leans across its leather-clad surface conspiringly.

'The collection is not complete,' he says, now almost in a whisper. 'Once we had begun making an inventory we quickly realised that this must represent only half of an enormous collection. You can imagine the hunt for the missing manuscripts that will get underway the minute this becomes generally known. And, lastly, there are plenty of dealers around who were deeply disappointed when the whole of the present collection came into the possession of the library.'

Giordano nods his understanding.

'We have been busy over recent years tracing the other half of the collection and, as you will understand, all this has to be done with the utmost discretion. That's why we have organised no more concerts or put out any other sort of publicity connected with Vivaldi. He has to remain "buried" for a while longer.'

'And has your search borne any fruit?' asks Filippo with real interest. He has by now also adopted Alberto's pose of mutual confidentiality.

'Oh yes it has, thank God! It was not easy, but absolutely worth all the effort. I have been able precisely to trace the other half of the collection and now we have arrived at the point at which I must appeal to your charitable generosity.'

Sensing the way the discussion is heading, the manufacturer leans back in his chair, bringing to an abrupt end the atmosphere of intimacy established between the two gentlemen.

'The documents that complete the collection are presently in private hands. It looked as though a purchase would prove impossible, but the owner is showing increasing signs of agreeing to a sale. However, it is the finances that are the problem. The library holds insufficient funds, and that goes for the local authorities, too. Our director has even contacted central government, but it seems Mussolini has other priorities just now.'

'That's absolutely right,' replies Giordano with irritation. 'Look what happened last week. A pantomime treaty containing the so-called ratification of the Holy See, wherein Roman Catholicism is elevated to the status of the national religion of Italy. Ha! Nothing but a publicity-stunt on the part of Mussolini to increase his sphere of influence among the people. But what nobody realises is quite what a costly joke this is. In my view, Mussolini has bought the Pope, despite official declarations to the effect that the state wants to compensate the Vatican for all the church property we once appropriated.' He slams his fist down on the desk, concluding furiously, 'Stuff and nonsense!' Professor Gentili recoils in shock, particularly since Signor Giordano has risen to his feet, gesticulating threateningly with his right index finger in the air.

'The only thing Il Duce has assured himself of is Vatican support for his administration! Do you know, Professor, this country is slowly going down the drain like a lost traveller sinking in a quagmire? Everyone follows along behind Mussolini like sheep but not one of them sees as far as the end of their own nose. And I tell you it is industry – the thing this country should prize most highly of all – which has to pay for his 'administration'. You are about to ask me for money. But if 'our leader' carries on the way he is going I have to ask myself seriously how much more room there still is for 'charitable generosity', as you put it just now.'

Professor Gentili feels a first hint of concern. Politics have never interested him, but he knows the economic situation in the country is far from rosy, and donations for cultural acquisition are low on the current list of priorities for industrialists. It is time to play his last card. The chair he has been occupying all this time has finally become too much for him and he gets to his feet. He can now look Signor Giordano straight in the eyes; the two men are of equal height, though Filippo is clearly more heavily built.

'I don't think we need worry, Signor Giordano. Politicians come and go like leaves on the trees. History has taught us that. It should not surprise me if twenty-five years from now Mussolini were long forgotten. But who will certainly not be forgotten ...' the professor pauses significantly ...

'Ha!' interrupts Giordano with a laugh, 'Antonio Vivaldi!'

But the professor is not laughing; indeed, his expression is grave as he softly replies, 'Vivaldi, yes, possibly. But also Renzo Giordano!'

The director stares back at him half-stunned. At his right eye he feels the involuntary tic that always comes when he is under pressure.

'What did you say?' he asks in amazement.

'I named your deceased son, and the possibility of making Renzo immortal. I know for certain that this way you would be doing your wife a great service and an honour.'

'But I don't understand what you mean,' stammers Filippo.

'Signor Giordano, this collection, this music carries the potential once more to conquer the world. Your name and that of your son will thus never more be forgotten; they will be synonymous with that of this great composer.'

It looks for a moment as if Giordano can glimpse the future, for he smiles fleetingly at this alluring idea. But then he shakes his head. 'Nonsense, Professor. No one would take on such a proposal.'

'There is a precedent,' Professor Gentili volleys back at him. 'The first half of the collection is in fact financed by Roberto Foa in memory of his son Mauro, who died very young.'

'I see that you have done your homework, Professor.'

Gentili continues unperturbed. His arms thrown wide in an all-embracing gesture, he declaims, "The Mauro Foa and Renzo Giordano Collection". That is how our library will designate it.. What is more, a suitable vignette will be designed for the new bindings, incorporating an image of your son. *In Memoria Di Renzo Giordano*.'

The professor folds his arms, giving the other man the chance to respond. Filippo's forehead is deeply furrowed as he gazes at the photograph of his son in its heavy silver frame upon his desk.

'What sort of sum are we talking about?' Giordano breaks the silence.

Professor Gentili raises his shoulders. 'We are still in negotiations, Signor, but what interests me right now is whether or not you agree to the idea.'

Francesco has meanwhile appeared in the doorway again.
Filippo walks up to the professor and, already gently shaking hands goodbye, draws him towards the door. He thanks him for their discussion, and then pauses before finally letting the professor go.
'I would like to invite you to spend the weekend at our mansion,' he says. 'My wife would enjoy meeting you and I am quite sure she will be interested in what you have to say.' He turns to his secretary, 'Francesco! Ensure that transport is arranged for the professor, and send in my next appointment in a minute or so.' Giordano again shakes the professor by the hand, heartily this time. Then shuts the door behind him and turns back to his desk.

The professor takes his coat and hat from the still hostile-looking Francesco, who informs him coolly that his taxi is waiting below. As he swiftly descends the marble staircase, Alberto Gentili wonders whether or not he should rejoicing. Will Giordano be prepared to unite the two halves of the collection and so preserve it?

Filippo Giordano stares transfixed at the photograph of his son. Might this be a way, after all, to alleviate a little of his his wife's grief? He has little time to consider, for Francesco ushers in the government representative. Giordano takes an immediate dislike to this stunted, balding figure: a stereotype of the classical accountant. In an unpleasantly sour little voice, and without deviating for a moment from his mission, the man announces that the majority of revenue profits from Giordano's business are to be reserved for the new and self-evidently promising plans of Il Duce. It is naturally a great honour for this factory to be allowed to make such a contribution.

Hands behind his back, Filippo stands at the window watching the professor's departing taxi. The bland drivel emanating from the government representative barely reaches his consciousness. Filippo smiles to himself. 'The time has come,' he muses, 'to allow Antonio Vivaldi to return to life. In glory and in commemoration of my son, Renzo Giordano!'

1

Venice, Epiphany, 1709

It is bitterly cold and the night unusually dark. Despite *carnevale*, it is also remarkably quiet. Even the usual soft splash of water against the quay has been numbed into silence by the chill. Over the past two days an icy north-easterly wind has frozen solid the entire lagoon and all the canals in the Republic. Now that the lacerating *Bora* has died down, a clammy blanket of mist shrouds the terracotta roofs of *La Serenissima*, suffocating the brilliant and most serene Republic of Venice, deadening her streets with unprecedented cold.

The priest's breathing is heavy and irregular, like that of a wounded beast. The world spins about him, a sensation that only worsens when he closes his eyes. He is no longer aware that in his search for home and longing for the safety of his warm bed he has arrived for the third time at the same bridge. He has already vomited twice this evening, all over his specially bought cloak. Even this he hardly notices. Blind drunk, he totters on the bottom step of the bridge with glazed, unfocused eyes, unconsciously pressing his left hand to his painful chest. Then, as if having arrived at a momentous decision, he takes a step forward and stumbles. Before he knows what is happening he has fallen, groaning, to the ground, rolled from the bridge and landed with a crash on the ice. Like a drowning man he sinks into unconsciousness.

The couple of passers-by who have crossed the bridge in the last hour and a half have completely ignored him, perhaps themselves too far gone to notice the comatose form. It is well past midnight when quick footsteps again approach. Their flickering torches do not provide enough light for the two half-running men to inspect all the porches and doorways of the narrow streets.

'Father!' shouts the younger man in shocked tones as he reaches the bridge. 'What is it?' calls the other man, a slight tremor in his voice.

The boy holds out his torch to illuminate his brother, spread-eagled on the ice. 'My God,' stammers his father, 'has he frozen to death?'

Tomaso has already jumped onto the canal and is slithering and sliding his way towards his brother. He holds the torch nearer the motionless man and leans over to see if he is breathing. A filthy stench of alcohol and vomit hits him in the face and the younger man recoils in frightened revulsion. 'Bloody hell!,' he exclaims, pulling a face and gasping for air. In the meanwhile his father has followed Tomaso onto the ice. Giambattista Vivaldi dives forward to press his ear against his son's unconscious lips. Tomaso gazes at his brother, holding his nose in disgust. For some seconds all is still. Giambattista mutters something and undoes the priest's cloak, pulling open his tunic so roughly that the top two buttons fly off. Worming his fingers quickly beneath the tunic the father feels the warmth of his son's inebriated body. 'Thanks be to God and Mother Maria,' he mumbles, 'he's still alive!' Giambattista shakes his son's head back and forward and hisses his name. 'Hey, Antonio!... ANTONIO! Come on, wake up!'

A loud belch is the only response from his unconscious son.

'Damn it all, this won't do!' Giambattista's voice betrays a trace of the angry humiliation he feels rising in him. 'We'll have to carry him home, Tomaso. The whole neighbourhood will be awake soon, and that's all I need. Come on; let's get him on his side to start with. Then I'll carry him on my shoulders.' Tomaso props the torches against a wall and helps his father get the limp body of his brother up onto the wharf. Luckily Antonio is quite small of stature and his father is able to swing him up onto his shoulders like a sack of old rags. 'Show me the way home, Tomaso.' Antonio's younger brother again picks up the two torches, now almost extinguished; it doesn't matter, Tomaso knows the winding streets of this part of town like the back of his hand. To his father's great relief they meet no one they know, and after ten minutes' brisk march they are at their own *campo*. Before crossing the square Giambattista stops to glower about him. He doesn't want anyone to see them; certainly not that old gossip Gianatta, because then the whole neighbourhood will have something to talk about for the rest of the week. But the square is asleep, along with all its houses and their inhabitants. The icy cold has ensured that nobody has left his or her bed without good cause tonight. Giambattista crosses himself and lurches at a jog trot across the deserted square. One more corner and they will be safely home. Tomaso opens the door for his father and Giambattista hops inside like a rabbit escaping from a fox. The door is closed silently. Venice sleeps on.

There is music playing in his head, but it is not his music! On and on the rhythmic strumming of the harpsichord continues stubbornly hammering, only to make way now and then for a hellish pounding. It is as if a horde of German blacksmiths were beating simultaneously on an enormous anvil. Germans! A wave of memory rises in the clouded brain of Antonio Vivaldi. *Il Sassone*... a harpsichord, and... the image is gone again. The thumping in his head continues mercilessly, contorting his face with pain. Slowly his hands move to his ears in a crude attempt to stop the noise. It does no good. He tries with difficulty to open his eyes and, still hovering on the fragile cusp of drunken unconsciousness, rubs his temples, moaning. His breath is no less irregular and feverish. With every sigh his parched throat gets drier and it seems as if his tongue, already partially stuck to his cracked lips, will shrivel away forever. Bit by bit Antonio begins to realise that he is alive, and with every minute that passes he becomes more conscious of the pain. Once his eyes are open it is a while before he realises that he is lying in his own bed. The room is almost dark, but a strip of light entering through a chink in the blinds allows him to get orientated. His right arm waves wildly out of bed in its search for the tumbler of water that always sits next to him on the floor. After a bit he has a good hold of the tumbler and with a shaking hand can bring it to his mouth. But as he lacks the strength to lift his head off the pillow, half the water misses his mouth and goes over his shirt. The other half reaches his lips and tongue and he greedily gulps down the balsam, miraculously escaping death by choking. He puts the tumbler back, or rather it slips out of his hand and rolls across the stone floor. Antonio does not notice. He has lapsed back into his oblivion. Deep down somewhere inside him the steady jangling of the harpsichord goes on and on... Uggh... *Il Sassone!*

Chirping sparrows, the hoarse scream of a seagull and the cooing of doves foraging in the gutter. Thumping around in the house. A door slamming shut and the slow chiming of a church bell. Slowly Antonio becomes aware of the world around him following unperturbed its own rhythm. The music has gone from his head but the syncopated pounding continues unabated. He opens his eyes and sees in the twilit room the portrait of the Holy Maria, who today seems to look down upon him with disapproval. '*Domine... Domine...*' he murmurs, attempting to make the sign of the cross. He tries to summon together his thoughts. My God, he thinks, what have I done? He leans out of bed to get some water, but seeing the empty tumbler lying some distance away falls back on the pillows with a deep sigh. 'Oh, Mother Maria, have mercy upon me!' He touches his elbow, which still feels sore. As do his ribs on the left side. 'My God, what time is it? I can't stay lying here!' He pushes the blankets from him and swings his legs out of bed. The stone floor, so deliciously cool in summertime, is now ice cold. With another sigh he tries to stand, but as soon as he is upright the room begins to spin about him again. He takes a quick step forward and grabs hold with both hands of the table upon which stands a big porcelain ewer. Normally he would use warm to wash with, but now he doesn't care. He cups his right hand and splashes a little cold water on his face. The fresh feel of it does him good, and he guzzles a couple of big mouthfuls from his hand. The pale sunlight, its source not yet visible through the mist, blinds him; with a groan he pushes aside the wooden shutter and looks in the mirror. 'Mother Maria!' he exclaims, horrified. There is an enormous lump on his forehead. But that's nothing compared to his eyes, dull and lifeless as a drowned sailor's and afloat on thick, blue-grey bags that remind him of the dead fish on the market-stalls of the *Rialto*. An expression of hopelessness hangs about the slack mouth that is usually so shapely. Pushing back the red curls that he has to thank for his nickname of '*Il Prete Rosso*', 'the red priest', he rubs his brow. Despite his mere thirty-one years, he looks old, and oh, how he hates himself like this. Full of remorse, he shuts his eyes and turns away from the mirror.

'I have to get to work,' he slowly realises. But the moment he tries to stand straight the dizziness returns and a wave of nausea almost has him throwing up. Retching, he stumbles back to bed and falls in. Clinging as if to a lifeline, he holds onto the sheets and tries to take long, deep breaths and overcome the sickness. Through half closed eyes he can see his clothes lying in a crumpled heap in a corner. His beautiful cloak! He realises for the first time that he is only in his underwear and suddenly feels how cold it is. Pulling the blankets up over himself he racks his brains to recollect the events of the previous evening. He has no idea how or when he got to bed. Equally mysterious is the bump on his forehead and his bruised ribs. He turns carefully onto his back in an attempt to escape Maria's penetrating stare. The minute he closes his eyes, the giddiness comes back so he at once opens them again and peers upward at the beamed ceiling. At first the wooden rafters seem to be dancing, but each time he blinks they move more slowly, and finally assume their proper place. Only now can Antonio begin to order his thoughts. Fragments of the previous evening come back to him. Disjointed memories of the party, dancing, lots of happy people and wine, a great deal of wine. And the king of course, the king had been there; but there is something, someone else, a woman...! He closes his eyes and tries to picture her face. Instead, he sees a young man with an arrogant smile, an insolent grin. And then the music comes flooding back to him again. That music! The sound of the interloper! Fury arises inside him, accompanied by the cramping in his chest. Damn it all, it had been a terrible evening! When it should have been his own. His chance to show everyone that he, Antonio Vivaldi, reigned supreme!

Yes, now everything begins to fall into place. Oh, my God. What a disaster!

All the indications had pointed to a great breakthrough for him last night. So what had gone wrong? Vivaldi orders his thoughts, no mean task considering the unrelenting hammering in his head, and manages somehow to recover his memory, right back to the moment when it all began, just a couple of days ago. Last Sunday, to be precise.

Antonio sees himself again standing on the small podium, prepared for the start of his first motet. The little auditorium of the *Ospedale della Pietà* was, as usual, full to capacity. Just as the performance was about to begin there was some disturbance at the entrance and, under the direction of one of the governors of the *Pietà*, some of the audience had to make room for an extremely sumptuously attired gentleman and his entourage. Chairs were hastily shifted and one of the governors, Piero Frascari, had scurried up and winked at Vivaldi, who leant down irritably from the stage; he did not like untoward incidents during his performances. 'Don Vivaldi,' whispered Frascari excitedly, 'hold on just a moment until these people are seated. We are honoured by the presence of important guests this afternoon!' Vivaldi furrowed his brow and waited for the governor to offer further explanation. But the latter simply laid his finger on his lips and turned back to join the unexpected company. With no clue as to the identity of the newcomer, the priest turned his back contemptuously. What an hoo-ha, thought Antonio, casting a glance up at the *cantorie* where the inquisitive faces of the female musicians, the *Figlie di Coro*, peered through the wrought-iron balustrade trying to catch a glimpse of the goings-on below. A gesture from Vivaldi was enough to send them jumping back to their places before the governor behind him coughed, apparently to draw his attention to the fact that the unknown guest was now also seated. Turning a couple of seconds later to confirm that he might begin, Vivaldi had to suppress a laugh at the sight of the governor diligently waving his handkerchief. Vivaldi gave him an abrupt nod and signalled to the musicians. When all were ready he picked up his violin and drew a deep breath. Fine, thought the priest, we'll give our guest something to listen to! He placed his instrument under his chin and with a gracious sweep his bow settled upon the tense strings.

'*Grandioso! Grandioso!*' was the spontaneous cry as the final notes died away. The unknown visitor had stood up and was heading straight for Vivaldi, in his wake the governor. 'I am told you are the composer,' said the stranger in a distinctly foreign accent. His carnival mask hung daintily from the little finger of his left hand, planted firmly on his hip.

'Don Antonio Vivaldi. At your service, your Excellency.' Vivaldi gave a slight bow and descended from the podium. Now he was looking straight into the face of a tall man, done up in a magnificent wig that enhanced his height even further. The aristocratic figure had an enormous nose and a powerfully prominent chin. A rather cool expression played about his mouth, giving an initial impression of severity. But his moist eyes and slightly flushed cheeks clearly betrayed the soft side of this foreigner. 'We have enjoyed your compositions, and the remainder of the performance,' he said. 'Your choir,' he waved his right hand in the direction of the *cantorie*, 'is extraordinary, quite sublime.' The compliment delighted Antonio, who loved nothing more than to hear how people liked his music. But who was this man? Where did he come from? It was plain from his dress that he was extremely wealthy. Perhaps Antonio could interest him in the purchase of some of his compositions? The priest bowed once more. 'You are too kind, your Excellency. Might I on a future occasion dedicate a *concerto* in your honour and glory? Or is your stay in *La Serenissima* to be of too short duration?'

'A *concerto*?' The stranger looked pleasantly surprised and cast a quick glance around his masked entourage. They nodded in dumb acquiescence.

'A *concerto* dedicated to...? Vivaldi paused. 'My sincere apologies, your Excellency, forgive me. I have not in fact properly heard your name.'

'*Ach, so,*' the man paused significantly and the person standing at his left stepped forward and bowed to the priest. 'Don Antonio Vivaldi,' he declaimed in a remarkably deep voice, 'it is an honour to introduce you to... His Royal Highness Frederik IV, King of Denmark and Norway.' Antonio's heart missed a beat, but he tried to disguise his amazement. Falling at once upon his knees before the sovereign he stammered, 'your Excellency! Forgive me! Your most devoted and faithful servant offers you his true apologies for not having recognised your Majesty.' The king laughed and pointed out that this was hardly possible since the two had never before met. 'Don Vivaldi, the honour is all mine.' The priest again lowered his head. 'You will do us the great pleasure,' added Frederik IV enigmatically, 'of not divulging to anyone our true identity. For the duration of our informal visit to your lovely city we shall be known as the Duke of Olemburg. It is our desire to participate in your *carnevale* without the burden of formal duties.' Vivaldi made a third bow, his brain working feverishly. A king! Dedicate a *concerto* to him? I have pretty well an entire *opus* lying there finished. This is my chance!

Antonio cleared his throat discreetly. 'Your Excellency, Sire, your Highness. A *concerto* I would dedicate to a duke, but a king deserves nothing less than an *opus*! Next week a 'royal' concert is to be given in honour of the Feast of the Epiphany.' The priest gazed now almost beseechingly at the king. 'Your presence there and the dedication of my work to your Royal Highness will commit me for all eternity to prove myself your humble, devoted and obedient servant.' To underline his request Don Vivaldi made a sign of the cross whilst watching from the corner of his eye the reaction of the king. Just behind Frederik IV, he saw the face of the governor of the *Ospedale della Pietà* colour and it dawned on Antonio that he had violated every rule of protocol. Who was he to issue a concert invitation to a ruling head of state?

The person standing next to Frederik IV, he who had introduced Vivaldi to the king, now broke the silence. 'Thank you for your submission, Don Vivaldi,' he said concisely. The king gave a quick nod and turned away, leaving Vivaldi on his knees. 'Sire,' said the priest in farewell. But Frederik IV, King of Denmark and Norway, was by now far out of earshot and making straight for the exit where, already guessing who he might be, people stood aside to let him pass. Behind him shuffled Frederik's courtiers, among them a relieved Piero Frascari. As he passed Vivaldi the governor made sure to stick his finger in the air as final warning.

Silence descended upon the auditorium and Antonio Vivaldi got stiffly to his feet. All the excitement had brought back the pain in his chest and it hurt him to breathe. God was his only refuge in such moments. '*Domine*? What will the king think of me? Did I overstep the mark? But what a chance! It's too good to be true.' His second piece of work was almost ready for publication and thanks to this personal encounter he was able to dedicate his *Opus II* to none other than the King of Denmark and Norway! Mother Maria! What will my father think? I have to get home as fast as I can! The sounds of soft movement and feminine whispering reminded him that the musicians were still at their post upstairs in the gallery. Oh, my God! Completely forgotten! He duly thanked and dismissed the *Figlie di Coro* and, with his head in the clouds, walked quickly to the back of the hall.

'This is great news!' cried Giambattista Vivaldi, elated. He poured himself a glass of wine whilst Antonio cautiously tasted the hot chocolate made for him by his mother. Father and son had withdrawn together to their shared workroom on the ground floor of the moderately sized house, occupied for the past couple of years by the Vivaldi family. Before they moved in, this room had been a fish-shop and on hot summer days you could still smell it. But now a wood fire crackled in the hearth and, as always, the chimney was not drawing too well, so now and then the room filled with smoke. The shutters were usually left standing open all day, but the wind had changed direction this morning, bringing a sudden drop in temperature. The little mirrors behind the burning candles reflected their warm glow across an enormous work table covered with music paper and clean pages. At one corner lay piles of music neatly lined up and ready for collection. The cold had forced Giambattista to stop his copying work earlier than usual today; his fingers had become so stiff that he was no longer content with the notes they formed on the manuscript page. Giovanni Battista Vivaldi, better known as Giambattista, had a reputation to uphold. For many years now he had enjoyed a place among the undisputed best *copisti musica* in Venice and, self-critical as he was, he wished to keep it. 'You seem to have really moved the king with your music, my son. You're right, this is a chance in a million! It would be wonderful if Frederik IV came to the concert; that would show all the *Veneti Nobili* what sort of stuff you're made of. Fantastic!' He sniffed appraisingly at his wine, approved it and took a sip.

'I wonder what the *Congregazione*, the *Pietà* administrators, will make of it,' Antonio anxiously speculated. 'Piero Frascari clearly disapproved of my behaviour.' 'Don't you worry about him, son,' advised his father. 'That Piero has always been oversensitive. No doubt he feels he's been passed over, and so would I in his position. But I know the governors. If Frederik IV really does decide to come, they'll all be there, elbowing each other aside to make sure of a place next to him. And as for the monarch, well, that fellow Frederik IV could have done us the honour of leaving his winter weather back home in Norway,' he quipped, taking another mouthful before putting his wineglass down on the mantelpiece. Giambattista sat down beside Antonio, close to the fire, and rubbed his hands in the warmth. 'Brrr, it really is cold. How can a man be expected to think straight under such barbaric conditions?' Antonio, staring into the fire, seemed not to hear his father's words. He was wondering how long he had to get everything ready; could Bortoli get the work printed in time? And when was Frederik IV leaving for his homeland again? The more the composer thought about it, the more problems he saw looming on the horizon. He felt the old pain returning and sighed deeply. 'Are you all right, son?' asked Giambattista. 'Yes, everything's fine.' But even as he spoke Antonio was rubbing his sternum, a clear sign to his father that he was upset. 'Tell me, son, what is it that's bothering you?'

'Maybe I've been too impulsive, father. My work is far from ready. I'll have to find out how long Frederik IV is here for. Only then will I know for certain whether or not I will be able to present him personally with my *sonatas*.'

'Of course,' responded Giambattista, 'that speaks for itself. Do you have any idea how you would like to present the work? It could be a problem to get it printed in time. As you know, Antonio Bortoli is not so nimble these days. To be frank, his work isn't any the better for it either. Just this morning I was looking at some new stuff in from him and it was awful. There were smudged notes and in some passages I couldn't see if it was an A or a G. How can anyone read the music properly when it's in that state, let alone play it? If the printer rushes the job and makes a mess of it, we'll be left with a dilemma. You can't really present a king with work in that condition. But fine, if we run out of time I can make a really beautiful clean copy of your original, and if you give him that, with a hand-written dedication, you'll make an indelible impression on the king and everyone else too.'

'Yes, but that'll never be ready for next Sunday.' There was panic in Antonio's voice. 'I still have to write two *sonate* before the work is complete.'

'Well then, I'd get on with it, if I were you,' encouraged Giambattista. 'I'll drop in on Bortoli tomorrow morning. See if he can help us out. Come on; let's see how far you've got. Maybe I can give you a hand.'

Antonio finished his cup of chocolate and scratched his head. Giambattista poked the fire into life again and followed his son to the table, where together they pored over the manuscript in which Antonio had made a start on a new *Sonata da Camera*. The priest put all his concentration into the music, living it again, feeling where he wanted the piece to go. Without a word he picked up his pen and dipped it into the inkpot his father pushed towards him. After a moment's hesitation a first note appeared on paper, and then another, and another. Until a single fluent movement of his hand produced a torrent of notes capable of withstanding Giambattista's most stringent scrutiny. And the pain in the Antonio's chest was as good as gone.

That Sunday morning was colder than ever. Over the past few days the temperature had plunged below freezing every night and this morning again the sun had not had the strength to lift the mercury above zero. On his way to the *Pietà*, Antonio Vivaldi was assailed by the scent of freshly baked bread and *pìnza*, a cake that for a thousand years had been made especially for the Feast of Epiphany. Before entering the auditorium of the *Ospedale della Pietà* he paused for a moment on the quayside, pulling closer around him his *tabarro*, his beautiful new woollen cloak. The wind had died down but there was still a wild, razor-edged breeze. From where he stood he could see the Slavonic seamen and hear them swearing as they hacked away the ice from around the keels of their ships. He was more used to the sound of them singing at their work: lovely songs from their Dalmatian fatherland, sometimes sentimental, sometimes full of passion, but always a source of inspiration to him. Vivaldi had heard that the ice could be so powerful that it could crush even these great ships, so he understood why the men were labouring so furiously.

 His glance moved along the quay towards the place where muted morning sunshine shone upon the dome of *Santa Maria della Salute*. The landing stage was nearly deserted. Many skippers had taken their ships out early, apparently afraid of getting stuck, icebound in harbour for they did not know how long. Even on the *Riva degli Schiavoni* itself there was almost nothing going on. The unexpected cold was obviously keeping most Venetians at home. Beyond the moored cargo vessels and as far as the eye could see, the entire *Canale di San Marco* was frozen solid. Starving gulls flew screaming back and forth above the quay. There won't be much scavenging for you today, thought Antonio, filling his lungs with freezing air. He felt tense. This afternoon was the Epiphany concert and he was still not sure whether or not King Frederik IV would be there. Earlier in the week Antonio had asked another of the *Pietà* governors, Giacomo Faresinna, whether any more was known about the possible attendance of the King of Denmark and Norway. Faresinna had given Antonio a contemptuous look, as though he was not even worthy of a satisfactory reply. And the patrician had not been able to resist relaying how unimpressed the *Congregazione* had been with Vivaldi's forwardness the previous Sunday. The administrative authorities were very busy at present with the current festivities. 'But,' warned Giacomo, 'you will be hearing further from us about this matter, Vivaldi!' For once Antonio had held his tongue.

Normally it would have been Francesco Gasparini who, as *Maestro di Coro* of the *Pietà*, led the festival for Epiphany. But this year he had delegated the task to *Il Prete Rosso*. Over the past year the *Maestro* had offloaded other work onto Vivaldi's shoulders. The worst disaster that could befall him now was for the administration to recall Gasparini from his sabbatical. All the work of the past few days would then have been in vain. But there was no point in counting his chickens before they hatched. All his trouble would also be wasted should the king decide to put off his visit this afternoon. Vivaldi rubbed his sore chest. He would go indoors.

With plenty of time left before rehearsal began, he sat down in one of the places reserved for members of the *Congregazione* and their guests. Looking about him he could see nothing to indicate whether or not Frederik IV and his entourage were expected this afternoon. The rest of the hall was empty and the general public would, as always, remain standing. Vivaldi loved this place, even when it was unlit. He gazed, humming, up at the ceiling, at the paintings, each and every one of which meant so much to him. The work of Loth made him sad, but he adored that of Palma Giovane and especially that of Mazzoni. Despite the present cold the auditorium was an oasis to him. This, after all, was the space in which his music came to life, each piece for the first time!

Antonio was to include in today's programme his two best *sonate*, even though he had requested no official permission for this. They could always be dropped from the programme should King Frederik IV fail to appear.

Yesterday afternoon his father had attended the rehearsal and had clearly been impressed. Of course, Giambattista had his usual few critical remarks, and not without reason. Antonio agreed that the amendments he suggested greatly improved the whole. Both father and son had relinquished the idea of all twelve *sonate* being ready in time. Antonio was not satisfied with the last composition, and printer Bortoli had notified them that he had no time to spare for them over the coming weeks. Giambattista had made a superb copy of the first ten *sonate* and Antonio had composed a dedication in his best handwriting that could later be reproduced in the printed edition of his *Opus II*.

The silence was suddenly broken by the shrill tones of a young girl shouting 'Father!' and a roguish little face peeped round the doorpost. 'Father Vivaldi, we're ready for rehearsal,' she called again, more softly this time but with no less verve. As Antonio looked round she vanished as suddenly as she had appeared, the sound of her running footsteps growing fainter as she ascended the staircase. Vivaldi, rubbing his hands together to get the blood circulating, followed the echo at his own speed. The dress rehearsal went without a hitch. His ladies never let him down, and certainly not today, when the rumour was about that King Frederik IV might come this afternoon. The choir had been quite happy to run through the two extra *sonate*. Only the *Maestra*, the head of the *Figlie di Coro*, had looked somewhat askance. She knew this would mean trouble with the administrators.

Deep was Antonio's disappointment when the concert was about to begin and there was still no sign of blue blood. The hall was pretty full of people, many more than usual. In Venice a secret never remained a secret long, and obviously word had got out that there would be a king at the concert.

Vivaldi had delayed the start as long as possible. He had given the orchestra as much time as he decently could to tune their instruments, and then proceeded in a leisurely manner to resin his bow. But this did not please the audience and they had begun to get restless. King or no king, Il Maestro must begin! Halfway through the allegro, Antonio Vivaldi sensed the entrance of Frederik IV. Excited whispering, the rustling of cloaks and shuffling of feet told him enough; he did not need to turn his head. Only at the end of the first concerto did Don Vivaldi turn and bow deeply to his audience and, as soon as he caught sight of him, extra deeply to Frederik IV in particular. The king nodded almost imperceptibly. Antonio turned resolutely back and made an energetic start on the second concerto. From now on he kept up the tempo, giving the public what they had come for, an unforgettable Epiphany concert. As the performance progressed Il Prete Rosso became so lost in his playing that he failed to notice that the king and his court had left the hall. With the dying notes of the finale echoing in his ears, Antonio looked proudly out into the audience and his heart turned over to find no king among them. He swiftly scanned the entire audience: sure enough, no Frederik IV. Panic-stricken, he turned back to the orchestra; sweat was pouring from his forehead despite the chilly concert hall. He thanked the coro and left the podium. What on earth could have happened? Bystanders were clapping him on the shoulder; queuing up to shake his hand and compliment him on the magnificent performance. Vivaldi heard nothing. He pushed his way through the crowd towards the exit in the hope of catching sight of the Scandinavian king. Perhaps he had gone to sit somewhere else? Then he bumped into the person he had seen earlier in the company of Frederik IV. The man surveyed him coolly and Vivaldi gave him a tongue-tied and rather foolish grin.

'The Duke of Olemburg would let it be known that he was delighted with this performance,' intoned the man. 'His engagement diary did not allow him to remain until the end but the Duke would like to hear more from you and offer you a due reward later this evening. The Duke expects you at the ball to be held at the house of Procurator Sebastiano Foscarini.' Not even waiting for a reply, the man pushed his way out of the hall, leaving behind a bemused but greatly relieved Vivaldi. For an awful moment he had actually thought the king had disliked his music enough to abandon the hall. With an immense sigh of satisfaction Antonio turned to embrace the praise being heaped upon him.

He had been to the music room to thank the *Figlie di Coro* for their efforts, for they had really done him proud this time. His father was waiting for him in the lane behind the *Pietà*. From here it was only a short way home. Full of excitement Vivaldi described the king's invitation. 'Will you come too, father?' he asked exuberantly, 'Then he can hear us playing together.' Giambattista thought a moment. 'It is you the king wants to see, my son, not your old father.' Giambattista knew himself; he would not feel at home among all those aristocratic patricians and princes. 'Don't forget your violin,' he added with a wry smile. Antonio gave him a wink and stormed back inside. Again Giambattista waited. Antonio rushed back out into the lane and they walked a little way together. Once on the *Riva*, the father clasped his son's hand and wished him luck.

With the gondolas lying impotently at rest on the ice, Antonio had to walk the rest of the way to his destination. With a wave to his father he made off down the quay in the direction of Procurator Foscarini's great house. He walked gently and thanks to all the adrenaline at first hardly felt cold. Who will be there this evening, he wondered. The Memmos, the Trons, undoubtedly the Mocenigos, and certainly all the Grimanis. What amazing luck! If the gentry see how a king appreciates my music it will open the door to a lot of work! Once he had passed the *Palazzo Ducale* the thoroughfare became busier and he slipped like an otter through the festive crowds. And yet it was less hectic than usual here and he was even able to walk at normal pace. Some daredevils had taken a short-cut over the ice, but Vivaldi was not tempted and left the frozen canal to the reckless.

By the time he arrived at his destination he was panting. The walk had been longer than he was used to. The wooden landing-stage next to the house had been stacked with marooned gondolas and the main entrance on the water closed, so that all the guests had been forced to walk the long way round to this evening's festivities and make use of the small entrance on the landward side. Darkness had descended early that afternoon, but so much light streamed out through the windows that it seemed the sun itself had been invited to the ball. Antonio wanted to catch his breath for a moment; after all, it would not look good to make his entrance gasping. The cold air sliced deep and painfully into his lungs, so that he felt himself becoming even more short of breath and decided it would be best to get indoors. Pulling his cloak around him, he pushed back the hood and stepped resolutely in the direction of the entrance. The two ushers posted on either side ignored the priest, letting him enter unhindered.

Before climbing the big staircase he again paused; after the bitter cold it was warm here in the rowdy foyer and the sudden change in temperature completely robbed him of breath. He leant against the wall, making himself as inconspicuous as possible while every kind of brightly coloured creature pushed past him. This large entrance hall seemed to offer a foretaste of the *piano nobile*, the great ballroom on the first floor, for here the scene was already one of frenetic coquetry, drinking, hilarity and mutual admiration. A cacophony of foreign languages and strong dialects filled the air, all melting into an unintelligible din. Costumes stood out in a kaleidoscope of colours against a monotonous background of black worn by the gentlemen. The women were without exception lovely to behold, and must have spent many hours before the mirror perfecting their appearance for this evening. Vivaldi found himself treated to a procession of voluptuous bosoms in deeply swooping decolleté, immaculately dressed hair adorned with diamonds, pearls and golden pins, cooing laughter, brightly painted fingernails and wafts of delicate perfume. Each woman had made the most of her own unique features. Some sported the *appassionata*, a subtle point drawn at one corner of the eye and visible only when the mask was slightly drawn aside. Almost as exciting were the *coquette* and the *galante*, an exquisite spot placed just above the lip and on the chin. But most irresistible of all was the *assassina*; the 'murderer' that sat at the corner of the mouth, yearning, demanding to be kissed but only visible when the lady in question suggestively but discreetly lowered her richly embroidered fan. The priest surveyed with admiration one after another awe-inspiring gown. He had a definite predilection for beautiful clothes and respect for those who could wear them with fitting elegance. He unbuttoned his own new mantle so that everyone could see his sober but stylish attire.

In the meanwhile the priest had recovered his breath, and now proceeded in a leisurely manner up the stairs. The higher he went, the busier things seemed to be around him, and once in the semi-lit *piano nobile* he quickly looked for a quiet corner. Nobody seemed to be listening to the small group of musicians playing a *concerto* by Corelli; a relatively old piece, but still pleasant on the ears. Antonio let his gaze roam around the enormous ballroom, trying to find the king; an apparently impossible task, for his view kept getting blocked by high wigs and gorgeous costumes. On either side of the ballroom, doors opened on to other, smaller rooms and what was probably a gallery. With his violin still clamped under his arm, Vivaldi made his way along the edge of the ballroom, peeping into each room. Everywhere there were people drinking, laughing, but especially conversing while waiters made sure their glasses were never empty.

The next room he looked into was filled with people leaning excitedly over a card-table upon which lay a small fortune, including several ladies' jewellery that had by now changed hands several times. There was flirting, lovemaking and dancing. But also someone lying half-comatose in a chair, concentrating hard on balancing a glass of wine. Vivaldi had to smile. Time and again he had refused the drinks offered him; if he was going to play he had to have a clear head.

It was in the last room that the strains of Il Sassone met his ears for the first time; the harpsichord was being played with pace and professionalism. Who could that be? These melodies were new to Vivaldi and he knew it could not possibly be a Venetian, let alone an Italian, performing them. But before he was able to reach the musician's side the piece was over and there was enthusiastic applause and calls for an encore. This time Vivaldi instantly recognised the opening notes: it was that old Scarlatti! He tried eagerly to catch sight of the player over the heads of the crowd assembled around him. The king! Antonio was looking straight into the eyes of Frederik IV. He got no reaction. The Danish sovereign was obviously relishing the music and drinking deep draughts from a wineglass that was being refilled as fast as he emptied it. A great wave of disappointment engulfed Antonio. It was clear that by now the king had probably forgotten all about having invited him here this evening. The room was again filled with thunderous applause. Who was this harpsichord player? Vivaldi looked about him, asking one or two of his neighbours if they knew the musician's name. One shrugged in ignorance, another probably understood no Venetian dialect and a third mumbled something incomprehensible. Increasingly intrigued, Vivaldi pushed his way though the crowd, repeating his question.

'Who cares what he's called?' retorted one man, dressed as a Turkish admiral. 'This is the best musician I have ever heard play!' The response irritated Vivaldi. How could anyone say that when they had not heard all the world's music, let alone HIS music?

'Isn't he fantastic?' swooned one young lady. 'This is what I call music,' followed another. Vivaldi got more and more annoyed as he fought his way forward. Eventually he was at the front and saw a man, not as old as himself, seated at the harpsichord. 'Viva il caro Sassone,' was the cry from a multitude of mouths as the last chord died away. The young player sprang to his feet and bowed deeply, especially to the wildly applauding King Frederik IV.

'Who is the harpsichordist?' asked Vivaldi, this time of an older man standing just in front of him. The man turned and through his mask gave Vivaldi a piercing stare. 'You are wearing no mask,' he observed authoritatively. Only a patrician could speak like that. 'I am a priest,' responded Vivaldi. He found it nonsensical to hide himself behind a mask. He deliberately wanted everyone to see him! The nobleman looked him up and down and turned his back without a word. 'Do you know who he is?' tried Vivaldi once more. 'Everyone knows that he is Giorgio Haendel,' said the patrician with ill-hid arrogance, 'everyone, that is, but you.' The man turned his back again as though to make clear that for the rest of this evening he intended to ignore this ignorant priest.

Haendel, Haendel? Vivaldi racked his brains. It suddenly came to him that he had heard the name before. Was it not at the performance of *La Resurezzione* in Rome? He had a vague memory of his father telling him about the sudden success of this youthful German composer. But Antonio had not pursued the subject further and after this brief spell of fame neither Vivaldi, father or son, had heard anything more of the German. No more of Haendel's music had reached Venice. It amazed Antonio that he was attracting so much attention this evening. Who was interested in that dry style of German music anyhow? Those folk up north had no idea about modern music! What he had heard of it were just a few artificial embellishments that bore no relation to the line of the melody. Moreover, he had never been able to trace a spark of spontaneity in the work of a German composer. But Antonio was worried, nevertheless.

The young Haendel had taken his seat at the harpsichord again and was surrounded by people whispering, demanding silence. The German waited for the right moment and began to play. Antonio shuffled a bit closer but still could not get a clear view of his face. Instead he watched the player's hands and saw how fluently his supple, powerful fingers moved over the keys. Vivaldi was impressed; for a German, this man played in a very Italian way. It was not perfect, of course, but he certainly had individuality of style. And Il *Sassone* had no trouble holding the attention of his audience; only rarely could someone be heard whispering excitedly in another's ear. Antonio found himself wondering if this young man had equal mastery over the violin. He looked once more at the king and found him completely absorbed in the music. The priest's mood was sinking by the moment. Would he still get a chance to play this evening? Would Frederik IV and the nobility present still be sober enough to appreciate his music if he did? He knew from experience that it no longer mattered what was played later in the evening; people would enjoy anything. You could get a monkey to tinker on the harpsichord and they would still applaud to high heaven and swear through their tears they had never heard anything so beautiful in their whole lives before. And the next day they'd have forgotten it entirely.

Vivaldi gave the whole evening up as a bad job and took his first glass of wine from a passing waiter. Without tasting the contents he emptied the glass and took another. The room was filled with applause and 'bravos' and Il *Sassone* bowed extravagantly to his grateful public. Vivaldi clapped rather coolly but managed nevertheless to shout 'bravo'. As far as he was concerned, Haendel was simply an intruder who had managed to commandeer all Frederik IV's attention. Antonio's envy was further awakened when he saw how the German and the king stood chatting, almost informally, like two old friends! They must both speak German. Good grief, is this what they had come to Venice for? The sovereign slapped the musician good-naturedly on the shoulder and appeared to ask for more. Il *Sassone* tried politely to wave aside the request, but who can refuse a king? With a huge smile spread across his blushing features, Haendel resumed his seat at the harpsichord.

For a moment he seemed to be considering, and then he turned to the audience, 'Ladies and gentlemen, especially for you, but also in honour of the Duke of Olemburg...' He paused, seemingly to savour the amusement of all who had long known the true identity of the Duke. 'I shall play a piece from my much-appreciated composition *Il Trionfo del Tempo e del Disinganno*. This *cantanta* in the style of an oratorio has been extraordinarily well received both in Rome and in Naples. But the real music lovers are to be found here in Venice,' he flattered, 'and it is your opinion that I shall most respect. I hope that it will meet with your approval.' This was greeted with roars of applause from the audience. They love him! Vivaldi realised, piqued beyond measure. He did not feel in the mood to listen for any longer, and anyway it was getting far too close in this room.

He made his way back to the ballroom and sought out, as far as possible, a quiet spot. Far away from Haendel and all his admirers he found a couple of empty seats. Slumping onto a sofa, he wiped the sweat from his face. Despite the vicious hold of winter on the Republic, it was hot indoors. The many human bodies together produced plenty of warmth, although happily it was cooler here in the spacious ballroom than it had been in the claustrophobic music-room. Vivaldi took another drink and wondered what he should do now that the chance of introducing himself to the *Veneti Nobili* had well and truly passed him by. Nor did he yet know when the king would be leaving Venice, and Vivaldi wanted personally to present him with his *Opus II*. He must talk to Frederik IV! I'll wait here, thought Antonio, taking another swig of wine. He pushed his violin-case under the sofa and relaxed back into the soft upholstery, tipping the wink to a waiter for another glass.

In a serious attempt to suppress his disappointment, Antonio immersed himself in his surroundings. His eye was caught by the colourful frescos ornamenting the ceiling. He saw companies of angels hovering around clouds that broke open to reveal a charging chariot-of-war drawn by three white stallions, foaming at the mouth. In the chariot, flanked by yet more balloon-cheeked angels blowing trumpets, sat a dignified lady. Above her head a slave held a laurel wreath. Nearby, on a great cloud, stood an elderly man gazing respectfully at the lady, who proudly held aloft a family crest. The wine began to do its work; the whole spectacle seemed slowly to come to life, the horses descending amongst the partygoers at a slow gallop.

Vivaldi was distracted by the voice of the master of ceremonies requesting attention for the formal opening of the ball. In response, people gravitated towards the edge of the dance floor to stand, or sat down to recover their breath. From all the side-rooms and galleries masked ball-goers streamed laughing into the main hall. Frederik IV came into view, with *Il Sassone* in his wake. To his huge annoyance Vivaldi saw Frederik IV pass Haendel a number of gold coins, for which the latter bowed his gratitude. His chest felt dangerously constricted and Vivaldi knew he should stop drinking. But common sense had already taken its leave of him two glasses ago.

As the ballroom fell still, Vivaldi recognised in the master of ceremonies the stern features of Procurator Mocenigo. His crimson ceremonial robes swept noiselessly over the polished stone floor as the procurator took his place solemnly at the centre of the huge ballroom. Antonio, who had got to his feet, discovered that he was better sitting down after all and did so; he would just have to watch the proceedings from his sofa. On the longer side of the hall, host Sebastiano Foscarini took his place alongside his ravishing wife Caterina Querini on the richly carved wooden throne that stood upon a raised dais. Foscarini nodded permission to Mocenigo for him to speak. A single gesture and the sound of his powerful voice were enough to silence any remaining noise in the hall. Now that he had their full attention the procurator bid everyone welcome in the name of the host, with a particularly warm welcome for the guest of honour this evening, the Duke of Olemburg. A wave of sniggering passed around the hall. How much longer was this pantomime to go on, Antonio asked himself. In stilted Italian, the 'Duke' thanked the procurator for his warm words and for the wonderful reception that had been given in his honour. The ball was declared open and Procurator Mocenigo propelled his wife somewhat precipitously onto the dance-floor.

Stiffly, the elderly matron allowed Frederik IV to lead her in the first minuet. The king was not impressed. She was short and fat and did not look as though she was enjoying the evening. This was a sharp contrast to the many other Venetian women he had met over the past few days. He knew already that he would miss Venice when he got back to Copenhagen. Not just Venice, but all its beautiful, proud women who in their self-confidence did not hesitate to initiate a conversation with him. Frederik IV already had a quiet eye on Caterina Querini. He had made her acquaintance earlier this evening, but the many guests had meant their encounter had been only fleeting. She was young and had a lovely figure and perfect teeth. With every smile they seemed to compete with the shining string of pearls she wore draped over her gown in the latest fashion. He had not been able to see her eyes properly through her mask but he was confident they would be in keeping with the rest of her. The minuet seemed to last forever. Applause and thanks to the procurator's wife were courteous but brief.

Frederik IV did not even have to approach the dais, for Caterina had already stood up and stepped elegantly onto the dance floor. As a matter of course she accepted the invitation of the 'Duke' who, thrilled, took her cool and silken hand in his. She looked boldly at him and it was Frederik IV who had rather shyly to avert his eyes from her gaze. This dance was faster than the last. The king and Caterina spun merrily and ever closer about one another. Caterina, a mischievous sparkle in her green eyes, made sure their bodies never touched. This so agitated Frederik IV that he made a somewhat over-enthusiastic movement, thereby catching Caterina's pearls in his lace cuff. Before either of them knew what was happening the string was burst and the costly pearls scattered themselves over the floor and into every corner of the hall. Frederik IV recoiled so violently that the music came to an abrupt halt. At first nobody could make out what was going on, but the hall soon felt that something was amiss and all fell still. Vivaldi sat bolt upright and watched whilst a huge pearl rolled straight towards him. It rebounded off his shoe and came to a halt. Well aware of the value of the gem, he had to suppress an urge to pick it up. Instead he remained sitting motionless.

Frederik IV gazed helplessly at Caterina. The hall held its breath and the king was at a loss. He stared shamefacedly at the floor whilst Caterina Querini looked at him and burst out laughing. Frederik IV shifted his glance to his host for possible direction and watched the blood rise to his face. My God, what have I done, agonised the king. He abandoned his regal role and fell upon his knees to gather up any pearls still in his vicinity. This was too much for the patrician Foscarini. What sort of king went down on his knees in public for a woman? Furious, he marched out of the hall with not a thought for the precious pearls crushed beneath his feet. Caterina, still laughing, did not follow her husband but clapped her hands, calling out to the musicians, 'Continuare!' She took a step towards the Danish sovereign, still busily humbling himself, and stretched out her hand towards his face.

'Let be, sire,' she whispered, 'it is nothing!' The Danish king glanced sidelong upwards and her look was enough for him. He got to his feet, his hands full of pearls. 'What shall I do with these?' he asked softly. Caterina waved her fan and a girl appeared at her side, obviously her chambermaid, who relieved him of them without a word.

'I am so very sorry,' he murmured with sincerity. 'Might we now finish our dance?' Caterina commanded in return, entirely dismissing the episode. Still ill at ease, Frederik IV took her hand again and the pair awkwardly resumed their dance. But the charge formerly built up between them had vanished, never to return. Quickly the floor filled with other dancers. By the end of the evening there would be not a pearl left lying. There were plenty among the ball-goers this evening who knew the value of the jewels and would not be able to resist temptation. Antonio saw the whole evening fall apart before his eyes. First Haendel, and now this. The king had clearly made a complete idiot of himself, as well as insulting his host. Would it still be possible to speak to Frederik IV, or would the king avoid all contact with Vivaldi, knowing he had witnessed this shameful incident? Let him dance himself into the ground first, thought Vivaldi; most people, including the king, would soon have forgotten the whole thing. Meanwhile the pearl still sat at his feet like one of the temptations. The priest pretended not to look. Now and then he scratched his calf, glancing about him shiftily to see if anyone was watching. He had already reckoned how much the gemstone was worth and how much he could ask for it. Nobody seemed to be watching him; they were all dancing, talking, flirting, bragging and admiring one another. Might he take a chance?

'Got it!' The female voice came out of nowhere and a hand snatched up the pearl from his feet. 'May I?' asked the young lady, and without waiting for a reply sank down beside him on the sofa. His heart had missed at least two beats. Where on earth had she appeared from, and had she guessed his intention? 'What a shame, isn't it? Such a gorgeous string! I've found far from all of them, and fear my mistress has seen the last of most of her pearls.' Looking at her, Vivaldi was surprised to find something familiar in her face, although he could not quite place it. She had wavy, dark blond hair and he thought the eyes behind her mask were blue. It was plain from her accent that she was not from Venice. The moment she began to speak he had become aware of a dimple in her cheek just beneath her mask. Although she clearly did not belong to the aristocracy, she was still a remarkable looking girl. She was sliding the pearls protectively one by one into a blue velvet pouch. She has beautiful long slender fingers, thought Vivaldi, perfect for playing the violin. He kept on trying to think from where he knew her features but her mask did not help matters. 'What an evening,' she sighed. 'What an evening indeed!' he returned.

She sat upright, looked directly at him and asked, 'Are you all right?' Vivaldi was still not certain whether or not she knew he had wanted to appropriate the pearl. But he reassured himself that he had nothing to worry about; he had not even touched the thing! He transformed his expression into a smile and replied, 'I could be better.' 'You wear no mask, sir,' she observed. 'I am a priest' he responded. 'Oh!' This apparently required some thought. 'Are you here in a professional capacity?' she asked curiously. He had to chuckle. 'As a servant of God I am always acting in a professional capacity, but I don't think I have much to add to these festivities.' Again he winked at a waiter for more wine. 'What then did you want to contribute to the ball?' the girl persisted. 'You're very inquisitive!' replied the priest.

She smiled but continued to fix him with an expectant stare, awaiting his reply. What does it matter, he thought with indifference. He might as well tell her. 'Do you, madam, know the true identity of the Duke?' 'Of course!' she spluttered with laughter. 'Everyone does!' Vivaldi shrugged his shoulders nonchalantly. He should have known better and now felt very stupid for having asked. 'I'll tell you what my contribution could have been!' She looked smilingly at him, but in such a way that he felt the tension slipping from him to be replaced by pleasure in having found a willing ear. He told her the whole story, from his first encounter with the king the previous week in the Pietà, up to and including the meeting with Haendel this evening. But she was not satisfied. She went on questioning him about his work, his compositions, his family and the girls of la Pietà, and Vivaldi gave her the answers happily. It was wonderful to have someone show such an interest in him; he could not recall it ever having happened to him before.

The wine kept coming, and she kept pace with him glass for glass. It was some time before he realised that he knew nothing about her. But what did it matter? On the floor the dancing grew more and more wildly abandoned. Vivaldi leant ever closer to the young woman to make sure he was understood. He found himself momentarily distracted by her perfume. She smelled delicious, as fresh as spring. 'What did you say?' She grasped his arm as the din in the hall grew louder. 'Come on,' she added, 'I know a quieter spot.' Criss-crossing her way through the horde, she found her way infallibly through the house. There were people everywhere. Antonio, already quite befuddled with wine, wavered his way behind her, barely able to keep up. She paused a moment and glanced invitingly behind her, before neatly lifting a carafe of wine from the tray of a passing waiter; then she was off again, followed by a puffing Vivaldi.

After countless corridors they finally arrived in a cool chamber, amazingly enough empty of people. Breathless from his long journeying though the vast mansion, Vivaldi saw by the light of the single lamp that they were in the anteroom of a bedroom. In the half-dark he discerned a small sofa and collapsed into it, rubbing his chest. 'My old trouble,' he sighed in explanation. She sat down next to him and poured him some more wine. Her next question was already upon her lips when it dawned on him from where he knew her face. She was the Holy Maria from the panel next to the altar of *San Martino*! Watching with the utmost attentiveness, he asked her to remove her mask. She uttered a small giggle, visibly hesitant. But then the disguise slipped off, along with much more besides. 'Mother Maria!' muttered the priest respectfully, making the sign of the cross.

Her face dissolves slowly, like mist over the lagoon on a bright summer morning, and he cannot bring it back. 'Maria?' he whispers softly. He doesn't even know her real name. There is a gaping hole in his memory... What else happened? He hears footsteps ascending the stairs and recognises his father's unmistakably heavy and decisive tread. My God, Vivaldi wonders, will he forgive me this? Already ringing in his ears is the sermon to come. He turns over quickly in bed and as the door opens feigns deep sleep. He does not have the strength yet to face his father. Giambattista leans over him and shakes him repeatedly by the shoulder. Antonio growls. 'Drunken heap of junk!' mumbles Giambattista, and slams the door so hard shut behind him that Vivaldi curls up like a foetus, hugging his knees.

2

Venice, January 1709

'Have you gone out of your mind?' roars Giambattista at his eldest son. 'You could have killed yourself. If it were not for the ice you'd have drowned!' Mute and miserable, Antonio avoids his father's eyes. He had come downstairs with knocking knees, hoping the old man would be out. But no such luck. Giambattista, industriously copying, does not even have to lift his head to know it is this son who has come down. 'ANTONIO,' issues the summons from the workroom. 'Sit down,' the father orders peremptorily, indicating the chair with a wave of his left hand whilst continuing to write. There is no way out and Antonio knows it; he can only wait stoically to be deluged by his father's tirade.

'I don't know what happened and I don't want to know either. But you need to realise once and for all that in a single evening you can lose everything we have built up until now! Unbelievable ingratitude! I never had a father who offered me the chances I've given you. You weren't put through seminary just to walk around in nice clothes. The idea was to better your social status, allow you to rise above the station you were born into. And what does his lordship do? Get completely plastered at the house of one of the most important families in Venice and end up sprawling covered in puke in a canal. Unbelievable! Pathetic, that's what you are!'

His father's pen meanwhile does not cease its moody scratching across the surface of the paper. But in his rage the scribe presses down too hard on the nib and ink flows suddenly much too heavily. Furious, he slams the pen down on the table, crumples the spoiled and blotted page into a ball and hurls it into the fire. He begins to pace back and forth before the hearth, his hands clasped behind his back. 'Did you manage to speak to the king?' he snaps. Antonio shakes his head. 'You're not going to tell me you blew it completely?'

With a weak shrug the priest mumbles something inaudible.

'And do I have to expect a visit from the *sbirri* to arrest you?' Antonio shakes his head. 'Out with it!'

'No, father.'

'Hmm.' Giambattista carries on nervously striding, thinking back on the previous evening. He doubts anyone saw them so there shouldn't be any local gossip. But what on earth could have happened at the ball? Giambattista had played often enough for the patricians and without fail it ended up in a mass booze-up of which nobody the following morning had the slightest sensible recall. He looks down at the figure of his son, meekly bowed before him. He can pretty well imagine how grim Antonio must be feeling, and even has some sympathy for him. Oh, yes, he has no trouble remembering the misery of a monstrous hangover; he'd been quite a lad too, in his day. The only difference between him and Antonio was that he hadn't had a father to get him back on track. And his mother was always so disappointed in him when he came home paralytic yet again. 'I'm only glad your father isn't here to see this anymore,' she would tell him, a remark that made a less than vivid impression on him. His wife Camilla had shown less patience. Returning home after a wild night out with friends he would catch the full force of her fury, and the following day's hangover would be greeted not with sympathy but more likely a bucket of cold water. So that his outings with friends had become few and far between, though Giambattista held on to his pleasure in a glass of good wine.

Camilla had an enormous sense of responsibility and found it unbecoming that the children should get up in the morning to find their father sleeping off the night's revelries at the breakfast table. But one lives and learns, and Giambattista had grown a great deal wiser with the years. What was more, they had their worries over the young Antonio, who had been a very sickly child. It had become increasingly clear that the poor health of their firstborn would stand in the way of a career as a manual worker. But Antonio was bright, and so they began to think more in the direction of training for the priesthood. And it had not taken Giambattista long to discover that, despite being backward in physical development, his son was musically gifted.

'Perhaps one day he'll play as well as his father,' Giovanni Legrenzi had laughingly remarked one afternoon in March, soon after Antonio's seventh birthday. Giambattista would never forget that day because it was the same occasion that Legrenzi, friend but more significantly *Primo Maestro* of the *Cappella Ducale*, had asked him to join his orchestra as violinist - the orchestra of the Basilica of *San Marco*. It was huge honour. Since then it had been much easier for him to get invitations to play in one of the theatre orchestras, but a real breakthrough had never come his way. His brushes with the aristocracy had been just enough to give him a tantalising taste of the life led by the upper classes, whilst reminding him that his lowly status excluded him forever from their ranks. This awareness was only confirmed when Antonio, no sooner had he had got his tonsure, was appointed *Maestro di Violino di Coro* at the *Ospedale della Pietà*. The son was thus suddenly earning a salary twice that of his father. Giambattista did not mind in the least. It only proved that Camilla and he had been right about the young man. And what might yet be in store for Antonio?

Well, not so very much just now.

'Come on, son,' his father chides more softly. He ruffles Antonio's hair. 'Go outside for God's sake and get a breath of fresh air. But whatever you do, don't stand still and get into conversation with anyone. Because you stink to high heaven.'

Antonio gives his father a grateful look and stumbles out of the room. The old man gazes after him, shaking his head. 'Enough of that daydreaming now!' Picking up a clean sheet of paper, he strokes it flat and concentrates on work again. He has wasted too much time as it is.

A couple of days later the weather thaws. No one in the

Vivaldi household has again mentioned the recent spat between father and son, and daily life is back to its old rhythm. The lump on Antonio's forehead is shrinking nicely and his bruises beginning slowly to fade. He is on his way home. Twilight has fallen and the shopkeepers are busy clearing up their stalls and closing the shutters. From the gaiety of their song can be deduced how well they have done today and one has obviously sold much more than another! As every day, Antonio steps inside the church of *San Giovanni*. It's always quiet at this time of day, just as he likes it best. For days now he has been wondering if he should go to confession. But what does he have to confess? God will certainly forgive him for coming home drunk one night. But something else nags at his conscience. Is it his violin?

It was more than a day before he missed his instrument. The last he remembers is shoving the violin under the sofa. His first instinct was to rush to Foscarini's house, but something has held him back. He postpones the decision until he is absolutely certain he did nothing to humiliate himself. Whole days have passed without rumours or complaint, but you never know! Maybe tomorrow he will go. He stares at the red marble font in which more than thirty years ago Father Giacomo baptised him. Oh yes, the *abbate* would be surprised alright to hear that Antonio Vivaldi was planning to dedicate at least twelve sonatas of his very own composition to a foreign monarch! It is clear by now that Frederik IV feels so at home in *La Serenissima* that he will be staying a while longer. Waltzing from one party to the next, the king has fallen in love not once but several times, and commissioned artist Rosalba Carriera to paint a series of miniatures of the loveliest women in Venice: no easy choice for the sovereign. Despite not having spoken again to the king, Antonio is determined to dedicate his second *opus* to Frederik IV. Giambattista is busy putting the finishing touches to the manuscript, and this evening Antonio will draft his dedication. He already has in mind a few well-turned phrases that he hopes will impress not only the king but anyone who sees the manuscript.

Once home, Vivaldi goes straight to the workroom. He greets his father, who is deeply immersed in work on the new opera he is copying for the impresario of *San Angelo* theatre. He softly hums the melody, keeping time with nods of his head. 'Not bad,' he admits, and lays the score down on the table next to his son's violin.

My violin! But how did it get here, wonders a dumbfounded Antonio, whilst all the possibilities chase each other wildly through his mind. Has his father been to the Foscarini house? Surely not, for how would he have known the violin was missing? After all, Antonio is always leaving it behind at the *Pietà*. Vivaldi goes up to the table and lays his hand tenderly on the case before opening it. Seeing at a glance that the instrument is unharmed, he gives a deep sigh of relief. His father looks at him expectantly, awaiting an explanation. But Antonio wordlessly closes the lid of the case.

'You didn't tell me that, son.'

'What, father?' Antonio's asks guilelessly.

'That you forgot to bring home your violin.'

'I thought no more about it, father.' This is clearly not the answer his father expected. 'Thought no more about it,' he snorts. 'If your grandfather could hear you now he would be turning in his grave! He paid a goodly sum for that thing back then.'

'I'm sorry, father,' apologises Antonio, meaning it.

'Lucky for you there are still some honest people in this world. A young woman came to the door this afternoon, asking for this to be returned to you.' Antonio feels himself blushing. But his father is absorbed in his music again.

'Oh?' ventures Antonio. 'Did she have anything else to say?'

'Hmmm, pom-pom-pommm. Wonderful stuff!' His father's mind is definitely back with the music. 'Eh? Did she say anything? Let me see... No, nothing in particular. Well, she asked if you lived here and who I was. Then she asked me to make sure the violin got back to you, and that was that. Before I could ask her anything she was outside again. Is she a friend of yours?'

Maria! If he shuts his eyes he can still smell her, but all their conversation still eludes him. What sort of nonsense had he babbled? He cannot imagine; he can't even remember her name. 'Oh, no. She's just someone I know.'

'That's fine then,' says Giambattista. As far as he's concerned the matter is obviously closed. Vivaldi offers quiet thanks to the Lord and opens the violin-case again. Perhaps she's left a message for him. But he finds nothing there. He has to put her out of his head. More important business awaits his attention. Selecting the most perfect sheet of paper from the sheaf, he begins writing in an immaculate and decorative hand: Dedication to King Frederik IV of Denmark and Norway.

After applying several times for an audience, Antonio is at last granted access to the king's secretary. The priest steps excitedly inside. The moment has finally arrived for him to present the sovereign with his *Opus II*.

But Frederik IV does not appear. Instead the secretary notifies Vivaldi that to his deep regret His Highness has no time to receive the musician personally. Vivaldi lays his music hesitantly on the table and a couple of seconds later is outside again. He looks about him in dismay, turns and stares up at the windows in the hope of catching a glimpse of the Scandinavian king. But there is no one to be seen. Devastated, Antonio quickly takes the shortest route home, his tragic expression contrasting sharply with the laughing faces of the milling carnival-goers, all looking forward to yet another evening out. Vivaldi will have no part in it. *Carnevale* has never really appealed to him; it is a flight from reality that he, most especially this evening, has no use for.

Life for the majority of Venetians carries on as normal despite *Carnevale*, the festival that each year brings more and more tourists to the city and for a couple of months swells the population by a fifth. Among the ordinary folk of Venice, children are born and people die. People go about their daily work; bakers bake their bread. It may look to outsiders as though the Republic is held together by a string of parties but behind the scenes the economy runs on, business as usual. At least, so it seems. For just as some gullies in the lagoon get choked with slurry, so it goes, too, with trade in Venice. But how many people realise this? The splendid *palazzi*, the wonderful theatres, the imposing *Piazza San Marco* and the endlessly teeming casinos give the visitor to *La Serenissima* an impression of immeasurable and eternal wealth. But nothing is farther from the truth. Fewer and fewer cargo vessels are calling at Venice. There are periods when warehouses stand empty and the exchange markets are increasingly quiet.

The patricians whose families have belonged to this community since the birth of the city have for a long time failed to live up to the sharp business practice for which their forefathers were famous over centuries. The spice trade has been taken over by Dutch and English merchants, without the *Doge* and the Senate being able to do a thing about it. In a mood almost of resignation, people are investing in land and vineyards on the mainland. The tourists, of course, bring in a certain amount of revenue. But nothing compared with the vast profits from a ship returning laden with pepper and cloves from Constantinople a hundred years ago. Behind the façade of festivities and partying, concerts and operas, the first hairline cracks are becoming visible in the Republic. Here and there, belts are having to be tightened, not least at the *Ospedale della Pietà*.

The twelve members of the *Congregazione* of orphanage La Pietà, home for foundlings and children without parents, sit grave-faced around a large table, at their head the stately figure of Procurator Lorenzo, chairman of the administrative committee. They are halfway through the agenda, but things are moving slowly today. It is once more the first full meeting of the committee since *Carnevale*, and they have plenty to discuss. The weightiest matter before them is the budget; donations in the form of gifts and legacies have again fallen over the past six months compared to the preceding term. What is more, there's been a drastic drop in income from musical performances over the same period.

'It's been far too cold,' opines Andrea, one of the older

governors. Most of his colleagues nod in agreement, despite a feeling that this offers scant comfort. Giacomo thinks they have to rein in the expenses. 'That's the only way to tally the accounts.' Everyone mumbles their assent, but nobody comes up with an idea for economies. 'As far as I'm concerned we can sack *Il Prete Rosso*,' says Piero Frascari, breaking the silence. 'And what possible reason would you give for such a thing?' asks the chairman of the committee, bemused. 'Apart from the fact that this priest does not know his place, he made a ridiculous spectacle of us during the first visit of Frederik IV. Moreover, I have spoken to the *Maestra* and she's told me that she and the *Figlie Privilegiate di Coro* are more than capable of teaching our pupils.'

'Is she absolutely sure of that?' asks the chairman, scratching his beard in doubt. Lorenzo is aware how good a teacher the priest is, and has a great deal of respect for him as a violinist. 'Absolutely,' insists Piero. 'And she is quite prepared to put it in black and white.' The chairman looks up and down the table and decides to follow protocol and put the proposal to the vote. The result is six for and six against. Even Lorenzo's vote is insufficient to save Vivaldi. But he makes one more attempt to champion the *Maestro di Violino*. 'It is true that Don Vivaldi has trouble knowing his place, but we must not overlook his enormous pedagogic skills. We have seen, have we not, the huge progress he has led over recent years? It's a fact that the quality of our *Figlie* stands head and shoulders above the other institutes. And as his salary represents only a tenth percent of the budget, his removal will have almost no effect on the figures. I consider keeping Don Vivaldi for the *Pietà* to be nothing less than an investment in our future!'

But the seeds of doubt have been sown and there is a great deal of murmuring among those present.

'Your honour...' Eugenigo addresses the chair. 'I should dearly love to find myself in accord with your wise words. But, with your permission, I should like respectfully to add a note in the margin which I hope all members will take into consideration.' Seated next to Piero Frascari, Eugenigo has just voted against

Vivaldi. Lorenzo knows little good can come of it, but has no option but to let Eugenigo speak. 'An investment in the future can only be guaranteed if it poses no risk whatever,' continues the latter. 'Well, I have reason to suspect that this respectable institution would be running considerable risk by retaining Il *Prete Rosso*.' Everyone's eyes are alert and fixed on Eugenigo. 'My cousin, who a few weeks ago laid on a fine reception to welcome the King of Denmark and Norway, has informed me that our priest's conduct on that occasion was far from unimpeachable.'

Lorenzo's face assumes a fastidious expression. 'What precisely do you mean?' he demands impatiently. Must he really listen to yet another of the thousands of sordid little rumours in constant circulation around Venice?

'Well, chairman, it's as I said. He fooled around with one of my cousin's wife's chambermaids there. And we all know where that might end; today a chambermaid, tomorrow one of the choirgirls!'

'Did your noble cousin himself witness this incident?' asks Lorenzo with concern.

'Do you doubt my words?' responds Eugenigo, reddening.

'Not at all. But before we take any important decision I should like to establish whether your honourable cousin really saw this incident with his own eyes. After all, it was *Carnevale*, and I understand it to have been in many respects a very good party! Apparently, things got quite entertaining.' Lorenzo winks roguishly at the governor sitting to his right, who roars with laughter.

'You may laugh, chairman,' persists Eugenigo, 'but will we still find it so amusing when this PRIEST,' he accentuates the title, 'gets his hands on the choir?' His words echo round the stuffy little room.

'Come, come Eugenigo,' replies Lorenzo in measured tones, 'that would seem to me to be something of an exaggeration. In all the years Vivaldi has been with us there has been not a single incident. With this in mind, I should like to put the matter to the vote once more.' 'Fine!' Eugenigo nods his head. Then, emphasising every word with a vitriolic slam of his fist upon the table, adds, 'But if the vote changes and he is kept on, I should like my warning to be recorded in the minutes.'

But the clerk does not have to put anything down for posterity. The new vote is decisive. Seven votes against. Subdued but always prone to thinking along straight lines, Jacopo has changed his vote and the unsuspecting Vivaldi is summarily dismissed.

Hardly any secret can survive in Venice, and even fewer in the *Ospedale della Pietà*. The meeting of the *Congregazione* is hardly disbanded before the first rumours filter out, gathering strength as they go. It is only a matter of time before the whispers are out on the streets and the following morning every baker between the *Arsenale*, the Republic's shipyard, and the *Pietà* is regaling his customers with the news that *Il Prete Rosso* has been sent packing!

The door flies open and Antonio's youngest sister Zanetta rushes in, out of breath and shocking half to death the family still sitting quietly around the breakfast table. Camilla spills boiling water over the table and Cecilia swallows something down the wrong way. Only Antonio remains immune to the drama; as usual, he's miles away.

'What in heaven's name is going on?' demands Giambattista, stooping to pick up a couple of still warm *bovoli* dropped by his daughter in her consternation. Francesco, one of Antonio's brothers, unimpressed by all the excitement, breaks a *bovolo* in half and takes a bite of the fragrant bread.

'It's Antonio', stammers Zanetta. 'They say Antonio's got the sack.' Waking up at the sound of his name to what is happening around him, Antonio stares in disbelief at his sister. Many raised voices fill the little kitchen: 'What did you say?' Zanetta repeats the news told her at the baker's. 'Gossip,' pronounces Giambattista decisively. Antonio sits on in dejected silence. His brother Francesco eats steadily, harvesting the crumbs from the table on a licked forefinger. Giambattista decides to put an end to all uncertainty by an immediate visit to the Pietà. 'Come on, Antonio. Let's go and find out what the game is.'

'But you haven't finished your breakfast,' protests his mother. 'Later,' barks Giambattista, throwing on his cloak. Antonio is reluctant to move. He knows this is no gossip but longs with all his being to avoid hearing it confirmed. 'I'm not feeling so well, father,' he complains with an expression of pain and rubbing his chest, where indeed he feels the cramp returning. 'Too bad,' returns his father. 'It's your job and your future. GET GOING!' The threat in his voice tells Antonio there is no point in arguing. He gets to his feet with a sigh and just has time to put on the tabarro thrown at him by his father. His mother says nothing more, but wipes a tear from the corner of her eye. Running a damp cloth swiftly over the table, she prays to Mother Mary. But in her heart she fears the worst.

'What is said cannot be unsaid and I am the last person who can do anything about this!' Unmoved, the governor of the Ospedale della Pietà stands behind the door, holding it open just a crack. 'But why?' shouts an enraged Giambattista. 'You can at least give us a reason!'

'There's a letter on its way and if you disagree with the decision you'd better lodge an objection with the chairman of the Congregazione.' The man has hardly finished speaking before he slams the heavy door in their faces. The bolts are shot, rendering the institute as impregnable as one of the fortifications in the lagoon. Stunned speechless, Giambattista hammers furiously with his fist upon the wooden door whilst the desolate Antonio stands watching. He knew it would turn out like this. Finito. The end of everything. Now he will be a laughing stock. Everyone will treat him with contempt. But why have they thrust him aside so savagely? Utterly humiliated, he prays, 'My God, my God, help me find my way through this'.

On the other side of the door, a little way up the staircase, two teenage girls lean sadly against the wall. Tears trickle down the cheeks of the younger, and she bites angrily on her forefinger. 'It's not fair,' bursts out Anna Maria. The other girl puts her arm comfortingly around the shoulders of the younger. They listen to the banging on the door below. Anna Maria sobs even harder. How can she live without Don Vivaldi? As far as she's concerned the redhead priest is the best violin teacher in the world. She has never felt so angry; the arrogance of her *Maestra*, who thinks she can play just as well as the *Maestro* himself! In Anna Maria's view the *Maestra's* fiddle playing is pathetic, complete rubbish. Mother Maria, do I really have to take lessons from her from now on? Maybe I'll just give up playing altogether! But she is not totally convinced of this idea, afraid of missing her music terribly.

Father and son Vivaldi walk briskly over the *Riva*; the one man livid, the other simultaneously relieved, angry and sad. 'This way,' snarls Giambattista, turning off left on the other side of the bridge, in the direction of the *Torri dell'Arsenale*. They cross another higher bridge and Antonio, clearly feeling the climb and his father's lively pace, falls behind and watches as Giambattista strides ahead and into Benno Belluno's wine-bar. Benno looks up with surprise from his cleaning. 'Hello Rossi, you're early today! What can I get you? Hi there, Antonio, welcome, welcome. Well, this is a treat so early in the morning.'

The cheery landlord, real name Benito Gazonni but known by everyone for years as Benno Belluno, pulls out a bench from under a table and wipes it 'clean' with the greasy cloth that he wears slung over his shoulder.

Benno arrived in Venice many years ago from a tiny village in the Dolomites to seek his fortune. His childhood dream had always been to become a shipbuilder: a remarkable ambition for someone born and bred among steep and rocky mountain crags, knowing the sea only from stories told him by gypsy pedlars. But somehow these travelling people always had the time to tell a thrilling yarn, and the young Benno had many a time hung on their every word as they spoke of the city in the lagoon; of the thousands of ships that voyaged all over the world under the flag of *San Marco* and the craftsmanship of the men of the *Arsenale*. Benno dutifully served his apprenticeship as carpenter, but had no desire to make tables and chairs. His aim was to build ships, ships large and strong enough to withstand the roughest storm and the most terrifying sea monsters. Ships that would return safely to their home port laden with riches. The moment he was old enough he set off, without a glance behind him, down into the flatlands at the feet of the mountains. Once in the lagoon he was amazed at how quickly he found a job as apprentice carpenter at the *Arsenale*.

But alas, his luck was not to last. One morning whilst a mast was being erected a badly fitted pulley came crashing down and without warning landed with a dull thud on Benno's left shoulder, crushing it to smithereens and bringing to an abrupt end his career as shipbuilder. His left arm was as good as paralysed. But, optimist that he was, after nights of high fever Benno began to show signs of recovery. The doctor had decided against amputating the arm, for which Benno was to be eternally grateful. And with the tiny, one-off compensation payment awarded him he took over the tenancy of a small tavern across from the entrance to the shipyard. He had found his place in life.

A magnificent view of the ships and air drenched in the scent of freshly sawn wood, hemp and tar had made a more and more contented man of him. At the end of every day, as the gates of the shipyard opened like the jaws of a mythological sea monster to spew out a wave of workers, his tavern would fill up within seconds. And he was blessed with the help of Rosa and Maretienna, who with a happy smile kept the wine-beakers of the thirsty constantly refilled. Visitors could always be assured of a bite to eat, and even if they weren't hungry the smell wafting from the kitchen would soon have their mouths watering. Benno always had something on the stove, mostly a recipe from the village of his birth, and the rich aroma of herbs, casserole of rabbit or smoked capon escaping the warm kitchen seduced everyone within range.

Benno knew his regulars, and that meant he also knew which wine to put in front of Giambattista and his son. He instructed Maretienna to bring them a bottle of the best Cypriot, and two glasses instead of beakers, then left his guests in peace. He too, by now, had heard the news concerning the priest.

'What a cheek,' grumbles Giambattista. 'Not even the civility to let you know in a decent manner. It's a bloody shame Gasparini is still away. He would have warned us. That's for sure.'

'But would he have been able to do anything, father?'

Giambattista shakes his head. 'I fear not. It's the management committee that takes such decisions. But I've seen things like this happen before, when I was working for the *Ospedale dei Mendicanti*. The minute they think their own people can play better than the teacher, they chuck him out. They're such arses; they can never resist economising left right and centre. As long as it's not on their own bonus, of course!'

Father and son have agreed there would be no sense in lodging any objection. The management committee will have to discover for itself how difficult it was to uphold standards of musical performance. 'You'll see son, one of these fine days they'll be back with their tails between their legs. Ah, but then it'll be our turn. Then we'll be the ones calling the tune. We're going to make sure your name is known far and wide. You have the talent, and the day will come when everyone will know that you're the supreme *Musico di Violino Professore*. Not just within the borders of the Republic but far beyond them!'

Thanks to the efforts of Viennese agents such as Matthias von Regaznig, some of Antonio's early works have already found their way into the hands of a few music enthusiasts north of the Alps. This, according to Giambattista, is where the future lies: the royal music ensembles of the Bohemian and German regents, princes and dukes. Father is soon back on form and it's business as usual, planning Antonio's future for him. Antonio, helped by the wine on an empty stomach, finds his enthusiasm matching his father's. The more he thinks about it, the more he feels that after all it's good to be gone from that place. All these years shut up in the straitjacket of La Pietà and now he's free to do as he pleases. You can bet the administration will regret their decision! But they've seen the last of him. The Pietà is too small a world for a Vivaldi!

He listens intently to all the plans his father lays before him, his cheeks flushing deeper and deeper. Together they shall conquer all the concert halls of Italy and the people will pour in by the thousand to hear him play. For this is Antonio's future; it stands to reason. All will be well. Leave it to father!

Benno puts another bottle on the table, but Giambattista waves it away, produces his purse and settles the bill. Outside, a sobering shower of rain serves to dampen father and son's spirits somewhat. Each mulling over all their plans in silence now, the two make their way through the puddles homeward.

After the raw February rains and March showers, spring has arrived at last. The sun begins to shine with more conviction, soon banishing the memory of a long, cold and wet winter. Church, cupola, tower and richly worked façade stand sharply contoured against a brilliant blue sky. The whole of Venice comes to life. Shutters are flung open and each house gets a good spring clean. Every corner is scrubbed and mopped. In the narrow lanes is heard the chirrup of brightly coloured birds hanging from the shutters in their cages, their song perhaps restrained by the longing to spread their wings. But the prisoners get no sympathy from the cheeky street sparrows, free to choose under which roof-tiles they build their nests. And even less from the newly arrived swallows swooping like lightning along the eaves, on the lookout for last year's brooding place. Everything seems to be following the repeating rhythm of life itself.

And that goes, too, for the inhabitants of San Marco. The annually recurring rituals, stemming from very early times when the first primitive settlements were established upon the boggy islands of the lagoon, are once more followed through. The only difference being that each year they are carried out with more pomp and pageantry, as if reflecting the increasing power of Venice.

But the grandiose ceremonies have assumed ever greater proportions since the Republic passed her zenith and her influence in the Mediterranean has been on the wane. It is almost as if the Senate is trying to pull the wool over the eyes not only of its own citizens, but definitely also of the many foreign visitors. Over the course of the year, more than forty great processions are scheduled to pass through the streets. Whereas most Italian cities make do with a single patron, Venice is content with no fewer than fourteen.

All this show means a busy time for Giambattista. The necessary rehearsals and performances in San Marco always take up a great deal of time. Now that May is here, he will have more time to work with Antonio on their strategy. In the meantime the priest has been building up new contacts. Helped by publication of his Opus II, his name is now known to all the foreign agents in Venice. The fact that the new work is dedicated to King Frederik IV of Denmark and Norway has, to the great joy of printer Antonio Bortoli, endowed it with some measure of success. And this has brought with it increasingly frequent invitations to play at the many embassy receptions that take place with the regularity of ebb and flood.

But large-scale commissions and recognition still elude Vivaldi, not least because the patricians of La Serenissima continue to snub Il Prete Rosso. He may be a priest, but his humble background is not to be denied, born as he was an operari. Moreover, there exist among the circles of the Veneti Nobili plenty of dilettanti who, in the view of the aristocratic gentlemen, probably play better than Don Vivaldi.

His search for recognition leaves Antonio little inspired to compose anything really new. He toys with various new violin positions and bowing techniques but cannot find what he is looking for. Perhaps the answer lies in the past?

When they still had the time, father and son together studied the work of Corelli, Alessandro Scarlatti and Legrenzi, but also many whose work Giambattista had copied over the years, including such old masters as Girolamo Frescobaldi and Claudio Monteverdi. Soon after beginning work as a scribe, Giambattista had started a habit of keeping a copy of anything that interested him. He enjoyed playing these compositions in his spare time and later, when he saw that Antonio showed above average ability as a violinist, used them as studies for his son.

The past offers Antonio no immediate way out of his impasse. Indeed, it represent a road leading backwards and that is the last thing he is looking for. Luckily his father will have time for him over the coming weeks.

With summer in view, so too the *Villeggiatura*. The homes of the patricians are bustling with preparations for the annual escape to their summer villas, located at the loveliest spots to be found in the *terraferma Veneta*. It's a perfect moment for Antonio and his father to set out upon their search for a musical style that will take all Venice by surprise. But, alas, all plans are brought crashing down by the sudden death of the *Doge*. Eighty-first birthday celebrations for Alviso II Mocenigo are no sooner over than he expires, leaving the Republic to elect a new leader and throwing into complete disarray all normal social order. Receptions and large parties planned at country mansions on the mainland have to be cancelled and newly packed suitcases regretfully unpacked. Plainly, nobody looks forward to spending summer on the lagoon. The combination of heat, stink and malaria offers no pleasant prospect.

The election of a new *Doge* is a complicated and time-consuming process. In the meantime, in the basilica of *San Marco* memorial services are held in honour of Alviso II Mocenigo. Only after these are over can the investiture of a newly elected *Doge* take place, followed by Alviso's funeral. Giambattista sees his planned free time go up in smoke. The next few weeks will be packed full of rehearsals and performances with the orchestra of *San Marco*.

The weather soon warms up until it is too hot for Antonio to think clearly. His daily routine begins with a short morning walk along the *Riva degli Schiavoni*, always pausing for a moment at the building housing the *Pietà*. From where he stands on the bridge above the *Rio del Santo Sepolcro* he gazes down and along the façade behind which lie the music hall and the lodgings of the *Figlie di Coro*. Peering inquisitively in at the windows, he hopes to catch a glimpse of one of his pupils, but to his sorrow it seems as though the massive building has devoured them forever. He strains his ears for any sound of singing or music lessons, but the thick walls of the ancient institute let no sound escape. It is only if by chance the shutters are standing wide open that a strand or two of music sometimes reach him, and then he knows instantly who is playing. But what he hears does not make him happy. The heart and soul is gone from the music, and that hurts him so! There are few concerts in these months, so that Antonio has no idea how things are going with the choir. But he has his suspicions that all is not well here either. True, in the beginning he was still so full of rancour that he would have quite enjoyed hearing how the quality had deteriorated. But the longer he is away the more his attitude changes towards it all, and every day that he passes the *Pietà* his painful nostalgia for the place increases.

He worries about the fate of little Fiorina and Basilia. They're still so young, so fragile! It doesn't take much to push an emerging talent in a wrong direction. And he notices that he is concerned too about Lorenza. With the right guidance she would make a *virtuoso* cellist. But it is Anna Maria over whom he frets most of all. How old will she be now... twelve or thirteen? And yet already so far along the path and so very talented. But Anna Maria is an extremely sensitive child. He recalls how years ago he first saw her, how she had stood out from the other girls in her shyness and diffidence. And how struck he had been. Not by anything she said, for she never opened her mouth. The other girls had stood giggling at the redhead priest, hardly listening to a word the violin teacher told them, so that the *Maestra* had to bang with her wooden stick on the stone floor several times to rally their attention. It was only Anna Maria who stood quietly, taking in all he said. So that she was the obvious and only choice to join the *Figlie di Coro*. The gigglers would continue to attend music classes, but the rest of their education would be focused on household tasks in preparation for life outside the *Pietà*.

Much to his own surprise, Antonio had discovered in himself a real gift for selecting the right girls. Sometimes he had no rational explanation for a certain choice, and often had a terrible job finding arguments to convince the *Maestra* and the governors that his decision had been the right one. 'Did you not see how she held her bow?' crowed the *Maestra* when Antonio had once more picked someone out of the group who was apparently not her own first choice. 'She'll never get anywhere; that must be obvious to everyone? A pure waste of time.'

Antonio always got wound up over such short sightedness; of course the girls were still just children, but it was his task to teach them. 'It is a great shame so few people recognise true quality, whilst we offer such enthusiastic applause for so much less,' he would remark with as much restraint as he could muster. Up until now it had appeared that, to the great discomfort of his superiors, his judgement had been infallible. Such moments had not added to the popularity of the young priest. But gradually the quality of the choir had improved and *Maestro di Coro* Francesco Gasparini, clearly satisfied with both musical and pedagogic qualities in the young Vivaldi, had offloaded more and more tasks and responsibilities onto his shoulders. All these Antonio had eagerly accepted, leaving Gasparini with his hands free to compose operas and perform them in the theatres of Venice.

The younger girls did not always find their life easy. As yet unconscious of their own musical talent, they often had at first to contend with the jealousy of their sisters. They might make an angelic impression upon their audience; among themselves they were more like wolves, continually fighting for their place in the pack. Choir members knew how to use their womanly charms on most of the music teachers so as to win solo parts; but unfortunately no such ploy worked with the 'red-haired priest'. Flattery and flirting, for so far as these escaped the notice of the *Maestra* and her stick, got them nowhere with the violin teacher. Everyone soon learned that Don Vivaldi's only love was music and that he would be impressed only by musical qualities in his pupils.

More and more doubts assailed him. Should he attempt an approach to the *Congregazione* with a humble and courteous request to return to their service? He had even considered doing so for a reduced salary, when his father brusquely brushed aside any such notion. 'If you return,' he told Antonio resolutely, 'it's at the request of the institute. A Vivaldi, my son, never goes begging.'

Antonio turns his back on the *Rio del Santo Sepolcro* and stares out through the forest of masts towards the horizon. Ships are negotiating a wary passage between the shallows of the lagoon, arriving or departing for far-flung places. Dreamily he watches a great three-master weaving its way beyond the Lido. His spirit travels with the ship as it swaps the shelter of the lagoon for the rough heave of the Adriatic Sea. More sail is hoisted, a gruff order comes to haul the sheets, and the ship makes more headway. The bows plunge deep into the waves, showering the foredeck with a fine rain of silty brine flecked with foam. Antonio has never in his life ventured beyond the lagoon. He is not sure whether the rough life of the sea really appeals to him. But the idea of travel does. In spite of all its promises, he has not found the past six months very inspiring. A concert here, a performance there, and now and then a commission put his way by an agent; but generally it has been a pretty hand-to-mouth existence. The quest for something new, the inspiration to compose something that will secure his fame throughout the courts of Europe, up until now it has evaded him. And the harder he racks his brains for a solution, the more it seems his creativity is ebbing away. Perhaps he too should travel; literally broaden his horizons and break the stagnant pattern of his days. Away from Venice and out from the shadow of the Pietà that is increasingly gnawing away at him. What would he do once he arrived at a new destination? Nobody would know him there. Who would be expecting him? Not a soul.

No, he must find his way here in Venice. He wanders dejectedly off the bridge to seek the shelter of home, for the day is becoming more stiflingly hot by the minute. The swallows, too, are returning to the cool of their nests, to emerge again only as late afternoon sinks into evening.

Venice has a new *Doge*! The complex election procedure has gone smoothly this time, and as soon as protocol allows, the investiture will take place of Giovanni Corner and the patricians will be free to go off to their summer residences. The ferries have been waiting weeks for their summer passengers and the one *burchiello* who freed his vessel to embark this morning has very few for the mainland. A rather surly-looking man, he stands on the after-deck and gives a short order to the young fellow on the foredeck to loosen the bow-rope. Gently, but at an even tempo, they row the boat out in the direction of the mouth of the Brenta. In the stern sit two young noblemen, whispering softly to one another. The remaining passengers are seated beneath the canopy. A solicitor from Padua sits motionless, looking earnestly straight ahead of him and it sounds as though the two men busily talking together are on their way back to their homeland in France. There is also a young woman with beside her on the seat a large wicker basket fastened with two leather belts. Across from her is an almost toothless old lady, in her lap a small basket containing fresh *sardela* and crusty bread that her daughter-in-law made ready for her this morning before wishing her a safe journey.

Lucia comes only twice a year to Venice to visit her youngest son and her grandchildren. She used to come a lot more frequently, but these days the summers there are too hot for her and the winters too cold. Lucia has lived her whole life in Padua. After her husband's death seven years ago, she moved in with her eldest son who owns a busy shop. She still regularly helps her daughter-in-law behind the counter. Of the seven children the old lady has brought into the world only two are left, the eldest and the youngest. The latter, Francesco, moved to Venice years ago and enjoys reasonable success as an architect. To visit him is a big undertaking for Lucia, but she loves her son; and her grandchildren perhaps even more. Yet she notices that every visit takes a little more out of her. The long journey and the stay, surrounded on all sides by boisterous grandchildren anxious to show grandma everything, takes its toll. She regrets seeing so little of her family these days. Her son has promised often to come and see her in Padua, but Francesco has too much on his plate to be able to leave Venice with a quiet mind, even for a couple of days. Looking out ahead, Lucia sees the contours of the mainland becoming clearer by the minute. Just another little while and she knows she will be able to smell it again, the spicy perfume of its resinous trees, the rustling grass and grazing cattle. She has to admit she feels safer on the mainland. In Venice you never know if the land will sink away from under your feet. She finds it impossible to sleep well there and sometimes wakens drenched in sweat from a dream in which the rising water is already sloshing against her bedstead.

Lucia has been looking across at the young woman who has sat so silently for the whole of their journey. She wears a simple dress with a white shawl thrown about her bare shoulders to protect them from the sun. Beneath the strong nose her small mouth is pursed. Lucia thinks she does not look happy.

Less so, in fact, with every stroke of the oars. Staring out at the receding silhouetted churches and cupolas of Venice, and unconscious of Lucia's scrutiny, the younger woman brushes away a tear.

It is not yet a year since the unhappy girl arrived in Venice for the first time. Her good references had led her quickly to be given a position as a chambermaid in a very respectable household and all her dreams seemed to be coming true. The glamour and glitter of Venice was even more spellbinding than she could have imagined. She spent her precious spare time visiting one church after another, deeply impressed by their wonderful paintings. The bustling city was for her one huge treasure-trove of new discoveries. Her employer was kind and generous, often giving her chambermaid a book to read, later to discuss its contents with her. The girl could not have been happier. But after a couple of months Venice began to pall on her. She saw it was nothing more than a huge, richly filled cake and, having tasted it, you had soon had enough. Behind the décor of art and *concerti*, architecture and opera, she found only a great desert of plain superficiality. Art here had become something that one person had to possess in order to trump another. The music was as ephemeral as the sea air; everyone breathed it in without giving it a moment's thought. Everything was transitory and more and more superfluous. It was a relief when she came across a like-minded spirit, but such meetings were few and far between. Carnival, she had discovered, provided moments of fascination and unexpected encounters, but some of these had unexpected and unwelcome consequences. Oh, how she would miss the city! If only she did not to have to leave, but there was no other way.

She had taken some while to realise it. At first she had thought her sore and swollen breasts might be due to the weather. But when her monthly 'curse' failed to appear she soon realised the condition she was in. She tried to hide it for as long as possible; after all, something could always go wrong. But the time came when her rosy cheeks and rounding figure could no longer escape the notice of the rest of the house. People were already whispering, and once that happened in Venice a secret was very soon a secret no more. She knew the rules of the household, sorrowfully packed up her few belongings, including the two books bought out of last year's earnings, and left. The morning she left, using the door onto the street, only a couple of the staff came out to say their goodbyes to her, sobbing and with a hug and a good luck wish. Her mistress, with whom she had spent so many hours on intimate terms, almost like best friends, stayed out of sight.

She knew there was no way she could stay in town. The family with whom she had been in service dreaded the idea of their name being blemished in any way. They had given her three months' salary and a clear request, or rather, a clear demand, that she get on the first boat back to the mainland. She had hesitated before acting on their wishes. She was not to be dismissed that easily. She could, of course, have gone to ground, and after the birth of the child simply lowered it in a jute sack into one of the canals. But the very thought of it made her blood run cold; indeed, she nearly died of shame that she had for an instant entertained such a notion. She could also have taken the child to the orphanage, but that would surely have been too great an irony! And anyway, her pride would never have allowed her to go knocking at his door.

No, she felt herself alone responsible and she would see what fate God dealt her. At last she had made her way to the landing-stage and stepped aboard, still with no idea where she would go when she disembarked. Best of all she would like to return to her father, but that is her last alternative. My God, she wonders, will I ever return here? She brushes away a tear and folds her hands in her lap, near where lies hidden the tiny souvenir of Venice she is taking with her.

Meanwhile, Lucia has gestured to the elder of the two oarsmen to bring some drinking water. Without a word, he fills a beaker from the vat and holds it out to her. She takes the beaker with a smile and nudges the young lady, 'Here you are, my sweetheart, take some water. You'll soon feel better.'

The girl sips the water thankfully, despite its vague taste of algae. Lucia has, in the meantime, opened her basket and dipped some bread in the sauce from the sardines. She offers it to the young lady, but she politely declines. Lucia takes a mouthful herself, and then continues enjoying her meal. To the accompaniment of her chatter all about her dead husband, her children and grandchildren, the flat-bottomed ferryboat soon covers the distance between *La Serenissima* and the mainland. On the banks of the slow flowing Brenta, Lucia bids the young woman a fond farewell. She has not discovered the cause of her unhappiness, but she will certainly pray for her. Now she has to step smartly aside, for the next load of passengers are jumping aboard, craning their necks impatiently to search the eastern horizon for their first glimpse of the famous city of *San Marco*.

As unhurriedly as the Brenta empties itself into the lagoon, so passes the summer. Antonio has had a strong sense of his brain also being lulled to sleep by the heat. The summer has brought him no intimation of innovation, and even his father is beginning to doubt if his son has it in him to create anything new. Clearing up at his desk, Giambattista gloomily wonders whether perhaps he has set his sights too high. Before long the first commissions will once more begin to flood in upon him. The theatres are putting together their autumn programmes and that means another influx of copying work. Fortunately, Antonio can lend a hand this time, and perhaps it might even help inspire him.

Autumn also brings the patricians back to Venice. The landing-stage on the Brenta is busy, for also arriving are the first tourists of the new season. The ferries are jam-packed with *Veneti Nobili* exchanging their summer news and asking what they can look forward to in the way of theatrical spectacle during the coming *carnevale*. There is, in any case, one man on board in a position to give them an answer. Giorgio Frederico Haendel, now widely known in the city as *Il Sassone*, is for a second time honouring Venice with his presence. Over his shoulder hangs a leather bag that he holds clamped to his left side. A little afraid of falling overboard, he has seated himself in the middle of the vessel and takes a deep breath as the *burchiello* casts loose from the shore. His expectations for this visit are very great, for in a couple of weeks one of the theatres of the Grimani brothers will be the venue for the premiere of his second Italian opera.

'I'll leave!" storms Antonio. He has just heard that *Il Sassone* is to perform an opera in his city. 'In the greatest theatre in town, no less! What a bunch of corrupt beggars they are! Listen to this, father,' he continues, fiercely ironing flat with his fist the small pamphlet carrying the news, '*L'Agrippina, dramma per musica*, to be performed at Grimani's *Teatro San Giovanni Gristostomo*. Libretto by his Eminence Cardinal Vincenzo Grimani, Nobleman of Venice. Music by Giorgio Frederico Haendel.'" He practically spits out the name.

'Cardinal Grimani?' exclaims Giambattista, astonished. 'He's in Naples, isn't he?'

'Maybe, but he still part-owns that theatre with the rest of the family. Why in God's name do they have to look that far afield for talent?'

'Perhaps this Giorgio really is good. We've heard his name before, haven't we?' says Giambattista lightly. The father has been around a long time and seen strangers come and just as quickly go again; he isn't going to let this get to him.

'Good? How good can a German be? Frigid, bad-tempered and soulless: voilà, *Il Sassone*! Just you wait and see, the first night he'll be jeered off the stage and sent packing back to Germania with his tail between his legs.' Brave words, but deep down Antonio is less sure of himself. He remembers very well that evening, already nearly a year ago, on which Haendel had indeed made an impression upon him. But how come such a fledgling gets given a commission like that? He grits his teeth. How come everything falls into the lap of this foreigner whilst the Grimani family turn their noses up at him? Elitism; that must be it! The more he thinks, the more frustrated he becomes. What in heaven's name does he have to do to get in with the nobility? Maybe it really is a lost cause and he should simply up sticks and seek his fortune elsewhere. The idea gathers strength and each new day increases his frustration with this narrow-minded, parochial city.

L'Agrippina is a resounding success. Right from the first performance on the evening of the twenty-sixth of December it attracts bigger audiences than the theatre has known for many a long day. *Il caro Sassone* receives more applause than the vocalists. Antonio has attended three consecutive performances in *San Giovanni Gristostomo* and it is still beyond him why the public is reacting with such uncharacteristically delirious delight. Usually the theatre is the scene for a series of tableaux with the audience at centre stage rather than anything taking place on the podium. Now instead everyone seems to be completely carried away with the performance; the curtains are even pulled back on the boxes and there are people hanging over the balustrades to listen. There is hardly any swearing in the hall, almost no gossiping and nobody is spitting over the balcony on the heads of those below. If anyone does venture to talk during the performance, their neighbour swiftly silences them. Only during the short pauses after an aria does the hall fill with uproar. A unanimous cry goes up of 'Viva il caro Sassone!' and the foot-stamping audience thus sends its approbation thundering through the hall like a horde of wild boar under fire. And why? In God's name, what's it all about? For the life of him, Vivaldi cannot find a reason. The music carries Roman elements, a whiff of Naples, of Corelli and Scarlatti. But of course, Scarlatti! Antonio has heard that Haendel is a friend of Domenico, one of the sons of Alessandro Scarlatti. But once having set aside his feelings of jealousy enough on the third evening to really listen properly, he discerns something else. Is that German? He allows the melody to imprint itself upon his memory so that he can play it later to his father.

Antonio has become more than ever convinced of the profits to be made from opera. It is rumoured that Haendel has received two hundred ducats for this performance. Imagine! Four times the priest's annual salary from the *Pietà*! For a production lasting less than a month.

A plan is slowly ripening in his mind. Might opera offer a way out of his difficulties? If he could only see a chance to write a successful score, he'd be made. His name would be established and *scritture*, commissions for new operas, would come pouring in. But would he have Haendel's luck? Not only did Il *Sassone* have a good librettist, the same author has provided the German with the chance of a lifetime: Cardinal Grimani, Viceroy of Naples, member of one of the oldest families in Venice and owner of his own theatre to boot!

It's not what you know, it's whom you know, concludes Antonio, having traced in his mind the trajectory taken by Haendel. It's hardly credible how high and fast this German's star has risen. Once you've found the right person willing and able to patronise you, you're made. The German's certainly proof of that. The public is completely mad about him and performances of *L'Agrippina* are to run twenty-seven nights in a row. The young stranger from the north features as hero in all the girls' dreams, while the men admiringly discuss the musical talent of this foreigner so suddenly shot to fame.

But anyone who thinks Haendel might be resting on his laurels is sorely mistaken. Giorgio Frederico Haendel has spread his wings still farther. Like a young swan amazed at his own strength in his first flight across the lagoon, he already has another goal in sight. Before anyone knows what is happening, and at the very height of his fame, he vanishes, apparently unaware of the trail of broken hearts he leaves behind him. A day later or sooner, and he and Antonio would have been sharing the same ferry. Each has booked his passage to the mainland quite unconscious of the other, but once on the other side their paths will not cross. One is to travel north, the other westwards.

Antonio has finally made his decision: he will seek his fortune elsewhere. His father Giambattista is at first sceptical of the plans unveiled by his son. All the way to Rome? For hours on end the father sits making notes and adding up the figures. The family coffers are reasonably full, but a journey of this length and duration will cost a coin or two. Giambattista agrees with Antonio that it will be inspiring to see more of the world and be surrounded by new people and places, but Rome? 'The theatres are still closed there,' reasons the father. 'Wouldn't it be better to go to Florence? That's closer, and hasn't Haendel also been received at the court of the Medici?'

Together father and son decide that Antonio will request an audience with the son of Cosimo III de Medici; Prince Ferdinando is known to be a good musician and lover of the fine arts. Once all the travel documents are in order and a courteous response has arrived from Florence to the effect that Don Vivaldi may pay his respects, all is ready for the priest's departure. On the quiet morning following the one on which Haendel has taken his leave of the lagoon, Antonio also steps on board the ferry to bid his first farewell to his homeland.

Florence is quite different from Vivaldi's imaginings. The city suddenly becomes visible, emerging from the mist that has enshrouded the country for many weeks to reveal buildings dating from the Middle Ages and streets characterised by their heavy, small-windowed façades. The byways themselves are very different from anything he is used to; in stark contrast to the city of the Medici, there is not a right-angle to be found in Venice. All the canals, lanes and pavements follow the lines of old waterways and streams. It is also quite obvious that Florence is past her prime. Antonio has spent this, the final morning of his journey, sharing a carriage with an old textile trader, and Ottavio Squarcialupi, who enjoys a chat, has found a willing listener in the redheaded priest.

'Florence will never regain its former stature,' complains the old salesman. 'Every day they come up with new tax reforms and enforce new laws. When it comes to that, Cosimo's powers of invention certainly know no bounds. It's almost like the reign of terror we were under with Savanorala.' He sighs and looks sadly out of the window before going on to tell Vivaldi how his family has been in textiles for centuries, but just as a ship must steer a middle course in a variable wind, so the family Squarcialupi has had regularly to change tack. They made a great deal of money in the wool trade, but that was two hundred years ago. 'There were years in which the family had more than a thousand employees,' murmurs Ottavio, pausing in his story as if lost in memories of past glory. But the world changes and Florence with it: from wool to silk, from production to trade... and now?

'Now it's a matter of sitting it out until we can shut up shop,' says Ottavio with a mournful look. 'Taxes are creeping up and the competition is murderous. No, it's all over with the trade. And that goes not only for me, you may be sure of that,' he tells the priest, forefinger raised. 'It's the same for all of us! The youngsters are smart. They take themselves off, leaving the trade behind them. But you know, once you get to my age it doesn't make much difference anymore. I'm just glad I don't have a daughter, because then I would have had to sell my house. Nobody can afford to give their daughter a decent dowry these days without getting themselves halfway into debtors' prison. You should see the houses standing empty! No, it's just as I said; things will never be the same again.'

So, the carriage rattling over the cobbles, they arrive in the centre of Florence. As soon as they step out onto the square, Ottavio makes himself scarce so as not to have to offer Antonio a bite to eat or a roof over his head. His journey has left Ottavio with an empty bundle, and his is not the only one. Looking about him, Antonio is aware for the first time of the many beggars. Rather uneasily he pulls his cloak more tightly about him and crosses the square to the entrance of the *Galleria dei Lavori* that the coach-driver has pointed out to him.

To his great annoyance, it has taken days for Vivaldi to be summoned to an audience with the Grand Prince of Tuscany, Ferdinando de Medici. In the meantime he has made the acquaintance of the other musicians attached to the court. Thus, he has spent a whole afternoon in the company of Lodovico Erdman, whom Antonio met a few years earlier when he was oboe teacher at the *Pietà* in Venice. Not that this abrupt German appeals greatly to the priest, but he is at least a familiar face in the strange surroundings of the Medici court.

Lodovico has given Antonio a guided tour of the great building. It appears from their conversation that Lodovico has met his countryman Haendel on several occasions when the latter was a guest of Ferdinando. Antonio grasps this chance of interrogating his ex-colleague and intrigues Lodovico with his obsession concerning the organist from Halle. Lodovico has also introduced Antonio to instrument-maker Bartolomeo Cristofori, for years attached to the court. Apparently he has made a nice instrument, one that will certainly be of interest to Vivaldi.

'Interesting' is the first word Antonio utters after hearing the elaboration offered him by Cristofori and feeling beneath his fingers the keyboard of the *Arpcembalo*. Like a child at a harpsichord for the first time, Vivaldi strikes arbitrarily with his forefinger on a key, softly at first and then pressing down harder. 'There you are,' says the delighted Lodovico. 'It's up to you how much volume you use and so you can give more expression to a note.' Puckering his brow, Vivaldi allows his hands to glide over the keys, picking out a tune. Cristofori stand quietly behind his instrument, studying the face of the priest as he excitedly explores every octave before suddenly lifting his hands clear of the keys.

Then comes his verdict: '*Piano*, too soft.' The instrument-maker looks up, stunned.

'What do you mean?'

'Much too soft! Even if the volume can be varied, at its loudest it is still too soft to hold its own in a *concerto*.' Antonio walks over to a nearby harpsichord. 'Listen!' He plays the same melody as before, but now much louder. Cristofori remarks timidly that it is not the loudness that is at issue, but precisely the variation in volume. 'Perhaps,' adds Bartolomeo, 'the *Arpcembalo* is more suited for chamber music.'

'Hmm, then the chamber won't need to be too big,' retorts Vivaldi with scorn, 'or else the music will evaporate before it reaches the ear of the listener.' *Il Prete Rosso* is clearly unimpressed and Lodovico has long ago regretted ever having introduced him to Cristofori. Antonio turns on his way out of the room and throws over his shoulder, 'The idea's good, but unless you can get some more sound out of it, that instrument will never catch on.'

'Cardinal Ottoboni has ordered one,' remarks Lodovico dryly.

'Glad to hear it,' is Antonio's response. 'But I find it too affected; it's impossible to get any expression out of it. I'm sorry, gentlemen, nothing, but nothing, touches the heart like a stringed instrument in the hands of a competent player!' To illustrate his words the Venetian priest makes mock sweeps of a phantom bow, watched by a somewhat crestfallen Bartolomeo Cristofori. Lodovico, by now properly embarrassed by the whole affair, finds it high time it came to an end, rounds off the conversation and whisks Vivaldi away to the gallery.

Behind them the instrument-maker once more doubtfully presses down a key. Yes, it could be louder, but how?

Despite the glory on show in her churches, the offices and palaces of the Medici, Florence begins to lose its allure for Antonio. His main anxiety is the freakish conditions under which the Florentines are living these days. Everywhere he hears the same story: people abandoning the city, and ever rising prices. And just as the place itself is sinking to its knees, so, too, are the Medici. The power once held by the family is waning fast and with it the respect with which they were once regarded. Antonio has read with amazement the motto on a pamphlet stuck to the wall of *Palazzo Pitti*: '*Appigionasi in quest' anno - Che i Medici se ne vanno*', 'Palace to rent this year, after disappearance of the Medici'. No one in Venice would dream of putting up such a thing on the palace of the *Doge*! Can there be a future here for anyone at all?

Antonio Vivaldi is bid welcome by Luca Casimiro, right-hand man and close personal friend of the prince. Luca is familiar with Vivaldi's work because, as he tells the priest, the King of Denmark and Norway called in on the Medicis on his return journey from Venice the previous year and proudly displayed the *Opus II* dedicated to him in Venice. Antonio feels himself grow an inch or two taller and notices the increase in his own self-esteem as he is introduced to the Grand Prince of Tuscany, Ferdinando.

Cosimo's son is forty-five but looks old and worn out. For years he has been in failing health, a fact the court keeps from the outside world. His voice is so rasping that it is impossible to imagine he was once a fine singer. Yet as Antonio produces his violin and plays a sonata the prince's spirits seem to revive. Ferdinando suggests jovially that they make some music together and, without waiting for the priest's reply, takes his place at the harpsichord. The music the prince selects to play is simple enough and offers no challenge to Antonio, but he sees the enormous pleasure it gives the sick man, and that is all that matters.

'Oops,' exclaims the prince, hitting a wrong note. 'Tut, tut,' he shakes his head disapprovingly, but the further the tune progresses the clumsier becomes the playing of His Royal Highness. 'It's far too hot in here,' declares Ferdinando suddenly, tearing off his wig and throwing it into a corner. Antonio blinks in sheer amazement but, given the circumstances, says not a word. The prince has got to his feet and is staring at Vivaldi with a vacant look in eyes remarkable for their unequal and constricted pupils. There are beads of sweat on the royal forehead and the prince seems to have been transported to another planet.

He looks as if he's gone out of his mind, thinks Antonio shaken. What should I do? The priest glances over at Luca, who gives him a clear sign. 'Shall I play something more for you, Your Highness?' asks Vivaldi softly.

'You're lucky to be a priest,' mumbles the heir of the Medici dynasty. *'Che disse donna, disse danno,* women are a plague, priest, women are a plague.'

His meaning is lost on Antonio, but the prince suddenly seems to emerge from his trance and his amiable mood inexplicably returns. 'Ah, yes. Play for me, my Venetian priest. Take me back to

La Serenissima. Ha, ha!' He laughs aloud and smacks his legs. Sinking into a sofa, he commands in now slightly slurred tones, 'Come on, man, let's hear something!'

Vivaldi no longer knows what to make of it all. He looks around the other faces in the room, but nobody else seems to find the prince's behaviour at all out of the ordinary. The priest closes his eyes and mind to everything, and simply plays. Effortlessly improvising links between adjacent melodies, he produces a flow of music that streams on for twenty minutes.

'Bravo!' claps Ferdinando, as enthusiastic as a little child at the end of his first puppet-show. He rises with difficulty, unaware that he has left behind him on the sofa, and carries on his trousers, a large patch of wetness. Antonio is so excruciatingly embarrassed, he does not know where to look. But the prince thumps him amicably on the shoulder. 'Fantastic, priest! That's just what we need around here, a bit of fun. But play on, I want to hear more!'

The odour of urine hangs in Vivaldi's nostrils, sickening him. Lodovico had warned him that the heir to the Medicis was not altogether himself these days. But this is worse than that. The man is very far from well! It costs Antonio more effort this time to invent a recital and he keeps getting stuck in the same ritornellos. By now the emphatic and omnipresent stench of urine is affecting his powers of concentration and when at last, with a final flourish, he brings his piece to an end, Vivaldi notices with relief that the prince has nodded off to sleep. At least now he may be sure of beating a safe retreat. Luca Casimiro accompanies the priest outside. Pressing fifteen ducats into his hand he hisses, 'I am confident that His Royal Highness much appreciated your presence. I put my full trust in your discretion as a priest not to divulge further anything you have seen today of the prince's behaviour.' Luca rests a heavy hand on Antonio's shoulder and looks him penetratingly in the eye.

'Absolutely. You can trust me,' Antonio assures him.

'As you are aware, the prince has not been feeling so well lately. But we are confident that he will soon be himself again, and your music has most certainly contributed to his recovery!' whispers Luca with a firm handshake. 'Our thanks to you. Do let us know if we may be of any further service.'

Without awaiting an answer, Luca turns and disappears back into the room, leaving Vivaldi alone in the hall.

That's great, thinks Antonio, disappointed. What are those words worth? And suddenly he knows that he has had enough of Florence, enough of the misery and the hopelessness of having no future to look forward to. Is he a failure too?

He is obviously getting nowhere like this. He needs to get home. There's no point in travelling around with no clear goal in sight. He needs a plan of action, and the place for planning is Venice. It doesn't take long to pack up his few belongings, and the same day finds him in a carriage on the road out of Florence.

Grand Prince Ferdinando of Tuscany stares out through the small window without registering anything he sees. In a far corner of his brain not yet affected by the syphilis there echo some last lingering notes of Vivaldi's violin. Then comes a sudden, piercing shaft of pain in his leg and even these are vanquished.

The return journey does not go to plan. A change has come in the weather, rain giving way to snow and making the badly maintained road so slippery that the horses can proceed only at a slow walk over the icy paving stones. Luckily this coachman is experienced and cares about his beasts; all too often horses are driven to their utmost, often resulting in bizarre accidents. One wrong step and a broken leg may mean not only the end for a horse; passengers also run a terrible risk of being crushed beneath an overturned carriage or disappearing fatally into a wayside ditch. There are few travellers on the road at this time of year, and certainly now that the weather has taken a turn for the worse most people think twice about leaving home. Antonio has only one travelling companion; with him in the carriage is a well-dressed man of middle age who has introduced himself as Andrea Farsetti from Vicenza and then buried his head in his book for the rest of the journey. Now and then he makes a note in tiny handwriting, no easy task given the lurching carriage. Antonio looks out of the window, asking himself what he has achieved with this journey. The fifteen ducats given him by Luca Casimiro are not even enough to cover his return fare to Venice. How is he to earn a decent income? He will have to achieve success as a composer before he is invited to write *concerti* and give performances in the palaces of regents and the aristocracy. Damn it, I keep going round and round in circles, he thinks, rubbing his hands to warm them.

It is already dark by the time they arrive at their lodgings for the night, and the landlord is clearly not expecting such late guests. The coachman has to give a couple of good thumps on the door before it is answered. Antonio and his companion are ushered inside and the horses taken to the stable. It is warm indoors, and the three men sitting enjoying themselves noisily at a table turn round to welcome the frozen Andrea and Antonio. The group apparently comprises two Englishmen and a guide, all on their way to Florence. The landlord pokes the fire into life and in a generous gesture throws on more two logs. He offers the two new guests a most welcome chair beside the fire and soon the clothes of the priest and the traveller from Vicenza are steaming and their cheeks have regained some colour. They have been offered soup, and although Antonio is not quite sure what it is made of he is more than grateful for the warm liquid. After putting away plenty of bread as well, he makes his way to bed, tired and rosy-faced from the fire. The inn is small and cramped, with just two upstairs rooms, so that he is going to have to share a bed with Andrea Farsetti. And actually the term 'bed' is a misnomer for the heap of straw covered with a damp and dirty sheet. The lantern gives very little light, which Antonio considers no bad thing: 'what the eyes don't see the heart doesn't grieve over!' This inn surely can't be any filthier than the many others he has slept in during his travels. But he keeps his clothes on and uses his cloak as a blanket.

Downstairs the Englishmen are in fine fettle, giving

boisterous voice to their songs from home. Barbarians! Vivaldi tries with closed eyes to ward off the smell of musty straw and stale urine, and quickly falls asleep.

He awakes the following morning with a slight headache and hears the wind tugging at the roof. It is cold. Next to him lies Andrea Farsetti, snoring and also wrapped in his cloak. Vivaldi feels his way downstairs and tries to blow new life into the fire; the huffing and puffing make him dizzy but he manages to get the tiny twigs to burst into flame and after a few minutes the fire begins to give out a pleasant warmth. Scraping a window clean, he glowers outside. It is still hardly light, but Antonio sees that snow must have been falling all night. Now and then the wind picks up a whole drift of the stuff, scatters and deposits it in a cloud elsewhere. Things do not look too promising. Both landlord and coachman looking outside a while later arrive at the same conclusion: there's no question of travelling today. The Englishmen are still in bed sleeping off their hangovers. Signor Farsetti sits by the fire reading. Antonio tunes his violin in a leisurely fashion then plucks lazily on a string, trying out a new melody. Time slowly passes.

By later that morning the Englishmen and their guide from Turin have appeared and, very subdued, joined the others at the fireside. Vivaldi, restless from idleness, feels the urge to play and, unperturbed by his audience, tries out some of the tunes he has invented during the course of the morning. 'You appear to have an extraordinary gift for the violin, priest,' observes Farsetti. It is the first time this morning that he has opened his mouth. Vivaldi gives a short laugh. Farsetti has shut his book and is attentively following the priest's playing. The Englishmen mumble at one another; it's unlikely that they are in any state to appreciate the violin this morning, anyway.

'Your ability is clearly far above average,' says Farsetti, flattering now, but with genuine interest. 'I also play the violin, but always have difficulty with the changes in position you have just executed.'

Ha, that's nothing, thinks Antonio. But with polite formality he responds aloud, 'I am a violin teacher and composer.'

'Oh, really?' says Andrea convivially. 'I am very sorry, but I have never heard of you before.'

'My last published work is my *Opus II*, dedicated to King Frederik IV of Denmark and Norway,' says Vivaldi, with a very slight swagger. 'I am a music teacher in Venice, both private and at the *Ospedale della Pietà*.' He sees no harm in naming his former employer.

'All that at once, priest. Your Reverence will have a busy life,' is Farsetti's response.

'Indeed. I have just come from the court of the Medici and am now on my way to Venice to put the finishing touches to my next piece of work.'

'Ah, how very interesting. And what might that concern? I shall most certainly look out for it, when it is published,' promises Andrea with sincerity. Antonio now appraises this man properly for the first time. Andrea Farsetti is certainly a good ten years his senior, with a friendly, gentle face; his hair is greying but shows no sign of thinning, and he returns Antonio's look with friendly brown eyes. Vivaldi decides that he likes him. 'To be honest, I'm far from finished with it,' he admits. 'I'm searching for a new mode, a new sound. But I can't find the right inspiration,' explains Antonio, rather taken aback at his own openness.

'Sometimes it is better not to seek, but to find,' responds Andrea.

'That's a fine philosophical thought,' the priest returns, 'but how can you find anything unless you look for it?'

Andrea sits up straight in his chair. 'It surprises me that I have to explain this to a priest. I believe that every individual experiences a turning point in life that gives him a new view on it. One person calls it a heavenly intuition, another a vision. But I call it simply inspiration, or the power of the imagination.'

'Ha, you should have been a priest,' remarks Antonio with

a chuckle.

'Hmm, funny you should say that. As a child I had certain aspirations, but our family does not go in for the priesthood. The Farsettis have for centuries been great landowners, and as an only son my fate was already sealed. Not that it has always made me happy, for my interest lies elsewhere, more in the region of literature and music making – although as far as the latter is concerned I should never dare to measure up to you, Don Vivaldi.'

'I would be delighted to give you a couple of lessons. You would be amazed at the progress you could make.'

Farsetti nods, apparently considering this suggestion. 'We may well have to remain here a while, and I shall certainly take advantage of your offer!' he says.

The bad weather has persisted. Although the snow has stopped, the wind still rages undiminished round the house and nobody at the fireside is the least bit tempted to put their nose out of doors. The landlord has killed a couple of ducks and baked fresh bread, and apart from plenty of cheap beer he also evidently has some decent wine in the cellar. As the day wears on the English guests begin to swap a few words again and it's not long before the landlord puts some beer in front of them. Andrea and Antonio refuse the same. They both know from experience that the beer in this sort of establishment is not the most salubrious drink in the world; it has often sat around too long, and you wouldn't believe what you found floating around in it. But none of this deters the Englishmen. Andrea enquires what sort of wine the landlord has in the house and, hearing the bottles named, orders a *Roscali*. 'An excellent wine,' Andrea assures Vivaldi, adding as he pushes a glass towards the priest, 'but one day you must taste the wine from the Farsetti vineyards.'

So the day passes in a leisurely fashion, Vivaldi now and then playing a piece and explaining certain passages to an eager Andrea; Andrea, in turn, sharing more of his own interests. He writes poetry, he says, and offers to read from his notebook some

lines written over recent days. Antonio likes them. They are lovely verses. The last is so vivid, evoking memories of their recent journey in a swaying carriage with its poor suspension. The priest claps softly and gives voice to praise that seems almost to embarrass the poet. 'Have you ever written any poems yourself?' Farsetti asks.
Vivaldi shakes his head. 'That's a bit of a pastime for the aristocracy, is it not?' he muses out loud.

'Nonsense,' laughs Andrea. 'There's a poet in everybody, if one only lets him speak. It's the same thing we were talking about earlier today,' he persists. 'Everyone is born with certain talents and creative power. Only a few do anything with them. We pray for redemption and look to others for help, while often the answer lies hidden in our own soul. It's all about making manifest the hidden part.' He takes a sip of wine, then gets up and wrests a log of wood from the pile just brought indoors by the landlord. Brushing the melting snow off it, he hands the log to Vivaldi.

'Well, what do you feel?' he asks the priest.

Antonio frowns. 'Nothing. A block of wood.'

Andrea takes the wood from him, runs his hand over the raw grain and taps on the bark. 'Listen! Solid, hard, wood. At the moment it feels cold, but look...' Throwing the log on the fire, he waits whilst sparks fly upwards and the block bursts into flame. 'A cold, hard log is transformed into warmth, and see what remains.' He rakes his fingers in the grate, blows the ash from his palm. 'Dust! Who would have thought it? I'm sure that's why so many talents and ideas never see daylight. Because we don't look for them, perhaps out of fear of what we might find. The tragedy is that people are all too good at standing in their own way, while the power of the imagination is, in fact, a door opening onto a more beautiful world!'

'Well said, sir!' interrupts the landlord, setting a great steaming pan down on the table. 'Watch out, gentlemen, the pot's boiling hot.' He goes off, returning with a couple of deep bowls and spoons. The ducks, long overcooked, are afloat in an unseasoned, soupy concoction of *polenta* and bread. As far as the meal is concerned, only the wine saves the day.

The next morning there is a clear blue sky and the wind has subsided. The coachman wakens the guests early, anxious to make up for lost time now that the weather has cleared.

Before travelling on to Venice, Vivaldi spends two days as Andrea's guest. They use the time philosophising, and Antonio helps his host further with his violin playing. In thanks for the hospitality, Antonio has spent the evening before his departure writing a sonata, and this Andrea accepts the following morning with tears in his eyes. The two embrace, promising each other faithfully to continue their new friendship by corresponding regularly.

But sadly nothing is to come of this, for later the same spring Farsetti's housekeeper finds him dead in bed. It is sudden and completely unexpected. On his chest lies a notebook, open at the page containing an unfinished poem.

The moment he gets home, and as yet ignorant of Andrea's death, Antonio plunges into composition. He's well and truly finished with that old stuff! Inspired by Farsetti's words, Antonio is determined to do something new. Giambattista, delighted to see his son at work with so much energy and enthusiasm, tells Antonio that he has heard from Francesco Gasparini, *Maestro di Coro* of the Pietà, that the management has still not gone in search of a new violin teacher.

It is now more than a year since the termination of Antonio's contract. Rumours that Il *Prete Rosso* has been sacked under suspicious circumstances have eventually died away and everyone by now agrees money lay at the root of his dismissal. 'Have patience, my friend,' Gasparini assures Giambattista. 'It is only a question of time before your son is brought back into the fold. I've mentioned several times to the management committee that musical standards are falling and we're losing audiences as a result, as yet with no response. Take my advice: get playing as much as you can in other churches here in Venice. I know it doesn't pay well, but I'm sure once the *Congregazione* realises that people are flocking to church specially to hear Don Vivaldi play, there'll soon be a climb-down.' Whilst he is talking Francesco's eye falls on the *concerti* Antonio is currently working on. Curious as to the reaction of the *Maestro di Coro alla Pietà*, Giambattista pushes into his line of view the remaining sheets of music. 'Interesting,' concludes Gasperini. 'A lot of new elements, very surprising. But if he really wants to make a name for himself, he needs to let go finally of Corelli.' In clarification, the *Maestro* points out one by one the passages he is alluding to.

For his part, Giambattista tells his friend that he will take to heart all his wise words.

It is not so difficult to gain admission to the churches. The church fathers are perfectly aware that music is the definitive element in attracting congregations and keeping them coming! Indeed, to the majority of the inhabitants of the Republic, church is no more than a cheap alternative to the theatre. Outside the theatre season the same singers found on the podium during carnival earn a bit extra in the churches. Thus, the doors of the many churches in Venice, always busy trying to outdo each other with a better music programme, stand wide open for the Vivaldis. It soon becomes known that the former teacher from the *Pietà* and his father are giving regular recitals together. The *concerti* dedicated to the King of Denmark and Norway are now also accessible to mere mortals, so the services at which the Vivaldis play draw bigger and bigger public participation. It is an enormous joy to both father and son that so many people appreciate the music; they may not applaud, but the soft coughing and shuffling of feet demonstrate very clearly the enjoyment of these congregations. And the same relish may be attributed to the church fathers adding up the collection afterwards. Gasparini too is delighted to hear from Giambattista how things have gone over recent months. Some churches have even placed small commissions.

'Fine,' compliments Francesco, clapping Antonio on the shoulder. 'Things are moving in the right direction. But keep going! You've got somewhere now; make good use of it.' He points to the pile of paper gradually taking shape as Antonio's next *opus*, 'Don't get stuck in the instrumental work but develop your ideas on several fronts. You may be getting a bit of recognition, but you must always watch out people don't get tired of you. Surprise them! Stay a step ahead!' The *Maestro* gives an inscrutable smile, leans towards Antonio and whispers, 'Vocalisation! Write church music in the style of your present instrumental work. You're on the right path and I'm certain, once you've set the tone, the *Pietà* will come to its senses.'

Antonio looks quietly at the *Maestro*, and chews over his words.

'Listen,' Francesco continues, as the church bells begin to ring, 'I have to leave now, but next week I have some time free to help you further. Will you come along to my place on Tuesday morning?' And Gasparini rushes off, leaving Vivaldi nodding.

But he has his doubts. Antonio has devoted his whole life solely to stringed instruments and he is still busy exploring all the possibilities of the violin. Is it really such a good idea to start composing for the voice while he still has his name to make? He'll have to see.

Autumn again brings with it a busy time for Giambattista. There is a great deal of copying to do for the theatres and he is himself to play in the orchestra for several productions. Gasparini has advised Antonio against playing in the orchestra pit. 'You'll drown in anonymity,' is his contention. 'Carry on playing your own concerts and concentrate most of all on your own music.' It is all very well for the *Maestro* to talk, but Antonio lets a number of lucrative offers pass him by as a result. The theatre pays a great deal better than do church recitals.

The way one *barcarolo* voice carries better over the water than another's, it's as if the *gondolieri* compete with one another for who can sing loudest. Anything that floats seems to have been put into the water to manage the endless stream of visitors trying to get to the island of *San Marco*. Barges deeply laden with boisterous tourists, pleasure-seekers and courtesans ply their way up and down the waterways of the city as it prepares for the annual *carnevale*.

But there is one traveller whose serious expression conveys something other than the general mood. Estienne Roger left Amsterdam weeks ago, looking forward not to immersing himself in the partying so unique to *La Serenissima*, but to going hunting. In his role as music publisher he is always on the lookout for new material, and especially for music that sells! His present voyage, for practical reasons avoiding France, took him first to Rome. Here he held lengthy negotiations with the elderly Arcangelo Corelli, who is still working on his *Opus VI*, and making painfully slow progress. His health is meanwhile deteriorating and the veteran composer seems to have lost all real motivation for completing his work. A disappointed Estienne took his leave of Rome with empty hands and set off with a heart full of hope for his new destination of the Republic. He feels sure things will go better here. This is the second visit he has paid to Venice; his first, though almost a decade ago, he recalls with perfect clarity. He was then only just embarking on his career and did not yet have the resources to settle contracts with composers. In the years since he has built up his business through his skill in publishing good work by Italian composers; often, however, without their knowledge. These days it is quite commonplace to appropriate the work of other people and publish it under one's own name. But Estienne is ambitious and wants to conquer all of Europe with his publications. The era in which he bought earlier published work and reprinted it is behind him. Nowadays his modus operandi is most often to seek personal contact and negotiate directly with composers whose work is in demand. And the demand for Italian music in north-western Europe is growing fast whilst his agents are unable to provide him with an adequate supply. A great music lover himself, Estienne has a gift for recognising good music the moment he hears it; others may look askance, but he has an infallible ear for what will turn out a year hence to be a great composition. He must and shall return to the lowlands with new work in his portfolio; otherwise he stands to lose clients! His hope is that Tomaso Albinoni has more work ready. Estienne has received a series of *sonate* from Albinoni before, and his work sells well. There are another eight days before *carnevale* bursts loose upon the streets of the city, and the music publisher decides to use the coming days to scan the latest acquisitions of his Venetian colleagues. At best he might pick up a few ideas and at worst always find something to reprint. In any case, he won't return home with empty hands!

Estienne Roger has rented a small room in a neglected building hidden away in a back lane in the neighbourhood known as *Dorsoduro*. It has been hard enough to find anything reasonably priced, as most available accommodation has been booked in advance by regular visitors. But Estienne is not much bothered, as long as he doesn't have to share a room with a stranger. He needs rest and space in which to study the music he has gathered over recent days. There is plenty of new work, but much of it is of insufficient quality. Some is the vulgar bread-and-butter work of well-known composers and to Estienne's experienced eye immediately recognisable as such. A number of pieces seem to him original and pleasant on the ear and it is these he is now busy scrutinising. Having listened here, there and everywhere, he now compares these pieces with his purchases of this morning from the elderly Guiseppe Sala. The old bookseller did not have much on offer to surprise *Monsieur* Roger. The bookshop made rather a rundown impression, not helped by the presence of Sala, suffering from a heavy cold and keeping a suspicious eye on every client in case they might be tempted to pocket a page of sheet music. That's probably a competitor less for the very near future, thinks Estienne, without a trace of remorse.

Still impressed by Albinoni, the publisher is nevertheless

having trouble concentrating on the composition. He finds himself shocked and distracted again and again by the poor quality of the print work; you would never dare submit work in such a state nowadays in Amsterdam. He leafs on calmly through one composer after another. Hmm, he's heard that name Vivaldi before; he vaguely recalls having seen something earlier from the same composer. But it can't have made much of an impression on him, otherwise it would be in his catalogue by now. Smiling at the pompous dedication to Frederik IV, he thumbs on through sheets of *sonate*. They don't look too bad; even at a casual reading Estienne finds his interest awakened. And he's in luck, because tomorrow there's to be a performance of Vivaldi in the church just around the corner, the *Chiesa dell' Angelo Raffaele*. It seems to the publisher that it might just be worth his while to take this opportunity of hearing Vivaldi playing live.

The Raffaele is pretty full and Estienne has to work his way forward through the crowds. If only he had come on time.

The publisher had no way of knowing that Vivaldi had played here before and in the meantime built up quite a following. Embarrassed, Estienne allows the first half of the service to wash over him. If they knew back home that he had attended a Catholic Mass! As the first half of the service comes to an end and Vivaldi comes forward to play, it becomes instantly evident to Estienne how he has earned the nickname of Il *Prete Rosso*. The priest with the mass of red curls needs no further introduction. As Antonio begins energetically to play, Estienne Roger at once recognises one of the *sonate* from *Opus II*. Rather Corelli-like, he thinks... and yet, not quite. There follows a new *concerto*, and this time it is most definitely different! Estienne leans forward to listen more closely to the cellos. Wow! This is something! When at the end of his recital Don Vivaldi announces this *concerto* to be part of his *Opus III*, Estienne has obvious difficulty in controlling himself. Could Vivaldi be already committed to giving this new work to a local publisher?

Bowing deeply, Antonio thanks the public and stands chatting to his accompanying musicians. Estienne pushes his way forward as best he can and, before he knows it, is standing face to face with the priest. 'A publisher, you say?' repeats Vivaldi with interest as Estienne Roger introduces himself. The priest is quickly intrigued and impressed by the little Frenchman from Amsterdam as he proudly describes his publishing business, his publications, his unique distribution channels in the northern lands – but most of all his interest in the work of Don Vivaldi!

Estienne's candour soon wins Vivaldi's trust, yet Antonio remains on his guard. Is this man truly interested in him? What is there to be gained? Is he really to be trusted? Antonio decides to invite the foreigner to his home while his father is around and continue discussions there. Estienne hesitates. He has no intention of letting the priest slip through his fingers. What if Sala or Bortoli gets to hear that he has been talking to this composer? No, he must not let Antonio out of his sight before he has reached an agreement with him!

Is this over-insistence or determination? Antonio wonders as *Monsieur* Estienne offers to accompany him home straight away. He is not quite sure what to make of the interest shown by the publisher. Maybe this foreigner has his eye on the main financial chance and is going to make Antonio an offer for publishing his work that undercuts Boroli's last charge. On the other hand, he won't mind if the publisher takes it into his head to pay for the gondola!

Antonio has barely introduced the publisher from Amsterdam to his father when Estienne gets down to business. Giambattista listens quietly to what *Monsieur* Roger has to say. 'How long have you been in the business?' asks the father curiously at one point, breaking in on the publisher's story.

'Oh, well,' he laughs, 'let's see. It's more than twenty years since I ventured into the world of booksellers and publishing as an apprentice printer. But I've been working entirely for myself ever since 1697!' he concludes with pride.

'And how does a Frenchman come to live in Amsterdam?' pursues Antonio.

'Good question! Like many of my fellow countrymen, I was forced out of my land when our king more or less outlawed the Protestants. The choice was simple: convert to Catholicism or die.'

'Good Lord!,' exclaims Antonio in consternation. 'So you escaped execution by the skin of your teeth!'

'I wouldn't put it quite like that,' says the Frenchman with restraint. 'I was just twenty at the time and the circumstances provided me with an excuse to go and try my luck elsewhere. I already knew at that age that I did not want to spend my whole life in Caen, and now I am much happier in Amsterdam. Life is so much simpler there and it's unbelievable how open-hearted the Amsterdammers have been in their welcome. I think by now about a quarter of the inhabitants of Amsterdam must be French Huguenots, and I know not many of us wish ourselves back in France. But enough of myself.' And feeling instinctively that doing business with the father will be more complicated than with the son, he directs his gaze straight at Antonio. 'I should like to talk more to you about your new compositions.'

Estienne's intuition has not misled him. Giambattista is thinking things could turn out quite nicely. At least, if he plays his cards right. He gives his son a look that conveys exactly where the initiative belongs and that from now on Antonio must hold his tongue. 'Well now, *Monsieur* Roger, my thanks for your visit and for your interest in my son's work. You will understand that in the wake of his last publication he has become much sought after. You have heard him play, so I don't need to tell you what a *virtuoso* he is. And as for his new work, well, how should I put it...? Let's just say there is a certain amount of interest in *Opus III*, and although we have not yet decided which publisher we shall entrust it to, we do have our preferences.'

This is precisely what Roger was afraid of. It's a generally accepted fact that a Venetian will sell his own blood-bespattered mother if only he can get a good price for her. But no worries; this is a game Estienne has played before. 'Of course,' he says silkily. 'I take it as read that there are many eagerly awaiting this publication. Certainly if all the *concerti* attain the high standard of that which I had the honour of hearing yesterday, I am confident that you will arrive at an excellent agreement.' Estienne picks up his hat and gets to his feet. 'I shall take up no more of your precious time, gentlemen. Should you decide to make use of my services, please do not delay unduly. I depart in a couple of days for the Netherlands.'

Estienne makes as if for the door and Antonio glances panic-stricken at his father. Just one nerve-racking thought fills his head and it is that they are letting go of their big chance. Giambattista straightens a pile of papers on the worktop in front of him. Pretending to read and thus not having to look at Estienne, he asks nonchalantly, 'Why should we decide to make use of your services?'

Got you! Estienne turns round and removes his hat again. A sigh escapes Antonio's lips.

'For a number of reasons,' says Estienne softly. He does not wish to put all his cards on the table at once. The less he has to pay the Vivaldis, the bigger his own profit. 'I have described to you our distribution system, unique in the whole of Europe. We advertise in newspapers and catalogues and within a very short period of time the name of Antonio Vivaldi is known throughout Germany, Sweden, Denmark, the Netherlands, France and England. I do not have to explain to you what that might mean in terms of commissions. Moreover, I dare claim our print work to be the best in the world. Personally, I should consider it a great shame were you to make use of a local printer and have your new work appear in the same condition as the last.' He throws Vivaldi's *Opus II*, bought earlier in the week in Bortoli's bookshop, carelessly onto the table as if it were so much waste paper.

'Why, what's wrong with it?' Antonio wants to know, wounded.

Giambattista has raised his hand for silence. 'Elaborate, *Monsieur* Roger.'

From his bag Estienne conjures forth one of his own printed pages of sheet-music and sets it on the table before Giambattista. 'Why not look for yourself?' he invites the copier, brimming with self-confidence.

Antonio has got up and stands behind his father as he starts to skim through the pages. 'Mother Mary!' mutters the priest, his eyes growing ever wider with admiration. They have nevers seen such resolution and clarity before. Triumphant, the publisher describes how his books are printed. By employing a copperplate engraving process in place of lead typesetting he can achieve far greater sharpness and detail. The exact intention of the composer can be clearly made out from every note on the sheet, each of which is spotlessly clean. There is no bleeding of ink and the paper looks whiter than ever before in manuscript.

'It's beautiful work,' admits Giambattista. 'You've fully convinced us on that front. But there are other things at stake.' He pauses. Estienne grins, now confident he has his case half won. 'I agree entirely,' he says. 'I should like to make you an offer,' a trace of irony creeps into his voice, 'so that you may compare it at your leisure with others you have already received.'

Giambattista does not hesitate for a moment. He invites the publisher to resume his seat and asks Antonio to pour them all a glass of wine.

'If you write the work exclusively for me, I will give you an advance. I will then pay you a sum upon receipt of the manuscript, and the remainder will be paid as a percentage on sold copies,' Roger completes his proposal. It takes more than a bottle for the three gentlemen to arrive at a final agreement. There are handshakes all round and Giambattista puts everything down on paper immediately. 'Then there can be absolutely no confusion over it!' declares Vivaldi senior, strewing sand over the wet ink.

Carnevale has burst upon the city as violently as usual, but Antonio notices nothing of it. All his concentration is upon the composition of his *concerti*. For he has decided they will all be *concerti*. Four sets of three, a structure with which Antonio is exploring the farthest frontiers of traditional composition. Estienne has made plain that *concerti* modelled on the Roman, the sort composed by Corelli, will sell well. But, as he readily admitted, a whiff of fresh air through them could never go amiss. But how much is a whiff? What in the morning feels like a wondrous flash of inspiration is the same afternoon waved aside by a grimacing Giambattista. It begins to get on Antonio's nerves the way his father constantly rejects his work like this, without ever offering a sound alternative. What does his father know of the creative process? Giambattista certainly has no new musical ideas of his own. But despite everything the new work takes shape, Antonio refusing to accept some of the criticism aimed at him. The act of composing comes more and more easily to him and fewer and farther between are those moments in which the pen hangs motionless above the paper whilst the ink slowly clots.

Nowadays, whenever the priest feels himself falling into a vacuum he thinks back on the inspiring conversations with Andrea Farsetti. It had been a great sorrow to him that day when, with his returned letters, had come a brief note telling him that his friend was gone. The priest had prayed for his soul; it was all that he could do for Andrea now.

After Christmas the manuscript is ready to send off. Antonio intends at first to dedicate the work to Andrea, but his father will hear nothing of it. 'There's no money to be made from corpses,' is his definitive observation. Eventually father and son agree that the dedication must be to Grand Prince Ferdinando of Tuscany. 'After all, you never know,' Giambattista chuckles. 'Perhaps you'll be welcomed back to his court when he recovers, and that might be worth a lot more than the last fifteen ducats.' Picturing the sick prince, Antonio can't quite muster the same optimism.

In anonymous tribute to Andrea, Antonio has suggested to his father that they give the work a title. This is a not unknown convention, but usually it is the publishers who dream up increasingly florid titles to stimulate sales. 'What have you in mind?' asks Giambattista.

"The Inspiration", something like that,' replies Antonio.

'Hmm, not very original,' is his father's lukewarm response. 'Can't you do any better?'

Antonio casts his mind back to the snowbound inn. He can almost hear Andrea laugh, see his beguiling smile as he throws the log of wood onto the fire. The fiery power of the imagination... yes, YES, that's what it has to be!

"L'Estro Armonico!" shouts Antonio. 'New and old, hand in hand! Imagination, inspiration and harmony. That's it; that's what it has to be!' No shadow of a doubt in his mind.

Bemused, his father stares at his son, and then smiles indulgently. 'Fine, lad. L'Estro Armonico it shall be. I can live with that.'

Giambattista Vivaldi makes a careful copy of the original and takes the enormous paper parcel to the post.

It's a while before word comes back from Amsterdam that everything has arrived safely. Each week that passes deepens Antonio's agonised self-doubt. Reading through the original manuscript, not everything comes up to scratch. He would have liked to make improvements and now it is too late. News has spread that Don Vivaldi has found a foreign publisher for his next *opus* and the general buzz is, 'What arrogance; what's wrong with our own printers?'

The letter from Holland is waiting patiently for them on their arrival back from Brescia, where Giambattista has been paying a long overdue visit to his family. Antonio has gone with him this time because his father has arranged that the trip will include a joint performance by them at a service in *Santa Maria della*

Pace. This has proved a great success and Antonio, whose first time it is in Brescia, has made the acquaintance of many people introduced to him as cousins. The family, all proud to be related to this violin *virtuoso* and composer from Venice, is keen to press the church council to offer Antonio a commission. For although the redhead priest might have been born in Venice, he surely has Brescian blood running in his veins!

Giambattista quickly breaks the seal and opens the letter. A cheque flutters out, which Antonio swiftly retrieves from the floor. 'Fantastic,' is Giambattista's verdict a couple of seconds later. His eyes flit again over the contents of the letter. 'Estienne has begun on the first plates and has already sold some copies in advance!' Antonio reads excitedly along with his father, the cheque trembling in his hands.

His good fortune does not desert Estienne. He knows he has hit on gold. This is again confirmed as the first copies of *L'Estro Armonico* roll off the press and find their way directly into the hands of wealthy music lovers. The publication, running to more than two hundred pages, receives excellent reviews in Amsterdam. It is not long before the good news reaches Venice and the name of Don Vivaldi, otherwise known as *Il Prete Rosso*, is on everyone's lips.

But that is not to say that everyone is equally enthusiastic over the 'Master of the *concerti*'! There are plenty of conservative noblemen who enjoy looking down their noses at all this modern innovation. But the main thing is that the music is being discussed, albeit praised by one and abused by another. And one thing stands out like the *briccole* of Venice above water: *L'Estro Armonico* is clearly different, plainly something new, and it is to provide the priest with the recognition he has so long yearned for.

Whose idea it was we can no longer discover, but father and son are agreed that they need a bigger workroom, one with more light. If Estienne's predictions prove correct, demand for Antonio's compositions will soon be on the rise; already more and more people are knocking on the door for violin lessons while the house is too small to teach in. It is not long before a suitable place is found. The new residence stands on a pleasant square, just along from the monastery and church of *San Zaccaria*. Downstairs is a shop with a large working space backing onto it, lately occupied by a carpenter. Jacopo, an aged wood-carver, had worked less and less up until his death at the beginning of the previous month, and he has no successor. Apparently, no one is interested in taking over his business. There are already more than enough carpenters in Venice, and fewer and fewer ships are gliding from the launching bay of the *Arsenale*. Many a fine craftsman is being forced into other work.

This house is perfect! Two workshops and enough domestic accommodation on the upper two floors for the rest of the family. *Mamma* Camilla, after a thorough inspection of the kitchen, expresses her concern that the chimney seems to be full of soot. The rest of the house is none too clean either, but she is quite happy to give that a good going-over with a dustpan and brush. One huge advantage is the well, just outside the front door of the house. That'll save her a fair bit of running about! The workshops have not been cleaned for years; wood shavings and heaps of sawdust lie everywhere and every footstep throws up a new cloud of dust. This soon affects Antonio and sends him running outside, coughing and spluttering. Between gulping in one lung-full of fresh air after another, he manages to make it understood that he's staying out there until the place has been cleaned up. Giambattista soon has things organised, and towards the end of April, when the house has been more or less declared dust-free, Antonio Vivaldi takes possession of his very own studio.

From Amsterdam keep coming the enthusiastic letters carrying news of healthy sales of *Opus III* and requests for more work. Antonio is kept fully occupied meeting all these demands, while Giambattista throws himself not only into finishing off his own work, but also making increasing numbers of neat copies of commissions.

Lady Fortune is now smiling upon the Vivaldis, so that it comes as some surprise one fine afternoon to find standing on the step with his hat in his hand one of the governors of the *Ospedale della Pietà*. The *Pietà*!

What with one thing and another, it is a long time since Giambattista has given it a moment's thought. But the same cannot be said for Antonio. He often thinks about the *Coro*. How might things be going with his pupils?

The *Congregazione* has become aware of the fact that Don Vivaldi is attracting bigger and bigger audiences, for they are detracting from its own listener numbers. The chairman has now decided that enough is enough and swept from the table all remaining arguments against him. The result of the vote on twenty-seven September 1711 is unanimous. Don Antonio Vivaldi is to be reinstated in the position of *Maestro di Viole all'Inglese*. With an increase in salary!

The only remaining question exercising the chairman is whether the priest will accept the offer. He is not kept long in suspense; the very same day Antonio shoves everything else aside and, humming a joyful tune to himself, once more lets fall the heavy knocker on the door of the *Pietà*.

The news travels through the corridors like wildfire; *Il Prete Rosso* is back!

3

Venice, September 1711

'Maestro!' Anna Maria calls out jubilantly, rushing headlong into the music-room. 'Maestro!' She throws her arms about the priest as if he were her own father. Smiling, Vivaldi disentangles himself and holds her by the shoulder so he can look at her. 'You've grown, my girl,' he says softly. She looks back at him, tears of joy rolling down her cheeks. 'I'm so happy you're back. You don't know how much I've missed you.' Anna Maria clasps her arms around the priest again and he rocks her gently back and forth. From her chair, a disgruntled *Maestra* watches the pair. Anna Maria catches her eye and pokes out her tongue as rudely as she can, but before the woman can rebuke her, more choir members arrive and take turns embracing the disconcerted priest. He has not expected quite such a warm welcome and is surprised the girls and women have missed him so much. They bombard him with questions, so not much music is made this morning. Antonio takes the trouble to tell them all they want to know and listens attentively in turn to their stories. The *Maestra*, duty-bound to stay and keep an eye on things, passes the time in jealous speculation. This priest is a man, after all, and that's the one and only reason the girls make such a fuss of him. But she does not fool herself. Deep in her heart she knows all this affection is not due solely to Vivaldi's masculinity. She knows that Don Antonio Vivaldi is a superlative teacher, capable of nurturing to fruition all the hidden talent in the *Figlie*. It is a task in which she herself has signally failed, a painful fact she would rather not face and the true reason why she holds aloof from this joyous reunion.

The day of tumult soon passes, fading into the centuries-old rhythm of the *Ospedale della Pietà*. The first thing Antonio does is to audition everyone who plays the violin, noticing straightaway that most people have stayed at the level he left them two years ago. A couple of the string players have made clear progress but are playing very sloppily from a technical perspective, posture incorrect and holding the bow as though it were a fishing rod. There is much work to be done!

This afternoon he has an appointment with *Maestro di Coro* Francesco Gasparini to report his findings. Gasparini is relieved to have Vivaldi back as teacher. He has missed him, for the priest has shown enough ambition to take over certain tasks from the *Maestro di Coro*; his violin playing is still unsurpassed and the young man is making good progress with his compositions. This has all reduced the pressure of work on Gasparini, allowing him to direct his energies into more lucrative business, such as the writing of a new opera.

Before him lies the *libretto* handed him earlier this week by Apostolo Zeno. Quickly skimming through it at the time, Francesco had noted the title given it by the librettist: *Merope*, yet another ancient Greek tragedy. Francesco Gasparini has asked the priest to join him this afternoon on the small roof terrace of the *Pietà*. It is the beginning of October but the weather this week has been extremely warm, as though the sun can't bear to take its leave of the Republic. Whenever he gets a chance Gasparini is to be found up here on the roof, convinced that the farther away from the water he sits the better it is for his health. He cannot understand how people can spend their whole lives in such a steamy city. He hates the water, but has hit on a compromise by making his home in the city of *San Marco*. For more than a decade now he has been living in the lagoon and is proud of the fact that during this period the standard of the *Figlie di Coro* of the *Ospedale della Pietà* has improved beyond recognition. To the extent that everyone agrees the *Pietà* stands musically head and shoulders above the other institutes, and people come from far and wide to listen to the choir, his choir!

But the real money-spinner for him over recent years have been his operas.

His reputation having preceded him, Gasparini, soon after his arrival in Venice and appointment to the *Ospedale della Pietà*, had been offered the opportunity to compose an opera. Since then his hands had been full. Yes, Venice had been good to him, very good. And one side-effect of success had been to make him forget his chronic cold and the risk of malaria.

But now, after a decade of hard work, he is beginning to feel it all becoming a bit much for him. The daily pressure of having to write new motets, vespers and other compositions for the *Pietà* alongside his theatre work is increasingly burdensome. Added to this is a much more demanding public; while a couple of years previously one opera sufficed for the whole season, this is no longer enough. 'More, and yet more' is the motto of the day. As long as he got well paid for his trouble this was not too much of a problem for Gasparini, but deep down it disturbs him that today's theatre-goers seem to listen less and less no matter what the performance. Yet it has to be brand-new, or else completely revamped! Where will such superficiality end?

His ruminations are interrupted by the appearance at the trapdoor of Vivaldi, gasping for air and red-faced. When he invited Antonio to meet him up here Francesco had completely forgotten how badly the priest suffered from shortness of breath. Puffing and panting, Vivaldi slides onto the bench and takes thankful possession of the glass of wine poured him by Gasparini.

'I don't come up here very often,' manages Antonio, sucking in short, desperate breaths between each word. 'It's a whole pantomime for me, climbing those stairs,' he wheezes, banging on his chest. Francesco waits before answering, giving the priest a moment to recover. Staring out across the city and the *Canal Grande*, the choirmaster watches a slow procession of cargo vessels, smacks and *gondole* glide out over the water.

Once the priest's skin colour has returned to normal, Gasparini addresses him in his deep bass, 'So Vivaldi, tell me, how does it feel to be back?' Antonio smiles. 'To be honest, I've missed the place. It's nice to work with motivated people, and the *Figlie* are just like a dry sponge, greedy to mop up every word you say.' Gasparini nods, laughing. But the *Maestro di Coro* has other things on his mind. 'What are your plans, priest?' he asks.

Antonio is wary. He likes Gasparini, but he also knows how calculating the old bear can be and he's not absolutely sure what the motive is behind his being lured up here today. If it's only about work, then why couldn't they have discussed it downstairs? 'I'd like to concentrate on technique. There are one or two things that need polishing up,' says Antonio, formulating his reply with diplomatic care. He doesn't want to rush into criticising the string players of the choir.

'Ha!' Gasparini roars with laughter. 'I can well believe it! But what I meant was, what are your personal plans? What do you mean to achieve over the coming years? Last year you wanted to come back to the *Pietà*. *Voilà*, here you are back. But what's your next goal? Or are you going to spend the rest of your life showing people how to hold their bow properly?' The visage with its huge, bristling eyebrows glowers challengingly into Antonio's face. Momentarily dumbstruck, Vivaldi takes a sip of wine and directs his gaze over the balustrade out towards the horizon. 'I'm not really sure as yet,' he admits. 'I know I'm good at teaching, and the *Figlie* are rewarding students. But I find the success of *L'Estro Armonico* stimulating me to go on composing *concerti*. According to my publisher there is an increasing demand for them. *Monsieur* Roger even wants to reprint new editions of my first two works, you know. They may not be *concerti*, but they're still works by Vivaldi!' he adds with pride. 'I've started on a new collection, but I'm also very busy with smaller compositions; I get asked for more and more.' Gasparini nods approvingly. 'I'm glad to hear all is going well with you. You're obviously making a name for yourself instrumentally. But how are things with vocal work? I think I advised you once before to explore the possibilities in this area. Of course it's all very fine that *Monsieur* Roger is selling so much of your work, but where's it getting you? And naturally it's wonderful to be worldfamous, but you also have to earn your bread and butter.'

He rubs thumb and forefinger together significantly. 'Make no mistake about it, once you're on the road to success people start taking advantage of you. You can rest assured your publisher will make three copies of every piece of your work he sells. Great for your spreading your name, but you earn not a ducat from them! Scritture, commissions, that's what it's all about!' Francesco points at the myriad church spires rising above the terracotta-tiled roofs of the city. 'Look about you, Vivaldi. The place is alive with opportunities. Your Venetians have an insatiable appetite for innovation.' Again he sweeps an arm towards the many campanili, 'Over there. The "Teatri di Divozione". These theatres with all their festivals are screaming out for compositions that will pull in bigger and bigger audiences. Who's going to write it all?'

Antonio lets the words sink in a while. There's something in them, he thinks, although his church recitals earned him very little cash. But then he still has hardly any sacred music in his repertoire.

'Now that you're back at the Pietà you are in a privileged position in terms of composing for the city's churches and monasteries. Make use of it! But that's not all. How do you feel about theatre work?' pursues Gasparini, tapping the libretto before him on the table. 'Every year more and more operas. You want my prediction? Opera: that's where the future lies, man! And where there are audiences there's money! Much more than you could earn at the Pietà in a lifetime.'

A gleam comes to Antonio's eyes as he asks humbly, 'How much more?'

'Oh, that depends entirely on how successful you are. But say you can produce a decent dramma per musica; that will soon bring you in a good few hundred ducats. And if you can summon the energy and stamina to write several productions for a single season, ha!' Gasparini grapples grotesquely at the air as if gathering in an armful of Midas gold. His eyes are rolling wildly and in his excitement the Maestro has begun unconsciously to dribble.

Antonio sees the mountains of ducats heaping themselves on the table before him and empties his glass in a single greedy gulp. With a broad grin of satisfaction, Gasparini tops them both up with wine. Wiping his mouth on his sleeve, he probes, 'What have you done so far in the line of vocal work?'

Antonio shrugs. 'Not much,' he admits dubiously. 'I don't know, it doesn't seem to be my thing.' He recalls the *sonate* he wrote for Frances Quirini three years or so before. Despite all the compliments, he wasn't so very pleased with it. It was too contrived and far from harmonious. He hadn't even thought it worthwhile keep to the manuscript. The episode had seemed to him to confirm that vocal music was not his strong point.

'No,' says Vivaldi with more self-confidence, 'the more I think about it, the more I'm sure it's not for me.'

'Rubbish!' insists Gasparini. 'You just haven't had a serious go at it. As long as that's the case, you can't shut the door on it.'

Antonio fidgets uncomfortably on the wobbling bench. 'I don't know. My father shares my feeling. "Do one thing and do it well" is his motto.'

'And you always do exactly what your father tells you!'

Antonio grins. 'Well, not always. But he usually gets things right. What's more, I find it difficult working with vocalists. An instrument follows your instructions precisely, but a singer is a human being. So you can never be sure of them. They all have their little idiosyncrasies and you never know what's going to happen: a streaming cold on the very day they have to sing.'

'Rubbish!' repeats Gasparini. 'Pure exaggeration! The fact that a person is not an instrument is exactly what makes the human voice so unique. EMOTION! The trick is to find the right balance between instrument and voice. But once you've found that, ah, *toccare il cielo col ditto*, then you're in seventh heaven!' He looks skywards with glazed eyes and swiftly crosses himself. 'Listen,' Gasparini moves nearer Antonio. 'I'll give you a hand. I'll let you work on some new compositions for the *Pietà*. Have a look at some of the vocal work I've done over recent years and try doing something similar. You can find all the peace and quiet you need to rehearse with the *Figlie* within these four walls. Don't say anything to your father just yet. When the moment comes I'll have a word with him myself.'

'But have you time for this?' Vivaldi knows how busy the composer is already. Nor does Antonio feel entirely sure of himself, however seductive the promise of enormous future financial rewards.

'Don't you worry your head about that, priest. I've said it once and I'll say it again; you'll master this business in no time.' The *Maestro di Coro* pats Antonio encouragingly on the shoulder with his huge paw.

To Francesco's great joy, Antonio has wasted no time in embarking on their new project. The priest is spending hour after hour in the library leafing through years of vocal music written for the choir. He is also attending rehearsals, listening with interest and taking notes, which soon arouses the suspicion of the *Ospedale della Pietà's* singing teacher, Pietro Scarponi. What's Vivaldi up to? Scarponi keeps the priest under close observation and starts to have real worries. Surely Vivaldi can't be after his job? It begins to look more and more like it, as Antonio selects a number of vespers and goes through them with the choir.

Conducting choir and orchestra is a whole new experience for Vivaldi and he discovers he relishes it. He has now set to music a psalm and offers it proudly to the *Maestro* for his opinion. But Gasparini is not impressed. 'Read the text, man, read the text!' he mutters. 'It doesn't have to keep going off in all directions like a firework. Here, read this through carefully and let the words sink in.' The *Maestro* indicates some rather melancholic verses. 'You write as though we've just triumphed over the Turks. Your music fizzes and bangs and sends up cheers. But what I read here is a completely different story! Look at the words again and try to make your music strengthen and carry the message. That's what it's all about!' The criticism throws Antonio into an agony of self-doubt.

But just as hatred of having his work pulled apart is in Antonio's character, sensitivity to other people's feelings is absent from Gasparini's. 'Start again,' he orders, pointing at a pile of fresh paper.

More out of respect for the master than internal conviction, Antonio returns to the psalms. He remembers how years ago he studied the same texts at the seminary; and how he committed them to memory by giving each its own melody. The words bring the same tunes faithfully back to mind. But now they make him giggle; they're so childish, such artless devices. Yet one sticks, and as he starts to play with it he finds himself writing feverishly.

This time around Gasparini seems rather more pleased. Handing the music back to Antonio, he instructs approvingly, 'Go and rehearse it with the choir.' From now on things begin to flow and one psalm after another is set to music. 'I knew you'd get the hang of it,' the *Maestro* tells Antonio one afternoon as the last member of the choir is leaving the music-room.

The marriage between instrument and voice is a revelation to Antonio. He listens now with other ears than during previous theatre productions in former seasons. For the first time he analyses the tone and colour of each voice. He has never before realised the degree to which singers differ from one another. And this new awareness soon equips him to sort the wheat from the chaff. Some vocalists who enjoy an impressive reputation are, when you listen carefully to them, not actually so wonderful. This, however, does not bother the average theatregoer. Well-known artists are greeted onstage with deafening applause; when it is the turn of a new or unknown artist they find themselves upstaged by an audience happily amusing itself, as is its wont, with the many and colourful diversions practised and perfected by Venetian culture vultures over generations. And this Vivaldi finds a great shame, for the least known singers often sing better than the big stars. His lung problems have always prevented Vivialdi from being able to sing well, but the techniques of voice training and breathing are beginning to intrigue him. Gasparini, in his younger days himself an enthusiastic and trained singer, is pleased to answer in detail the priest's technical questions. Yet still Vivaldi holds back a little, retains his reserve. He does not know quite how to accommodate in vespers the energy and momentum that he pours into his fiery *concerti*. But, encouraged by Francesco Gasparini, he does discover a deepening understanding of the psalms, enhancing his ability to set them to music.

It is only a matter of time before Giambattista discovers his son is busy experimenting. 'What's the point of it all?' he asks, disappointed. Antonio does his best to reply, using sentences and arguments put in his mouth by Gasparini. His father is not satisfied and, waving in the air one of Roger's letters, goes on the offensive, 'Here in black and white is a request for more work that could have been answered long ago. It's all very well what you're doing behind my back, but it isn't bringing in a single lira. Get down to work this minute. Amsterdam's been patient enough already!'

Crestfallen, Antonio slopes over to the worktable and takes up his *concerti* again. But the work will not come back to him. His head is full of new melodies now, and texts, and most of all, emotion! And this last he finds irresistible. He is familiar with how his instrumental work can stir an audience, but now he knows he can do more. He is no longer satisfied with simply reaching people; he wants to touch, to move them! To stir the very soul; as if angels had engraved the words of the psalms upon their hearts for all eternity.

His music soon reaches a state of maturity surprising to all who hear it. When, during rehearsals, a member of the *Figlie* sings a vespers, Vivaldi is not the only one who feels the depth of emotion in his music. The soloist too is gripped by an intensity that often leaves her weeping. The priest finds doors opening in his comprehension as the music breathes new life into Biblical texts. No longer are vespers sung mindlessly or heard as background to an idle glance around the congregation. No! The priest's music becomes a religious experience capable of moving the most hardened churchgoer. Is it possible to come closer to God on earth than this?

Antonio has for a while been staring at the words:
> 'The mother stood, in sorrow
> and in tears, by the cross
> upon which hung her Son.'

The hymn *Stabat Mater* offers a sweet challenge, its poignant lines begging to be set to music. The father and son performance in *Santa Maria della Pace* in Brescia has brought them a commission after all. In conference with the church fathers it has been decided that the famous Antonio Vivaldi, grandson of Agostino Vivaldi of Brescia, shall write a composition based on the ancient song of praise to Mary at the crucifixion of her son. The premier will take place during the Feast of the Seven Sorrows, for which only the first eight of the full twenty couplets are to be set to music. This may at first sight seem no great task, but Antonio has something very great in mind.
> 'Who could fail to be moved
> watching that sweet Mother
> grieving with her Son?'

There is so much drama in the words; they need only the lightest musical touch to emphasise them.

The verses recall to Antonio's mind events surrounding poor Carlo Chiari, eleven days before. The man had been a good soul. People regularly poked fun at him, yet he either did not understand or refused to let it affect him, always running around with a loveable grin on his face. And over the years he had made himself invaluable at the *Teatro San Samuele*. It began with simple tidying up, but in the end he was sweeping and cleaning the theatre after every performance. He also helped build the sets, for Carlo might be deaf-mute and a little simple-minded, but he was also tremendously strong. Supple as a cat, he would crawl and climb over the scenery and sets and stroll along the high beams from which hung panels and backdrops. After every scene, complex mechanical equipment was used to change the set in seconds, leaving the audience gasping with amazement. To shouts of 'Oh!' and 'Ah', a storm at sea would make way for the inner courtyard of a great palace.

Whenever a new production was coming up it was Carlo who knew where and how everything should be put together, high up in the rafters. But this morning things went wrong. Nobody knew exactly how it happened, but a sudden dull thud resounded through the building and everyone working in the vicinity of the stage looked up in shock. A painter, furious that his canvas had been suddenly splattered with great blobs of paint, turned round angrily, ready to fire off a volley of swear-words. But his eyes were soon wider than his gaping mouth, for there lay the broken body. The brush slid from the painter's hand. Others rushed to Carlo's side as he lay face downwards on the floor. Gently they turned him over. Just above his left eyebrow was an ugly wound from which the blood pulsed in tiny crimson spurts, finding a course down the slightly sloping platform, mixing on the way with colours spilling from overturned paint pots. By now more of the company had gathered around Carlo. 'Call a priest!' cried one in panic. 'Bandage his head,' screamed another. One set-builder had torn off his tunic and pressed it to the wound. Carlo's face was by now white and drawn, and people made a sign of the cross, shaking their heads. Surely nothing could be done for him now.

Then, as if from nowhere, came a deep, tremulous murmuring. At first no one could tell where the sound was coming from and people turned nervously, half expecting to see some dreadful apparition emerge from one of the dark corners of the theatre. But as the volume increased it became obvious the noise was emanating from Carlo himself. 'He's alive!' someone shouted. But the sound soon became a keening, animal moan, utterly heartrending and inhuman. Nobody had ever heard Carlo utter such a din before. The horrible lamentation grew so loud that people stepped back in dread horror. Such was beyond the bounds of normality! *Santo Cielo*, it must be Satan's work. This was too much for the impresario. 'Get him out of here!' he yelled without mercy. If the story got around that his theatre was possessed by the devil he'd never get another audience in through the doors. 'Come on, pick him up and get him outside. Out of here!' More in terror than in anger, he gave a couple of lads a kick in the backside that made them stare at each other wide-eyed in wonder. 'Allora, get going,' raged the impresario once more. 'Otherwise you both lose your jobs.'

This got them going, for jobs were becoming less and less easy to find. It took four men to get Carlo up off the ground. Lorenzo, the one who had used his tunic to roughly dress the dying man's wound, walked outside with them, for the bleeding would not stop. Swearing, the impresario brought up the rear. He could not rid himself of the sad little procession fast enough.

Widow Elisabetta Chiari lived just behind the theatre. Nobody wanted to take Carlo to the hospital. None thought he stood a chance of making it. So the badly wounded man was dragged up the steps to his mother, giving her such a shock she nearly died of a stroke herself. Lorenzo was the only one to stay behind with her. Having dumped the wailing Carlo on his hysterical mother, the others ran away as fast as their legs would carry them. 'We're off to fetch a priest!' shouted one of the boys in excuse. Carlo's dreadful death song was like a cry for help that pierced Elisabetta's soul. Outside on the square, more and more people had gathered to stare up at the closed shutters on the first floor. There was whispering and gossip, people muttering prayers and crossing themselves.

The doctor, who had arrived at the same moment as the priest, was soon back outside again. None of his years of experience equipped him to help Carlo. There was nothing he could do. Shaking his head sadly and silently at the crowds, he made off as quickly as he could.

The priest remained indoors. It would be three long days

before the good man would leave again. In the meanwhile, peace had returned to the square. After a bitter struggle, Carlo Chiara had given up the ghost.

Elisabetta was distraught. All that time she had stayed at his side, talking softly to him, washing him, stroking his skin. She had kissed him and prayed for him. She could do nothing more. Helplessly she had looked on as her son's life slipped through her rheumatic fingers. 'My Carlo, my darling. *Perchè*? Why must you suffer so? Where is God? Oh Mother Maria, HELP ME!'

There had been moments when hope, both for herself and her son, had leapt up like a flame in her heart, whilst really she knew how things would end. After all, she had lost six children and a husband. She knew how it felt to have Death in the house; she recognised the chill of his shadow as it fell upon her again. Still she held fast to every movement her son made and every sound he uttered. Where there was life there was hope! The priest had few prayers to offer. He knew the end was nigh. And indeed, in the early morning of the third day after the accident the mother's last spark of hope was extinguished as the last fine wreath of mist is evaporated by the slowly rising sun. She had no tears left to cry. It was over.

A great emptiness filled her tortured body and soul. She could not let her son go, not yet. She could not bear the thought that this once joyous, thronging family home would henceforth be inhabited only by spirits of the past.

'Who shall not weep,
seeing the Mother of Christ
in all her anguish?'

Antonio feels the immortality of the lines echo down the centuries. Would Maria have received the support of those around her, he asks himself?

A collection had been made in the neighbourhood for Elisabetta , so that she could give Carlo a good burial and still have something left over for herself. But for how long would people stand by her? How long before it would be business as usual again for everyone? How long before she would have to seek help from the church?

More a matter of days than months, Antonio reflects bitterly. Life was hard; it rolled on remorselessly, without regard for mere mortal struggle. But Maria was the mother of Jesus, and she too was spared no agony. Yes, he ponders; everyone must undergo a moment of true suffering in life. None can escape it. The pattern is now clear to him. His *Stabat Mater* must remind everyone of Maria's true experience. But the work must also make each aware of what awaits them too. For a moment he considers dedicating the *Stabat Mater* to Elisabetta but he soon dismisses the idea. Who in Brescia will know Elisabetta Chiara? And anyway, what difference will it make? Is there not a fragment of Maria in every mother?

He dips his pen in the inkpot and scratches the first notes confidently upon the paper.

The work is completed with astonishing speed. So easy is the process of writing that he hardly trusts it and reads everything through again to make amendments. But, as his glance glides note for note over the music, his pen hangs motionless in the air above the page; a hawk relinquishing its prey. He lets go his breath, pushes the music away from him, and puts down the pen. 'Perfect!' he whispers.

'We'll do it downstairs,' says Antonio, taking the lead in front of his father and Francesco Gasparini. Both are intrigued as to what awaits them, for Antonio has been willing to let on nothing about the music. He could of course have served it up stone cold, but he is now so sure of himself that he has brought his father and *Maestro* Gasparini to the auditorium to hear the *Figlie di Coro* perform the piece in rehearsal. His father is still full of criticism that his son spends more and more time composing for voices. But he has to admit that, judging by what he has seen so far, it is not inferior work, if not up to the standard of Antonio's *concerti*.

The musicians have taken their places and one of the *Figlie* is standing out at the trellised balustrade in front of the choir. It is too dark, however, to make out the identity of the soloist. Francesco and Giambattista have taken up position in the centre of the empty church. Gasparini is extremely curious as to what he is about to hear, for he has had little time to nurse this work into being with his special attention. He has so much on his hands these days! As the violinists strike up the opening notes his mind is still full of all his new plans and productions. He comes to himself with a shock; what he is hearing is quite different from anything he had expected! Pushing aside all other thoughts, he listens now with the ear of the master. Francesco and Giambattista both find themselves momentarily caught off balance. Antonio's father has instantly recognised the text, "Stabat Mater dolorosa", but is this truly the work of the famous Vivaldi? Where is the energy so characteristic of the master of the concerti? The alto easily reaches every corner of the auditorium. 'Mater unigeniti, Mother of God's only Son'. Now that the melody has drawn him in, Giambattista feels himself deeply moved by the words of the ancient song of praise. And the melodic undercurrent streams on almost imperceptibly now, carried forward by the basso continu. Every couplet makes more palpable the suffering of Maria. 'Dolentem cum Filio?' 'Grieving with her Son?'

Tears well up in Giambattista's eyes and he dare not look at Francesco. 'Eia Mater, fons amoris': 'Oh Mother, source of love, give me a share in your grief, that I may mourn with you.'

The sung amen gives Giambattista a chance to recover himself and quickly dry his eyes on his sleeve. He draws in a deep breath and looks at the man standing next to him. Antonio's mentor is listening with half-open mouth, a tear trickling with agonising slowness down his wrinkled cheek. You can hear a pin drop.

'Mother Maria', whispers Francesco, respectfully making the sign of the cross. Giambattista follows suit.

The silence in the huge hall seems amplified by the dying notes of the ode to Maria.

One of the musicians coughs, the rest of the *Figlie* remain sitting motionless, with bowed head.

'Allora,' cries Antonio, breaking the spell he has cast on all assembled. 'What do you think of it?' He walks up to his father and Francesco, bringing them back to themselves. Both men look up and nod. 'Good, very good!' murmurs his father sincerely.

'I knew you had it in you. I always told you so', says Gasparini, shaking Antonio's hand with vigour.

Vivaldi heaves a great sigh of relief. How wonderful to see his father moved. That doesn't happen often. And the compliment from *Maestro* Gasparini is worth its weight in gold, too. Yes, even Antonio himself feels satisfied with this composition although some sections could do with a little improvement.

'Come on then,' roars Gasparini in his enthusiasm, 'Let's hear it again!'

Antonio smiles. 'With pleasure!'

He leads the *Figlie* through the couplets for a second time, perhaps a shade more dramatically. It feels to him like victory and revelation in one. He can do it! Who knows what may lie ahead for him now? He shuts his eyes and gives thanks to the Madonna for her gifts of grace.

Francesco Gasparini has been feeling a great deal better recently. He's pleased to see that Antonio Vivaldi has acquired a taste for composing vocal works and feeds his growing hunger with ever more commissions. The annual programme of the *Ospedale della Pietà* makes many demands upon the *Maestro di Coro*. Every religious festival needs a new *oratorio* or concert. One of the most important functions of the *Maestro di Coro* is the writing of new music. Psalms, songs of praise, oratorios; people can't get enough of them. Everyone, that is, bar Gasparini. After years of providing the *Pietà* with new music, Francesco is finding it harder and harder to find the enthusiasm and inspiration to meet the demands. The meagre income from his work for the institution forces him to subsidise it considerably by composing *Drammi per Musica*, mostly for the theatre of *San Cassiano* but also for theatres on the mainland.

With each year that passes, Gasparini is becoming more exhausted. His whole life has been music. By the time he was twenty he had mastered the organ. He also sang and played other instruments, as well as committing to paper his first compositions. He was soon taken under the wing of Benedetto Pamphili, Cardinal of Rome. Ah, Rome! Memories of the eternal city on the Tiber bring a smile to Gasparini's tired features. Corelli, Scarlatti and many other talented musicians had found their way to the palaces of Rome, where Cardinals Ottoboni and Pamphili offered them every chance to explore their potential. From here it had been a small step for him to the post of *Maestro di Coro* at the *Ospedale della Pietà*. Eleven years had gone by since Venice had embraced and welcomed him in like a Roman hero.

The early years he had enjoyed immensely, for nowhere had he found musicians as dedicated as those of the *Pietà*. Things were very different in the theatres he had known before! It was not long before his first opera opened in *La Serenissima*. He was hardly settled in his new city before Francesco Santurini, impresario of the *Teatro San Angelo*, approached him. Gasparini shakes his head at the thought of it. The impresario had promised him a good deal of the profits should they put on a new production in his theatre together. Gasparini, of course, was to write the music. A newcomer to Venice, he could not have known that *San Angelo* was regarded, certainly by the aristocracy, as a second-rate theatre. It was only much later that he discovered how Santurini had been involved for years in a legal battle with the owners of the piece of land upon which the theatre was built and that the impresario was the biggest shark in the business. Reason enough for certain composers and musicians to avoid this small theatre like the plague. But the forecast winnings had blinded Gasparini to everything. Santurini was not an unkind man, but he thought in black and white. One moment you were his best friend and the next he was baying for your blood, even if you hadn't the slightest idea what you'd done to deserve it. The only recourse was to stay well out of his way!

Preparations for the opera "*Tiberio imperatore d'Oriente*" were going fairly smoothly when it became clear to Gasparini how Francesco Santurini made his profit. Everything was done on the cheap: artistes unknown and low paid, sets and costumes worn out and so often repaired it looked as though they had been used and reused in productions over centuries. According to Santurini, none of this was a problem for nobody was looking behind the scenes.

But Gasparini had his own ideas about it all, for neither stage-sets nor costumes bore any relation to his *libretto*. And if this caused him consternation, surely it would also irritate the audience. The singers for this season were unfamiliar to Gasparini, most of them part of a group from Ferrara, and despite their low salary Santurini did his best to milk them for everything they had. 'Amateurs!' jeered the impresario mercilessly at the podium during dress rehearsal. 'Where in God's name did you learn to sing?' he thundered. The singers dared say hardly a word in their own defence. 'Now I know why you come all the way here from Ferrara. No sane person there would let you on the stage!' The string players, meanwhile, sat quietly putting the sheet music in order on their music stands. Most were local and long used to these tirades that belonged to the impresario's grand plan of docking money from the artistes' honoraria. 'Ugh, *fa schiffo!* Mother Maria, to think we're opening tomorrow! I might as well shut up shop here and now, because when the audience hears this they'll run away screaming and then I'm as good as closed down anyway!' And he slammed his fist down upon the podium in exasperation before resuming his place in the body of the hall. '*Su, andiamo!* Now let's hear something worth listening to!' The soprano began trilling her aria. Santurini sighed theatrically, shook his head and closed his eyes. The borderline between truth and fiction was difficult for Gasparini to discern, so he kept his mouth shut, having reached the private conclusion that the biggest actor in the hall was Santurini himself. In fact, he had never seen anyone give a more convincing performance. But this time the impresario had gone too far. The singers had been provoked beyond endurance. He had also failed to pay them their full advance and upon arriving back in their lodgings that evening, tired out and hungry, they decided enough was enough. 'Santurini can go hang himself, he can get on with it!'

The following morning the entire company packed its bags and was ready for the trip back to the mainland. Too bad about their pay, but there was a limit to how much insult and humiliation a person could take. That Francesco Santurini was an old hand in the trade became clear that morning. The door of Gasparini's workroom flew open and a furious Santurini stormed in. 'Come on!' shouted the impresario. 'They've taken off!'

Gasparini was stunned. 'Taken off? What are you talking about?'

'Our singers! Get a move on, otherwise they'll be at the boat.' With this the impresario grabbed Gasparini by his coat sleeve, but the latter brushed his hand away. 'Yes, but hang on a moment,' he said, bewildered. 'What in heaven's name are you going to do?' Santurini turned on him, his face flushed and swollen so that the whites of his eyes stood out against his tanned skin. From where he stood facing the impresario Gasparini could feel the damp warmth of his sweat condensing on the air. 'Listen to me, man,' panted Santurini, gripping the tunic of the shocked composer. 'If we have no singers this evening then we have no show! We're in this together, aren't we? Do I have to spell out to you what it'll cost us if we can't get these idiots back on stage again?!' He loosened his grip. Gasparini nodded, asking in a low voice, 'What do you want me to do?'

'Ah, that's more like it! Now, let's get going!' and Santurini thrust Gasparini roughly out through the door ahead of him.

They arrived completely out of breath at the lodgings, just as the door swept open. Upon seeing the impresario, the tenor's expression changed through amazement to shock. 'Ha, where do you think you're going?' bawled Santurini. Robbed of speech but not of instinct, the tenor slammed the door shut. But before the bolt could be thrown Santurini threw his full weight against it and struggled through. The company jumped back as a man from the impresario, who had a face like a hungry wolf about to devour his prey. Nobody dared make a move, not even when Gasparini stepped quietly into the room. Watching things unfold from the corner was the landlord, equally afraid to intervene. He didn't fancy making close acquaintance this morning with the famed fists of the theatre boss.

'And where would you all be off to?' enquired the impresario, still panting, but now in honeyed tones. Nobody dared reply until at last the soprano broke the silence. 'We've had enough of it all. You can keep your money, we're going home!'

She folded her arms emphatically across her chest, feeling pretty pleased with herself for having stood up to this old boar.

SLAP!

Santurini brought the flat of his hand down so hard on the side of her face that she pitched sideways and was caught halfway to the floor by the contralto. The remainder of the company screamed and the tenor stepped forward. 'Have you gone finally off your head?' he raged. Santurini instantly aimed a right hook at the singer, hitting him straight on the nose. The speed of response took Gasparini by surprise; after all, the impresario was a good few years older than he was. The tenor lay groaning on the ground with his hands to his nose, blood tickling through his fingers. The poor man received another kick for good measure, at which his colleagues crept into a cringing huddle, like a flock of lambs about to be slaughtered.

'I don't believe I need to explain to you what a very silly remark that was,' Santurini postured. Forefinger raised, he looked one by one round the faces of the singers. 'Well, everyone can make a mistake, so I'll let you off this time. But no more pranks. Get yourselves back to the theatre this instant!'

Weeping and wailing, the members of the company stared round at one another, wondering what they were to do.

Francesco Gasparini ran forward to help the tenor to his

feet. He felt slightly ashamed, but on the other hand he had also done the sums and knew that cancellation was out of the question. 'Come on, out you go,' shouted Santurini once more at everyone. 'Don't imagine I'm going to let you out of my sight for a single moment. Take your gear with you. You can sleep in the theatre for the next few nights.'

His threats were enough to galvanise the group slowly into action. But once outside, the singers came slightly to their senses. Surely this was unacceptable? Now they were on the street, what more could he do to them? Although she didn't sing much anymore, Cecilia had travelled with the group for many years. She now threw her suitcase on the ground. 'This is crazy. I'm not moving another step. We've made perfectly clear that we're going home, and we should stick to our word.' Looking around the group she felt her resolve strengthened.

Santurini stalked silently up to her and stared her in the face. He spat on the ground just at her feet. 'We can do without you, *donna'cchera*,' he growled in contempt, turning his back on her and driving on the rest of the company, 'Come on, keep going you lot.' But they were hesitating.

Cecilia began to bawl, attracting the attention of bystanders. People turned round to look or stopped in their tracks to watch what was going on. Gondoliers glanced up in surprise to see where the screaming was coming from. The singers came to a wavering halt and gazed at the impresario with triumph in their eyes. 'If you don't keep walking I'll break your legs, one by one,' hissed the theatre boss. Gasparini flushed with embarrassment. By now they had a full audience. Something had to be to be done!

But nothing was done.

A silent battle of wills began between the troop of singers and Santurini, who well understood that any further beating up of his employees would not go unpunished out here. Livid, he watched them through narrowed eyes. In the background Cecilia kept up her screaming, stamping her feet and hurling all manner of abuse at the impresario, so that more and more people stopped to watch.

That was it! With the speed of a hawk, Santurini dived at Cecilia, picked her up and threw her unceremoniously into the canal. The bystanders, oddly enough, all reacted differently. Some were obviously outraged, but plenty found the whole episode hilarious, spluttering with laughter and pointing at the woman thrashing around, still shrieking, in the water. Now that all the attention was focused on the drowning woman, Santurini ran back to the group. He gripped the soprano tightly by the arm and drew his dagger.

'The first person to deviate from his role from now on ends up on the end of this! COMPRENDE?! Now keep walking.'

Crushed and sobbing, the little procession got moving once more. They had learnt their lesson: you did not play games with Signor Santurini. Glancing timidly over their shoulders they saw with relief how, to the hilarity of the public, one gondolier was cheerily hauling aboard his 'catch'.

The singers from Ferrara sang from the first to the last note without another murmur and no one in the audience noticed that their roles were played with less enthusiasm than they should have been. A couple of arias were rewarded with applause and *bravos*, but for the majority of the performance the audience entertained itself. It was an evening out like any other, to see and be seen. A chance to exchange gossip and generally carry on in a manner not permitted during daylight hours. Eating in the theatres had, since last year, been forbidden, but nobody took a blind bit of notice of the prohibition. Whenever the audience got fed up with a singer or found an aria going on too long, chicken bones, apple cores and other inedibles would be sent hurtling towards the stage. This was the pattern on the first night of *Tiberio imperatore d'Oriente*, as Gasparini watched anxiously from the wings. What philistines! In despair he recalled his performances in Rome. At least there the *nobili* and cardinals knew how to show their appreciation for his music in a civilised fashion. But, he reasoned, glancing disdainfully through the wings again, this was after all just a public theatre.

Santurini summed things up for himself. 'Perfect show. You'll won't be sorry, Gasparini.'

Surveying the hall after the performance, the composer had his doubts. It was a battlefield. The floor of the theatre was covered in detritus and the mob had departed booing loudly. He was afraid not a soul would show up the next night.

'Nonsense!' Santurini brusquely brushed aside 'his' composer's worries. 'The public loved it. All that booing is quite usual. If they didn't express an opinion it would look as if they didn't have one, or knew nothing about it. You might not yet be aware of it, but our audiences are all musicologists!' Grinning broadly, he was busy counting up the takings. And the more he counted the wider grew his smile. 'Listen my friend, people come to the theatre only for pleasure, warmth and to pass the time, and whether or not they like it is a matter of the utmost indifference to me.'

He dropped the lid of the cash-box with a loud crash and turned the key in the lock. 'Only one thing matters in this business, and that's a full hall!' He rattled the box happily; obviously the only tune Santurini cared about was the one made by clinking ducats.

But the impresario had been right. Night after night the hall was reasonably well filled and every night the same scenario replayed itself anew. Gasparini began to ask himself what sense there was in launching so many new productions every season. For all that people listened, you might as well just repeat the same thing year after year.

One way and another, this opera had been a profitable affair. After all deductions, including the cost of the singers, Gasparini made a hundred and eight ducats. Easy winnings! But he had also decided that this would be his final performance with Santurini. The stress involved in this production was not something Gasparini wished to have to look forward to again. His youngest brother Michelangelo, a long-time resident of Venice, had warned him in advance about the sly impresario. And on this occasion Angelo, as he called his brother, had been correct. So, upon receiving a commission from *Teatro San Cassiano* to write another new work for Christmas, the first thing Gasparini did was to consult his brother. This time he fully approved.

Since then he had had more than a dozen compositions performed at *San Cassiano*. Yes, from this point of view those had been golden years. But gradually things had become a grind. He found too much predictability in the yearly rhythm of one festival after another. Moreover, he had had enough of the lagoon. Water, water, everywhere! In summertime when the heat rose, the air would become pregnant with moisture. Sheet music and other papers would start aggregating in clumps and mould would grow on the walls indoors. In the winter the mist could be as thick as pea soup, and hostile soup at that, seeping into every corner of the house! Everything would become clammy and any item of clothing put away damp would transform itself into a nutritious breeding ground for the most remarkable specimens of fungi, species to be found only in Venice. In summer you were bitten half to death by the mosquitoes, which led a charmed life in the meandering creeks of the lagoon. And then the stink! There were days when the tides lacked the conviction to transport away all the garbage produced by the inhabitants of *La Serenissima*. Then you would find excrement, kitchen-waste and the occasional inflated cadaver of a stray dog or cat, or worse, a mutilated baby, piled up at the dead end of a *Riva*. The gondoliers had to try to navigate as carefully as possible through the sludge. Any unlucky enough to let his oar come in contact with the stretched skin of a drowned beast was sure to be subjected to a torrent of abuse from bystanders. For then, with the ungenteel urgency of a belching water buffalo, rotten air would escape the bizarre balloon to fill the sultry afternoon air with a stench that was unbearable.

Winter is not much better. Coughs and colds are then generously passed on from one person to another, so that by Christmas everyone knows someone in Venice who has died from flu or pneumonia.

Gasparini reckons it's unbelievable he's held out here for as long as he has, and realises once and for all that the time has come to make other plans.

The light falling in through the stained-glass windows finds its soft reflection in the polished floor. Silk wallpaper of the latest fashion and coloured marble and alabaster pillars rise up towards the richly decorated plasterwork ceiling, great areas of which are painted with the most breathtaking scenes of gods, angels and wild creatures. Three immense chandeliers dominate the upper space, each bearing enough candles to bathe the entire hall in light as evening falls. Along the walls stand alternating superbly worked sofas and impressive statues of famous mythological figures. On one wall, far enough away from the windows to protect them from sunlight, hang precious masterpieces by artists long gone. The vast hall, unequalled in the whole of Venice, belongs to an enormous *palazzo* situated on the *Canal Grande* just over from the *Basilica di Santa Maria della Salute*. It is one of the few mansions with its own spacious grounds, well known for a rare collection of exotic plants. On sultry summer days its pools and fountains attract flocks of cooing doves which flutter their wings in the refreshing waters. Romantic arbours offer enough shade for people to sit outside through even the most sweltering hours of the day. Almost out of sight, but nonetheless ever-present, is a legion of servants ready just at the right moment to refill a glass, fan someone with cool air and ensure there is always enough food and fresh fruit on the table.

Antonio sighs deeply. The *palazzo* with its gorgeous garden slowly evaporates with the early morning mist that comes drifting in on the tide from the lagoon. How often has he dreamed about this house? In his heart he knows that he will never own such a palace. But one must have a goal in life. For the time being, commissions are still coming in, and with them money. He has had the family measured up for new clothes and bought some for himself.

He cannot get his dream out of his head. He knows a time will come when he will look out each morning on the *Canal Grande*. In the meanwhile Antonio's sisters are more than happy with their older brother and stand purring like the neighbour's fat cat in front of the mirror.

His mother Camilla too is proud of her son. Her old furniture makes way for modern, skilfully worked tables and chairs, and everyone can see that things are going well with the Vivaldi family. Who would have thought it? He was always such a helpless creature, that poor Antonio. When Camilla shuts her eyes she can see it all again: the long, difficult labour, and little Antonio hanging between life and death for days on end. It was only once he was weaned that things turned a corner and the wee fellow started to thrive a bit, better a weak scrap of humanity than the alternative. God had been merciful to her!

Apart from the theatre work, his father has his hands full writing out Antonio's commissions. When it is quiet he works ahead so that he can build up a small store of his son's better pieces. These Antonio Vivaldi sells as 'exclusive' items to interested foreign musicians, and none so far seems to have rumbled that the *concerto* written specially for them is actually not so exclusive after all. Antonio's days are filled with teaching at the *Pietà*, giving private lessons and writing music. And Gasparini piles on the commissions until questions begin to be asked.

The *Congregazione* has been wondering what might be the reason behind this. After all, it is not Vivaldi's task to compose music, and he certainly needn't expect to be paid a single ducat extra for doing so! Gasparini has had no difficulty in hushing their fears and assuring them that they need have no worries concerning money.

'It surely can't do any harm to let the violin teacher compose a bit?' the *Maestro di Coro* excuses himself. 'It's good for his development, and it gives Il *Prete Rosso* a chance to hear straight off how seriously his pupils are taking their music lessons.'

'But does Don Vivaldi have enough time left for his real task?' This is what really worries the management. 'What influence does it have upon his instrumental work?' they want to know.

'Do you notice any change?' asks Gasparini, slightly peeved. 'The *oratorium* is fuller over recent months than it has ever been.' So the management committee sees all its objections knocked on the head, criticism ceases and the discussion is closed, much to the regret of Scarponi the singing teacher.

That he has increasing numbers of listeners, and that people come to him for lessons, reaching deep into their pockets to do so, caresses the ego of *Il Prete Rosso*. But it is not enough. Both Antonio and his father have the feeling there is much yet to be achieved. They must change course, do the sums all over again. His father has entirely relinquished the idea that Antonio has to confine himself to instrumental music. The *Stabat Mater* is followed by other work featuring a glittering role for solo vocalist. Antonio is prevented by pressure of work from personally performing the *Stabat Mater* in Brescia but extravagant letters from the family and *Santa Maria della Pace* church council abound with praise. Giambattista reads them through time and again, his heart swelling with pride. It is on such an evening that Antonio brings up the matter of the theatre. Gasparini is so fired with enthusiasm for the possible triumphs awaiting him there that he has swept Antonio along with him completely. And being so utterly sure of the chances in store, Vivaldi has little difficulty in finding arguments to support his wishes. You only had to put your head into a theatre for five minutes to hear it. Some compositions were truly not worth the paper they were printed on and people still flocked to hear them.

'The aesthetic lies in the church, my son, but the fortune in the theatre!' contends Gasparini time and again. 'A vespers is for life, a *dramma per musica*, or "opera" as they call them, to make a living from,' insists the *Maestro di Coro* with genuine conviction. 'Nobody's really the least bit interested in opera, are they? Why else has not a single publisher dared publish one? Simply because it is too ephemeral, simple pleasure for the simple-minded masses. An innocent way to pass the time, and one that leaves no lasting impression. As fleeting as the scent of roses in full bloom; superficial as the gilding on a mirror that creeps beneath your fingernails at the slightest scratch. A brief shimmer of beauty and just as soon forgotten. But one thing it can do; under the right circumstances an opera can produce a very nice pile of money!'

Giambattista carefully folds away again the letter from the church council in Brescia and replaces it on the mantelpiece. He pushes his chair nearer the fire and rubs his hands to warm them. Antonio has brought up the subject with the greatest delicacy, not knowing how his father will react. But Giambattista hardly responds at all; he appears deep in contemplation. 'I think Gasparini is right,' he says eventually. 'Morally speaking, there's nothing to stop you from trying it out, but be careful! Have you thought about the consequences if it doesn't work, if your first opera should flop and you can't show your face on the street for the rest of the season? What kind of influence this might have on sales of your other work and, even more important, what influence it might have on your standing?'

'Oh dear. Typical of father to look on the dark side of everything.' But running the mental gauntlet of all these questions Antonio soon discovers there's something in them. He has to laugh. 'You're right, father. I'm aware of the risks. What we need is a good libretto. If that's sound, nothing can go wrong!'

But Giambattista is not so sure. 'Of course a good libretto is a prime concern, but you also need a decent audience. I would not want to foul my own nest.'

Antonio gives his father a quizzical glance. 'What do you mean, exactly?'

'Look for a theatre on the mainland willing to put on a first performance of your work. If it goes wrong over there, there's nothing lost on this side of the water.'

Antonio blows his nose to hide his disappointment. Does his father have so little faith in his abilities? What could go wrong?

'Agreed, a good *libretto*,' mutters Antonio, thus postponing any further discussion. He empties his glass and wishes his father goodnight.

But sleep eludes Antonio. He lies in bed, restlessly counting up imaginary riches and half-dreaming he is playing his favourite violin in the great hall of his waterside palace. An opera here, an opera there...pom, pom, pom. It must be possible! Pom, pom, pom. But suddenly the walls begin to shudder and pieces of plaster fall about him. The marble pillars tumble and land with a crash like thunder on the stone floor below. The heavenly frescoes crumble and gods disintegrate in a cloud of dust as they, too, land on the stone floor. Antonio backs towards the wall, but then the windows fall in, glass shattering and raining down in rainbow shards. He holds his violin in front of his face to protect himself, but then the floor itself begins to dance, bouncing up and down like a thin sheet of ice, before breaking with a characteristic creaking crack. He loses his balance. Beneath him yawns the green water of the lagoon. He just manages to grab hold of a windowsill, but then there is a roar and he slides, palace and all, into the water. He can't swim!

A twist of his body and he is spiralling upwards, using his hands to push away debris. He manages a deep breath, as if he has just broken the surface... and realises that he has been dreaming. A tremendous crash booms overhead. Thunder! His shutters are still standing open and the wind is madly driving gusts of rain into the room. He gets unwillingly out of bed to batten down the hatches. The thunderstorm rages its way across the city, taking long minutes to die away. Breathing heavily and sweating, Antonio rubs his tight chest. He can feel his heart beating far too fast for his own liking. He must try to breathe slowly and relax. The vice about his chest begins to loosen its grip. He sleeps dreamlessly on.

'Oh, how lovely!' exclaims Anna Maria in wonder, letting the lining of Antonio's new cloak glide through her fingers. 'Oh,' and a mischievous look comes to her eyes, 'may I try it on?'

'Why not?' says Antonio, helping her on with the tabarro.

'It's so beautiful. Mmmm. How fantastic it would be one day to parade along the quay and the Piazzetta.'

The Maestra, meanwhile, never takes her eyes from the priest and his young pupil. Those two, they're always chatting away together. She wonders if they ever talk about her. Sometimes she leans near, or even goes right up to them if she thinks things are getting a bit too intimate. But she never gets a chance to catch what they are saying, as if they have a secret language to whisper in. When it gets too much for her she taps spitefully on the floor with her stick, yet however hard she knocks, it never seems to bother the pair unduly. But now, now things have gone too far! She watches as the redhead priest holds out his cloak for the girl, and how, giggling, she slips the costly crimson cloth about her. Anna Maria is not much shorter in stature than the Maestro di Violino himself these days, so that the cloak looks far from ill on her. The young violinist struts around the room in a stately fashion, makes a sweeping turn and runs laughing into the arms of the priest.

'Enough!' cries the Maestra, beside herself. 'What is the meaning of this?' she shrieks, brandishing her stick above her head as if threatening to bring it down upon them.

'Don't get so worked up, madam,' intervenes Vivaldi with a severe expression. 'Nothing is going on here of which we need be ashamed.' With a wink he takes the garment back from Anna and drapes it over the back of a chair. Anna Maria, as has been her habit for years, totally ignores the Maestra, and quietly proceeds to remove her violin from its case.

The next half-hour is filled with hard work. Exercises are repeated, new positions tried and fresh pieces practised. They get through the lesson in record time. To the depths of her being the Maestro is incensed with jealousy; jealousy of Anna Maria's talent and envy of the attention she gets from Don Vivaldi. Their duets disturb, yet also curiously intrigue her. The end of the lesson has gradually developed into a playful war of sparkling *cadenze* in which they compete in brilliant virtuosity and daring. They are playing at a level far outstripping the *Maestra*, who thus finds her respect for this errant teenager growing in spite of herself.

She will never let it show of course; there is only one mistress around here!

'*Brava!*' calls Vivaldi as Anna Maria bows her final note. Panting from exertion, she stares at the priest with almost feverish eyes. As the concentration ebbs away she comes back to earth on the music-room floor. 'You're making great progress, my girl. I'm proud of you!'

And she reverts to the little, timid girl who looks up to her music teacher. 'Thank you,' she mumbles with flushing cheeks.

'I have something else nice for you to work on over the next few days,' says the priest, producing some music from his bag and leafing through it to find the right sheet. 'Ah, here we are.' He spreads the music out before her on the table.

'At the end of next month a delegation from the *Figlie* has permission to play in the monastery of *San Francesco della Vigna*. Make sure you master this perfectly by then and you can come along. You like to get away from this place sometimes, don't you?'

She gives a quick laugh, but her eyes are already moving swiftly over the notes, relaying them to her mind and inner ear where she hears the melody. As she reads, a frown comes and goes from her forehead, and when she reaches the end she looks somewhat disappointed. 'I don't know if I can play this,' she says humbly.

'Why don't you think so?' asks Antonio.

'Well, look at this,' she points at certain passages. 'That's technically almost not possible.'

'Ha!' laughs the priest, 'Not on your poor old beast.' He taps softly on the instrument she has just been playing, adding, 'I think he must be getting on for a hundred years old so you're probably right. But on this violin... all things are possible...' and Don Vivaldi hands her the instrument he has been using today. 'Voilà, madame. For you.'

Anna Maria takes the violin from her master, her eyes as big as saucers. She is almost incapable of breathing and completely lost for words. Her fingers run tenderly up and down the smooth neck of the instrument. 'For me?' she whispers incredulously. Antonio nods.

Anna Maria holds the violin as though it were a lover, her feet tapping impatiently on the floor. The Maestra has come across the room to them, for she cannot quite make out what is happening here. Do her eyes deceive her? Has that girl been given her own violin? Since time immemorial the instruments upon which the girls take turns to play have belonged to the Pietà. What sort of madness, then, is this? Anna Maria is completely overcome. The longer neck of the new instrument allows her to play in more positions, expanding her technique. And then the tone! Just listen to that! In ecstasy she moves the bow across the strings. Then hovers, not knowing what to play. She'd really like to play everything she knows, all at the same time!

'Oh, Babbo, Father, thank you!' Tears streaming down her face, she hugs the priest, who really does not know what to do with her. He raises his hand for moderation.

'You don't have to thank me. Thank the management. It was they who approved the purchase of this instrument.' There is a nod of approbation from the Maestra as he gives the answer she wants to hear. But her face is as contorted with doubt as ever; before she knows it, all the girls will be demanding their own instruments. Antonio collects the music together and lays the pile ready for Anna Maria. But she hasn't finished admiring her new instrument, examining it from every side, exactly as though her hands had never held a violin before. The Maestra, though, has seen more than enough. The next lesson is due and it is high time Anna Maria was gone. The priest too is finished for the day, and makes way for the singing teacher, who looks in astonishment at the sobbing, smiling Anna Maria. Never has she been so happy! Arms full of music and the new violin, she hops and skips her way out of the room, leaving behind her the head-shaking *Maestra*.

The new instrument offers Anna Maria the chance really to explore her own possibilities. It seems to her now as if her previous violin had cramped her style, hindering her further musical development. New vistas now open up before her and she again faces fresh and welcome challenges. Music, music... what would the world be without it?

As far back as she can remember there has been music in her life. She never knew her parents. Ever since she became conscious of her body she has known the scarred brand-mark of the *Pietà* on her upper arm. She must have been a tiny baby when she was abandoned to the care of the orphanage. Sometimes she tries to imagine how her mother might look, but all she sees is a great emptiness. It's hard for her to know what she has missed in life so far, but this matters less and less to her, for the void is filled with the warmth of music. Music is her rock, her pillow, her lover and her confidante. It can comfort, it can be her hiding place, but it can also give her pleasure. She honours the great organ, the bass notes of which roar like unearthly monsters, she sparkles at the sound of the mandolin. But it is the sound of the violin that melts her heart and fills her with sublime despair. Anna Maria sings just as naturally she breathes, all day long, and even at night while she is asleep, sweet tunes keep every demon at bay. She has grown up with music and she could no longer do without it. It is not a passion she can share with every other girl of her age. Not all are as sensitive to music. Those just a bit older look down upon her with contempt, unable to understand what moves her so. They have other things on their mind, freedom! Physically, they have made the transition from girlhood to young womanhood; their otherwise formless tunics are gradually filling out with rounding hips and breasts that long to be touched. But the road to freedom runs only via marriage. The regime of the *Ospedale della Pietà* is designed to turn the girls into good wives and housekeepers. But, despite their waggling hips and seductive necklines, not every girl is chosen.

Some are so marred by the pox and so little endowed with physical charms that potential husbands turn their heads away when introduced to marriageable members of the Figlie, and even the dowry offered by the Pietà is not enough to make him see otherwise and change the man's mind.

For those that have been repeatedly rejected there remains only a lifetime spent in the institution. Then it becomes their turn to initiate the younger girls in the art of household tasks and wifely duties: a dream world from which they themselves are forever excluded.

But there is one other possible route to freedom. Music! The most talented girls get the chance to join the Figlie di Coro. Depending on their gifts, they learn to sing or to play one or several instruments. The putte, as these girls are called, provide the music for all the religious festivities taking place in their church. Nobody's quite sure who started it, but at some point people were asked to pay an entrance fee for certain performances and, believe it or not, they appeared more than happy to do so! Over the years the Ospedale della Pietà, like the other three such institutions in Venice, has built up quite a name for itself. People come faithfully from far and near to listen to the concerts here. The management had soon realised that if this rich source of income was not to dry up, musical standards had to be attained and maintained. So, one teacher after another brings their expertise to bear upon the Coro, enhancing its success. By now it is impossible for any institution to manage financially without a choir. Every tourist that sets foot in Venice attends at least one performance at one of the ospedaletti. The concerts provide a constant stream of income from ticket sales, but programme booklets, spontaneous donations and legacies also bring in much needed capital. The extra income allows the orphanages to appoint the best teachers, so that standards keep rising. The women and girls of the choir are, however modestly, kept in clover; better and more food at mealtimes, good wine and more spacious accommodation than their peers. And chaperoned outings are organised for them, too, expanding their horizons beyond the walls of the institution. But most important of all, as far as Anna Maria is concerned, is that she now spends her life among soul mates.

Before she was in the choir she had to sleep in the big dormitory and was often bullied for being different. She was quiet and shy and her thoughts were often miles away. She would be swooping far above the lagoon like a swallow before the threatening storm, plucking as many tiny titbits from the air as was still possible. She would daydream to the melody of any music she heard playing in the background. She would take her time scrubbing the floor of the *oratorium*, trying for as long as possible to enjoy whatever rehearsal was going on there. She did not feel the slaps administered to hurry her, or care about the teasing and the slyly spilled bucket of water. Her only aim was to impress her *Maestro* when the time came, so that she would be accepted for the choir. So nobody knew quite how to react when Anna Maria was informed she was among the chosen few. Her voice was not particularly impressive, but *Maestro* Vivaldi had certainly been struck with the progress she had made over just a few lessons on the violin and cello. She cheered, leapt and danced around. She threw her arms about everyone's neck, including the worst of her torturers, and whilst they tapped their foreheads in mockery, they secretly doubted their own judgement now. She could not pack her things fast enough to make the move to the quarters occupied by the *Figlie di Coro*. At the dormitory door she turned and took in for one last time the empty beds and comfortless room that had been her home for almost ten years. Then she grinned broadly, stuck out her tongue and was gone, leaving the past behind her.

She had embraced every aspect of her new life, even if here too she found girls who dreamed of life with their *Nobiluomo* and saw the choir simply as a step towards a 'better life' outside the walls of the institution. Although marriage came at a price; musical performance in public would then be out of bounds. This was not something that ever kept Anna Maria awake at night. She knew she wanted to devote her life solely to music. She'd heard enough stories from the older women to make her flesh crawl. Once married, a woman had nothing more to contribute. Pregnancy was physical torture, and you were lucky to survive one delivery after another. And then the suffering! The least lucky were those who survived all their own children. And there was always a good chance that your husband would die, and then who would provide for yourself and your children? Before you knew it you were knocking at the door of the poorhouse or selling your own body to seamen and good-time tourists.

'Of course, there are happy moments too,' admitted the women. But what did they remember of those now? Love was a fine thing to dream about. But one thing had become plain over the years, and that was that the virgins of the Pietà were spared many a nasty disease. The sinning that began with love was all too often rewarded with sores, sickness and premature death. How could it be other than that the putte escaped all this? They enjoyed the direct protection of the Holy Maria!

In truth, the Pietà is like an ark afloat upon turbulent and dangerous seas. Safety dwells within her walls and membership of the choir endows unprecedented status. Within the boundaries of their own world, the women and girls have the chance to develop intellectually without posing a threat to any man. The regime of study and prayer within a secure environment is a good recipe for a long and healthy life. Look at Bastiana, Stella, Anzoletta, Ortensia, not to mention Marcolina, all still active choir members and every one of them more than sixty years old!

Maestro di Violino Don Vivaldi, nicknamed Il Prete Rosso, is the first man with whom Anna Maria has ever been in regular contact. He discovered her! She adores the priest, whom she alone lovingly but respectfully calls 'Babbo'. To her, he is the father she has always lacked. And now that Babbo has given her this chance everything will be wonderful! She has learned with equal flair to play cello, mandolin, harpsichord, lute and theorbo. But for both her own sake and that of *Babbo* she has poured heart and soul into the violin. His gift to her today comes as confirmation of her choice. She feels the jealous looks, but just as before they have no power to hurt her. Nothing, but nothing can come between her and her music.

'Ah, Antonio,' Francesco Gasparini greets the priest amiably. Quite by chance they have bumped into each other on the square in front of the monastery of *San Zaccaria*. 'Good to see you, I was just coming to look you up. Have you a moment?' With a nod Antonio suggests they find some shade, and together they walk to the church that stands beside the monastery and shares the same name. The door stands invitingly open. Inside it is cool and they can talk in peace. Gasparini apologises for the fact that they have had so little chance to speak lately. The *Maestro di Coro* wipes the sweat from his face. It's another stifling hot day. 'Oh, I don't know. I'm much too busy. That's the fact of the matter,' he broods.

Antonio says nothing. He's heard the story so often before. Gasparini looks quickly about him and shambles up closer to Vivaldi. 'Listen, my friend.' He glances round once more to make sure nobody is listening, but the towering, vaulted space is almost deserted. Only at the far end of the nave, near the altar, are one or two people wandering about, probably tourists, and someone else is busy cleaning the central chandelier. 'Listen,' repeats Francesco, leaning close to Antonio's ear. 'I've had enough. I'm leaving.'

'What?' Antonio recoils.

'Shhh! Nobody must know anything of this. You are the only person I am telling. Come here, closer.' And as if at confession, Gasparini entrusts his secret to Vivaldi in hushed tones. 'I have one or two bits of business to finish off, but my family went on ahead of me last week.'

'But why?' stammers Antonio, chilled and shivering with shock.

Gasparini tells him everything. The constant pressure to

deliver something new, the climate, and the provinciality of Venice. He's had it all, lock stock and barrel. And enough is enough!

The news does not please Antonio. He gets on well with Gasparini and still has much to learn from him. And then there's the Pietà; what will the Coro make of it all? A thousand questions flood his mind. He has an overwhelming sense of abandonment, but Gasparini is reassuring. He has absolutely nothing to worry about; with his talent, the priest can himself take over the post of choirmaster, certainly if Gasparini puts in a good word for him with the Congregazione. And, of course, the two men will stay in touch!

Antonio thinks hard. This is the last thing he had expected. He, Antonio Vivaldi, Maestro di Coro di Ospedale della Pietà! It sounds a great challenge, and yet it terrifies him. It is naturally a huge honour, but also carries with it massive responsibility. Right now his ambition is focused on becoming a successful composer and writing opere on a grand scale. But for this he needs Gasparini's help. And now the man is jumping ship. He feels his chest tightening.

'You can't leave. At least, not yet! I still have so much to learn from you, and I'm only halfway there.'

Gasparini smiles. 'Don't worry. I've promised to help you and I shan't go until you're good and ready. But that means you have to be quicker off the mark composing opera than you'd thought!'

Vivaldi breathes again. He tries to be candid with Gasparini concerning his worries about taking over as Maestro of the Pietà. Those anxieties, that is, apart from the question of whether or not the management will go along with the idea, for Antonio is certain they find Il Prete Rosso far too cocky already. He understands all too well what sort of dilemma faces the present Maestro di Coro and does not fancy ever finding himself in the same boat. Gasparini nods. 'You're right. Look, you're already on the right track! If you can foresee all this, I have no concerns about your future. Now then, let's get down to opera. Have you a libretto in mind?'

The priest shakes his head. He is still too unfamiliar with the world of theatre. And men like Apostolo Zeno, oh boy! He'd rather not pursue the unattainable. He doesn't have that kind of money. Gasparini rubs the back of his head thoughtfully. 'Ah,' a gleam comes to his eyes. 'I tell you what, pop in on the impresario of Teatro San Cassiani. He'll point you out a librettist who's wandering around at a loose end, the one who had a flop last year. With Elisa, you remember.'

The smile is back on Vivaldi's face. 'Ah, yes. The comic opera! Fantastic! It's just a shame the public didn't think so.'

'Indeed,' agrees Gasparini in sombre tones. 'Venice isn't ready for it. I think it's too modern. In any case, it's sad the production came off the boards prematurely.' He grimaces, 'Yup,' he continues with a sneer, 'you can dish up anything you like to the Venetians, as long as it's not too different from what they're used to. Anyway, it's Domenico Lalli who wrote the libretto for Elisa. He doesn't come from around here, but I've worked with him a few times and with pleasure, I must say. He's about your own age and I have the feeling you'll get on. His problem is that since Elisa he hasn't been able to find anyone willing to take a libretto from him. I'm sure you'd be able to agree a good contract with him, but should he prove difficult just say I sent you.'

That was that then! Vivaldi would have to try his hand at opera before he had thought he would. It makes him nervous, but on the other hand there is the thrill of the unknown. Terra incognita! New frontiers, new possibilities, new success... the thought of it is enough to make him giddy. Only there is so very little time.

'But where will I find to perform my operas?' he asks Gasparini. Without a theatre his work will have no audience. The current musical director smacks his lips as if anticipating a large glass of wine. 'Leave that to me, Vivaldi.'

'Lalli?' barks the impresario of Teatro San Cassiano forbiddingly in response to Vivaldi's question. Where might the librettist be hanging out? The man makes a face as of someone who has just trodden in something unpleasant. 'Ha! That filthy confidence trickster needn't show his face around here anymore. Go and look for him among the miserable beggars at the *San Angelo*. That's the only place for folk like him!' He slams the door shut, leaving Vivaldi fuming on the other side.

Confidence trickster? *Elisa* wasn't that bad, he thinks, walking back along the quay and hailing a gondolier to take him to *San Angelo*. It's not far, but Antonio feels he's walked enough today already.

'What do you want him for?' demands a suspicious Francesco Santurini. The old man rubs his cheek as if suffering from bad toothache, while Vivaldi stands at the foot of the stairs and looks straight up at the theatre boss. He has seen Santurini before but never had the pleasure of meeting him face to face. His father, who often plays in the theatre orchestra, knows the impresario better, and many a cold winter's evening at home has been enlivened by colourful tales of this old shark.

'I have a proposal for him,' answers Vivaldi.

'I see. You'll be Giambattista Rossi's son?'

Vivaldi nods.

'Hmm. Come on up then,' says Francesco, turning on his heels. Vivaldi climbs the wooden stairs into a long, dark corridor. It smells musty and there are cobwebs everywhere. He follows Santurini into a room badly lit from a single tiny window. Santurini slumps into a chair and pours himself some wine. He indicates another chair, covered in papers. 'Put those on one side and make yourself comfortable.' Antonio stands awkwardly with the papers in his hand, then puts them down on the floor and takes a seat. Peering curiously around the room he sees it is a mess. In one corner is an unmade bed, at its foot a cracked chamber-pot, the lid hanging half off. This Antonio identifies as the source of the all-pervasive sour stink in the place. The window is closed and the pane misted with dirt. An old, fraying curtain, perhaps even predating the theatre itself, hangs from a couple of rusty rings. The floor is covered in withered sausage skins and tiny black beads that

137

Vivaldi recognises as evidence of a multitude of mice. Santurini's balding pate is decked in scabs and he keeps scratching behind his ears. Gradually Antonio, too, begins to itch, beginning in his neck but gradually descending through his back to his arms and legs. He tries as discreetly as possible to ease the irritation by rubbing his back against the chair, but this only makes it worse.

'So, Signor Vivaldi, what is the proposal you wish to put to Domenico?' The impresario is busily digging dirt from beneath his fingernails with his knife and does not even do Vivaldi the courtesy of looking at him when he speaks.

'I think that is a matter I should like to put to Lalli personally,' replies Antonio quietly. This man is beginning to annoy him.

'Ha! There are two things people want from Lalli, money or a libretto. How do I know you're not after his money?'

Ludicrous! According to Gasparini – the man was penniless, where was he to find any money? 'Libretto,' replies Antonio curtly.

'For whom?' Santurini thrusts back, slowly slicing off a piece of sausage and watching Vivaldi through narrowed eyes. The impresario is playing with his knife like a circus artiste making his audience gasp by holding the trembling steel against the temple of a helpless girl in the stocks.

Antonio tries to ignore the blade. 'For myself,' he says, wondering meanwhile whether he is capable of standing up and walking out of here. Nobody saw him coming into the theatre and the whole place seems deserted.

'Ha!' the old impresario cackles with laughter. 'Another gold-digger! What makes you think you can write an opera? You might be able to do a few nice concerti, but if you want to keep an audience entertained for a whole evening you'll have to come up with something better than that! You're not the first, and you certainly won't be the last, to think there are a few ducats to be made from opere. Well I'm here to tell you, forget it! But if you did insist on being pig-headed enough to try, where do you think you could perform such a thing?'

For a minute the priest feels outmanoeuvred. 'My mentor

Francesco Gasparini, *Maestro di Coro* of the *Ospedale della Pietà* and composer of many operas has his own ideas on the subject and they differ from your own.'

At the mention of Gasparini's name, it is Santurini's turn to be surprised. He looks the priest up and down, recognising for the first time in his eyes the energy and determination that is so often taken for arrogance. The impresario grins grotesquely and puts his knife back down on the table. 'Which theatre did you have in mind?'

Antonio glances about him, frowning. 'Somewhere on the mainland,' he says, non-comittal.

'Seems a good idea,' laughs Santurini. 'Come back same time tomorrow and I'll see if Signor Lalli will talk to you.'

With a swift nod Antonio gets up and tries to find his way with as much dignity as he can muster, but as fast as possible, from the theatre. What a character! The thought of a return visit the next day is distinctly unappealing.

Giambattista Vivaldi quickly realises something is up. His son's mind is elsewhere. Instead of writing he sits staring straight ahead of him, tapping out a melody now and then with his fingers. 'Everything all right?' Giambattista asks with deliberately casual concern. No response. Giambattista shrugs. When his son is in this mood there's no point in cross-questioning him; the more he does so, the deeper Antonio creeps into his shell. At the sound of bells tolling from the nearby church Antonio stands up and, without even bidding his father goodbye, leaves the room. In his head Santurini's scornful words go round and round: 'What makes you think you can write an *opera*?' Antonio is reeling inside between uncertainty and pride. Could Santurini be right? He can't be. The man might be an experienced impresario, but does he have any real understanding of modern music? No! He's nothing but a damned arrogant old tyrant.

Antonio arrives the next day, punctual and sure of himself, and this time remains standing when offered a chair. 'Suit yourself,' says Santurini indifferently. 'Tomorrow late morning you'll find Domenico Lalli on the *Piazzetta*.'

'Fine,' replies Antonio with relief, 'but how will I recognise him?'

'Don't you worry about that, Red Priest. He'll recognise you alright!'

His business finished, Antonio makes for the door. As quick as a flash Santurini shoots from his chair and blocks the exit. 'Before we take our leave of one another, *Maestro*, a small gesture of appreciation would surely be in order?' Vivaldi feels himself shrinking. But why should he be afraid of the old scoundrel? Santurini is watching him with a smile as wide as an old lion that knows his prey can no longer escape him. 'Why, yes, of course,' says Vivaldi, producing his purse. He never has much money on him because his father always takes care of such things. He feels with thumb and forefinger for a lira coin and lays it in the grubby, open palm before him. Santurini tosses the coin playfully in the air and catches it. 'That's one!' he says, staring Vivaldi in the eyes. The smile is gone. Antonio hesitates momentarily then finds another lira.

'There we are, *Signore*, and many thanks!' He pushes aside the man's still outstretched arm, impressed at his own performance. Behind him he hears Santurini guffawing like the devil in a recurring nightmare. The priest starts to run, taking the stairs two at a time, his heart bouncing madly. Only once he is safely on the street does he look round and take in a great gulp of air. Never ever again will he set foot inside that theatre.

The canal seethes with ships, all fighting to secure the best place on the quay to unload their cargoes as fast as possible. The southerly breeze feels pleasantly cool and the air is full of the cries of mariners from the water mixed with a symphony of quayside voices. Snippets of many languages, most prevalent among them the broad dialect of the Venetian gondoliers and the men who, swearing and shouting, are busy loading and unloading the ships.

In the occasional moment of silence a hum of voices may be heard emanating from the *nobili* gathered to talk in the *Broglio*, the shady covered walkway of the *Palazzo Ducale*. Like the quacking of ducks, from left and right comes the chatter of groups of tourists gawping at the unique architecture of *La Serenissima*. Vivaldi laughs. The city sings. Everywhere there is music. Bump, thump, bump, the rattling rhythm of kegs rolling across the quay; swish, swash, as sailors hoist the heavy canvas. Stall-holders vying with one another for the attention of passers-by; here the best silk, there the most delicate spices! A melody may even now and then be heard threading its way amidst the swearing. And should you lose yourself amidst this cacophony of colourful sound, a *barcarole* from a passing gondolier will soon restore you to the true rhythm of Venice. Someone is tapping Vivaldi on the shoulder. 'Don Vivaldi?'

Antonio turns to gaze into the face of a large man with blonde curls and remarkably blue eyes. Offering his hand, he introduces himself as Domenico Lalli. Vivaldi is pleased. He had wondered whether the man would turn up. In retrospect, perhaps it had not been such a bad idea to pay Santurini the two lire.

'I'm pleased to see you,' says Antonio. 'Come, let us find somewhere to sit down with a drink.'

Lalli looks vaguely about, but Antonio points towards the bridge.

'I know a good place, where we won't be fleeced. Everywhere is much too expensive around here. Come this way, it's not far.'

They walk along the *Riva degli Schiavoni* and turn off left after a couple of hundred metres. Passing along a narrow lane, the two men emerge onto a small square and take a seat in the shade of the wine-bar belonging to Elena Mazzuro. It is quiet here, and very soon a carafe and two glasses appear before them on the table. A moment later Elena comes out again with a dish of *bussolai buranei*. She sets it down and Domenico peers curiously at the contents.

'Ah, you are not familiar with these? Wonderful! A biscuit

that is made only on Burano.' Antonio picks up one of the baked rings, dips it in his wine and sucks the liquid from it. 'Delicious!'

With a slight frown, Domenico follows suit. 'Hmm, not bad!'

Vivaldi wipes his mouth, scrutinising his companion. The first thing to strike the priest is that his clothing is not much to look at. It's also quite obvious the man is not local. Lalli must be a good head taller than the average Venetian. He has a big nose, but not as coarse as that of Gasparini. His smooth-skinned and close-shaven face is tanned. The eyebrows are oddly unpronounced, and it is the eyes beneath them that dominate the face. He could be Greek, but the accent sounds more like Naples. Then again, might he come from Sicily? For the first ten minutes the talk is of everything and nothing. Then the blond man gets down to business. 'You have a proposal for me?'

Antonio removes a last fragment of biscuit from his palate with his tongue and takes another mouthful of wine. 'That's right. To put you in the picture, I am *Maestro di Violino* at the *Ospedale della Pietà*, just round the corner from here.' Antonio jerks his thumb casually over his shoulder. 'I am also the composer of a number of instrumental works, predominantly *concerti*. This last year I have been exploring vocal possibilities and have decided to try my hand at writing an opera. My friend and mentor Francesco Gasparini, with whom you are acquainted, suggested that I speak to you. I understand that there is not much demand for your work at present.'

Lalli gives the priest a penetrating look, debating with himself whether or not to tell the truth. He could of course try to save face by declaring that his days are completely taken up with writing for certain famous composers. But he knows by now no secret survives long in this city. If he's found to be lying he'll lose this chance too. So Domenico decides to make the best of a bad job, and a sour little smile appears on his lips. 'Alas, you are right. I have all sorts of ideas, but I've discovered the Venetian public is extremely critical.'

'Mmm,' Vivaldi wades right in. 'I'm not sure that's the right word for it. Conservative, more like. You mustn't try giving them anything too different from what they heard yesterday.'

'It wasn't all my fault,' declares Lalli. 'With different music it could have been a success.'

Vivaldi shrugs. 'I don't know. Ruggiere may be a *dilettante* but his music isn't bad. I think it was more to do with the genre.'

'Look, if I'd put that on in Naples I'd be a celebrity by now!'

'Oh?' responds Vivaldi with eyebrows raised. 'Why then did you not perform it there? What brought you to Venice?'

Lalli colours. 'Oh, you know how things are. You want to see something of the world, spread your wings. And I honestly thought I'd find all sorts of chances awaiting me here.'

'You come from Naples, Signor Lalli?'

The priest watches as his blush spreads. The fellow is certainly hiding something. That could prove useful! Antonio leans back calmly in his chair and reassesses the man before him. Small beads of sweat have broken out on his forehead. Lalli is clearly ill at ease.

'Yes, that's right, from Naples,' he answers, confusedly. 'But it's a long time ago, you know!' he adds with a short, nervous laugh.

'I see.'

'Yes. I've travelled about a lot. Lived in Rome a while, and then ended up here.'

'Ah,' answers Antonio. There is another silence.

It occurs to Lalli that perhaps it had not been such a good idea after all, agreeing to meet the *Maestro*. Vivaldi looks him straight in the eye, as if capable of seeing down into the most hidden depths of his soul. Bloody hell, isn't being a composer enough for him? Does the man have to be a priest as well? Lalli can see no way out for himself.

'And what are your plans now, Signor Lalli?'

Domenico swallows hard and examines the glass he's rolling back and forward between his hands.

'To survive,' he declares softly.

'Well I never, and to think Santurini was worried I was after your money!'

'Money!' exclaims Lalli, shocked out of his reverie. He reaches under his tunic and produces the small bundle that hangs from a leather thong around his neck. Shaking it back and forth, he almost shouts, 'See, this is all I possess! And I even had to give Santurini a lira for arranging this meeting with you.'

'What?' It's Antonio's turn to be taken aback. He sits straight bolt upright in his chair. 'I had to pay him two lire. The dirty swindler!'

The two men burst into gales of laughter at the sheer audacity of old Santurini and the ice is broken between them. But, good humour apart, Antonio knows he has worked his way into a prime negotiating position. 'Right, let's get down to business!' he says, leaning across the table towards Lalli. 'I want to write an opera. Unlike your audience, I found nothing wrong with Elisa, but for my own premiere I'd like to be a little less daring. I'm looking for something traditional, yet with fresh appeal. What's more, it needs to be kept simple, not too many singers. Good, but not cheap and cheerful, if you get my meaning.'

'Absolutely,' replies Lalli, enthused. 'I've had a story in my head for some time that will suit you perfectly.' He takes a good draught of wine and shifts onto the edge of his seat. 'Love, jealousy, betrayal and attempted murder! And all in the country villa of the Roman emperor, Otho!'

'Fine. And how about the rest of the story?' enquires Vivaldi.

'Ah well, as I said, it all takes place in the country palace of Emperor Otho. We don't need an armed guard or large court, so the number of singers can be limited to just five. Despite the disapproval of his counsellors, Otho is madly in love with Cleonilla. But she is in love with Caio Silio, the young Roman who is in love with Tullia. Tullia is unhappy about all of this and disguises herself. Assuming the name of Ostilius, she becomes personal maid to Cleonilla, who falls for her instead of Caio Silio. Do you follow?'

Antonio nods.

'Silio is jealous and tries to get rid of the servant, not realising that Ostilius is actually his beloved. Luckily, Otho and Cleonilla manage to prevent the murder. But when Silio makes a last attempt, accusing Ostilius of betrayal, she reveals her true identity. Cleonillia then gaily admits she has known all along that Ostilius was a woman, and everyone lives happily ever after. What do you think of it? Fantastic, eh?'

Vivaldi ponders the plot. It all sounds a bit far-fetched but maybe something can be made of it. It certainly fits the bill as far as public taste is concerned. And well, why not? 'It might do,' he says cautiously. 'Can you let me see some text before I make a definite decision?'

Domenico is radiant. 'Of course. I'll get going on it straight away. When would you like to get *Otho* onstage?'

'I've no idea,' answers Vivaldi. 'I have to compose it first.'

He pays Elena and, having shown Lalli how he can find his way home, shakes hands with him. Next time they can meet at his house, Vivaldi tells the librettist.

'You'll hear from me as soon as possible,' is the grateful response.

Antonio puts on his hat and walks home. He can't quite get the measure of Lalli; what is this man hiding from him? He'll have to make some enquiries.

'Betrayal in Villa Otho?' Giambattista is nonplussed when Antonio reappears and tells him of the day's events. Opera? So that's what his son's been up to. Opera, indeed. My God, can this be a good idea? He knows what a competitive world it is. But Antonio prattles on so happily and so unstoppably about Lalli, Otho, the public and his imminent success that Giambattista has to relent. It all seems innocent enough and perhaps he shouldn't put a damper on things this time. 'I think I've heard that tale about Otho before. Hmm, let me see.' Antonio goes on talking while his father rifles through pile after pile of sheet music and libretti. 'Ah, here we are. Take a look at this.' He interrupts another stream of enthusiasm from his son and blows the dust off an old libretto. 'I knew it. Messalina!'

'What do you mean?'

'Here, have a look; Messalina, performed in 1680 in the Teatro San Salvatore. You were just learning to walk then. The text was by Francesco Maria Piccioli, set to music by Carlo Pallavicino. Yes, he was a good composer. It was his opera Vespasiano that was the first on the boards at the opening of Teatro San Grisistomo, you know. A real honour! He moved to Dresden later, and if I'm not mistaken he died there, too. I can't recall what sort of success he had with Messalina, but neither can I bring to mind a single flop for Pallavicino.'

'Perfect!' replies Antonio. 'That's a good omen to start with.'

'Hold on though, not so fast. I'd like to think about the possibility of an opera, but not here in Venice. You know my feelings about that.'

'I do, father, and I bear them in mind. But I have instructions from Maestro Gasparini to leave all of that to him. He actually has everything to gain from helping me.'

'Oh?' responds his father in surprise. But Giambattista will have to wait to know what his son means by this remark. Before he can probe further Antonio has gone off to his own room, his face alight with a mysterious smile.

As the days get shorter, so the libretto grows ever thicker. Vivaldi and Lalli meet regularly and become good friends. Antonio has still not discovered what Lalli is hiding from him, but it no longer bothers him.

The priest has enquired a couple of times of Gasparini whether he has any idea where the debut of his opera might take place. The Maestro di Coro assures him that he need have no worries on this score. Trust him and all will be well. In the meanwhile he is offloading more and more work onto Vivaldi. 'You scratch my back, I'll scratch yours,' he mumbles, handing the priest another list. Vivaldi unfolds the piece of paper: a Mass, two vespers and no fewer than four motets. He glances up, his brow deeply furrowed. 'And who's finding you a theatre?' booms Gasparini, before Antonio can open his mouth.

While Venice once more prepares for a new carnival season, both Gasparini and Vivaldi are frantically composing. Gasparini has received a *scrittura* from Milan but is also putting the finishing touches to *La verita nell'inganno*, to be performed later in *Teatro San Cassiano*. He works on the composition with a huge smile on his face: "The Truth behind the Lies" – what a superb title! Ah, if people only knew! With an enormous flourish of satisfaction he sets down the final note. *Voilà*, that'll be his last opera for *San Cassiano*. *Ciao, Venezia!*

Giambattista can hardly lift the stack of papers. Antonio, desperate for the day when he no longer has to give lessons or rehearse in his workroom, is producing one sheet of music after another. Apart from his work for the *Pietà*, private commissions also lie awaiting his attention. And then there are the little reminders that keep coming in from *Monsieur* Roger. The pressure on him to complete his *Opus IV* is increasing by the day. But Antonio has written enough *concerti*. Nine have already arrived in Amsterdam and are on the engraving plate. This evening he and his father are to select the last three works. There is so much to do that he has hardly had time to work on Otho. His father doesn't mind his writing an opera, but still regards such efforts as more or less a hobby. 'First the work that brings in some money, my son,' he prompts each time he catches Antonio putting aside his other commitments to work on Otho. And then he has to turn sullenly back to the list made up for him each day by his father. The amount of attention allocated to each piece of work depends on the rank of the commissioning client. If possible, already existent work is re-worked. This sometimes happens for the Pietà, too. Antonio often mines his father's archives for inspiration, digging up intriguing and long-forgotten or never properly published pieces. It then costs him little time and trouble to rework the melody so that it fits perfectly into his own composition, which makes a big difference to his workload!

In the 'free' time thus won, Antonio plunges back into reading Lalli's libretto. It's very different writing an opera to a concerto he has to admit, but he is learning. Whenever possible he attends a new theatre production and sometimes finds himself listening more to the public than to the performance. What does the audience really appreciate most? What's the difference between a BOO and a BRAVO? What quality is it in an aria that makes them sit up, shut up and take notice? The costumes, the stage-set, the backstage machinery used for set changing; what contributes to a successful production, or are the mob completely impervious to all? Vivaldi is fascinated to learn. Especially when he goes twice to the same production and sees the differing reactions of two audiences. Remarkable!

Over recent weeks the tourists have had to share Venice's flat-bottomed barges with flocks of sheep. Not the live version, but salted and smoked carcasses of the lambs that during the summer months grazed the meadows of the Brenta. At this time of year La Serenissima seems transformed into one gigantic kitchen, for wherever they walk none can escape the savoury smell of castradina and green cabbage. It is the feast of the Madonna della Salute.

'One of the few good rituals I'm going to miss!' whispers Gasparini in Antonio Vivaldi's ear. They are sitting side by side at an enormous table shared by staff from the Pietà. By tradition, every year after the service they all eat together. Today the church had been full to bursting. 'It's about time they built a new and bigger place,' remarks Gasparini provocatively. He hates a hall full of people packed together like sardines behind him when he is leading the choir. But, as usual, the public seems to have enjoyed the service.

'I've another bit of news for you, Vivaldi,' growls the *Maestro di Coro* in a low voice, trying with his little finger to extract a remnant of mutton from between his teeth. 'Vicenza.'

'What about Vicenza?' Antonio asks, his mind elsewhere.

'Oh,' Gasparini looks up at the ceiling and closes his eyes despairingly. 'Oh, Mother Maria! I have found a theatre for your Otho.'

'WHAT? But that's wonderful!' screeches Antonio. He gratefully embraces Gasparini whilst the choirmaster tries gently but firmly to push his arms away. 'That's enough,' he mutters, embarrassed at such a show and all the attention this is attracting from the rest of the table. Everyone is by now staring open-mouthed at the pair. Pietro Scarpari gives Antonio a dour look. The singing master is sure by now his premonition was correct; those two are definitely up to something.

'*Allora*, may we share in the celebration? Are we all getting a rise in salary or something?' calls out Scarpari, evoking a round of laughter. Vivaldi beats out a triumphant roll of drums on the table with his two hands, rises to his feet and strikes a pose with one foot on his chair. 'Signori, you will soon have the pleasure of hearing a new production, *Ottone in Villa*, a *dramma per musica* in three acts, written by none other than your very own Don Antonio Vivaldi!' He spreads his arms in the air as if already accepting the accolade of a standing ovation. '*Brava'ccio!*' hisses Scarpari between clenched teeth, clapping as hard as the rest of his colleagues, by now all offering Antonio their congratulations.

'I can live with that,' nods his father upon hearing his son's news. Although still part of the Republic, Vicenza is just far enough away. The *Teatro delle Garzerie* is fairly well established, but a new theatre is due to open shortly with two works by Pollarolo on the programme. Antonio is unperturbed. There will be plenty of public left to attend his debut. Somewhere deep down he has decided that should it be a washout he will blame Pollarolo and the new theatre.

His honorarium will not be great, Gasparini has warned him with care. But this doesn't bother the priest, either. He has a stage, and that's the main thing.

'How will you combine this with your work at the Pietà,' asks his father, practical as ever.

'All arranged! At least, Maestro Gasparini is going to make sure I get a month's sabbatical. That should give me time to rehearse as well.'

'Fine,' agrees Giambattista. Gasparini would seem to have everything under control. On the one hand, he's pleased that the Maestro di Coro is lending Antonio so much support. On the other, he wonders what the old fox is really up to. Like rats making their tentative appearance as evening falls, the first rumours are on the move. The father waits and watches. For the moment all his attention is focused on his daughter Cecilia's coming wedding.

'Not bad,' is Gasparini's judgement, having finished reading the last sheet of music. 'I think the public should be more than satisfied with this. It's well balanced and not as modern as your concerti. In short, fine.' Vivaldi proudly retrieves the composition from his hands. 'Hm, just one other little thing,' adds Gasparini as if it has just come into his head. 'I have something else for you.' Vivaldi's eyes begin to glisten. 'Now that I've seen the music for Otho, I'm convinced you can do this sort of work.' Gasparini has a sudden attack of coughing. He's been walking around for weeks wrapped up in a scarf but can't seem to get rid of his filthy cold. Antonio, meanwhile, can hardly contain his curiosity.

'I have a commission lying here for an oratorio.'

Gasparini clears his throat and takes a drink. 'Hm, you don't have to rush. It's for the beginning of June. A special Mass in the Santa Corona in Vicenza at which Pope Pius V is to be declared a saint. Round about then Vicenza will have got to know you in the theatre and I'm sure they'll be banging on the church doors to get in and hear your La Vittoria Navale.'

'*La Vittoria Navale*?' repeats Vivaldi reflectively. 'What a remarkable title.'

'Yes, don't ask me what it's about. There was no *libretto* enclosed with the letter, but I gather the piece describes the battle near Lepanto and the angel Saint Pius sings the main part of the story. Doesn't really matter much apart from that. I know you'll make something of it.'

'Thanks, *Maestro*. Thank you for all your advice and help up until now. Without you I would never have got this far.'

'Rubbish!' Gasparini glowers, trumpeting as he blows his nose. 'Oh how happy I shall be to be back in the hills. Away from this lagoon and all her swampy canals. A fire blazing in the hearth and a glass of good wine. You watch me, I'll be my old self again in no time!'

'When do you leave?' asks Antonio softly. He already knows how he is going to miss the *Maestro*.

'I'm as good as ready for off, Vivaldi. I hope to celebrate Easter at home this year.'

Once Gasparini has got the management to agree to a month's sabbatical for Antonio Vivaldi, the *Maestro* starts packing. He does so as discreetly as possible. Each day a small load of household items and books is dispatched to the mainland. A good week before Vivaldi is due to leave for Vicenza, the *Maestro di Coro* reports sick. Given his years of service, it's not difficult for him to get special leave of absence; and the management grants him six months off to rest. His farewell is brief. Gasparini has brought up to date all his accounts with the administrators of the *Pietà* and does not even take the time to say goodbye to the *Figlie di Coro*. They may not suspect the truth, but he knows he will never see them again and he cannot bring himself to tell them to their faces. He is leaving in the knowledge that as long as Vivaldi is attached to the *Pietà* he need have no worries about musical standards falling there.

Father and son Vivaldi are the only persons to accompany him to the quay that afternoon. Pale spring sunshine silvers the water splashing gently against the harbour wall. 'I shall think of you, my son,' Gasparini says, in a strained manner and with a catch in his voice. Saying farewell to *La Serenissima* is hurting far more than he had ever expected it to. Giambattista embraces Francesco, by now fully in the picture concerning the *Maestro di Coro*'s true plans. 'Thank you, my friend, for all you have done for Antonio.'

Gasparini manages to swallow another sob and shrugs his shoulders instead. 'Oh, that was nothing. The lad simply has it in him.'

Antonio presses his fingernails hard into the palm of his hand. He hardly knows how to master his emotions and is fighting back the tears. With a lump in his throat he waves desolately to Gasparini, who has by now climbed aboard the ferry. As the ship pushes off, Gasparini makes for the saloon. The morning air is still quite chilly. He opens the door, pauses and turns round. Father and son Vivaldi are still waving, behind them the *Ospedale della Pietà*.

'Keep writing,' shouts Francesco hoarsely over the water. Then his eyes fill and, coughing, he pulls the door closed behind him.

The journey to Vicenza has gone well. In fact, Vivaldi has noticed little of it, for his thoughts are fully occupied imagining himself in the theatre and playing his composition through and through again. So that it amazes him to see the coachman staring him questioningly in the face and repeating loudly as if he were deaf, 'VICENZA!'

The theatre is old but has been reasonably well maintained; the singers somewhat provincial, but courteous and kind. The members of the orchestra are obviously ripe for something new, possibly another career altogether, for never has Vivaldi heard people playing with so little imagination. Even after he has treated them to a couple of impressive *cadenze* they still give Antonio the feeling they've seen it all before. It's not that they don't play their lines; they do, but that's where their inventiveness stops. The leader keeps a weather eye on the clock and, when Vivaldi suggests going once more through an aria, stands up and wishes the priest a goodnight. The first time this happens, Antonio is left speechless and, more significantly, completely alone in the hall.

He has also taken the musicians through his *oratorio*. His leave is going to be too short to allow him to attend the premiere but he has the feeling he need not spill too many tears on that account. For a moment he wishes he had brought along with him a couple of *Figliole* from the *Pietà*. That would have given these miserable specimens something to listen to for a change. E *basta*, that's how you play an instrument!

The evening of the premier arrives and, as predicted by the impresario, attendance is not at all bad. In the end the hall is half filled. There are people enough, apparently, keen to hear Venice's *Prete Rosso* play. His name is quite well known as the famous master of the *concerto*. And isn't it Vivaldi who personally teaches the angels of the *ospedaletto*?

Antonio does not suffer from nerves. As if to the manner born he carries his orchestra and choir through the performance. As the last notes die away the calls of *bravo* outnumber the booing, and this he takes as a good sign. Subsequent evenings attract bigger audiences, and the impresario is clearly delighted. But the rigid attitude of the musicians continues to infuriate Vivaldi and one way or another each performance leaves him with a hangover.

'What a heap of sandbags,' Vivaldi bemoans himself once back in Venice. He and Domenico Lalli are mulling things over with a glass of wine. 'Useless ruddy musicians,' grouches Antonio again.

'But what did people think of the production, and my story?'

'Oh, that went down a treat,' answers Vivaldi, with so much self-assurance in his voice it seems he's never had a moment's doubt about the end result. 'Listen, the impresario is overjoyed with everything and wants me back in his theatre as soon as possible. What more could you want?'

'Nothing!' beams Lalli. 'So when is it?'

'Oh, he has to find me some better singers and players first. Our show only worked each night despite their performance, not because of it. But don't even ask me what I've been through on that score!'

Lalli flashes him a sympathetic smile.

'No, seriously. That was a truly charming introduction to the theatre. You could sit and watch while a village band like that poured your entire production down the drain. All by themselves.'

'Mm,' Lalli ponders aloud. 'Sounds as if you're not much looking forward to your next opera. Shame. I've such a nice narrative in mind.'

Vivaldi taps his glass. 'Listen, Lalli, this was just the start! But the next time I want better musicians and better singers.'

'That's easy to say,' interrupts Domenico. 'Your ladies are busy singing all day long and have nothing else to worry about. Music making is all they live for.'

'Nonsense. Anyone who plays in an orchestra should be equally motivated. If all you're doing is playing for your bread and butter, you might as well make your living as a baker.'

'Welcome to the real world, Don Vivaldi,' retorts Lalli with scorn and by now slightly inebriated 'Bad luck on you, but that's not how things are.'

Antonio shrugs. 'I'll show you how things can be.'

His head is teeming with ideas. 'I'll show you how things can be,' he repeats, getting to his feet. He gives Lalli a gentle, friendly tap on the head. 'Until later this week.'

Domenico returns his farewell and refills his own glass. Nice man, he smirks, but what a dreamer!

4

Il celebro Vivaldi! Antonio may consider the performance of *Ottone in Villa* sub-standard, but apparently the public does not share his view. The news seeps slowly from Vicenza into the lagoon, at first a tiny trickle but soon swelling to become a surging river of praise that threatens to burst its banks. People who have never even heard Vivaldi play, let alone been to one of the performances in Vicenza, are among the most wildly enthusiastic and proud of 'their' *celebro virtuoso de violino.*

Il *Prete Rosso*'s standing rises by the day, as do prices for his commissions. Most thrilled of all are Giambattista and Camilla Vivaldi. Not so much because of the money pouring in daily, though this is greatly appreciated, but more with the status and respect accorded their son. Camilla is proud simply to be pointed out in church or at the market as the mother of Don Vivaldi. The same goes for his father and, in some degree, everyone else in the neighbourhood. Antonio's success reflects on them too and it is remarkable how many 'friends' the priest soon gathers about him; each and every one full of exuberant tales of how this very great composer excels in so many ways and yet remains faithful to them as a simple comrade. Then there are the *brava'cci*, the bluffers who go a step further and relate how the *virtuoso de violino* actually comes to them for inspiration! But, it has to be said, not many people fall for this particular claim.

How different is the reality. In fact Antonio Vivaldi has very few friends. As a small child he was already an outsider. He had never cared for ball games in the square, or playing tag and hide-and-seek. After a few minutes running around he would be gasping for air and have to retire, half-fainting to his mother's lap.

He would be in real trouble when things got warm and dusty. And simply going upstairs too fast would bring on an attack of coughing and wheezing. His parents had regularly been reduced to prayer by one of his many fevers, sometimes so severe he could hardly draw breath. The doctor, called on such occasions, could do nothing more than write out his bill.

For whole days and nights after another such attack the child would be confined to bed, too weak even to lift a glass of water to his lips. As he grew older the bouts of fever gradually became less frequent. Bit by bit his health improved, although he remained slight in stature. The older he got, the fitter he became. He still could not play football, but the little Antonio did not very much mind. He had never seen the sense in kicking a ball around the square again and again. Even games of tag had no attraction for him, nor when the local boys with bloodcurdling shrieks chased each other round the fountain, getting soaked in re-enactment of battles against the savage Turks. He preferred to sit indoors with his father. There was always something to do inside. The neighbours would come to the house to be shaved, and for those who could afford it his father would sometimes make a wig. The latest gossip would be exchanged and world news discussed.

But there came a point when Giambattista began to spend more and more time copying music and rehearsing various pieces. He was being invited increasingly to play in theatre orchestras, and when Antonio was just seven his father was appointed violinist to the San Marco basilica orchestra. Fewer and fewer men came along for their daily shave. Giambattista had better things to do. Antonio soon learned to read and write, and as he worked his father taught the boy how to read music too. It wasn't long before little Vivaldi began to imitate his father. He was allowed to draw some lines to form a stave on the back of an old piece of paper and invent his own tunes. For his eighth birthday his parents gave Antonio a violin, made for him with endless patience by his father. And this was the moment when Antonio discovered his true love. To his classmates he was by now nothing but a boring idiot and they soon dropped the 'little red'. He was not worth having as a friend.

One day a couple of his classmates decided to pull a fast one on 'carrot-head'. Out of sight of the school they jumped on the unsuspecting Antonio. 'Hey, poppy! Take that.' And without any reason, as so often with boys of that age, they set upon Antonio. The gang soon realised something was up. Antonio did not react to their punches or defend himself against their kicks. They began to back off, seeing how Vivaldi's normally pale face grew still whiter until it took on a waxy blue tint. 'My God, we've killed him!'

'Hey, what's going on there?' came a gruff voice out of nowhere. The kids huddled together in fear. Swapping shifty looks, they decided without a word to get out of there. Allesandro the rope-maker knelt down beside the unconscious boy. He at once recognised the red curls, for the Vivaldis were neighbours of his. Pushing the hair back from the boy's face, he saw blood trickling from a split lip. Allesandro hesitated not a second but picked Antonio up bodily and carried him at a jog-trot to the fountain in the square. Pushing aside the women busily washing and gossiping there, whose chatter turned to screams as they caught sight of the wounded boy, the rope-maker sprinkled cool water on Vivaldi's face. Coughing, the boy began to come round. One shocked woman dropped her washing and rushed off to fetch Camilla.

Arriving at the scene, his horrified mother demanded to know what had happened and Allessandro told her what he had witnessed. Sobbing, Camilla took her boy into her arms. She was strong enough to carry Antonio indoors and put him straight to bed. Fighting back the tears she sat down beside him, soothing, stroking his curls. Once more she waited and prayed.

It was not long before the attack came on, this time worse than ever before, so that Camilla truly feared for her son's life. But once more little Antonio refused to give in and struggled valiantly until at last the breathlessness subsided. It would be some time before the child, exhausted and debilitated from his ordeal, was strong enough to return to school.

Once recovered, Antonio had resolved never again to

retaliate when persecuted. But the bullies had learnt their lesson too and decided to ignore him from now on. They were terrified. What if he had died? Then they would certainly have been had up before the Inquisition, put on the rack and hanged next day like common criminals from the outside wall of the *Palazzo Ducale*.

Antonio was only too happy to be left in peace, although he was still scared. Oh, how good it would be to have revenge on them! But how? He knew he was too weak to do anything about it now and had to bide his time. But all his fear and anger melted away when he played his violin. The warm tones of the instrument offered consolation and in his private dream world there existed neither teaser nor torturer.

The pattern of bullying and retreat recurred at the *scuole sestierali*, the seminary of *San Giovanni*. Antonio put up with training for the priesthood, knowing all the time that his only real interest lay with the violin and any teacher who could enrich his knowledge of it. His mother, always full of concern, very often had the idea that the world was passing him by completely. 'What in heaven's name will become of him?' she would anxiously ask of herself and his father time and again. Her husband was much more phlegmatic, calming his wife with the observation that once Antonio was ordained his future would be assured; a priest could always earn a living. And of course Giambattista kept his eyes and ears open, and when he heard that the new *Maestro di Coro* at the *Ospedale della Pietà* was looking for a teacher for the string section he wasted no time in arranging an audition for Antonio. But it was thanks purely to Antonio's own abilities that *Maestro di Coro* Francesco Gasparini gave him the appointment. Antonio felt as if awoken from a long dream. He took an immense liking to the *Maestro di Coro* and could not have wished for a finer position. He fulfilled his task with unparalleled enthusiasm and it looked as though he had found his vocation. For the first time in her life, Camilla stopped worrying about her son.

His father usually opens the post, even when a letter is clearly addressed to Don Vivaldi. If so, Giambattista reads it through carefully before relaying any news to his son. Mostly this concerns a commission for a *concerto* or *serenata* from some hitherto unknown client. Only very rarely does the pile of correspondence contain a personal letter.

Perhaps it's the sweltering heat, but it seems to Antonio that his father is taking an age to open the first letter. Giambattista makes a real business of it, whilst Antonio sees immediately that the communication is from Amsterdam. That's not the one he's expecting. Snatching up from the table the remainder of the post, he shuffles through it impatiently, trying to make out the senders' name. Again nothing!

He hurls the envelopes back down on the tabletop, surprising his father with his strange behaviour. 'You might at least ask my permission,' Giambattista upbraids him, gesturing pointedly at the letters. 'Are you waiting for something you don't want me to know about?'

Antonio shrugs wordlessly.

'Or have you met a nice lady with whom you've promised to correspond?' laughs the father.

'Tch,' Antonio clicks his tongue derisively. The only ladies he is interested in are musicians, as his father well knows. The rest are all equally empty-headed as far as he's concerned; look at his sisters. Although his thoughts do, very occasionally, return to a special encounter of a couple of years ago. And he does regularly pop into the church of *San Martino* to gaze at her likeness in the painting of Maria. He cannot understand how he has never seen her since; it's just as though she has vanished from the earth...

'Out with it, young man, what's the matter with you?'

'Nothing, forget it.' Petulant, Antonio dons his hat and leaves the house.

His father frowns briefly but does not look up. He is used to his son's moods.

It is not yet noon but already the day is very hot. Antonio

decides against a long walk and instead makes straight for the *Riva degli Schiavoni* and Signor Emilo's coffee-house. Inside the air is cool and laden with the aroma of freshly roasted coffee beans. Sitting at small tables to the left and right of the entrance are some elderly customers who greet the priest respectfully. Antonio acknowledges them with a swift nod of the head. This is no morning for idle chatter. He orders coffee and sits down at a little table that wobbles on the uneven stone floor. Signor Emilo serves Antonio his coffee with a flourish and, twirling meanwhile a point of his magnificent moustache, enquires like a true landlord after his health. Meanwhile, Vivaldi responds courteously that he is in excellent form, but Emilo gathers from his tone that a cosy chat is not really on the cards today. Antonio stirs his coffee furiously. Why has he heard nothing yet? It is already two months since he returned from Vicenza. He is the talk of the town over there, and rightly so! But why still no word from the big theatres? Why no news from *Teatro San Cassiano* and *Giovanni Gristostomo*? It only confirms his suspicion that the Grimanis will never offer him a *scrittura*, not even if he was the last composer left on earth.

For years now the brothers have kept their stranglehold on the theatre world. The death a couple of years ago of Vincenzo Grimani had done nothing to mellow his brother Gian Carlo. Old Grimani moved in circles in which there was no place for modern composers of humble origin such as Vivaldi. *Antici*, that was what they were! And this attitude Antonio finds blocking him at every turn; he can move neither forwards nor back. He had thought seriously about the possibility of going to the mainland, living perhaps in Milan or even Vienna. Italian composers were apparently doing very nicely there these days. But then came news of an outbreak of the plague in Vienna, and Vivaldi had quickly rejected the idea of journeying to the Habsburg capital. Yet whilst he feels he is going round in circles, the very process of weighing up all these pros and cons has manoeuvred him into a new frame of mind. Why shouldn't he award himself a commission? Find his own singers and musicians?

Keep hold of the reins. Stop depending on unsophisticated impresarios who can't read a note of music and dopey local bandstand players who cut corners at every opportunity? His pride forbids him to go down on his knees to Gian Carlo Grimani for a commission. No way! He'll show him! Of course, he'll have to talk to his father about it all. He'll be bound to have a fit! But earlier this week an amazing chance had presented itself, one of those that comes along just once in a lifetime. The sort you have to grasp with both hands or spend the rest of your days regretting it. All his ideas have fallen suddenly into place, exactly as if it was meant to be. Since then he has been doing the sums, drawing up estimates, calculating the risks, and whichever way you look at it, it cannot fail.

The old theatre boss of the *San Angelo*, Francesco Santurini, had finally got his comeuppance. While Antonio was having his premier in Vincenzo, *Teatro San Angelo* was playing an opera, *Le Passioni per Troppo Amore*, by Johann David Heinichen. Venice had been home to Heinichen for a couple of years and he was one of Antonio's private students. Two operas by the German were running this season; Heinichen, however, had not quite reckoned on the cunning Santurini. After two days the impresario had unceremoniously swept *Le Passioni per Troppo Amore* from the boards, scrapping it from the programme and informing Heinichen that it was not to the public's taste. Standards, he announced, had to be upheld in his theatre. The truth was, behind the scenes Santurini had received a good offer from a dilettante who wanted to see his own opera staged. The impresario had not had to agonise long over this decision, especially in view of the large sum of money gravitating across the table towards him. But the elderly Santurini had badly misjudged both the young German and his audience. The public had been enjoying the Heinichen opera and was not to be bought off so easily by conciliatory noises from the impresario over how good the new performance would be. For the first time Santurini was feeling his age and heartily longed to be his fiery young self again, if only for a day. He knew what he wanted to do with these rebel-rousers! But their voices rose until they drowned out the impresario and as the first stones flew through the theatre windows he gave in and, much to the German's glee, put his production back on stage.

Santurini, though, would not have been Santurini if he hadn't tried to pull off another of his tricks. The audience having left the theatre happy night after night, Francesco smartly sacked the German. It was Heinichen's fault he'd lost out on a profitable deal and now the German could sing for his supper!

The news made Heinichen livid but, almost before he had fully taken in what was happening, Francesco's dogs-body had thrown him out of the building. What Santurini did not know, however, was that, before devoting himself entirely to music, Heinichen had studied law and worked for a few years as a solicitor. Johann Heinichen, delighted at last to be able to put to good use his long years of study, began a case against the impresario.

The lawsuit did not last long, for Santurini had been busy for many years building up a huge dossier of complaints against his own person. He had also managed run-ins with plenty of nobili, so that he stood not a chance in the courtroom. He was sentenced to a non-negotiable fine of sixteen hundred ducats, which meant final curtains for the theatre boss. The magnitude of the fine was enough to bankrupt Francesco Santurini, leaving Teatro San Angelo for the first time in ages without an impresario. But, despite it being almost impossible to make any profit from opera, the lease was soon taken over by Signor Modotto.

Tall and lean, Modotto is made of quite different stuff from his predecessor. He has no intention of working hard and like Santurini spending every day in the dusty theatre. Oh no, Modotto's plan is to sublet the theatre by the season. This is the way to make money, and here lies Vivaldi's chance!

The priest has been to see Modotto and put a proposal to him. Modotto has not directly rejected the idea, but neither has he rushed into accepting it.

'I'll think about it,' he's told Antonio. 'I'll drop you a line.' But time is passing without any word and the uncertainty is driving Antonio mad. He slurps his coffee, his thoughts elsewhere; perhaps Naples is still an option. He sets himself an ultimatum: if in five days he still hasn't heard anything, he will pack his bags. That might be cause for regret of course, but then it will be too late. Silent and grimly determined, but nodding amiably enough to all, Antonio steps outside. Blinded by the sudden fierce sunlight, he quickly dives into a shady side street.

'You've just missed your visitor,' remarks his father implacably as Antonio walks in through the door. Giambattista does not look up. He has a lot to do today.

'Visitor?' replies the priest in surprise. 'Did I have an appointment then?'

'I think he came along on the off chance. He left a note for you. Over there, beside that book.'

'Well, who was it?' asks Antonio, exasperated.

His father traces a couple of new lines on the fresh sheet of paper before him. 'Hmm, what was the name again? Oh yes, Modetto.'

'Modotto,' corrects Antonio, quickly unfolding the note. The handwriting is unaffected and so is the message. *D'accordo!*

'You're going to what? Have you gone soft in the head?' fumes his father. He has just heard Antonio's plan. 'It'd be safer to bet the family savings blindfold at the *Ridotto* than go along with this crazy notion. I know nobody who has got rich from opera. Forget it. Enough!'

Antonio has never seen his father this angry, but so completely convinced is he of his new direction that there is no way back for him. Keeping as calm as possible, he asks his father's permission once more to properly explain his plan. Giambattista is by now pacing up and down the room like a bear with a sore head.

'I don't want to hear another word! Where did you get such an insane idea?'

Outside on the square the neighbours are nudging each other and sniggering. The *Rossis* are at it again. Ah well, typical artists. Antonio comes out to fill the carafe with fresh water from the well and the crowd parts respectfully for him. He returns indoors with the full pitcher, drawing a deep breath as he goes. He fears it's going to be a long afternoon.

The minute he is back in view his father launches into a new attack, starting from the beginning and going over all the same ground again. Antonio calmly pours out some water and hands it to his father, who empties it in one gulp and holds out the glass for more. The spring water, combined with Antonio's quiet demeanour, begin slowly to have a cooling effect upon Giambattista.

'What in heaven's name did I do to deserve this?' the old man shakes his head in exasperation. 'Go on then, let's hear the whole cock-and-bull story again.'

Antonio laughs, but not too ostentatiously. He would hate his father to get the impression he did not take his views seriously. 'Well,' begins Antonio. He gives a short, nervous cough. 'We're going to take over the theatre. Not literally, of course. I want nothing to do with maintenance, only content. Choice of productions, selection of the libretto, auditions for singers and orchestra, stage design, lighting, costumes and ballet. In short, we will have in our own hands all the ingredients needed for a successful production.'

'But it's too daft for words. You'll be taking over the job of an impresario. Who's going to pay for it all?' his father wants to know.

'The public! As I said, it's only the stuff directly to do with the production that'll be our responsibility.'

'Your responsibility, you mean,' his father interrupts him.

'Fine, my responsibility. I have put a proposal to Modotto whereby we pay him a fixed sum per month, plus a portion of the takings per evening. Out of season we pay nothing, of course. Look, father, I've reckoned it all up. Here.'

Antonio smoothes and hands his father the estimate. Giambattista hesitantly accepts the sheet of paper and spreads it out on the table before him. Antonio holds his breath while his father runs an expert eye over the figures.

'Hmm, does this fellow Modotto agree with the sum down here?'

Grinning from ear to ear, Antonio pushes the note from Modotto under his father's nose.

'You do understand that you are gambling all our money on this scheme?'

'Only if we fail,' responds Antonio with confidence. 'But that won't happen, father. It's going to work, I'm sure of it! I'll make certain we have the best singers onstage, and by that I don't mean the most famous ones, with all their absurd salaries! Believe me, the public will be queuing at the ticket-office once a fresh breeze is blowing through the *San Angelo*. We'll alternate new shows with old favourites. Some I'll re-write, give them a new title and – *voilà!* Not a risk in sight!'

'Don't be too sure of it, my son. I've seen old shows in new clothing before now. And it doesn't always work.'

'If we just break even. And look at Vicenza. That was a great hit, but more for the impresario than for me! Yet I'm sure I can do a better job. Surely we can try it for a season? If it works we'll all be the better off for it. There'll be fatter earnings for both orchestra and copyist. You'll be knocking on our door in no time, father,' smiles Antonio.

'Very witty,' growls his father, still glowering over the figures. He holds the paper up and runs his eye down all the columns again. 'That's not right,' he declares, pointing ponderously at an item labelled 'lighting'. 'The income from the boxes is far too low, and I think you can ask more for sales of *libretti*.'

Giambattista's eyes are beginning to shine. They put their heads together over the calculations again, inventing various scenarios to test it, including minimal audience attendance and the worst possible losses. Eventually they get an idea of what their biggest debit might be over a season, given the tightest possible budget. Giambattista lets out a deep sigh and scratches behind his ear. Seeing the possibilities emerge, he too is getting excited. But it's still all a huge gamble and he has no desire to get into debt by a single lira. They go through all the sums again. Giambattista is still not a hundred percent convinced but he is pretty well persuaded by the statistics. Say it works! It'll be biggest challenge of his life so far. He takes another deep breath. 'Not a word of this to your mother,' he hisses, afraid that Camilla might overhear. Antonio leaps to his feet with a cheer.

'Sssh,' warns his father, succumbing silently but happily to his son's warm hug. Giambattista brushes away a tear.

'Come on, son. Let's go and take a look at our theatre.'

Dancing from foot to foot around his father, Antonio slaps him now on one shoulder and then on the other. What a day!

Things are quickly arranged between the Vivaldis and Modotto. The impresario has been very disillusioned by the number of parties interested in renting the theatre from him; there are far fewer than he had expected and so has little option but to accept Antonio Vivaldi's offer. The contract is signed and a preliminary payment made. The show can begin!

The family is now enlightened and everyone shares in the excitement. Only Camilla looks pensive. The sums of money passing hands are beyond her comprehension; she can only resign herself and trust her husband's wisdom in these matters. Everyone in the family is allocated a task and all join in preparations for the opening night of the season. Giambattista wants to begin cautiously, with an old production. Only once he feels completely confident he's got the new business up and running will the time be ripe for their own, brand-new show.

'It's too risky to try doing everything at once,' he tells Antonio. 'It'll take all our resources at first just to make sure each performance goes smoothly. What with everything else that's going on, to try staging a new opera as well is asking for trouble.'

Antonio, of course, disagrees entirely. But he is so overjoyed that his father has gone along with the whole initiative that for the time being he doesn't argue. And a good job too, for Antonio finds out soon enough what is involved in being an impresario; how it feels to have to chase up everything, from big issues to the tiniest detail. The writing of libretto dedications as part of each programme falls to him. Inexperienced as he is, Antonio finds it hard to estimate the number of programme booklets he needs to have printed. According to the printer, the order is always too small and the priest later discovers that indeed there are either too many or too few. Everyone's queries and complaints, to say nothing of the endless whining of singers, set-builders, painters, dancers and musicians, land in his lap. It soon dawns on him that he has lavished far too much attention on each individual in the first place. From the inanity of their questions it seems everyone routinely leaves their common sense at home, or else loses it on their way to the theatre; they certainly don't have it with them by the time they get there. Even his own brothers and sisters appear not to be immune, for their questions are as stupid as everyone else's. But then they have never run a theatre before.

Giambattista has assembled a good bunch of musicians, mostly old friends of his with whom he has played for years. All but two live locally, which forges a bond, certainly here in Venice. The same goes for the vocalists. It's already too late in the season to get together the very best of casts, but Antonio is far from dissatisfied with what eventually fills the stage. The whole operation is like an ocean voyage on which the crew needs time to learn to pull together. And just as every minute counts when preparing a ship for heavy weather, so father and son get no rest. They don't even have time for nerves. Before they know where they are the first performance is behind them.

The second night goes off more peacefully, everyone relaxes and at last the theatre runs like clockwork. So far everything is within budget, and it looks as if all will go to plan.

Another production is scheduled for January. Just to be on the safe side, the Vivaldis have asked Grazio Braccioli to write the libretto. *Dottore* Braccioli, who once studied law, hails originally from Ferrara but has for some years lived in Venice. He has published several libretti, all for *Teatro San Angelo*. His style is plain and conservative, precisely what the public most likes. He keeps his plots simple but is good at colourful characters that clearly appeal to audiences. Antonio would have preferred to write the music himself but has his hands too full organising the theatre. So for this he has gone to the youngest brother of his old mentor, and Michelangelo Gasparini, singer with the choir of *San Marco*, is quite happy to take on a bit of extra work. Michelangelo has written opera before and his music for *Rodomento Sdegnato*, based on *Orlando* by Ludivico Ariosto, is really not at all bad.

One way and another things have been hectic recently. But what a success! The best production so far is most certainly *Orlando Furioso*, another opera based on the narrative by Ludovico Ariosto; the hero and his beloved Angelica have kept the audience enthralled for no fewer than forty-six nights.

'Who said there was no money to be made from opera?' is Antonio's triumphant remark. Smiling equally broadly, Giambattista underlines the figures in his ledger. This outcome to their new venture exceeds their wildest dreams and they eagerly sign a new contract with Modotto for next season.

All the work involved in the theatre and the *Pietà* leaves little time for other business. Antonio has hardly had a chance to admire his own *Opus IV*, sent him with compliments by Estienne Roger. Entitled *La Stravaganza*, Roger has ensured the printed edition once again looks superb.

It has become clear to the management of the *Pietà*, meanwhile, that Gasparini will not be returning from his leave. Pietro Scarpari, who since early summer has been standing in for the *Maestro di Coro*, is being retained in this function until further notice. Antonio considers this far too great an honour for someone so completely devoid of creative talent. After all, it is Vivaldi and not Scarpari the *congregazione* has asked to take on the lion's share of its compositions. Since spring, Antonio's designation has been changed accordingly, to that of *Maestro di Concerti*; which sounds good but brings in not a ducat extra. Remarkably enough, this time the priest does not let it bother him. Coincidentally, he shares the celebration of his thirty-sixth birthday with a performance of his oratorio *Moyses Deus Pharaonis* in the packed church hall of the *Pietà*. It is a glorious occasion at which he is showered in praise. And it is another step on the way towards his new opera. In *Moyses Deus Pharaonis* he has consciously but surreptitiously experimented with a number of new melodies. The public loves it and Antonio now feels confident of using these innovations as the basis for his Venetian opera debut: *Orlando Finto Pazzo!*

Grazio Braccioli has produced a masterpiece. Giambattista looks on worriedly as *Dottore Grazio*, arms thrown wide, expounds his ideas. Antonio is enjoying every moment. This will be the most beautiful and best *Orlando* ever heard in Venice. New life will be breathed back into the hated sorceress Ersilla, bold Orlando, the faithful Brandimarte, proud knight Argillano, and Tigrinda, princess of the magic potions. Wondrous characters, perfect disguises, love, fidelity, and all played out in the fabled 'Kingdom of Organa'. Antonio, the story unfolding before his eyes, begins at once making preliminary notes. Fantastic scene changes, a huge ballet and the whole thing rounded off with a glorious choir. His father sees only the sums.

'Don't you think it's a bit too modern?' he ventures.

'Oh no! Not at all,' chorus Braccioli and Antonio decisively.

Auditions are underway. Because he wants the singers under contract before he begins writing the arias, Antonio has got the choir together relatively fast, making as much use as possible of local vocalists. He has drawn up a list of requirements for people taking leading roles and already has certain singers in mind for some. But everything depends on the availability, and especially on the honorarium asked by the artiste. For the main male lead the priest wants none other than public attraction number one, Antonio Francesco Carli. Antonio first heard this great bass sing in Haendel's *L'Agrippina*. How long ago all that seems now! The problem with Carli is that he sings almost exclusively for *Teatro Grisostomo* and is not the least bit interested in appearing in a second-rate establishment such as *San Angelo*. But Vivaldi is not going to let him slip through his fingers. He arouses Carli's interest by insisting what a very unique production this is to be. Francesco Carli is not only a fine singer with a broad register; he can also act. And Vivaldi is prepared to give him all the room he needs to show it. The bass, inspired by the freshness of Antonio's artistic approach to the project and as yet having no other engagements booked for the autumn, agrees.

The audition with Margherita Gualandi goes less propitiously. This much-loved diva from Bologna has on previous occasions sung at *San Angelo* but is also a celebrity on the mainland.

She arrives late for audition but going by her grand entry, with self-assurance intact. Margherita takes the stage without further ado, sending a mere cursory nod towards where Antonio has seated himself in the hall. Funny, she thinks, we've both got the same colour hair. That's a good sign to start with!

Vivaldi guesses her age at about thirty. Margherita is a well-built woman of elegant proportions. She has about her an aura of strength that suggests she is not someone to be played around with. Her normal speaking voice is hardly audible, the words sweetly articulated and caressing. But this is only half the story; once on stage she sings the rest of the company off the podium, a feat she also performs whenever she is not getting her own way. For then she can beat the lowest fishwife on the *Rialto* at screaming filthy abuse in fluent Bolognese patois.

'What do you want to hear from me Don Vivaldi? Shall I sing you my favourite aria?'

She is just about to start up without waiting for a reply, because everyone always wants to hear her best song. But Antonio has his hand up in the air. 'No, thank you. I've heard you sing before. I have no concerns about that. I want to see if you can act.'

Has she heard aright? Not sing? What has she come all this way for? What is this man about? She takes two steps forward. 'You don't want to hear me sing?' she inquires, choosing her words carefully but unable to hide the undertone of approaching storm.

'That's right, Signora Gualandi. What I want to know is can you act? I am looking for a singer capable not only of producing notes but also of animating the role she is playing. I am not interested in puppets playing out their own drama. I want to see Estilla the sorceress on stage and not Margherita Gualandi.'

Margherita gasps. Capable of producing notes? Who does the cocky cassock think he is? Any more of this and she'll lose her patience. 'Act?' she yells, 'Act? I thought I had to sing in an opera. If I'd wanted to be an actress I'd have joined some crappy company of *Commedia dell'Arte*. I'm a trained vocalist and of course I can interpret a role. That's obvious! And why don't you want to hear me sing, may I ask? Everyone wants to hear me sing! Oh, what's the point? I've wasted my time coming here to see a small-time impresario playing at putting on an opera. I'm off!' Antonio manages to contain his mirth, but only just. What a gorgeous creature, a perfect sorceress!

'Antonio Carli is playing opposite you,' he remarks in a throwaway fashion as Margherita stamps her way off the stage.

She pauses and seems to weigh up his words. Well, if Carlo's doing it. With a deeply theatrical sigh she turns back to face Vivaldi. 'Perhaps you could tell me something more about the piece?' she manages, her voice still trembling with suppressed passion.

'Certainly,' answers Antonio. 'But don't expect too much from a small-time amateur impresario,' he adds with a little, acerbic smile.

'Ah, Don Vivaldi,' she smiles seductively. 'I quite lost my

bearings there for a moment. One gets such days. It was not meant personally, I do assure you.'

Making her way slowly over to Vivaldi, she takes the seat he offers her. She looks straight into the priest's eyes, then drops her gaze modestly and sighs. Her next words escape her in a sort of sob. 'I've ruined everything, haven't I?'

Antonio can no longer restrain himself. He laughs out loud, so that Margherita really does begin to wonder about him. But Antonio recovers himself, takes her hand and plants there a respectful kiss. 'Signora Gualandi, if you will consent to play Estilla, you may stay!'

By the time he has finished going over his plans for *Orlando* with her, Margherita feels thoroughly ashamed of her former behaviour. But Vivaldi is having nothing of apologies and instead takes handy advantage of the moment to bring up the matter of her honorarium. They part on the best of terms.

Have to see about her, thinks the priest, scratching his head and looking about him. The theatre must still be crawling with lice; that'll be it.

Vivaldi has several people in mind for the role of Argillano, but one by one they get eliminated. Too dated, too rigid or too expensive. In the end he reaches agreement with Andrea Pacini, the alto *castrato* from Lucca, where Gasparini grew up. It had passed through Antonio's mind that this might bring luck. Andrea is clearly a rising star. He has produced scintillating performances in work by Scarlatti and Francesco Mancini and Venice took him lovingly to her heart about five years ago in Tomaso Albinoni's opera *Astarto*.

Giambattista reads through all the contracts once more. He is concerned about the honorarium offered the artistes, far higher than originally agreed. But Antonio brushes all objections airily aside. 'Open your ears to what people are saying, father. Everyone's talking about *Orlando Finto Pazzo* and we haven't even gone on stage yet. It's going to be a huge winner, father. Believe me!'

All hands are on deck at *Teatro San Angelo* building the sets. It's been a long time since the stage looked this good. Antonio Vivaldi has discussed each act with the renowned stage designer Bernardo Canal, who has then come up with some sketches. Vivaldi is thrilled with the stunning ideas put forward by the illusionist. Working with his son Zuane Canaletto, Bernardo transforms huge quantities of papier-mâché and metres of linen canvas into a positively breathtaking fairy-tale landscape. The conjuring techniques in which the Canals excel will ensure the theatregoer has a spellbinding experience of being transported to another world.

Everything is ready for the premier of *Orlando Finto Pazzo*. In the theatre final rehearsals are underway and the atmosphere is electric. The music is modern but with just enough traditional touches to offer a foothold for the more conservative among the audience. The soloists are raring to go. All members of the cast are content with their share of the arias, and Antonio has spared no expense on the costumes. It promises to be the glittering jewel in this season's crown, an opening night such as *San Angelo* has never known before. Advance bookings, to Giambattista's great relief, have gone well.

'You see!' Antonio cannot help gloating as he watches his father add up the figures again.

But, despite all the glamour, *Orlando Finto Pazzo* is a disappointment. The hall is full for the first week but then ticket sales begin to dwindle. And even when the death of Gian Carlo Grimani closes down the two big Grimani theatres, no extra seats are sold for *Orlando*. It is a mystery to everyone. Antonio has been overwhelmed with compliments for his music, and the singers, too, are perfectly happy with the public's response. Even Margherita has never before received so many bravos, and on the rare occasion a member of the audience has had the temerity to shout 'BOO!' they have brought down upon themselves the fury of the multitude. Carli has concluded people are simply not ready for a show like this; he himself has enjoyed the experience. 'True art is appreciated only by the few,' observes Margherita with a sigh.

'The person I'm most sorry for is Don Vivaldi,' whispers contralto Anna Maria Fabbri, who plays the role of Origille. 'I hope he won't decide to leave the theatre.'

It is not easy for Antonio to accept that his *Orlando* is failing to live up to his expectations. People like the show well enough; they just don't seem to understand it. Engulfed in a tidal wave of colour, music and dance, they can't cope. Ignoramuses! Disappointed as he is, Antonio remains pragmatic enough to transcend his feelings and keep a cool head. According to Giambattista's reckoning they will just about break even financially. As far as he's concerned this is an achievement in itself, for he has never been entirely convinced they would do so. In order to ensure some winnings this *carnevale* it is decided to re-stage *Orlando Furioso*, the opera that enjoyed so much success last year. Antonio re-writes and rearranges some of the arias so that the production can be advertised as 'new'.

'The public is always so very unpredictable,' remarks Antonio wistfully when night after night the hall is full to capacity again.

'Isn't it time you wrote a new opera?' probes Domenico Lalli. After months of silence, the librettist has sought Antonio out. He is impressed with Vivaldi's organisational talents and the success he and his father have had with the theatre. Lalli enjoyed and admired *Orlando Finto Pazzo* and in fact is still suffering pangs of jealousy that it was not his own libretto. But Antonio's response to the compliments Lalli lavishes on him is nothing more than a deep sigh. Domenico cannot help noticing how tired the priest looks and he empathises with his disappointment.

'From the artistic point of view it's perfect,' Lalli encourages his friend.

'Yes,' says Antonio flatly, 'but unfortunately artistry doesn't pay the bills!'

'Give me another chance to write a libretto for you. I've got a couple of ideas guaranteed to fill the hall.'

'You reckon so?' replies Vivaldi cynically. 'What makes you think you can judge?'

Lalli smiles cheerily, refusing to be put down. 'Well, look at Vicenza. Or have you forgotten that already?'

'Oh yes, a one-day wonder. More to do with people's curiosity about Il Prete Rosso than the story. Show me something worth looking at. Overawe and convince me utterly. Then maybe I'll be prepared to consider your libretto next time.'

Vivaldi's scornful attitude towards Lalli masks his true feelings. In reality he finds it hard to bear that the public has shown itself too stupid to appreciate his performance. Elementary melodies, plain lines, plenty of repetition and, most important of all, very little innovation. That's what the masses yearn for. But then the sheer audacious arrogance of them! One production is hardly off the stage before they're screaming for the next. What hypocrisy! Can't they see what fools they are making of themselves? A rehashed title, a few newly scribbled arias, another cast and voilà, a new opera! But in spite of all his grumbling, the theatre performances bring him in more and more work. Tourists never leave Venice without an edition of music by the famous Vivaldi. And it is the northerners who come back for more. Apart from producing compositions, he helps amateurs by giving them violin lessons during their stay, and these rich foreign pupils do not shrink from paying the fees asked by the renowned Vivaldi. They may not master every piece he gives them to practise, but most are delighted just to have the honour of playing with the great virtuoso.

A bonus comes Vivaldi's way this summer. For the management of the Ospedale della Pietà is more than pleased with its priest. Scarpari has produced not a single decent piece of music for the Figlie di Coro and so everything is falling on the shoulders of Il Prete Rosso.

Antonio loves it. All his new musical ideas he can try out with the choir. The *Figliole* are, after all, prepared to perform the best music from across Europe, all year round. Angelic voices emanating from veiled women half concealed behind a trellis and the fame of Don Vivaldi: it is a combination the public finds irresistible. The *Pietà* has meanwhile won a reputation as the most popular *Ospedaletto* of them all. The musicians cannot get enough of the new instruments introduced by Antonio. For Vivaldi the choir is nothing less than a wonderful playground in which he can experiment to his heart's content and give free reign to his artistic ideas. For the laws governing the *Pietà* are quite different from those of the theatre. Here he has no rich stage-set and the priest has to make do without the visionary ideas of Bernardo Canal. But within the sacred space of the *Pietà*, Vivaldi and the *Figliole* together weave their own web of mystery, one against which no décor can compete. With each new work it becomes more difficult to differentiate between an oratorio and a *dramma per musica*. The *Congregazione* has no trouble with this; the more paying audiences they get the better! And Antonio's bonus of fifty ducats makes a welcome contribution to the budget for a new opera. For a new opera is on the way, that's certain!

Despite the disappointment of *Orlando Finto Pazzo*, the Vivaldis are beginning to relish theatre life. The excitement attending on each new production is proving a pleasant challenge, even to Giambattista. But Vivaldi senior, a weather eye on all the risks inherent in every new venture, has also introduced some preventive measures. After every profitable production he puts aside a certain amount of cash, so building up a buffer to steer them through unforeseen eventualities such as a particularly bad season when no audiences appear. Giambattista learned early on how easy it was to lose a large sum of money. Incurring costs is a simple matter; it's always a lot more difficult to estimate how much will come in from audiences. Each new performance passes its losses on down the line, and this time Giambattista is going to make sure the budget does not get overrun.

'Old wine in new bottles' is Giambattista's laconic label for the reworked operas they put on, mostly with success. His artistic conscience being somewhat less well developed than that of his son, he doesn't really mind.

This autumn brings with it an amazing opportunity. The Vivaldis are offered the chance to stage the *carnevale* programme at *Teatro San Moise*. After some hesitation Giambattista has finally agreed to put on a new production by Antonio. It's not hard to find a libretto. Venice is full of writers and poets like Lalli, determined before they die to have their story put to music and performed somewhere in the city. But Antonio has no desire to work with amateurs. It does occur to him to ask Lalli, but Vivaldi has seen neither hide nor hair of him since their last meeting. To be on the safe side he at last approaches Antonio Marchi, a man who has written several successful librettos for Tomaso Albinoni. And this time even Antonio's father is happy, feeling confident the music will be familiar to the public.

That's something that deserves repeating, Giambattista ruminates, closing the ledger with a more than satisfied clap. Everything is going well. Perhaps too well, for suddenly Antonio is told his contract with the *Pietà* is to be terminated. No clear reason is given and neither can anybody imagine one. Especially not when at the next vote, in spring, the decision is revoked. A sigh of relief sweeps through the choir and Don Vivaldi is able to resume his activities as *Maestro di Concerti* as if nothing has happened.

Thanks to his enormous workload the whole episode has more or less passed Antonio by. But when he is lying in bed at night it begins to nag at him. What was the real reason for the dismissal? Does his work at *San Angelo* and *San Moise* pose too much of a threat to the Grimani theatres? Vivaldi knows better than to underestimate the power of the *Veneti Nobili*. These families that have inhabited the lagoon since the earliest days of the Republic have by centuries of intermarriage and alliances forged themselves into a single, strongly unified federation of patricians. It is impossible for outsiders to gain entrance to their closed community. A word here or a request there is sufficient for them to swiftly arrive at some complicit arrangement quite outside the laws they themselves establish. It goes completely against Antonio's grain to allow this cohort of inflated procurators to influence the course of his life. He much prefers to be in charge himself. Perhaps he should just decide to step down one of these fine days. That would be one in the eye for the *Congregazione*, to hear he no longer wished to work for them! He suddenly sees much more clearly what satisfaction it must have given Francesco Gasparini to do the same. But not yet. Not quite yet.

Close on the heels of *carnevale* comes the great spring clean. Most tourists are on their way home, satiated with culture; their luggage crammed with souvenirs of *La Serenissima*. Away with them they carry glasswork, paintings, bundles of sheet music and sometimes, sadly, an incurable venereal disease as well. Behind them the city breathes normally again, and every theatre, casino, coffee-house and brothel gets a good airing and scrubbing down in preparation for next season.

Coming in by boat against the stream of outgoing tourists there arrives in the spring of 1716 a small but colourful company. Each passenger gazing out at the nearing contours of the city in the lagoon cherishes his own hopes for this visit. There are excited exchanges in German about the miraculous city of Venice that seems to drift so '*wunderbar*' upon the water. Earlier this year the travellers departed snowbound Dresden, capital and domicile of August II, Prince-Elector of the Saxons. Under his leadership, Dresden, lying on the marshy banks of the Elbe, has been transformed into a baroque masterpiece equal to the court of Versailles itself. Artists from all Europe, but especially from Italy, feel themselves at home in this Parnassus of the North. The court orchestra, comprising no fewer than forty musicians, is ever thirsty for new compositions, and one of its violinists has himself begun composing for the great ensemble. He is Johann Pisendel. Elector August has dispatched this man, along with three other members of the orchestra, to hear with their own ears what Italy currently has to offer in the way of music. With them travels the sovereign's son. The twenty-year-old crown prince shares his father's love of music, particularly opera, and is looking forward hugely to the coming few months; he knows what to expect, for this is his third visit to Venice. Johan Richter, the Benjamin of the group, is not yet sixteen. It has been decided that, given his musical talents, the trip will be good for his development.

Pisendel has already met and played with Signor Albinoni and is keen to renew his acquaintance with the composer. But Johann Pisendel has other things on his agenda; at the top of the list the priest, Don Vivaldi. The *concerti* from *L'Estro Armonico* and *La Stravaganza* he knows almost by heart. He is a huge fan of Vivaldi and has set his sights on taking lessons in composition from the great master of the *concerto*.

Pisendel's first instinct as he sets foot ashore is to go looking for *Il Prete Rosso*, but he knows the more sensible thing is first to find their lodgings. The young prince is to be entertained in one sumptuous patrician villa after another; as a special guest of the Republic, his nest will be well and truly feathered. The musicians are staying in the house of one Christiaan Ritter, a German tradesman who has lived in Venice for nearly twenty years. Christiaan soon makes his guests feel at home, but no sooner are they installed than they are anxious to be off exploring the city.

It is not long before Johann Pisendel finds out where Vivaldi lives. The address is not at all far from Christiaan's house, but Pisendel still manages to make a full circle and end up back on the same square. What a maze! He asks the way several times in his stumbling Italian, but can't make out entirely what is said in reply. At last he arrives somehow at the residence of Antonio Vivaldi. But he is out of luck. A man claiming to be the father of the great composer tells his visitor he will have to come back again later in the afternoon.

So near yet so far away! Pisendel kills the intervening time tracing and retracing his steps through the many winding lanes that form a network linking the squares of Venice. In the middle of one he finds two fountains surrounded by the usual gaggle of washerwomen and their romping children.

On the other side stands a centuries-old church, its doors wide open. Back and forth from it across the square move swarms of people. Some go inside, re-emerging after a short prayer; others go into the church for a restful conversation out of the sun, or, as now, for a baptism. Intrigued by the sound of music, Pisendel hovers in front of the open doors, peering into the dim interior. The smell of incense wafts out, enveloping and almost making him faint. Bewitched by the plainsong and glittering Byzantine mosaics, he is just about to cross the threshold when something holds him back. With a jolt of shame he seems to come to his senses and, although not a soul knows him here, cannot help glancing guiltily about him. He peeps inside again and realises that this counter-reformation glory presents too great a barrier for him to overstep. Instead the Protestant Pisendel takes another of the little lanes that lead back into the labyrinth.

'Herr Vivaldi?' asks Pisendel rather uncertainly. Antonio is bent over some manuscripts. He looks up, disturbed from his task, and answers curtly in the affirmative.

Pisendel is taken aback. Somehow he has imagined the priest completely differently. His Vivaldi is a large, energetic man; extravert, with great fun-filled eyes and a wide, generous grin, all topped, of course, by a mass of red curls. The man with whom Johann now stands face to face is nearly a head shorter than himself and has eyes that seem almost to bore straight though him. Only the red curls correspond to his mental image. 'You will be Don Vivaldi, father of *La Stravaganza* and the genius behind *L'Estro Armonica*?' pursues Pisendel in softly flattering tones.

Vivaldi quickly sums up the young man. Standing before him is a well-dressed German who looks him intelligently straight in the eyes. He knows Germans to be good clients. We'll see what sort of stuff he's made of, he calculates, and assuming a faultless smile enquires, 'What can I do for you?'

Johann Pisendel introduces himself and gives the reason for his visit. He would like to have lessons from the master in the composition of *concerti*, and naturally he wants to purchase a great deal of music for the court orchestra of Elector August. Money is no object.

When Pisendel further enlightens Vivaldi that he has come to Venice in the company of the crown prince of Saxony, the priest is all ears. His faithful student Heinichen has told Antonio all about the court of Dresden and its great orchestra. 'Your sovereign is a noble man,' he compliments the visitor.

'Oh, that orchestra is just the beginning,' Pisendel goes on with mounting excitement. 'Our prince cherishes the ambition of forming his own opera company and is on the look-out for talent prepared to come permanently to perform at court in Dresden.'

Antonio is quite ambitious enough to perceive the potential here. He cordially invites his guest to partake of a glass of wine with him.

'Have you coffee too?' asks Pisendel.

'Alas, no, but if you would like a cup, let us walk round the corner to the coffee-house.'

'Oh, please do not trouble yourself, Herr Vivaldi. I am sure you are extremely busy and I can easily find my way without help.'

Not if I have anything to do with it, thinks Antonio. Impresario and composer at the court of Dresden, eh? There must be something in it for me. He grabs his chance. 'My dear friend. You have travelled all the way from Dresden to call on me. I am deeply flattered by this honour and would like to put myself entirely at your disposal; your servant for as long as you and your prince remain in *La Serenissima*. Come, I shall lead the way.'

Pisendel feels a slight prickle of embarrassment. My servant... the famed Vivaldi?

Passing the open doorway to his father's room, Antonio

winks. Giambattista gets the message and bursts into laughter.

'I understand that you also produce opera nowadays,' says Pisendel, savouring the fragrant aroma of coffee arising from the tiny cup held elegantly between his thumb and index finger.

'Another of my many activities.' Antonio haughtily waves a hand. 'When I have time over from my work in the *Ospedale della Pietà*, my dedication to private students and composing new pieces, I use it to write *dramma per musica*!'

'Really!' Pisendel is impressed. 'I must indeed introduce you to Prince August. It just so happens that he is looking for someone capable of managing a theatre. A person capable not only of composing and selecting singers, but who also has some understanding of stage design, a feeling for drama and choreography; somebody who can lead the company and guarantee the best performance ever put on in Saxony and Poland.'

Antonio almost chokes. This is too good for words. 'What a shame you have arrived only now in Venice. The theatre season has just closed. But if you are planning to extend your stay a few months, then I shall show you how a theatre is managed!'

'*Wunderbar!*' exclaims Pisendel in delight. Antonio continues, 'I have staged many successful productions in this city. It would be a great honour for me to play host to yourself and your prince. More! I can offer you the opportunity of playing in the orchestra. You will then be able to show your master what you have learnt during your months here. I shall provide a suitable composition, one fit to perform in honour of yourself and the son of the Elector of Saxony!'

'*Herr* Vivaldi,' says Pisendel in rapture, 'you do me too much honour. And we have hardly made acquaintance!'

'Ah, I know a committed musician when I meet one. An intelligent man and open to new learning. Well now, *Monsieur* Pisendel, I am more than prepared to assist you in your search for new harmonies. When shall we begin?'

Johann Pisendel has obviously seriously misjudged Vivaldi. In all sorts of ways the redhead priest manifests himself the kindest of men and a teacher of enormous patience and dedication. Pisendel is deeply impressed with the composer as a violinist, and it humbles him to know that he will never himself attain such a level of virtuosity. With an ease that seems effortless, Vivaldi demonstrates how something should be played and amicably describes step by step how a given composition came into being.

If Pisendel feels ashamed at having underestimated the priest, the same is true the other way about. Antonio at first regarded Pisendel merely as a rich source of income. Another one of those who thought money could buy everything. But ducats are not enough if one wants to master an instrument; perfection in playing comes from the depths of the soul and many hours of practice!

The longer he knows Pisendel the more respect Antonio has for this well-mannered German. The man learns quickly and asks deeply intelligent questions. Every explanation outlined by Antonio is punctiliously – *pünktlich* – noted down – in his notebook. The man is so gravely attentive during lessons that he sometimes misses it when Antonio cracks a joke. *Per le coglione*, copies down Johann, tongue wagging between his teeth in concentration. Antonio has noted this on the bass line of a composition he is writing for the German. After carefully filling in the timing a few times, Antonio leaves it, feeling he's spent too long writing already. Every professional musician is able to sense for himself how the bass should proceed further and Vivaldi considers it a waste of his time to have to annotate this throughout the piece. Seeing Johann meticulously copying every mark he makes, Vivaldi asks in astonishment what he is doing.

'Oh, well, you see, I was just going to ask you what that meant. I've never come across this musical term before.'

Antonio looks at his pupil and bursts out laughing. Oh my God, he thinks, how I am going to explain my way out of this in polite language? Feeling his way very carefully, he says, 'Umm, it is not precisely a musical term... my apologies... more a remark directed at the copyist, certainly not intended for you! It means something along the lines of "feel free to use your own discretion from now on..."

'*Coglione?*'

'Ah. That actually roughly translates as "fill it in yourself from now on, twit".

'*Ach so,*' responds Pisendel dryly, deleting the word with emphatic strokes of his pen. Blushing, Antonio continues the lesson.

Vivaldi does not see much of the crown prince. Once summer arrives in its full scorching glory the Elector's son is whisked away by some eminent patriarch or other to his summer villa on the Brenta. Far from the stinking canals, in the leafy shade of forested country estates, Crown Prince August flutters like a butterfly from one reception to another, barely resting a wing upon the verdant lawns and ballroom floors of Venetian aristocracy.

Concerts and opera performances, the young prince cannot have enough of them. And no chance is missed to enhance the comfort and pleasure of the future Saxon Elector. Eyes and ears alert for talent ripe for plucking and taking home to enrich his own company, he is open and willing to be impressed by any artiste. This summer cannot go on too long for him.

But while the higher echelons pass their time in pleasure, other Venetians are fighting for their fatherland. It is more than a year since the Ottoman Empire again declared war on the Republic of Venice. The war has less effect upon the inhabitants of the lagoon than former clashes; it is plain that they have fewer interests than in the time of *Doge* Enrico Dandolo. People on the street are less easily alarmed and the idea that Turkish galleons might sail into the lagoon is evidently quite unthinkable. The legacy that underpins the patricians' parties, their gambling for higher and higher stakes, comes from the profits of trade with the Orient. Few see, or want to see, that the end is nigh for *La Dominante* in her role as supreme world leader. The Republic is beginning more and more to resemble one of those sandcastles built by the fishermen's sons on the beaches of the Lido: great thick walls, breakwaters and strong dikes, towering turrets and magnificent *palazzi*, and at the centre of it all a proud *campanile di San Marco*. But the wind only has to blow from the wrong direction and the moon stir up the sea to surge against the shore for the walls to give way. And grain by grain the great castle comes sliding down while its proud little builders lie fast asleep nearby.

The Senate, however, is considerably worried. Each day that passes sees further erosion of Republic-owned territories, and what are they to do about it? What do they want to do?

The grand state receptions given time and again in honour of visiting foreign dignitaries to the Republic should now be bearing fruit. But, alas, it seems none is inclined to lend Venice their support. The Senate has assumed that other great nations would join Venice shoulder to shoulder to defeat the Muslims. But only the Pope and Maltese knights have offered their assistance and this is far too meagre to turn the advancing tide from the East. The scorching summer of 1715 sees an unbroken chain of Turkish victories that serves at last to show the Habsburgers the danger from this quarter. Reminded of the siege of Vienna around thirty years before, still indelibly engraved upon their memory, they smartly form an alliance with Venice. And not a moment too soon. For heavily armed Turkish galleons laden with troops have set course for Corfu, the last Republican stronghold on the Adriatic coast.

Like a sentry asleep at his post, the island of Corfu lies strategically at the entry to the Adriatic gulf. The island is the maritime port of entrance to Venice and its vanquishing would imply slow death for the city of *San Marco*. The gulf is the Republic's main artery and the Turkish invading army of Sultan Achmet III is now holding to it a razor-sharp scimitar that threatens the continued existence of *La Serenissima*!

Recognising their peril, the Venetians have spent the winter literally digging in. The hope is that the sight of these huge new buttresses and apparently inviolable fortifications will persuade the Turks to turn back.

But this they do not do. Landing, Sultan Achmet III has quickly surrounded the citadel with his vast army and he does not plan to return home without a victory.

Upon hearing the news that his land forces, under the command of Grand Vizier Damad Ali, have been defeated in a battle with the Habsburgers at Petrovaradin, the Sultan's rage is indescribable. An advance on two fronts has proved fatal for the Turks. His blood boiling, Achmet III on the eighteenth of August orders an assault upon the massive ramparts of the city. The Venetians find themselves with their backs literally up against the wall and dare not imagine their fate should the Turks, maddened as they are with lust for revenge, break through. Bravely but forlornly the Venetians try to repulse the Turks; the day promises to be a long one. Suddenly, after six hours fighting, during which they have hardly won an inch of ground, the Venetians launch a sortie. Defending forces, under the command of daring mercenary Duke von der Schulenberg, mow down everything in their path. Completely taken by surprise, the Turks panic and flee. In the chaos left behind them the defending soldiers collect a vast and valuable booty in the form of weaponry and ammunition, and morale is simultaneously reborn.

This night it seems that God, too, comes to the rescue of the Venetians. Out of nowhere there arises an almighty storm and all hell breaks loose. Whirlwinds whisk into shreds the tents of the attackers. Rain torrents unremittingly from the heavens, filling the trenches and soon transforming the battlefield into an ocean of mud. Lit by great flashes of lightening, the citadel glitters with joy.

The sea becomes a rolling, foaming turmoil, so that none of the retreating army dares to row out to their ships at anchor in the bay. The wind howls and beats against the cliffs where the soaked and terrified besiegers are trying in vain to find shelter. Then, slowly, a new drama begins to unfold before their eyes. The tempest has so gathered strength that their ships begin to drag at the anchors. Once one ship is in motion, there is no holding them. The light reserve anchors soon give way, losing their grip on the sea-bottom. The Sultan can do nothing but look on helplessly while one after another of his galleons rams into the next, so that within a couple of hours the whole beach is littered with pieces of wreckage and the corpses of his drowned men. It is a night of horror for the Turks, sure at every moment that their hour has come. As morning arrives, driving away before it the last storm clouds, the gale drops as quickly as it rose and once more the sun shines calmly supreme in the sky. There is not one among the surviving invading soldiers who wants ever to set foot upon this cursed shore again, and the Turks cannot board fast enough one of the few vessels left after that ghastly night.

Borne high upon the wings of a new day, the citadel trumpets its triumph. Corfu is saved. The Turk vanquished. Venice is victorious!

The relief felt by *La Serenissima* is unsurpassed. Out of the bottle once more leaps the genie of *La Dominante* and the city is full of rejoicing. With the taste of blood still upon its tongue, the Republic digs deep into the kitty and instructs the *Arsenale* as fast as possible to commission twenty-seven new vessels for the navy. Venice is determined to show anyone still in any doubt that it remains a power to reckon with; all island territories lost to it must be won back. In the mood of public euphoria that pervades the city even Antonio Vivaldi, averse as he is to all forms of politics, is caught up in the fever. He launches himself energetically into work on the commission he has received from the *Congregazione* of *La Pietà* for a special oratorio dedicated to the great victory.

It has to be magnificent, unique! 'The ultimate expression of love for the fatherland possible from the *Figlie di Coro*', according to the wording of the commission given to the priest. For the first time since he began composing for the institute, Vivaldi has a sense of the respect and appreciation with which they regard him. This works real wonders for his self-esteem and he is determined not to disappoint his employer and patron!

One Jacopo Cassetti, a name unknown to Vivaldi, is to write the libretto, based on the Biblical story of Judith. The tale tells how Judith cunningly repels the Assyrian invaders by brutally hacking off the head of the enemy commander as he sleeps. The maiden Judith here of course symbolises the triumphant Venice, and the enemy leader Holofernes the Turkish sultan. Whilst he quietly awaits the text Antonio's own head teems with a thousand notes that gradually find each other until, like threading beads, they turn into a flowing, harmonious spectacle.

The aristocracy return from their country villas in jubilant mood and, anticipating extra festivities this year, earlier than usual. There is so much to celebrate. Prince August has had a wonderful time in the country but also looks forward eagerly to the first of the new season's theatre performances. Antonio Vivaldi tests the water regularly with Johann Pisendel as to any news about the appointment of a theatre impresario and court composer. But Pisendel, who has seen little of the crown prince over recent months, merely shrugs his shoulders. He simply does not know.

Rumours spread fast. Antonio's ears have been flapping and everything indicates the truth of what he has heard; fragments of conversation echoing through the narrow lanes, abruptly discontinued dialogues and glances turned aside. Prince August has made his choice. Great is Antonio's disenchantment to hear that it is Antonio Lotti who has been selected to establish an opera company in Dresden. There follows a haemorrhage of Venetian artistic talent: in the wake of the organist of the *basilica di San Marco* a whole host of musicians, including the violinist Veracini and the castrato Senesino.

'No loss,' is Giambattista scornful reaction when a

dejected Antonio reports back to him. The father is preoccupied with replacing a broken string on his violin. 'Don't you worry, my son. They'll be back for you. Francesco Veracini may be a good violinist but he's got a screw loose. The man is as suspicious as the pox. Yep, they'll have the time of their lives with him in Dresden. Who else is going?'

'Oh, a few less important players and some singers,' replies Antonio condescendingly. 'Oh, yes, and Alessandro Mauro, Grisostomo's impresario.'

'Well, well, that's a bit of a letting of life-blood for the city; all artistes for the Nobili. Things are going to be quiet at the Gristostomo; all the better for us, anyhow. What's more, life at court is worse than a prison sentence. The Pietà has nothing on it. One rule after another; and that's not for you, my son. You just keep your mind on the theatre work.'

The theatre! Antonio mopes to himself. He's well acquainted by now with how risky the theatre can be. Submitting yourself to the public's every whim. You can make a huge profit on one production, it's true, but only to have it all swallowed up by the next. He'd rather have the advantage of a job at court. He's nearly forty, after all! Security and a nice, fat, safe income. What's wrong with that?

This choice on the part of the prince he attributes once more to having the right connections. Vivaldi knows that his concerti are listened to and loved by all of Europe's royalty. Yet without the right references he will never move a rung up the ladder. The Veneti Nobili continue to treat him with contempt. I might be a priest and famous violinist, reflects Antonio miserably, but I'm still the son of a poor down-and-out from Brescia. And God himself can do nothing to change that. He looks sadly at his father, still busily attending to his violin. Yes, a down-and-out, that's how the Foscarinis, the Memmos, the Trons, the Mocenigos and the whole damn lot of them regard my father. Even if the Vivaldis were rich as Croesus and able to fraternise with the patricians it would still take generations before their name would be treated with due respect. What good would it do him today?

Giambattista lifts his bow to tune his instrument. The horsehair moves tenderly across the strings and his father swings into a gay cadenza. Antonio uses his sleeve to wipe a tear from the corner of his eye. It's not fair! Thousands of ducats are thrown away on mediocre musicians who can barely play or sing a note, just because they have the right background. Where in the world will there ever be a place for him? A position in a great court, where not his lineage but his talent, knowledge and skill earn him all the success and respect that he deserves. And even were he able to find such a position, should his father be prepared to come with him? For Antonio cannot, in the name of his Lord, imagine what he would do without his father. Over the years the two have grown so close that they now form an almost indivisible unit. Giambattista's lack of creativity is richly compensated for by his pragmatism and organisational talents. Antonio's sense of injustice sharpens his resolve. Down-and-out? They can think what they like; we can do without the patricians!

The precise nature of the initiative the proud priest has in mind is unclear as yet, even to him. But time will tell.

The meetings with Johann Pisendel go ahead as if nothing has happened, although it is quite clear that he, too, is deeply disappointed that Vivaldi will not be travelling back to Dresden with them. Whenever Pisendel tries delicately to raise the matter, Vivaldi waves it indifferently aside. He has more important things to consider. Cassetti is as good as ready with the libretto of *Juditha*. It is looking good, and Antonio shows it to Pisendel, keen to know what the German would do with it, were he in his shoes. But, feeling more at home in the world of *concerti*, Pisendel refuses to comment. Johann knows the limits of his own talent.

It's taken a while, but Domenico Lalli has finally been able to bring Antonio round. The priest agrees that the libretto is well written. It lends itself easily to the composition of a straightforward piece, perfectly suited to the taste of the great public. *Arsilda, Regina di Ponto* is due for its premiere in the middle of October.

Antonio has the feeling he can put on whatever he likes, for the city is full to bursting with carnival tourists. The victory over the Turks seems to have inspired many to come to *La Serenissima* to discover for themselves the gate-holders of Christendom. These are golden days, not only for casinos and courtesans, but also for the theatres! Lending his presence at the opening night of *Arsilda* will be Crown Prince August, and Antonio vows to himself that hearing his composition will make the regent regret his decision. Vivaldi has written a *concerto* for the *entr'acte* in honour of his friend Pisendel. The German is very touched, especially when Antonio invites him to lead the piece himself. But he is also nervous; the *concerto* remains a challenge to play, despite his thorough rehearsing, and one particular cadenza goes on posing problems. Prince August cheers from his box, urging on his own violinist as Pisendel begins, proceeding as self-confidently as possible so as not to disappoint his master. On he plays towards the greatest hurdle of the piece, his accompanists maintaining perhaps a little more tempo than he could wish for. But he is the leader of the orchestra and they should be listening to him. He feels himself begin to sweat, and panic rises in his breast. He must not mess this up! Softly tapping with his foot, he indicates the tempo, but the other musicians take no notice and seem instead to increase their pace. He looks round at them, but they are not looking to him for leadership; instead each is focused stoically on his sheet music. '*Verdammte Italiener!*'

He taps harder on the podium, until he is stamping so hard that the people at the front of the audience can hear it. Finally Pisendel shuts himself off from everything going on around him and concentrates entirely on his part and his own syncopation. If they don't want to listen, damn them! The stubborn hard-headedness of the German eventually gets through to his accompanists and they are forced to slow down. So much for their attempt to sabotage Pisendel's performance.

To thunderous applause the German stands and looks triumphantly up at August's box. The prince is in hysterics. 'What a joke!' roars the crown prince. 'But you've proved your bravado now! Dresden is proud of you!'

Pisendel bows graciously. Out of the corner of his eye he sees Vivaldi get to his feet and stick up a thumb to him. Upon the priest's lips he reads the word '*Complimentissimo*'. He makes another deep, relieved bow, this time to the composer.

Unhappily for Johann, Prince August has decided to end his overseas tour. The city is becoming more and more congested and the crown prince, although never shy of a good party, hates the sluggish movement of the masses along the narrow streets of Venice; it reminds him of the contents of some giant bowels.

The company from Dresden, departing Venice prematurely, is to miss a huge spectacle. Connoisseurs are eagerly anticipating the widely advertised '*Sacrum Militare Oratorium - Juditha Triumphans Devicta Holofernis Barbarie*'.

Anyone up early enough to lean on the parapet of the bridge next to the *Ospedale della Pietà* and listen to rehearsals comes away more than amazed. Out from the open windows float the sounds of instruments never before heard in Venice. So powerfully sings the choir of four voices, so much like opera stars and such impressive ones at that, the bridge is soon packed with its impromptu audience and thus becomes impassable. Vivaldi has selected the popular Barbara for the role of Vagaus, servant to army commander-in-chief Holohpernes. Barbara is one of the older sopranos in the choir, but at sixty-six still a big audience favourite. The role of Holohpernes is played by the manly voice of mezzo-soprano Appolonia. And Catalina graces with her crystal-clear and vitally seductive voice the part of Juditha herself.

No one without an advance ticket stands a chance of getting in. City elders and nobles have all waited in eager anticipation of the premier of Juditha. Once the doors are open it is simply a matter of pushing and shoving. Even the mutual courtesies normally observed amongst the patricians are abandoned as all try to bag the best seat. The general hustle and bustle betrays the tension among the public, and excited babble bounces back and forth between the cool walls of the *oratorium*.

Like highwaymen lying in ambush for their prey, the *Figlie* peer through the trellis down on the audience below. Never before have they heard such a racket. It unnerves the girls, for what on earth is the public expecting from them tonight?

The unrest in the hall means the audience does not even notice the orchestra tuning up, and finally the chairman of the *Congregazione* has to raise his voice to calm the hall. A few words of welcome from the governor, and the *oratorium* belongs to the *Figlie di Coro* and their *Maestro*.

Words do not suffice to describe this performance. Vivaldi's composition employs a palette of musical colours so varied in range and texture that it dizzies his audience. The combination of so many instruments, many as yet unheard in Venice, stuns into silence his greatest critics. Accompanying the choir are theorbe, salmoe, clarinet, trumpet, mandolin, oboe, organ, flute, fagot, drums, violin, viola, cello, bass and harpsichord. Everyone is deeply impressed, but for the true Venetian it goes deeper. This music, this narrative strikes right to the heart. *Santissima Maria!* This is Venice. *La Dominante*, city of the sea, Queen of the Adriatic, conqueror of the barbarians!

As Giulia embarks upon her final recitative in her role as high priest Ozias, the hall feels like a simmering volcano.

Veniti Maris Urbem
Inviolatam, discerno...
'I declare Venice, city of the sea,
To be inviolate for all eternity'

Erit nova Juditha...
'Venice, the new Judith'

Applaudite Judithae Triumphanti
'Raise the roof for Judith the Triumphant!'
In a complete departure from normal protocol and before the choir can even begin the finale, a wave of tumultuous applause fills the hall. Tension has been building up among those present over the past hour and now it reaches the supreme moment. The patriotic pride of everyone in the hall explodes in one huge mutual orgasm of emotion. Men weep and embrace one another, and cries of bravo ascend in an unbroken stream up towards the choir.

Like a general surveying his troops, the priest gazes transcendently over the heads of his delirious audience. '*Applaudite*, Don Vivaldi,' he breathes softly to himself.

Antonio Vivaldi is deluged with praise in the aftermath of the concert and it looks as if the *Veneti Nobili* have at last thrown wide their portals to him.

But in the clear light of day it becomes clear that just one door has opened, and that a mere crack. His moment of glory is short and sweet. Briefly he may have been allowed to walk with head held high among the great and good, but for a moment only. As the church empties not one of the *nobili* invites him to join them to continue the celebrations elsewhere. Indeed, it does not even cross the minds of the many, whose one desire is to get back to the gaming tables. In the end, *Juditha* is nothing compared with the goddess of fortune.

But, despite the cold shoulder of the patricians, *Il Prete Rosso*'s fame increases with every performance of *Juditha*. A visit to the Republic is now incomplete without a trip to the *Ospedale della Pietà* to hear the priest and his female musicians. And each evening, the renowned composer is to be seen playing at *Teatro San Angelo* or *San Moise*.

After all the small commissions that Antonio has had to content himself with up until now, it comes not only as a surprise but also an honour when he is offered a *scrittura* for the reopening of the *Teatro della Pergola* in Florence.

The social status of the priest-composer is a matter of the utmost insignificance to Luca Casimiro degli Albizzi, impresario of the old theatre and long-time acquaintance of Vivaldi. Luca remembers the violinist with the red curls as if it were yesterday. As far as he can recall, the priest's conduct has on no occasion been unseemly. Antonio has never breathed a word concerning the shameful details of his encounter with the incontinent heir of Tuscany. Moreover, Luca Casimiro has heard tell that Vivaldi's productions at the *San Angelo* pull in more than average crowds. And that is precisely what he needs in Florence!

Scanderberg, the title for his new production, is the name of a fifteenth-century Albanian prince who leads a successful rebellion against the Turkish oppressor. *Juditha* has clearly rung some bells.

Soon after the Christmas of 1717, Antonio hears from the adjutant of Prince Philip, Count of Hesse-Darmstadt and Habsburg governor of Mantua. Prince Philip, a great music lover, would like to inquire, quite without obligation, whether or not it would please Don Vivaldi to consider a position as *Maestro di Capella di Camera* at the Court of Mantua.

'Give it some thought,' advises the adjutant. 'Prince Philip will be glad to meet you at the embassy to discuss the conditions with you personally.'

Antonio does indeed need time to consider, and replies to this effect. He must first talk to his father! But the wildest ideas are already racing through his head. The governor of Mantua is the port of entry to the Court of Vienna! The Habsburg Empire offers such an array of opportunities, and is Vienna not far more interesting than Dresden?

But what about the *Pietà*? Antonio has not forgotten how much he missed the *Figlie* when his contract with the institute was terminated so abruptly. And given that Scarpari is incapable of composing, who's going to take over his duties there?

One by one he enumerates to himself the pros and cons.

The fact is that his work for the *Pietà* is never going to make him rich. What exactly does his future hold? Four theatre seasons have actually pretty nearly cured him of his curiosity on that front. He is beginning to appreciate the mind-numbing effect of the treadmill that makes its predictable progress from one theatre season to the next. But worse is the lack of respect and appreciation, and the unfair criticism of the patricians is sticking more and more in his throat. The longer he thinks about it, the more he realises that it is the latter that is prompting him to broaden his horizons.

His father fully understands the dilemma facing his son. 'Perhaps it is time to move on,' falters Giambattista, for on the other hand he is used now to theatre life and the regular income it provides. But he soon relents. 'Well, come on then. Let's pay a call on Prince Philip and see what he thinks your talents are worth.'

A soft thrill of pleasure goes through Antonio as he senses already the rejuvenating effect of a challenge ahead. He fills his lungs powerfully with air. '*Avanti!*'

5

Venice, December 1717

Prince Philip, better known here in Italy as *Langravio* Filippo, stands erect, waiting in the spacious reception area of the Imperial Austrian Embassy. His Dutch adjutant, Walter Coopman, has announced the Vivaldis and now throws open the double doors. Father and son approach somewhat diffidently, whilst the count assesses the pair rather like a predatory animal eyeing its prey. Filippo is a professional soldier and, although it's a while since he saw active service against the French, in his forty-seventh year he still radiates all the power and authority of a military commander.

A slight tremor goes through Antonio as the doors shut behind them with the soft but decisive click of a trap. 'Gentlemen,' *Langravio* Filippo greets them with formal cordiality. He nods quickly and relaxes, planting his legs akimbo and standing with hands clasped behind his back. He continues, 'It is an honour to make your acquaintance, Don Vivaldi, and your father too.' His rather staccato Italian is nevertheless almost faultless. Antonio bows deeply, and his father follows suit. 'Your Excellency, the pleasure is entirely mutual,' declares Antonio.

Walter Coopman has meanwhile gone over to the table and is smoothing a sheet of paper.

'You have met my adjutant already,' Filippo gestures towards Coopman. 'We have no secrets from one another and I shall speak freely.'

Antonio and Giambattista both turn their eyes towards the Dutchman. The tall, powerfully built man has a long scar running across his face from ear to mid-forehead. He smiles silently in return.

'I wish you to be my *Maestro di Capella da Camera*.' The statement sounds more like an order. 'Mantua is like a wilting plant in need of tender loving care to bring it to life and make it blossom once more. I want the crème de la crème. Music, theatre, concerts... and you,' the count points his index finger at Antonio, 'you will achieve this for me!'

The priest frowns and Giambattista stares up at the frescoed ceiling.

'But Your Excellency,' begins Antonio, 'You are aware that I have ongoing commitments here in Venice. In a couple of days there is the premier of a new opera. And I have also committed myself to composing for the *Ospedale della Pietà* and responding to requests for new work from all over Europe. However much I should like to be of service to Your Excellency, my hands are tied.'

Filippo walks up to the priest. 'I understand that your contract with the *Teatro San Angelo* ends with this *carnevale*. I can offer you a theatre with a better public and no financial risk to yourself.'

'That may be true, Your Highness, but I am accustomed to arranging everything on my own behalf and to making my own decisions. I work with a permanent company of vocalists and I should not like to put on an opera without them.'

'Who is asking you to?' parries the prince.

'And, as I have explained, my work for the *Figlie di Coro* is extraordinarily important to me.'

'Even if you are compensated in two-fold?'

Giambattista coughs. 'Sire, there is too much work that simply cannot be set aside. My son receives requests daily for music. My task is to assist him with this and to ensure that such demands are met in a structured and efficient manner. An enormous responsibility, as you may imagine, and one impossible to execute were my son to reside at your court.'

The Count laughs. 'The *Palazzo Ducale* is quite large enough to accommodate you as well, *Herr Vivaldi*. I foresee no problem whatsoever.'

'But my father also plays in the orchestra of *San Marco*. He would not even be granted permission to leave Venice.'

Filippo marches over to the window and resolutely turns on his heels to face them again. 'My request is simple enough,' he states firmly and categorically. 'I ask you to be my choirmaster, and what do I hear? Problems, problems and more problems! I think I am correct in believing that you are a man famous all over Europe, and yet treated with contempt here in Venice. I am offering you a chance, let us say a podium, upon which to arise from the marshy depths of this lagoon. An orchestra awaits you of more than twenty musicians. You shall become more closely acquainted with the Habsburg Empire and I shall introduce you to personages of note, of influence. Of course, there will be no objection to your fulfilling commissions for other people. And if your father is refused permission to abandon Venice altogether and for all time, then let him commute back and forth between the two cities. Walter shall arrange this. You may bring with you your musicians and singers, for the choice of artistes will remain entirely your own. My only demand is that you give me music that will be talked about. I want Mantua restored to the cultural centre it once was. Or greater!'

Silence reigns. Giambattista feels his moment has arrived. 'What are your conditions?'

'Ah, now we are beginning to understand one another!' booms Filippo with a clap of his hands.

Two hours later the prince feels as if nothing would be finer than to be back facing the armies of Louis the Fourteenth again. At least he knows where he is when he's on the battlefield. Never before has he done business with a Venetian and after today he never will again.

To his astonishment, Vivaldi the elder produces a list to work through point by point. He has clearly seriously under-estimated this filial partnership and deliberations sometimes very nearly get out of hand. Each time Filippo seems disinclined to give in, father and son threaten to walk out on the negotiations and Walter has to intervene.

After much humming and hawing the Vivaldis succeed in securing a monthly salary of six hundred and eighty lire. Many times the honorarium Antonio is currently receiving from the Pietà. In addition to his salary, as impresario he is entitled to keep all the profits from theatre productions and remain free to compose for third parties. There is no objection to him travelling to Florence this summer to stage Scanderberg. In short, the prince is prepared to pay any price to lure Antonio to Mantua. The men shake hands and Walter draws up a provisional contract. It is agreed that after the last performance of Armidda al Campo d'Egitto in Venice the production will move straight on to the Teatro Arciducale in Mantua.

From this day forth Antonio is officially appointed Maestro di Capella da Camera to Filippo, Langravio d'Hassia Darmistath. The prince wishes the Vivaldis a hearty farewell and takes himself out onto the balcony. Once there he unbuttons his cloak so that the refreshing breeze may cool him off. That went extremely badly from my point of view, he confesses to himself. But what nobody knows, including Walter, is that the prince has dealt with this matter in the spirit of his dead wife, Maria Theresa.

After the peace of Utrecht the future had looked bright and his appointment as Imperial Governor of Mantua was the crowning glory of Filippo's career. Together with his wife he had made plans to restore Mantua to her former glory and to give their children a good upbringing in an environment rich in art and culture. The prospect looked a lovely one.

Thinking of her, he is again stricken with grief. It is more than two years since his wife's sudden death, and yet it seems like yesterday. The couple's four children, the youngest just six years old, would have to live on, deprived of the sparkling presence of their mother. Maria Theresa von Croy und Havre had been a great music enthusiast. She was herself extremely skilled on the harpsichord and had loved to sing cantate. Her demise had left the vast palace echoing and silent. Prince Filippo, watching his children bereft and pining away before his eyes, had lit on one possible remedy: music! And very soon he came across the name of Antonio Vivaldi. This *Maestro di Concerto* of the *Ospedale della Pietà*, famed composer of countless *concerti* and much discussed *opere* was the very man the prince was looking for.

He knows today's decision was the right one and pictures with tender joy the day he will see his children's faces light up once more and hear their carefree childish laughter.

The departure from Venice is rushed. Antonio has had no trouble in obtaining permission to leave the Republic. Deep down he still longs for someone to beg him to stay, but no such thing happens and somehow this confirms his feeling that the time has really come to break the bond with Venice. Antonio does not even glance back over his shoulder as the ferry casts off from the pier. He has not taken much with him, just a few bare essentials and his best violin. His father is to follow in a couple of days, together with most of the soloists who played in *Armidda al Campo d'Egitto*. As the ferry approaches the mainland it seems to rush to meet him with a bouquet of burgeoning spring. The sweet scent of the land prickles his nostrils, inviting the priest to take deep breaths of meadow air. It is as if strength is flowing into him with every inhalation, as if he could rise, take wing and fly straight to his destination; Mantua, birthplace of Vergilius, poet of ancient Roman times. It feels like a rebirth, carte blanche for a new chapter in his life.

Propelled onwards by his fame, Antonio shrugs from his shoulders the burden of his humble birth and watches it sink like so much rubbish into the muddy shallows of the lagoon. How could he have been so naïve as to fester for so long in the land of the *Doge*? The light becomes more limpid by the minute and in it he sees the world lying at his feet. He swears faithfully to himself that he will return to Venice only when its noblemen, princes and kings regard him as an equal.

The journey proceeds uneventfully via Padua and Parma, and he passes through customs without problems. While his fellow travellers have to dig deep in their purses so as to avoid a time-wasting search, the priest is greeted respectfully by the overzealous frontier officers and allowed through without question. A few days later Vivaldi is passing by stage-coach through the city gates of Mantua. Like Venice, the city is surrounded by water. But more like a rock rising out of the ocean than a sinking sand dune, this city stands ringed by walled escarpments in the middle of the River Mincio. Another thing that distinguishes Mantua from La Serenissima is that her many bridges make Mantua more accessible, certainly in hot, rainless summers, when the banks of the river lie exposed and dry. Then, even in the absence of the natural protection afforded by the water and when the croaking of the frogs is stilled, the citizens feel secure behind the citadels and massive buttresses of their fortress city. Although not even the mightiest fortification can repel the mosquitoes that plague the place each summer, every year spreading a new epidemic of malaria that claims its share of victims.

It is a huge relief to Antonio to get the journey over; the long hours by horse-drawn vehicle over uneven thoroughfares have worn him out and his muscles feel paralysed. He steps stiffly down from the coach, as the door is held open by a palace guard. Entering a huge courtyard, he gazes about him trying to take in his surroundings, but hardly has he had time to adjust his tired eyes to the unfamiliar scene when Walter Coopman himself comes out to welcome him. The adjutant enquires politely after the priest's health and his journey, and chatting together the two men make their way along a shady arcade to another courtyard. Here, leaning into the mediaeval palace walls stands the *Teatro dei Comici*. Like many such buildings of its time, the theatre does not look much from the outside. But Coopman is keen to show the priest to his quarters now and promises a servant will later provide a full tour. This arrangement suits Antonio very well; he longs to lie down for a little while and rest his aching bones.

Only later does Vivaldi fully appreciate how exhausted he must have been on arrival at the palace, for the full glory and splendour of its frescoes, its statuary and paintings, had almost been lost on him.

And indeed, time to luxuriate in all this wonder is sorely lacking, for his own arrival and announcement of the imminent opening of the opera *Armidda al Campo d'Egitto* stirs up huge excitement in the little city.

The capture of Mantua by the forces of the Habsburg Empire in 1707 had brought to an abrupt end the exorbitant life led at court by the last Duke of Gonzaga. With the appointment as governor of *Langravio* Filippo has come resurrection in the arts, so it is no surprise that there is a full house night after night for Vivaldi's opera, one audience after another rewarding composer and cast with a long barrage of applause. Antonio Vivaldi discovers himself the pet of prince, duke and ambassador, and cannot imagine a grander reception. It takes a five full weeks in production before almost the whole population of Mantua is fully satiated.

Signorina Tessieri is one of the few not to have attended a performance of the spectacle. Many years have gone by without her being reminded of the past, and now suddenly she is confronted with the name Antonio Vivaldi. It releases inside her a maelstrom of emotions, more than she could ever have expected, and plunges her into confusion. So that when word goes round that Il *Prete Rosso* has left for Florence directly after the final performance of *Armidda al Campo d'Egitto*, she really does not know whether to feel pleased or upset.

It is nearly eight years since he was here, yet Antonio Vivaldi's last visit to the city of the Medici is still fresh in his memory. For Giambattista, who has prolonged his leave to attend the performance in Florence, this is his first visit. He finds a certain charm in the place, but agrees with his son that it feels moribund. Old Cosimo de Medici, now seventy-five years old, still rules the roost. But what is left for him to crow over?

There are those that still deny it, but the city is slowly

rotting underfoot like a patch of autumn leaves in the damp shadow of an ancient chestnut tree. The smell of decay is omnipresent and the silent streets and deserted squares have no cheering effect upon the priest. Death stalks this city, and not even the most convinced optimist can avoid recognising that this is the end of the road for the Medici dynasty. Ferdinado, eldest son of Cosimo, has been dead five years. He was quickly followed to the grave by his uncle, Cosimo's brother Francesco Mario. Cosimo, aged and embittered, has long relinquished any hope of an heir, for the malfunctioning marriage and bizarre lifestyle led by his youngest son Gian Gastone will certainly produce no children. A highly divisive and spectacular change to the law has allowed Cosimo's widowed only daughter Anna Maria to assume the title of Grand Duchess and heir to the Medici household. This has caused uproar among such great powers as Spain, France and Austria, and these nations now prowl like wolves around the city, slavering to get their hands on it.

But not everyone shares the sombre outlook. Some continue to see a positive future and, avoiding politics and speculation, apply themselves happily to the tasks of each new day, coping with the problems along the way. This goes too for the members of the *Accademia degli Immobili* whose job it is to reinvigorate the old *Teatro della Pergola*. Here it is the honour of Antonio Vivaldi at the end of June 1718 to preside over a performance of *Scanderberg* before an enthusiastic audience. For a brief moment Florence regains her old sparkle.

With *Scanderberg* over and done with, father and son Vivaldi have no further reason to stay on in the city. Antonio has not yet had time to settle in Mantua and Giambattista has his head full of all the work piling up back home in Venice. So, another success to their name, their carriage leaves Florence, the horses heading bravely for the hills.

It is by now the height of summer and the many-plumed rushes crowding the muddy banks of the Mincio wave lazily back and forth with the warm breeze. Here and there stand cattle, motionless in the slowly flowing waters, their tails occasionally whipping away a multitude of flies. It is hard to imagine worse weather to be bumping over the dusty highway in a coach and horses; stiflingly hot and so humid one can hardly draw breath. Giambattista decides to stop for the night before continuing on his journey homewards. At the parting of the ways he promises his son he will be back in October to help with the new theatre production.

Coping alone with everything over the next few months Antonio soon appreciates just how much his father normally does for him. The priest has devoted more and more of his time over recent years to the pure art of composing. Not just writing music but also experimenting with unusual instruments. Any spare moments have been taken up in auditioning vocalists and musicians and taking full responsibility for fulfilling commissions. Everyday matters such as sustenance, clean clothes, financial affairs and correspondence, and arranging appointments left, right and centre, all of this has fallen to his father. Now he realises just how much the structure of his life has lain in his father's hands and thinks perhaps it is no bad thing to stand on one's own feet for a change.

Before leaving, Giambattista has made the some preliminary preparations and jotted down all sorts of instructions for his son. He has also drawn up a ledger and shown Antonio how to keep it up to date with detailed and correct financial entries. But although his son enjoys negotiating a singer's honorarium and the cost of a libretto, he considers filling in a cash-book a scandalous waste of his time. As long as there's money enough, what's there to worry about?

It is weeks before Antonio finds his feet in Mantua. He gets to know Filippo's children, but is not over-impressed with their interest in music, let alone their achievements. Only the youngest daughter, Theodora, shows some slight sign of responding to the music teaching of the Venetian priest. He has been allocated some spacious accommodation with a view out onto one of the palace courtyards. The thick walls and high ceiling ensure that his rooms stay cool, however sweltering it is outside. These months – not the most pleasant ones to spend in Mantua – are quiet at court. But from the beginning of October, when the leaves begin to turn from green to gold, the palace starts to buzz with activity. Guests begin flooding in from all corners of the Austrian empire to fill court apartments in the anticipation of a frantic six months filled day and night with hunting parties, balls and music.

But first comes a little calm before the storm. Every morning the priest takes a short walk, just as was his habit at home. It keeps him fresh and inspires him with new ideas for when he starts work later in the day. Antonio makes sure he is back indoors by the end of the morning, when the heat makes it unendurable to stay outside, even in the shady arcade of the inner courtyard. After a fortnight he has seen the whole city and is seriously wondering whether the place can keep him amused in the long term. Mantua is so much smaller than Venice, and so different. He misses the hustle and bustle of the *Riva degli Schiavoni*, the curses and song of its seamen, the scream of gulls. Every day anew the *Riva* offered a fresh vista of ships at their moorings, setting down as if with a sigh their heavy deck-loads of cargo on the quay. And then came the swarms of dealers and tradesmen fingering the newly unloaded goods, sniffing the exotic perfumes and tasting everything that came ashore before the bargaining began.

The only shipping crowding the tiny harbour of Mantua are the daily arrivals of flat-bottomed river barges laden with vegetables, fruit and cattle. It is only a couple of steps from the landing-stage to the market, where everything is laid out on stalls each day. And though this is not the *Rialto*, Antonio's morning meanders nevertheless make a colourful interlude in the endlessly long, slow summer days. Early, the square and surrounding streets still smell sweet and fresh. The fragrance of newly picked fruit and sliced vegetables mingles with the heavy scent of newly slaughtered pigs. In just a couple of hours this pleasantly-charged air will turn into a foetid stench of rot and decay, welcome only to the many flies come to feast on discarded fruit and the detritus of butchery. But by then the market will be over for another day and people will be busy clearing up as best they can for tomorrow. And so time flows imperceptibly on.

Antonio has bought strawberries. Each day he takes some fruit back with him to the court. The sun is approaching the zenith, beating mercilessly down upon the inhabitants of Mantua. Half-naked children run about, happily splashing one another while their mothers do their washing at the wells and swap the latest news. Antonio hardly hears their chatter as he passes by, anxious to get back with his fruit and rinse it while it is still fresh. He is in high spirits. What luscious strawberries! He pops into his mouth the crimson beauty of the season, so sweetly ripe! Surely he has never tasted berries so deliciously soft and delectable. He puts the basket down on the stone ledge of a fountain and thinks he will rest his legs a moment.

'Oops!' squeals a girlish voice. The remainder of the fruit is rolling away from the upset basket next to him and down the steps; one strawberry already lies cruelly squashed beneath the feet of a boy in his mad dash around the well. Perturbed, the priest turns his attention to the child standing at his feet. She is about ten years old and stares at him startled, her hand clapped to her mouth. Vivaldi starts. Those eyes! For a split second it is as if he is looking at himself in a mirror. She stares silently at him for a couple more seconds and then shyly averts her gaze. Snatching the little basket from the ground, she begins quickly to fill it with as many whole strawberries as she can find. Her small companions stand around laughing and pointing, while she carefully washes each berry in the fountain. No longer daring to look the priest in the eyes, she hands him the retrieved treasure.

'What's going on here?' asks a female voice behind Vivaldi. He turns to find a woman standing with her sleeves rolled up, presumably the mother of the girl, for the child has swiftly taken refuge behind her skirts. Vivaldi is so taken with the little girl he hardly notices the mistrust in the older woman's eyes.

'Why nothing, signora, nothing much at all,' Vivaldi answers, showing her the basket of strawberries. 'Your daughter?' The priest's question is uncertain.

'My little sister,' the woman corrects him.

'I beg your pardon, signorina. She quite by accident knocked over this basket of wonderful strawberries as she walked by.'

The woman bends down and whispers something in the child's ear. Very timidly the little blushing face reappears. 'I'm sorry,' she lisps. Antonio can do nothing but smile at the innocence of her confession. Kneeling, he offers her the basket. 'That's all right, my child. Here, take one.'

Sunshine softly returns to the small features and quick as a flash she claims the biggest and juiciest strawberry. Entranced, Antonio watches her face, especially the eyes. How extraordinary! Before he knows it the child has scampered off to rejoin the game as if nothing has happened. Getting to his feet the priest proffers his basket to the sister. She declines.

'How is Mantua suiting you?' she asks, friendly, but with the slightest touch of sharpness.

Used by now to strangers addressing him in the street, Antonio readily responds. He is aware that everyone in the little town now recognises him as the red-haired priest from Venice, the famous Vivaldi.

'Very well, thank you. How kind of you to ask.'

'Have you never wondered how things were with me?'

Antonio recoils as if hit in the solar plexus. What sort of question is this?

'Do we know one another?' he asks nervously. Shading his eyes with one hand from the fierce sunlight, he scrutinises her anew. Beneath the upswept hair her face is open and, despite her bare arms, still glistening with soap in the sunshine, there is something about her that sets her apart. Is she perhaps a singer who has auditioned for him at some time? No, that cannot be, for then he would have recognised her voice. He easily forgets faces, but never voices. Perhaps she has mistaken him for someone else.

'Know is perhaps an exaggeration, but we do have something in common,' she responds cryptically. Confused, the priest searches his memory for clues, staring helplessly at her meanwhile.

Her dark blue eyes betray her disappointment.

She offers him her hand. It is cool and yet, at the same time, feels warm to his touch. A shudder passes through him. 'Goodbye, Antonio Vivaldi,' she whispers softly, leaning subtly towards him. That perfume, the scent of her skin! It brings her back to him from the darkest depths of his memory. As her hand glides out of his he holds it fast for an instant, examines tremulously the long, slim fingers, hardly able to believe his eyes. Those hands, *Santa Maria*, it is she!

He stares at her, wide-eyed with wonder. He opens his mouth, but no sound emerges. Sweat pours from his forehead and down over his face, giddying him. 'I must go,' he stammers. 'It is the heat, it is...'

As fast as his legs can carry him he makes his getaway, pushing and shoving past people who swap bemused looks at this rude and distraught priest, elbowing them aside without apology.

Behind him, the woman takes a deep breath and watches him go. Should she follow? No, of course not. Her pride will not allow it. But will he come back? Or will he, as before, ignore the whole episode as if nothing has happened?

'Paolina,' shrills one of the washerwomen, 'what are you doing daydreaming over there? We're waiting for you.' Paolina packs up her things and calls her little sister to her side.

It is the warmest night of the summer so far. At least, so it seems to Antonio. His afternoon nap was disturbed today when he awoke with a shock. The woman visited his dreams. It is years since this happened. He used to meet her here in his dream world under every sort of strange circumstance. She would often be wearing a mask, when just that enticing smile proved powerful enough to lead him on, her white teeth and lovely full lips so seductively close that he would surface violently from their devouring presence and awaken bathed in sweat. Then it would be some time before his heart rate returned to normal and he could sleep again. These sudden and surreal encounters were a mingling of suspense and voluptuousness, revulsion and affection, but ended always in a sense of shame. All these years later he still has no idea of her identity. Sometimes he can smell her, so real a dream presence is she to him. Her voice sounds ever far away, veiled, as if she speaks to him from the bottom of the lagoon.

In busy times of his life he can easily go months without her awakening him. It seems a century since he last dreamed of her. Indeed, he had practically forgotten all about her until this morning. But now she is real!

So disturbed and distressed is he it seems the only solution is to banish her from his thoughts. But he hardly dare shut his eyes in case, sleeping, he glides straight into her arms. The very idea is a nightmare to him, a crushing blow to his vocation, his training as a priest. Women have never interested him as such, and an acquired rationality enables him easily to repress his latent feelings and concentrate his energy upon work. Naturally there have been times when a particular face, a certain personality, have stirred him. But then he has always been able to put on a smile of self-possession and laconically enjoy the passing moment without falling prey to the uncontrolled and primitive emotions that govern other people's lives.

Yet is he really so different? Trembling, he steps out of bed once more to pour himself another drop of wine. Going over to the window, he takes a gulp of cool night air. Is he so much better? For half his life now he has suppressed thoughts of this woman, turned her into a dream presence of the dark hours, a demon that tries time and again to seduce him – and so nearly succeeds. Does the shame not lie more in her failure to do so?

Exhausted, he falls back on the bed and is at last overpowered by sleep. After a little while he enters a room in which everyone is feasting and dancing. Suddenly the music stops and everyone retreats from the dance-floor. Thousands of pearls are rolling in all directions, and in the middle of the enormous ballroom Caterina Querini bursts into laughter as pearls continue to spill from her hands and find their halting way into every corner of the hall. At Antonio's feet lies a wealth of the world's most precious pearls and he can hardly resist the urge to pick one up. But just as he reaches for the biggest and most beautiful it changes into a strawberry. Astounded, Antonio watches the slow metamorphosis. The strawberry looks so lush he lifts it slowly to his mouth. But a gloved hand softly clasps his wrist. Glancing up, he meets those eyes. Without a word she guides his hand gently to her own lips and sucks the berry from between his fingers. Her eyes never leaving his, she flicks her tongue to lick the juice from the corner of her mouth. Antonio springs upright in the bed. In despair he rubs his face with his hands.

'Father, forgive me my sins,' he prays breathlessly. All is now fully apparent to him. She has stayed with him ever since that bitter winter night when ice lay thick upon the canals. It is she who haunts his dreams. What was it she said this morning? Something shared; something in common?

No, it cannot be. Not that. The little one was her sister; her words had been clear as daylight. No, he surely need not worry on that score.

But Vivaldi spends the rest of the night plagued by doubt. He is unable to recall in any detail what happened on that fateful night so long ago. What exactly took place? He has dreamed so often of her that he can no longer tell fact from fiction. He thanks God his father is not here. What would he make of it all?

Splashing his face with water the next morning, Antonio tries to order his thoughts. The emotions churning inside him are entirely unfamiliar. *I must see her again!* This he ascerts a hundred times, and just as often dismisses the idea a second later. Of course I must do no such thing! That way I might as well forget my appointment here. I must put her out of my head. She has no need of me, and anyway, who says she is waiting for me? Very probably she is married and I might as well forget all my crazy notions.

Pacing up and down the room, he returns each time to the window where dawn is slowly lightening the sky. At one point he slides behind his worktable and selects a fresh sheet of paper, but his thoughts are too much in chaos to write two consecutive notes. He goes back to bed and tries to rest again instead. I have to forget her, stop thinking about her. It was all so long ago, after all, so very long ago.

Breathing deeply and clearing his mind, he stares for some time up at the great timbers bearing the ceiling. *I have to see her!* The decision overwhelms him. Leaping from bed, he pulls on some clothes while outside the first thrushes serenade a new day.

It will be hours before the market gets going, and even then it is far from certain he will find her there.

Three days! Three days have gone by without Antonio seeing her again. Every morning he has stood at the lookout post, beside the well, on the corner of the arcade, and wandered between the market stalls. It seems she might be deliberately avoiding him and he begins to ask himself if this has indeed been nothing more than a prolonged dream. Just as he is about to return once more disappointed to the cool refuge of the court, he recognises the familiar figure. He goes straight up to her, but deep in his heart he is afraid, terrified that she will evaporate into mist again and he will awaken in his bed.

But this time it is no dream, and the warmth of her skin when he takes her arm is real, and as she turns to look at him her image does not shatter into a thousand tiny pieces. But she appears taken aback; she has obviously not expected to meet him like this.

He speaks hastily, 'I have to speak to you.' She frowns and then seems to recover herself.

'What about?' she asks carelessly.

'I must apologise for taking my leave of you so abruptly a few days ago. Our encounter took me quite by surprise; it is, after all, so long ago since we last met. In any case, I should very much like to speak further with you.'

In her eyes there is both triumph and mistrust. 'And what might you want to talk to me about?'

'You said that we shared something in common. I have given much thought to your words.' His glance moves to where her small sister is gallivanting across the square with the other children. Antonio draws a deep breath and closes his eyes, mentally reciting a brief prayer.

'Is it she whom we share?' he asks very softly, making sure his words reach no other ears.

'I beg your pardon?' she replies with evident amazement.

'Is she you call your sister actually your daughter?' he persists, assailed by doubt as he sees colour rise to the woman's cheeks and her eyes begin to spit fire.

'Listen, priest, had we not been standing here on this busy square you would have got a slap in the face for that. Who do you think you are? And where do you get such obscene ideas?'

If only the ground would swallow him up. Vivaldi is mortified. What has he said? What has he done?

'We once had a pleasant evening together,' she continues, prodding him in the tunic with her index finger. 'We enjoyed ourselves as most adults do on such a special night. But that does not give you the right to nurture all kinds of weird delusions!'

'Forgive me, lady, in all honesty, I beg your forgiveness. I have spoken about this with no other soul. I had, myself, as good as forgotten that evening.'

'Forgotten?' His words have wounded her pride.

'Yes. I mean, no. I mean...' Antonio resolves to hold his tongue before he sinks any deeper into the quagmire, for every word he utters feels like a millstone dragging him down further.

'Do you think I give myself to anyone who chances along?'

she demands of him, clearly deeply insulted.

'Absolutely not,' he rushes to reassure her. My God, why had he ever tried to find her?

'What do you remember of that evening?' she asks more mildly.

Antonio smiles tenderly. 'Your hands! And the multitude of questions you put to me, so many that I thought they would never end. And how I enjoyed your company, and how I loved having someone take such an interest in me. Do you understand?' He looks her straight in the eyes and clearly sees returning his gaze the person of ten years before. Slightly older, but with the same aura that back then seemed to envelop him in warmth, offering protection from all the ills of the world.

He is suffused with a strange mixture of alienation and shame. Never before has he admitted such feelings to another human being. 'Do you know,' he confesses, 'what has preoccupied me all this time?'

Watching him closely, she shakes her head.

'Your name, I do not even know your name.'

With a quick laugh she drops him a little curtsey, so that the tension between them is broken. 'Paolina Tessieri. How do you do?'

'Paolina.' He breathes her name, never to forget it again.

The two agree to drink some tea together in the shade of a coffee-house. From where they sit beneath the arcade, Paolina can keep an eye on her sister while trying to resettle her mind. Where do they go from here? Neither she nor Antonio brings up the subject of their former encounter. 'I never saw you again after that evening. Were you only in Venice for a short time?'

'I returned your violin, but unfortunately you were not in. Shortly afterwards I travelled to Ferrara and then on home to Mantua. Since my mother left our father I have been taking care of Annina.'

'A huge responsibility! What are your plans once Annina is

grown up?' Antonio cannot contain his curiosity. He still has no idea whether or not she is married. She wears a ring, but that means nothing. Paolina looks about her vaguely. 'Oh, travel... get away from here, anyway.' Her tone tells Antonio she is not happy. 'Come on.' She gets to her feet. 'It's time I was off again.'

He tries by any pretext to delay her; he still has so much he wants to ask her. 'What is it that we share?' he asks hurriedly as they cross the square.

She stops in her tracks and seems to weigh her words. 'Perhaps I'll tell you tomorrow,' she smiles mysteriously, suddenly planting a kiss on his cheek. She calls the child and they wander off together chattering, watched by a bewildered Vivaldi. He can hardly credit the turmoil inside him.

He plunges into work with renewed vigour. Early each morning he awakens with the pleasant prospect of seeing Paolina. So the weeks pass by, a chance meeting in the market, followed by coffee, always at the same place beneath the arcade. They talk about all and everything, but Paolina evades the question of what it is they share. Like ten years before, she shows a fascinated interest in his work and life, but, as then, gives little away regarding her own. It soon becomes plain to the priest that something lies hidden behind her warm façade and charming smile. But as relations between them deepen, Paolina little by little reveals glimpses of her life. For years she has helped her father in his wig-making business, assisting him on the clerical side with orders and deliveries. But business is going downhill, due not so much to a reduced demand for wigs, for there is plenty, but more because Pietro Tessieri cannot stay off the drink. Paolina confesses this with shame. Her father's habit has worsened over the years, she tells Antonio, and it did not help that her mother had abandoned the family. Her two younger brothers are still at home but they hardly lift a finger. The elder finds a job every now and then, but the younger seems intent on following in his father's drunken footsteps. Antonio listens with mounting horror as Paolina's story unfolds. So dreadful is it that he finds it a miracle that she and her sister keep smiling. But Paolina soon explains, 'If I gave in I would be finished. I keep going for Annina's sake. I can't let her down and neither can I just go somewhere else to live. People see you coming with a child. So I'll wait a couple of years until Annina can stand on her own two feet, and then I can think about what I want to do.'

'Have you no other family who might offer you a safe haven?' Vivaldi asks. She shakes her head and stands up, ready to go. As if by unspoken mutual consent, the priest has never accompanied her home. But this time he wonders if he should. He is deeply concerned, despite the cheery wave Paolina and little Anna give as if to assure him that nothing is amiss.

Once back in the insular world of his workroom, Antonio forgets his worries over Paolina. With the end of summer in sight, work begins to pour in. From his father he receives regular letters containing a list of pending commissions. These keep flowing in, providing welcome extra income to supplement his generous salary from *Langravio* Filippo. As the days shorten, a new winter season's programming begins to make demands on Antonio's attention. He is eager to get down to writing a new opera, one fully worthy of an imperial governor. Money is, in principle, no object; a nice position to find himself in. Not that it will tempt him to go looking for the most fashionable *castrati*. This he has never done and does not intend to do now. There is more than enough talent about and over the years Antonio has assembled a fine company of vocalists who are only too happy to continue working with him. Slowly but surely he gets back to work with the orchestra, for although the court greatly appreciates the cantatas he has been producing, he, personally, is not satisfied with these pieces. He finds them too simple, too transparent. He would like to spend all his days rehearsing with the orchestra, which now comprises no fewer than twenty players. What a sound! So thinking, he begins to search for a piece of work written earlier in the week, something he now wants to dispatch to his father. Piles of paper and music are strewn everywhere, cluttering every surface as if in mass migration from the overloaded table to the floor, and even to the bed. He has a perfect filing system in his head, and can usually lay his hands on whatever he is looking for amidst the apparent mayhem. But it's just as well his father isn't here to see him now; Giambattista has a real aversion to this kind of havoc.

Maybe the time really is ripe for a clear up, reflects Antonio, for that manuscript has gone well and truly missing. He begins to get irritated, rifling again through one pile after another and scattering papers everywhere. Finally he finds what he is looking for under a heap of other stuff. Who put it there anyway? He hears the chiming of the bells calling him to the marketplace. For two days now he has not seen Paolina, and he misses her. She has failed to turn up before; either too busy or there has been something wrong with the child. But she has never stayed away for longer than a day.

The market traders are taking down their stalls and people are making their way back home with baskets full of purchases. One by one the shutters are coming down on the houses surrounding the square, in the hope of excluding the worst of the noonday heat. Vivaldi has waited with growing impatience but caught no glimpse of either Paolina or little Anna. What could have happened? This time he does not turn homewards. He cannot rid himself of the sense that something is amiss and he wants to know what has happened to stop her coming to meet him. What if she is sick? Perhaps she has caught malaria? A vivid picture comes to him of her lying feverish and hallucinating. Might she even already be dead? He shakes the terrible thought from his head and masters himself; she is a strong woman. She must simply have been too busy lately.

His feet carry him from the square in the same direction she always takes, and he turns off right at the same corner. The street becomes increasingly deserted until the priest find himself accompanied only by the skinny cats that skulk with scabby noses and eyes in each portico and slouch upon every windowsill. On the next corner is a small tavern with one or two late diners lingering at its tables. The priest goes inside and asks at the first table if anyone knows where *Monsieur* Pietro Tessieri lives.

'Tessieri?' comes the shrill response. Vivaldi finds himself looking at a flabby man with an empty plate in front of him. 'You'll be meaning Girò, the wig-maker.'

'Giraud?' repeats the priest, his resolve wavering.

'Yes, don't ask me why, but that's what he's been calling himself for years. Pretty weird bloke. But what would you expect from a Frog?' The man roars with laughter at his own joke and the rest of the table soon join in. 'Walk straight on, priest, over the square, turn left at the corner then it's the... er, fifth house on the right.'

'Fourth,' says the man sitting next to him.

'No. That's Bottieri's place.'

'What are you talking about?' And a hefty discussion breaks out as to who actually lives where. Frowning, Vivaldi bids them a good afternoon. 'Oh, and priest, don't forget to bang good and hard on the door. He's probably still sleeping off last night.' The whole table again erupts with raucous laughter.

Antonio begins to wonder what in heaven's name he is doing here. Should he take this any further? What sort of scene will he encounter if he does so? But then he remembers Anna's innocent laughter, the little girl for whom Paolina feels such overwhelming responsibility. And his feet carry him on down the street according to the instructions until he arrives at Giraud's premises.

The shutters are down, but what else would he expect at this time of day? Antonio knocks softly. No movement or sound comes from within. Crossing the street, Antonio scans the upper floor. There too the shutters are closed. It makes no sense to go banging on the door or calling anyone. Every sensible person is asleep by now.

'It's a dreadful state of affairs, that it is.' The quiet voice comes from behind him, but when he turns round he finds only wooden blinds, badly in need of a coat of paint at that. Then comes a hiss from above.

'Here I am, priest.'

Taking a step backwards, he gazes up into the face of an old woman.

'What did you say?' he asks loudly.

'Shhh!' she hushes him, disappearing from the window.

Muffled footsteps on the inner stairs. The sound of a bolt being thrown inside, and the door swings open.

'So I was right. I thought I saw a priest down here. And about time too!' mumbles the old dame, and before Vivaldi knows what is happening she has hold of his arm and is pulling him inside. She shuts the door and darkness envelops them.

'Follow me,' she snaps peremptorily, leading the way upstairs. The room she takes him to is dimly lit from the windows, where the shutters are open a crack. The woman sits down at a small table. There is only one chair, but she points with an arthritic finger at a footstool for Antonio to sit on. The only other furniture in the parlour is an old dresser; the plaster walls have not seen whitewash for years and are beginning to peel.

The old woman opens fire on him at once. 'So the church has finally decided to do something about this dreadful situation, has it?'

'Would you be so kind, signora, as to explain to me what exactly is going on?' Unease and disorientation make his reply sound impatient, but actually he is feeling unpleasantly confused. The old woman sighs and lifts her arms heavenward. 'What, again? I've told Father Gianfranco so often about it all and he's always swearing something will be done. Now, what ARE you going to do?' Vivaldi taps nervously on the table with his fingertips. The one thing he must, on no account, do is let her know how superficial are his relations with the church. How long is it since he last celebrated Mass? Not since his dispensation. He only continues to wear the cassock because it gives him some standing in society.

But to be truthful with this old woman will surely ruin his

chance of learning what has happened to Paolina.

'Before I tell you what plans there are I must be brought up to date with developments. Come, madam,' he lays his hand confidentially upon her own, 'be so good as to tell me what has occurred.'

She looks the priest sidelong and suspiciously, obviously weighing up whether or not to confide further in him, then makes the sign of the cross and embarks on her story. 'It was in the air, you know, you could feel something was going to happen.' Vivaldi smiles benignly despite his inner turmoil. When will she get to the point? Hurry UP woman!

She peers through the blinds at the house on the other side of the street, still shrouded in silence, then moves closer to the priest and says in a low voice, 'It must be the devil's work. Must be.' Vivaldi nods again in encouragement.

'He was always a bit of a strange man, right from the moment they first came to live here. That must be fifteen years ago. Yes, because my husband Giorgio was still alive. He was a wig-maker too, you know, the best in the street. Even after the Frogs arrived. Oh yes, *Monsieur* Pietro was planning to make his fortune here with his fine French ideas. But nobody wanted that around here. He might as well have gone back to his own country, taking his stupid new styles with him, but there you are. It's a crying shame!' she pauses, her thoughts apparently wandering.

'What's a crying shame?' asks the priest

'Oh yes, he was a good man, my Giorgio. He's left me well provided for. Always set money aside and didn't mess me about. He was a fine man. No woman could have wished for better.'

How long have I got to sit through this, wonders Antonio in desperation.

'I knew right away, the minute I clapped eyes on that man Giraud, as he calls himself, I knew he was a completely different kettle of fish from my Giorgio. Oh, dear, oh dear,' she murmurs, once more crossing herself. 'Could that man drink, my heavens! And then the trouble started. Constant rows; it drove us mad.

220

Giorgio was always at their door, and in the beginning they took some notice and quietened down.. Because I can tell you, that woman was not a scrap better than her husband. No, once she walked out on him, and I don't blame her for that, things calmed down a great deal. But what kind of woman leaves her children to fend for themselves? What sort of world are we living in, priest, what sort of world?'

'It is indeed dreadful,' affirms Vivaldi, 'but what happened then?'

'Dead. Just like that, dead!'

'Who?' asks Vivaldi in alarm.

The woman stares at him in horror. 'My Giorgio of course! Worked all day as usual. Comes upstairs for his meal and collapses halfway without so much as a hiccup.'

'I am very sorry to hear it,' commiserates Vivaldi.

'Not a dying word passed his lips. Is that not remarkable, Father? But at least he didn't have to suffer like his brother. That poor boy, did he suffer!'

'Well, signora,' interrupts Vivaldi, running out of patience altogether. 'The *famiglia* Giraud, how did things proceed for them?'

'Oh, yes, well, as I said. His wife was gone and then he only had the kids. And they didn't fancy fighting all the time. So everything went quiet and things got even better once Paolina came back with the baby.'

'Ah,' frowns Vivaldi, 'her sister Anna.'

'That's what she calls her, yes, but I'm not so sure. I don't know where the mother is nowadays, but I'm pretty certain she wasn't pregnant when she disappeared. But then who am I to know what happened? Nobody knows everything, do they? But I must say Paolina has taken good care of Anna. Like a real mother. But what did they come back for? I mean, everything went fine at the beginning. Paolina had the whole house organised in no time, the shop and the workshop, and she even got those good-for-nothing brothers helping out now and then. But the real miracle was Pietro. He started working seriously again, and with Paolina in the shop it soon looked almost like a proper family. But you know what, priest? Well, I don't need to tell you, a leopard doesn't change its spots.'

Vivaldi nods briefly, terrified of stopping her story with another question, even for an instant.

'Back on the drink, of course. And the brothers every bit as bad as their father. Then all mayhem broke loose again. Oh, I am so glad Giorgio isn't here to go through it anymore. But it's worst for that wee Anna. You wouldn't believe, priest, what I've been through. The neighbours round there all the time. But those boys, well, they were getting bigger by the day and so you needed to watch your step with them. I went to see Father Gianfranco and he had a word with Giraud. But that only made things worse. If you ask me, it's revenge, priest. That Giraud is still mad at his wife for running off, and he takes it out on the child. It's a scandal the church hasn't done anything about it! And now it's probably too late. But don't say I didn't warn you. May God and Holy Maria be my witness, I warned you!'

The priest takes a deep breath. 'Tell me now what has happened recently?'

She makes another sign of the cross. 'I saw it happen, priest, from here, through that very window. It was early in the evening and my shutters were open, and so were those on the other side of the street. That's the sisters' bedroom and... oh, priest, it's too ghastly for words.'

The old woman has begun to shake. Vivaldi's heart heaves in his chest at the thought of what might have befallen Paolina and Anna. He lays his hand on her wrinkled one again.

'Go on, good woman, your secret is safe with me.'

'That animal! Giraud must have been out drinking the whole afternoon. I was having my lie-down and had fallen asleep, but then I got woken up with the screaming. It was really bad this time. I heard Annina screeching in fear and Paolina shouting at her father; he must have been outside their room. When I opened my blinds I looked in and saw the moment that monster broke down the door and fell in upon them. Completely out of his mind, you could see it. At first I couldn't think what was going on, but the bastard was obviously going for little Anna. Can you imagine, priest? Paolina jumped on him and managed to stop him, probably just because he was so drunk she could fight him off. But then I saw her brother, the oldest one, coming to his father's aid, and laughing his head off, too. But not for long, because Paolina had found a knife from somewhere and she stabbed it in him until he was crawling out of the room screaming and swearing and yelling blue murder. Then she literally kicked her father out of the room behind her brother and barricaded the door. Those poor lassies. What a terrible state they were in for hours afterwards.'

'When did all this take place?' Antonio demands.

'The day before yesterday. I ran straight to Father Gianfranco and he was going to get the police in.'

'And then?'

'Oh, what use are that lot? They finally got their backsides over here the following morning. That Giraud must have slept off his hangover by then and managed to convince the officers nothing untoward had happened. Then off they went again.'

'But what about Paolina and Annina?' Vivaldi feels his anguish must be audible. She shrugs. 'Nothing. They must still be in their room for all I know, because I haven't seen them on the street.'

'But this is crazy. Things can't go on like this!' Vivaldi rises to his feet. He can feel his heart thumping and the familiar compression clamping his ribcage. 'I'll be back at once,' he calls, already charging down the stairs, leaving the old woman still sitting, shaking her head.

Opening the door, he sees facing him the house hiding its dreadful secret behind closed shutters. Without stopping to think, he runs as best he can in the direction of the palace. But after a hundred metres he has to give up. He knows he can't make it and the attempt has made him dizzy with exertion. The vice-like pain in his chest worsens until he feels as if his heart will burst. Staggering back across the deserted square he finds the restaurant still mercifully open and all the customers gone. The landlord, busy mopping the floor, looks up shocked as the white-faced priest stumbles in.

'What is it?'

'Water,' gasps Vivaldi.

Pouring a tumbler full, the landlord helps him sip and takes him to a seat. He is breathing so fast and shallowly that he can hardly speak. Instead he fumbles for his purse and takes from it a ducat.

'Quick,' he wheezes, shoving the money across the table. 'Fetch Signor Coopman here immediately, adjutant to the Count. I am Don Antonio Vivaldi. This is an emergency, a matter of life or death!' The landlord wastes not a second in snatching up the coin from the table.

'You'll get another the minute Coopman gets here,' pants Vivaldi.

Shouting something into the back kitchen, the landlord throws off his apron and is gone. Antonio leans forward over the table and rests his head on his arms to ease his breathing. After a few moments he removes his hat and drags his sleeve across his forehead to wipe away the sweat. He closes his eyes. *Per l'amor del cielo.* Please heaven let them be safe. Mother Maria, what can I do? Just wait!

It seems hours before Antonio Vivaldi hears the clatter of galloping hooves. Slightly recovered, he puts on his hat and goes outside to see Walter Coopman approaching, another rider close behind him. Recognising the priest, they immediately slow their horses.

'Don Vivaldi,' Coopman calls out, slipping lithely from the saddle, 'what's going on?' Antonio quickly explains. The adjutant scratches his head thoughtfully.

'I'm not sure if I have the right to walk unannounced into someone's house, even given the seriousness of the present situation,' he says.

'Does there have to be a murder first?' demands the

outraged Antonio. Coopman shrugs. 'I'm afraid I'll have to consult the Governor first,' he replies, remounting with supple ease. Stricken, Antonio takes a step forward and catches hold of the rider by the leg. 'About what I have just been telling you; the head of the family is a Frenchman.' Vivaldi, in panic and offering the arbitrary information purely as a delaying tactic, has no notion the effect it will have upon this Dutch soldier who has been fighting the French for years.

The adjutant's eyes narrow. 'A Frenchman, you say?' With his fingers he unconsciously traces the long scar disfiguring his face.

'Absolutely, my lord.'

Coopman's face contorts with rage. 'Show me the house,' he orders grimly, spurring on his horse. The priest strides as fast as he can back the way he has come, until the landlord bars their path, himself short of wind and holding his hand out for the rest of his reward. Antonio slows his pace and throws the money at the man, who makes off at once.

'Here,' Vivaldi, wheezing hard once more, indicates the house of the wig-maker. Coopman halts at the front door and hammers on it loudly with the butt of his pistol.

'Hey, *Monsieur* Giraud, open up, in the name of the Governor!' Vivaldi sees on Coopman's face the tension that breeds violence. A full minute passes before there comes the sound of bolts being drawn. Gaping through a tiny crack in the doorway is a boy, almost certainly Paolina's brother. Coopman at once spurs on his stallion until its weight throws the door almost off its hinges. He now stands, horse and all, in the wig-maker's workshop. Nimbly he reaches down, grabs the boy by the scruff of the neck and demands to know the whereabouts of *Monsieur* Giraud. Dumb with terror, the boy can only howl. Out from the shadows emerges the master of the house.

'Who dares to intrude so rudely upon my business premises and talk to my son like that?'

Walter Coopman's blood rises at the mere French

intonation in this piping little voice addressing him so arrogantly. He lets the boy drop from his hand like so much dirty washing and momentarily tenses his calf muscles, so that his mount takes another step into the room. The older man stands with arms folded, not batting an eyelid as horse and adjutant tower over him.

'"In the name of the Governor"?' mimics Giraud derisively. 'You will show me your papers.'

Coopman is a man of deeply hidden passions. But a moment such as this makes him see red. His ears begin to ring with the cacophony of war, the roar of cannon, as if he were back among his troops and leading an assault upon French infantrymen. As vividly as if it were yesterday he sees in his mind's eye his comrades trampled beneath the feet of the enemy, and with each loved and bloodied face his hatred of the French grows more virulent. He hardly hears what Giraud is saying to him, the man's demand to see his papers. Does this Frenchman have any idea what sort of situation he has got himself into here? Coopman looks down on the wig-maker and notes with revulsion the stench of stale alcohol rising to meet him like a cloud. What? Does this alcoholic Frog think he can get away with mouthing his insolent sermons at him? He, the hero of Oudenaarde and adjutant to Prince Philip von Hesse-Darmstadt?

The Dutchman replaces his pistol in his sash. He will not be requiring it today. With meticulous care he draws his poignard from its scabbard. Ah, how many Frenchmen had felt the cool touch of this bright steel soothing their last breath? Smiling sardonically, he presses the tip of the blade against Giraud's chest. 'Listen, Frenchman, you give me the slightest excuse to slit your throat and I will do so with pleasure. Now give me straight answers to the questions I put to you, or before you know where you are you will be looking at the pearly gates. *Comprende?*'

It is becoming evident to the wig-maker that he is not dealing here with a common soldier or one of the idiots who turned up at the door yesterday. Who is this fellow?

Then he catches sight in the doorway of a figure, slight of

stature but nonetheless self-assured. He can't see the face, but from his headgear he recognises a priest. Bloody hell, who's been telling tales to the church? He swallows hard. It hurts.

Vivaldi takes up a position next to Coopman's horse and looks at the wig-maker. Before him is a dissolute face that bears no resemblance to either Paolina or Anna.

'Where are your daughters?' asks Antonio.

Giraud points above his head muttering, 'In their room.'

'Get them down here,' orders Coopman roughly.

The wig-maker shrugs trembling shoulders. 'They won't listen to me.'

Vivaldi glances at the adjutant. 'You there,' Coopman shouts at Giraud's younger son, 'show the priest the way.'

Scrambling to his feet, the boy lurches ahead of Antonio. But halfway along the gallery on the first floor the lanky lout comes to a standstill and, with a silent, dirty look at the priest, shows him a door before running off down the corridor and vanishing. Putting his ear to the door, Vivaldi listens. There is no sound. He taps respectfully.

No response. He knocks more persuasively. 'Paolina, Don Vivaldi.' He thinks he hears movement. 'Paolina, please open up. In God's name, are you all right?'

'Are you alone?' a weak voice answers from the other side of the door.

'I have brought help. Do not be afraid. Everything is going to be all right,' replies Antonio in agitation.

He hears furniture being dragged across the floor. The door opens a hand's breadth and Vivaldi stares into the scared eyes of Paolina. First checking the corridor in both directions, she pulls open the door and, stifling a cry, falls weeping silently into Antonio's arms. Over her shoulder Vivaldi surveys the ravaged room.

'Where is Annina?' he asks at last.

Paolinia blows her nose. 'Is it really safe?' Her mass of dark-blonde hair tumbles in disarray around her face, partly obscuring it.

'Yes, your father is downstairs, under guard. I suggest you pack up some things and both of you come with me back to the palace. You are not safe here.'

She leaves his arms and pulls open a cupboard. There lies little Anna, crumpled like a rag-doll, well hidden under a heap of clothes. She has her eyes shut tight and her hands over her ears. Paolina bends over and lifts her carefully from the press, the child clinging like a toddler to her big sister. With her free hand Paolina pushes the hair out of her own eyes.

'My God!' Vivaldi exclaims, aghast. As Paolina brushes the hair aside, exposing her face, he sees a thickly clotted scab where her lip should be. One eye is purple and both lids bruised and swollen with crying. My God, what must she have been through?

She shakes her head as if awakening from a nightmare.

'I want to go. Please let us go,' she sobs.

Taking her arm, he helps her downstairs step by step. Seeing the priest enter with the two girls, the adjutant arrives at his own conclusion. He leans forward, digging his dagger a shade deeper into Giraud's chest. 'Well now, incest is a hanging offence, you dirty little rat.'

Giraud appears to be singularly unimpressed and even beams happily.

'Incest, did you say? I've no idea what in God's name you're talking about!' The wig-maker meanwhile looks triumphantly at Coopman and throws Paolina a glance of contempt.

'Not one foot, do you hear me? Not one more foot shall you set in my house, you worthless slut!' he spits at his daughter.

Vivaldi feels Paolina stiffen, and draws her outside.

'And that goes for that imbecile child of yours, too!' screams her father after them.

Anger wells up inside Vivaldi. How dare the man say such things? With practised self-control the priest turns his attention to the sisters, but the father's brutal words burn themselves into his memory.

228

Coopman returns threateningly to the Frenchman. 'Listen here, you little shit. If anyone should happen to file a complaint against you it'll be me personally who comes to arrest you, and once the law has finished with you, I'll button your mouth for good, and with pleasure.'

He pushes his boot into Giraud's abdomen so that he falls backwards over his own feet. 'And one more thing! If any misfortune befalls either of these two ladies I'll run you straight through with this knife.' Coopman waves the blade once more at the Frenchman before regretfully allowing it to glide unused into its sheath. The adjutant turns his horse and steps outside, leaving Giraud laughing scornfully. But once the company is out of earshot his mirth drains away as fast as the colour from his face. On the other side of the street a shutter softly closes.

No case is brought against Giraud. The two sisters have no wish to talk about what has happened at home and Vivaldi does not pressure them. He wants to give them all the time they need to tell their story. The adjutant has offered them temporary accommodation. Beside the theatre are a couple of empty apartments usually used by artistes working here temporarily on a current production. The room is simple but lies safe within the walls of the court, and Paolina assures Coopman she feels secure here.

For his part, Antonio has one or two things to explain to the prince.

Filippo is not entirely happy with developments and at first blames his adjutant for taking the law into his own hands.

'You must understand, Don Vivaldi, that however honourable your intentions the palace cannot offer shelter to every woman in need. Before we know where we are we should have hundreds of women and children under our roof, and that we cannot do. Is it not the responsibility of the church to watch over its parishioners?'

'It most certainly is, Your Highness, but the church was in

fact aware of this situation and apparently had no power to intervene. The most important reason, indeed, for my calling upon the aid of your heroic adjutant is that Paolina has meant much to our family. Years ago she was working in Venice and cared lovingly for my mother on her sickbed,' Vivaldi feels he has no option but to mislead the prince, he is so afraid Paolina and Anna may be sent back to her father. 'I should have been renouncing my own mother had I turned my back on the girl. It would have been impossible for me to get another note of music to flow from my pen. The knowledge that these sisters remained day and night under the tyrannical rule of their father would not only have gnawed at my conscience but also have eroded my right to the priesthood. Had we,' and here Vivaldi pauses significantly and looks his benefactor straight in the eye, 'had we averted our gaze, were we not then as bad as any Pilate, washing his hands of guilt?'

The words hit their mark. Filippo is clearly moved. 'Fine then, Don Vivaldi, it is obvious to me that this business is justified. But what are your plans now?'

Vivaldi breathes freely again and Coopman also stands more at ease. 'Ah, sire,' Antonio offers, 'I should be only too pleased to pay for their lodgings. Paolina can help me with clerical work. She might take over many a task normally performed for me by my father. I can provide her with enough income for her to live an independent life.'

The Governor of Mantua rubs his chin and stares outside. 'Very well, Vivaldi, for the present she may remain here as my guest. Let them both recover somewhat, and in a couple of months you may come back to me with your plans for them. Should the girl wish to bring a case against the father, so much the better. I hope for both your sakes,' and here he gives his adjutant an uncompromising look, 'that her father has no desire to prosecute us himself for housebreaking, because in that case I think you would have no leg to stand on.'

Both Vivaldi and Coopman bow deeply. The priest waits for his chance, and when it presents itself assures the adjutant over and over again of his indebtedness to the military.

A few days later Prince Filippo honours Paolina and little Anna with a personal visit. 'For as long as you wish, you may remain my guest,' he reassures Paolina, observing with distaste the wounds on her face. The girl falls on her knees at the feet of the governor, who waves aside her thanks. 'You are lucky to have befriended the red-haired priest. He speaks highly of you, and I understand he has rescued you both from an utterly unendurable predicament.' Paolina nods, choked once more with pain and anguish. The prince stares at Annina. She reminds him of his youngest daughter, Theodora. 'Let me know if I may be of any further service to you,' he says, turning to leave. It gives him pleasure to offer them his hospitality, although he has no desire for Vivaldi to make a habit of such gestures.

With each day Paolina recovers a little more the habit of speech, although she manages to avoid all questions concerning her former domestic situation. Her wounds are soon healed and in appearance she is as lovely as ever. And yet something in her is broken. Her proud, joyous and self-assured outer shell has suffered a devastating blow. Any sudden loud noise sends her running pale and skittish for a corner, looking round nervously to make sure Annina is safe. It's always a false alarm, of course, and she ends up laughing apologetically, telling Vivaldi how silly she is. But he senses her fear and anxiety and knows he cannot leave her alone for long.

Annina is the first to recover. She does not fancy being cooped up in her room and prefers to be off all day on outings of discovery, chatting merrily with the other occupants of the gallery. She soon establishes a special relationship with the lady vocalists, and exploits to the full this surprising new world she finds herself in. Paolina takes longer to adjust. Vivaldi visits her each day and makes sure there is always enough to eat in the house. In his own way, he looks after her, and as her strength and confidence return he asks whether she might be interested in working for him; it would provide her with an income and give her a change to shape her own future. She promises to think about it, but has not so far come back to him. Thus Antonio is caught by surprise when, fresh and lovely as the dawn, she walks into his room one morning. 'So this is where you hide,' she says, her eyes widening in wonder as she surveys the table completely covered with papers, the littered room and the bed, apparently left unmade or changed in ages. She does not like the smell in here, and no wonder. In one corner, beside a bowl of rotting apples, sit a couple of beakers and a plate covered in mould. Piles of unwashed clothes lie stiffening at the foot of the bed. Mouse droppings have joined the small accumulations of breadcrumbs shoved aside between piles of paper. Paolina opens the shutters, welcoming in daylight and wafts of fresh air. Without a word, she begins clearing up. Dirty clothes she gathers together in one place, and scraps and leftovers of old food are swept into a basket. She labours the whole morning and gradually Antonio's living quarters are transformed into a habitable space. Empty inkpots are washed and refilled. Pens are rinsed and sharpened, and sheets of manuscript paper cut and placed ready in neat piles. It is exactly as if Giambattista Vivaldi had been through the place, setting everything in order.

'Fifty ducats per month, to be paid in advance.' Paolina states her terms at the end of the day, setting down beside the bed a basket of freshly laundered linen.

Antonio looks up. 'That's a very great deal of money, my lady,' he laughs.

'There is a very great deal to do. And trust me, I'm capable of a good deal more than washing underwear. Don't forget; I did my father's bookkeeping for years,' she glances at him, her expression serious, and holds out for scrutiny his ledger, empty of entries. It is the first time Paolina has mentioned her father. 'Agreed,' replies Antonio. 'Consider yourself appointed.'

Vivaldi now gets to know a completely different Paolina. The household chores seem to get done effortlessly, and very soon she has time to get to work on Vivaldi's administrative affairs. Long overdue correspondence is caught up with and she introduces some scheduling into his workload. Vivaldi now begins each day with a fresh worksheet, already beautifully laid out for him with clean paper and ink. He is awe-struck at his own reaction. It always drove him mad at home when his mother or sisters went into his room to clean it. Yet Paolina's presence causes him only pleasure. Not that they talk much; both are completely preoccupied. But the manner in which she brings order to his world appeals to him and adds to his sense of wellbeing. As the day draws to its end there is always time for a few words, and then she will inquire, with undiminished interest, about what he is working on; whether he has answered his letters or begun on the next commission for a new client. He can't tell what her feelings for him might be, dare not intrude emotionally, and makes absolutely no demands upon her. For the time being her presence is enough; trust will return in its own time.

And these weeks are no less revelatory for Paolina. There is another Vivaldi. She has always liked him, even before they knew each other. Their conversations in the marketplace had been pleasant enough, but now she discovers a whole new side to him. Working, he disappears into his own world, becoming completely unreachable. But the moment he finishes a new piece, he is up and out of his chair and clamouring for everyone to stop whatever they may be doing, to pay attention. For they have to listen, and before they have a chance to compliment him he is busy himself expounding the virtues and beauty of the work. It can get tiring.

But she has also found in the priest a valuable friend, and one who has taken the trouble to give new direction to her life without asking for anything in return. He remains chary of her feelings and keeps just enough distance, yet asks with unfailingly sincerity after her welfare and Annina's. While she remains closed he is sensitive to her silence, feeling when and on which subjects she does not wish to speak. Deep inside she prizes his letting her alone so honourably. For his own part, Vivaldi lets it be known when he requires solitude, and so a respectful friendship grows between the two.

Annina feels completely at home in her new environment. She gets singing lessons from 'Aunt Angelica', one of the older sopranos who has taken the little one under her wing. Anna knows she must not wander beyond the bounds of the court, and feels no need to do so. The surroundings of the theatre and palace offer a safe haven for the two sisters and neither feels the slightest pang of homesickness.

As the days shorten the court begins to bustle. Each morning the shrill blare of hunting-horns and wild barking of dogs accompany a new hunting party assembled for the chase. Concerts are given at regular intervals for the rich array of imperial guests. An opera is on the programme for the end of December, and Giambattista Vivaldi arrives just in time to assist with final preparations. He is immediately struck with how well his son is looking, for he has been somewhat concerned about Antonio. This is the first time in his life he has been without his parents. The older man ambles around the workroom inspecting with increasing incredulity the order he finds there. How can this be? The priest winks at his father and right on cue Paolina walks into the chamber, so that Antonio can introduce her as his secretary. His father looks dubious but says nothing. He recognises her at once as the girl who stood on the doorstep all those years ago, holding out to him Antonio's lost violin! Paolina responds politely to all his discreet questions. He can't wait for her to leave the room.

'What's she doing here?' he demands as Antonio shuts the door behind her. Without going into too much detail, Antonio outlines to his father what has occurred. The old man hums and haws and can't seem to say anything intelligible. Could he be jealous? Unable to accept that this woman has taken over his function and thus his place in his son's life? Maybe he feels he has lost his son to her. For it is as plain as day to him that Antonio is fond of her. But whatever, he has no time to worry about such things just now; there's too much work to be done. It's not every day, after all, that he has to transcribe all the parts for such a huge orchestra.

A couple of days before the opera Il *Teuzzone* opens, and after Mass at the *Duomo*, a magnificent Christmas banquet is held in the *Palazzo Ducale*. The place is packed with guests and it is some while before the Governor is able to hush the great hall and make himself heard. The moment there is silence *Langravio* Filippo makes the sudden surprise announcement of his engagement to Princess Eleanora Luisa Gonzaga, daughter of the Duke of Guastalla and Sabbioneta, widow of Francesco Maria, the extravagant and corpulent Grand Duke Cosimo de Medici.

Everyone is stunned, not least Countess Margherita Pavesi Furlani, who for years has served as governess to the Count's children. She had heard the rumours of course, but there are always those, and nothing had indicated that such gossip was founded in reality. Deep in her heart Margherita had cherished a hope that she might win the Count's love. Thus her smiles and applause, apparently in accord with everyone else in the hall, hide a heart filled with bitter tears.

Filippo wastes no time in broadcasting the news that his Princess Eleanora is already making preparations for her journey to Mantua. She is expected to arrive at court here in about a fortnight and the wedding is to take place soon afterwards.

This marriage has been negotiated in deepest secrecy as a union in the political interests of the Habsburg Empire. Fortunately for Filippo, the thirty-two-year-old princess is still an attractive woman – and one who each day thanks her lucky stars that she has been blessed with widowhood so soon.

She had been forced into her first marriage by her own family, and thinking back on that vile cardinal of a husband still appals her. Not surprising, considering it was common knowledge that the filthy man was more interested in young boys than in the company of a lady. What sort of woman would want to share a bed with so truly repellent a creature?

Up until his marriage the cardinal had led a life of blithe bestiality, a bizarre existence of gluttony and paedophilia. That he must abandon his post as a cardinal in order to marry a young and healthy princess he had considered an act of treachery against him by his brother Cosimo. But the cardinal and his young bride had represented Cosimo's only hope for male progeny and an heir to the Medici name.

However, to Eleanora's great joy and relief, the ex-cardinal was dead within two years of their marriage. His outrageously decadent lifestyle had fatally undermined his health and in destroying him had also robbed the Medici dynasty of its last chance of survival.

The Habsburg rulers have for some time had a sharp eye on Florence, feeling they have a reasonable claim to the Medici fortune. But anything that might strengthen such a right is carefully weighed in the balance and added to the ammunition. Eleanora is in all aspects a good marriage for the Governor of Mantua. Not only as widow of Francesco Maria de Medici, but also as daughter of the Gonzaga family, the former rulers of Mantua. Prince Filippo has never met Eleanora face to face, but she is known to be a beautiful woman and one of great individual charm. The prince is not desperate to re-marry, but the request from the Emperor in Vienna, in combination with a number of other interesting prospects, has been enough to persuade him of the wisdom of such a move.

News of the coming wedding spreads like wildfire through the streets of Mantua, and the city needs little to whip it into festive mood. Everyone stands to profit; the many guests will guarantee a good income for each innkeeper and wine-bar. The city receives a good clean and tidy-up and is duly festooned with gaudy decorations. Antonio Vivaldi is commissioned to produce a fittingly grandiose new opera. A couple of weeks earlier he has begun reading *Tito Manlio* and feels this may offer a suitable narrative. The libretto, written by Matteo Noris, was set to music twenty years ago by Carlo Francesco Pollaro and staged for the first time as a *dramma per musica* in Florence. This premier was followed by a successful two-year run at the *Teatro San Giovanni Grisostomo* in Venice. Giambattista can still recall a performance and warns his son that it has a very sad ending, absolutely not appropriate for a wedding.

But this poses no problem for Antonio. As so often before, he feels free, in view of the intervening death of the librettist, to produce an adaptation of his story. Instead of the main lead character coming to a bloody end, he is now liberated from his trials and tribulations in time to marry his beloved. Giambattista reads it through and can find no fault. The days fly by as Antonio planes and polishes the new work, while evening after evening *Il Teuzzone* plays to a full house.

The moment it is officially confirmed that Princess Eleanora is indeed to arrive in Mantua in two weeks' time and the wedding to take place in three, an outbreak of nerves begins to percolate though the court. So little time! How can a wedding be organised so quickly? Vivaldi feels the strain just as urgently, for he knows *Tito Manlio* has to be ready in time for the big day. The music begins to take real form, based on the story of Roman consul Tito Manlius Torquatus and his daughter Vitellia, who is secretly in love with Geminio, leader of the Latin rebels. Servilia, sister of Germinio, finds a way of cooling the conflict between Rome and the Latins by marrying her brother to Vitellia. But, unhappy with this outcome, he challenges the consul's son Manlio to a fight in which Geminio sadly loses his own life. Manlio, who has promised his father to approach the Latins in peace, has thus disobeyed his father and the consul has no alternative but, in the name of the senate, to pronounce the death sentence on his son.

Just as the execution is about to take place there is an army uprising and Manlio is rescued from the scaffold to marry his

Servilia. Vitellia is wed to Lucio, a Latin knight who has remained faithful to Rome. The Latins are subdued and their loyalty to Rome rekindled, and the whole drama up to and including the death of Germinio is certain to offer a theatrical spectacle of unrivalled glory.

Antonio agrees with his father that the latter will lead the orchestra over the coming days, so that his son is free to compose the new piece. The clock ticks relentlessly on, but the story is by now so vivid in Antonio's mind that it is simply a matter of filling up the many blank pages before him on the worktable. Hour after hour he works without pause.

Paolina brings him food at drink at regular intervals, makes sure that the lamps are kept burning brightly and catches the candles before they get too low. There is little more she can do for him; the priest is entirely caught up in his own world of ancient Rome.

After every orchestral performance Giambattista comes in to check how Antonio is getting on with his work-in-progress. In silence so as not to disturb his son, the father's gaze flits over the pages as fast as the notes flow from Vivaldi's pen and every couple of seconds he nods approvingly. The nights are long for Antonio, who has lost the art of sleep. Arias rehearse themselves over and over again in his head and send him jumping from bed to make a change or scribble a note for elaboration the following day. But before the week is over he is able, with huge satisfaction, to inscribe the word FINIS.

Later he adds 'Musica del Vivaldi fatta in cinque giorni': written in five days!

'Stupendous!' proclaims the priest, before his father has a chance to say anything.

Giambattista shakes his head good-humouredly. 'Nobody needs to try offering you a compliment, my son. Who would ever get the chance?'

Antonio doesn't even hear his words. He is already mentally occupied with the coming rehearsals. Just twelve days to go! The utmost demands are being made on the artistes, for every evening after rehearsing *Tito* all afternoon they must perform again in *Il Teuzzone*. This is where the good relations that Vivaldi has established with his vocalists bear fruit, and the promise of future reward for all their hard work adds to ensuring their full co-operation. Even the eloquent Margherita Gualandi carries on singing without complaint. And thanks to the herbal concoctions circulating among the artistes, the recipes for which remain a closely guarded secret, nobody goes down with a cold. Two days before the wedding performance comes the orchestral rehearsal. All goes well and the whole theatre dares to look forward to the great evening. Neither money nor trouble has been spared, and the fabulous costumes, also used for *Il Teuzzone*, are wonderfully set off by the magnificent stage design, a masterpiece by Antonio Mauro.

Thus the frustration and disappointment in the theatre is almost indescribable when it is learned that Princess Eleonora, within sight of Mantua's city walls, has called off the forthcoming nuptials and turned tail. Confusion reigns. This must be some cruel joke!

But it is not long before the Count himself confirms the news: 'The marriage is off!' No reason given. The mood is one of resignation, but a sense of angry grief settles on each and everyone who has worked so hard to make this wedding day an unforgettable occasion. The artistes themselves feel insulted. Have they laboured to learn arias and memorise recitatives, and in barely ten days committed all to memory, merely for the performance to be cancelled on a whim because this princess has changed her mind?

Langravio Filippo cannot make any sense of the princess either, or, come to that, of the effect of her jilting him. Meanwhile Eleanora's servants courteously return his bridal gifts. Are they trying to make him look a fool? In fact he is more relieved than saddened; this marriage was, after all, never his idea. His sympathy lies more with his court, the members of which have pulled out all the stops in the brief period of preparations. He decides to let a number of festivities go ahead anyway. It is in any case *carnevale*;

the celebrations will simply be rather more elaborate this year than in preceding ones.

The planned production of *Tito Manlio* is thus saved from oblivion, even if the empty chair next to the Govenor's does rather remind everyone of the wedding that never was. Directly behind the prince sit his daughters in all their finery, in the midst of them a radiant Margherita Furlani. It is the happiest day of her life.

By the end of the carnival season memories of both Eleonora and the defunct wedding have been consigned to history. *Tito Manlio* has proved a huge box-office success for the Vivaldis. The majority of soloists are on their way home, all with bulging purses. It has been an excellent season, but, for Antonio especially, an exhausting one. He is more than happy that there is no big project on the agenda for the near future and has vowed to use the coming weeks to recover. Giambattista is busy packing for his return to Venice. But for once, having got to know Paolina better, he feels fully confident that he is leaving his son's business affairs in safe hands.

Spring arrives, mild and soft. But in the wake of his father's departure Antonio has suffered a collapse. A bad dose of flu has kept him in bed for more than fourteen days with a high fever. Paolina nurses him with all the skill she can muster. For the first few days he sleeps, hardly conscious of what is going on around him. Once his temperature drops there is an improvement in his condition, but he remains weak and the tightness in his chest is almost as bad as ever. Paolina forces him to eat despite his unwillingness to do so. In the afternoons she reads a little poetry to him. Eyes closed, he listens with pleasure to her voice, its gentle modulation acting as balm to his soul. Glorious! For now he has no need of any other melody. Sometimes his attention wanders from the text, but often, entranced by some combination of words, his mind flies back to Andrea Frasetti, the dilettante poet with whom he was once snowed in when first he visited Florence. And then it strikes him how close her intonation is to his.

'Do you also write verses?' Vivaldi interrupts her.

She looks up; clapping shut the book from which she has been reading, her forefinger still between the pages, marking their place. 'How kind of you to ask,' she murmurs. 'I once resolved to write one or two lines each day. But alas, little has come of it. I keep a diary, but I usually lack the time to finish my entry with a poem. Some of what I have done is all right. Perhaps, when I have more leisure...' her voice trails off.

'I should like to hear some.'

'Mmm. I don't think they are good enough to recite.'

'A long time ago I met a man who told me that there was a poet in everyone, if only one gave voice to it,' Antonio repeats Andrea's long-lost words.

Paolina gives a short laugh. 'If only it was that easy! Then the world would be stuffed full of poets and none would stand out from the rest. No one would be able to tell himself apart or appreciate another's work. So perhaps it's as well not everyone is aware of the truth you have just kindly shared with me!'

Vivaldi shrugs. There's something in what she says. Who can produce music like he does, after all? Not a soul. 'You may be right,' he concedes, 'read on.'

She reopens the book and resumes reading the poem where she left off.

Antonio would really like to turn over and doze again, but Paolina has other plans. This morning she has laid out fresh clothes for him and thrown open the shutters. The sun pours in like molten gold and the day promises to be a glorious one. 'Get up, lazy-bones,' she calls out cheerfully to him. 'I'll come and collect you in half an hour.'

'What for?' he enquires, very slightly put out.

'Surprise!' She turns and winks as she leaves the room.

Antonio looks sullenly out of the window and allows into his consciousness the chatter of birdsong. He shuts his eyes again briefly, but decides nevertheless to make a huge effort and get out of bed. It is impossible to sleep on now that he knows Paolina will reappear in a little while expecting him to be up and ready. Splashing his face with warm water, he begins to wake up. It is weeks since he's been outside and he still feels very uncertain on his feet, but he manages to get dressed and eat some bread and nuts before Paolina comes back to collect him. Rushing in without knocking, she takes him happily by the hand, picks up his coat and together they descend to the arcade, she supporting him on the stairs. Down in the courtyard they find waiting for them a decorative open coach, harnessed to a mare. 'Voilà', laughs Paolina as Vivaldi stares at it in astonishment, 'We're going to take a drive.'

Greatly relieved he is not expected to walk anywhere, Antonio steps up into the *baroccio*. It is small and compact, just big enough to seat two people, and there's a small hamper tied to the back. Paolina springs up beside him and takes the reins. Clicking her tongue she urges on the mare and, as if she's been doing this all her life, takes the carriage neatly through the gate. The priest gazes in wonderment at the young woman seated next to him, so self-assured and relaxed, the reins held loosely in her hands.

'I didn't know you could manage a horse and carriage,' he remarks rather shyly.

She looks at him with triumph. 'I told you I was capable of more than just washing clothes.'

At a gentle trot they traverse their old haunt of the market-square and ride on out through *Cerese* Gate, leaving the city behind them. Passing the buttresses of *Palazzo Te* they canter westwards towards Parma. But Paolina is not going that far; after a couple of miles she turns off right. The mare paces quietly over a sandy track. There is no one in sight. The land around them is brilliantly verdant, newly grown crops standing emerald, two hands high. Now and then they pass a farm and wave to folk at work in the yard, but the mare is less friendly disposed towards the dogs that run barking alongside the coach, sometimes for hundreds of yards at a stretch. After an hour or so the track divides and Paolina turns off right once more. Soon they reach the riverbank. By now the sun is high in the sky, spilling its welcome spring warmth down upon the earth. Where the River Mincio curves in its course Paolina stops and tethers the horse to a tree. She loosens the bit and leaves the mare enough rope to enjoy cropping plenty of succulent young grass. She takes the hamper down from the back of the carriage and opens it, rolling out a blanket beneath the leafy shade.

'Sit down,' she invites Antonio with a generous gesture. From the hamper she brings all kinds of delicacies: freshly baked bread, smoked meats and dry fish from Venice, choice cheese, little round pastries and a bottle of fine wine. The fresh air is reviving and Antonio's cheeks glow. When everything has been skilfully unpacked, Paolina serves the priest with a selection of delicious food. He recognises his own choice of wine, and it tastes especially good to him today. And so together they enjoy a leisurely picnic lunch, while the river glides softly past. Herons arise on great grey wings low over the water, disturbed from their fishing by yet another boat drifting lazily downstream. The first swallows skim the reedy banks, screeching, scooping from the air a tasty harvest of insects. Sometimes the hum of a mirrored mayfly reaches their ears, at least, when the clamour of the ducks allows it. The fragrant grass stands tall with myriad flowers: golden buttercup, sorrel, wild marguerite and lady's smock. And all most delicious, it seems, at least as far as the sheep are concerned, for, grazing along under the protection of their shepherd, they glance up not once at the human picnickers.

'Ooh,' sighs Paolina ecstatically, 'if only it could be springtime forever. All this new life and everything bursting with colour, mm...'

'I prefer autumn myself,' responds Antonio languorously.

'But surely you wouldn't like it always to be autumn,' replies Paolina after a little pause.

'Oh no, certainly not. I don't need the last bit, when the mist changes to ice, all the leaves have fallen and the days are so short. And I can do without the whole winter as well.'

'Me too, but then perhaps we should get rid of summer

too... it's far too hot!' she laughs back at him. 'This is perfect. It doesn't need to get much warmer than this.'

Vivaldi nods his assent. The wine and food have made him sleepy. He lies on his back and for the first time in weeks hears music playing in his head again. Yes, spring is here. The birds are welcoming it with a joyous anthem.

Paolina looks down at Antonio, asleep and softly snoring. Sipping her wine, she looks about her. What will she do once they are back? She misses the wig-making shop not one bit, but the way she has to make her way so stealthily through the town and market grieves her. She is happy that Angelica has taken Anna so securely under her wing. Annina is convinced that she has found her vocation as a singer, and for now Paolina is quite content to go along with the girl. It makes a distraction, and it's very nice for her not to have to keep an eye on the child every minute of the day. The work she is doing for the priest she finds very satisfying. It's not too heavy and nowadays she even has time to read. Antonio Vivaldi has shown himself to be a good friend. She remembers how he never took advantage of her when she was at her most vulnerable. He is a priest, of course, but still a man for all that. She finds it difficult to guess at his true feelings. His liking for her is obvious, but is it love? And does she love him? Looking at his curls, she has to smile at the memory of their first meeting. Whoever could have imagined that ten years later he would be lying snoring at her feet on the banks of the Mincio?

She cannot make out what her feeling for him is. She knows she likes him very much, but is not sure if she is in love with him. He has so many different faces; she will have to get to know him better! But is that possible? Today is special; tomorrow will be a day like any other, and she likes the thought of that much less. Best of all she would like to leave Mantua today and never return, but she knows she has nowhere to go. Several times she has tried to coax Antonio to share his own plans, but these seem completely vague and even vary from day to day. All she can do is wait and see!

She opens the book she brought with her. The sun is still high; there's plenty of time yet.

It pleases Paolina to see how Antonio has enjoyed their outing. He is clearly much the better for it and soon gets back to work. They start going out regularly together, and sometimes Annina squeezes into the carriage with them. Spring has made way for summer and Vivaldi is fascinated to discover the ways in which nature responds to the changing year. In Venice one was far less aware of the passage of the seasons, and this is really the first time he has been conscious of how the weather influences people. In a big city one hardly noticed where one's food came from. Why should one? The market stalls were generally loaded with produce the whole year through. Yet now he sees how a wet summer results in harvests failing, just as a prolonged dry spell can mercilessly wither crops on the stalk.

As summer reaches its height their outings become shorter and take place later in the afternoon. No one wants to be out in the heat of the day, let alone galloping over dusty highways. Antonio is by now completely recovered and writing at full pitch, *sonate* and *cantate* for the court, and in the time that remains to him each day answering the requests of an ever increasing number of admirers. He lets Paolina keep an exact record of the date of starting each new piece of work, not only to prevent duplication but also to ensure that the same piece is never sent to near neighbours. This way of organising things allows him to keep up with the demand for his work.

But the moment arrives when he has to come up with something really new. It is for one of his best patrons, the Bohemian Duke Wenzel von Morzin. The fact is that the duke is a close advisor to the Habsburg Emperor Charles VI, and who knows, this might even lead to writing for the emperor himself one day. Morzin has a weakness for Vivaldi's *concerti*. The trips with Paolina to the river landscape of Mantua have provided the composer with plenty of inspiration for a piece to be called La Primavera, 'The Spring'. Vivaldi has fun creating a vivid instrumental sketch of the riverbank with its birdsong, the murmur of water and a breeze rustling through the trees and reeds. So he is displeased to find his first listeners fail to recognise his musical landscape. After the required polite applause the small, informal audience of court noblemen return without further comment to their conversation. But they are not getting away with it this time. The priest asks outright if they have understood the imagery with which he has just regaled their ears, and they have to admit they have not. A short, explanatory talk follows, in which Vivaldi gives examples of musical description, and finally the light begins to dawn. Never before have they heard such things. He gets the orchestra to repeat the entire performance, and now it is greeted with exclamations of recognition and delight. For this is surely more than mere entertainment – this is art!

Later in the evening, when Antonio and Paolina are alone together again, he takes the opportunity to share his concerns with her. 'The trouble with people nowadays is that they have no imagination,' he moans. Paolina looks up from her reading and nods. 'Perhaps you should write it all down for them,' she suggests, returning to her book. A surly Antonio continues packing up a set of new work ready to post to the Bohemian duke. He is curious as to what his lordship will make of it.

The summer creeps by with agonising slowness. As always, things are quiet at court, far too quiet for Antonio Vivaldi. He misses Venice, the dynamism, the tourists, the gossip and the plotting and scheming, and most of the theatre. Although, if he is honest, life in Venice was hard; every production meant new financial risks. Here at court he can grow old gracefully; put on operas to his heart's content without ever worrying about the cash side of things; all that is taken care of in advance. And he has no competition. So what more could he want?

Maybe it is just that. Perhaps it's the lack of competitive

edge that makes life here so dull, without the tension and excitement that rivalry brings. For was it not always a fantastic moment when, halfway through a production, his father breathed a sigh of relief and announced they had covered their costs again? From then on, everything that came in was profit! Stress and risk, were not these the ingredients that made life really worth living? Perhaps this is the thinking that underlies his decision to shelve the role of impresario for the coming season; it will save him a whole lot of trouble. The novelty is gone from the role of *Maestro di Capella da Camera*, and his motivation is on the ebb. Antonio finds himself openly pondering an answer to the question posed him so often by Paolina, 'What are your future plans?'

Choirmaster to the imperial court at Vienna? Or a similar function in Rome? He has no idea. But reading the latest letter from his father, he realises how much he has been missing his family. And the *Figlie di Coro* and all the sights and sounds of a Venice rampant with a life all its own. The city in the lagoon begins to beckon more and more poignantly, exerting such a pull on his heartstrings that he finds it increasingly difficult to maintain his loyalty to *Langravio* Filippo.

So that it comes to Vivaldi as a sign from God when an imperial courier appears one dark January day with the news of the death of Eleanore Magdelene Theresa, widow of the late Emperor Leopold I and Charles VI's mother. Protocol dictates that theatre performances be cancelled the length and breadth of the Habsburg Empire and people observe a statutory period of mourning.

It is a few weeks before the priest summons together the courage to talk to the Governor. For the umpteenth time Vivaldi offers the count his condolences for the loss of the empress-mother. Prince Filippo immediately senses that this is not the main reason for the priest wanting to speak with him. Digressing endlessly from his message in order to soften it, Antonio tries to tell the prince what he already knows; that there are no theatre performances on the programme at present and he has thus no opportunity to fulfil his artistic commitments or practise his skills.

It is plain to Filippo that he cannot hang on to Antonio Vivaldi, however much he wishes to do so.

'I can offer you unlimited leave of absence,' says the prince. 'Not, of course, for the same honorarium, but at least you will have the freedom to come and go as you will. You may retain your title, and I hope that we shall one day welcome you back to our theatre with a new opera.'

Antonio can hardly believe his ears. He thanks the prince profusely. He had never dared dream he would get away so easily, and now shares with the Governor his plan to depart at once for Venice.

The prince demonstrates his high regard for the composer by sending him off with a sum in payment, in addition to letters of recommendation for the imperial ambassador in Venice. Filippo seems to find it quite natural that Paolina and Anna should be accompanying Vivaldi back to the Republic.

'She is of inestimable value to me,' the priest assures the prince. 'Without her my work descends into chaos.'

Filippo laughs and entertains his own quiet thoughts. He cannot guess what sort of relationship exists between these two, but he has never been privy to an unsavoury rumour concerning them. And that is surely quite something in such a tiny enclosed world as the court, where nothing goes unnoticed and the slightest whisper is soon blown up out of all proportion to reality.

When towards the end of February the roads become passable once more, a carriage belonging to *Langravio* Filippo is seen leaving the *Palazzo Ducale*.

Annina is the only occupant looking over her shoulder with tears in her eyes. She will miss her singing lessons, in spite of the promise by the priest that in Venice there await them more than a thousand singing teachers, all falling over one another to instruct her.

6

It is still very cold on the water, despite the sun shining more strongly than might be expected for the time of year. A brisk spring breeze keeps the sails well filled, sending the vessel and her passengers scudding across the foam at a good five miles per hour towards her destination. Wind and sun have quickly dissolved the fine mist that covered the lagoon this morning, and there ahead shines the city – La Serenissima in all her shimmering splendour! Annina has already forgotten Mantua. From the railings she strains to make out the strange silhouettes of buildings mysteriously adrift upon the green waters. She is enjoying the boat trip, completely unperturbed by the rise and fall of the deck on the swell. How thrilling to ride the waves so fast and soundlessly; no dust, no hooves rattling over cobbles, and especially no stinking, sweating travellers all packed together like sardines in a tiny carriage. The only sound out here comes from the gulls swooping and crying in the vessel's wake, diving now and then into the spray to catch a gleaming fish.

Antonio Vivaldi does not share her enthusiasm for the voyage. He hates the pitch and roll that keeps his stomach churning and he'll be happy only once his feet are on dry land again.

Paolina gazes at the horizon with mounting excitement. She is back! Home again in the city that she was forced secretly to leave. With head held high she now proudly surveys the forest of towers and masts growing nearer and taller with every moment. She has always known she would return but never dared hope the time would come so soon. And yet her future feels full of uncertainty. She glances at the pale priest, staring grimly and silently ahead. Poor Antonio, she thinks, and her heart goes out to him.

Vivaldi has no plan of action beyond his return to Venice. What then? Paolina's greatest fear is that Giambattista Vivaldi will step straight back into his former role. For where will she fit in then? Antonio has dismissed her concerns and promised her everything will be all right. She will have to see. For the moment she can revel in her freedom. Radiant, she drinks in the sea air and licks salt from her lips, a delicious sense of liberation flooding her being. At last! In Mantua she had lived as a prisoner, always with the sense of being spied on by her father and brothers, ever fearful of one of them coming for his pound of flesh. It had been impossible for her to walk carefree through the streets. Here in Venice she could wander at will again, without constantly having to look over her shoulder.

Back on *terra firma* Antonio stretches his limbs. Home at last! The Venetian dialect is music to his ears. All the passenger baggage is unloaded and Vivaldi finds a face among the porters he vaguely recognises so as to avoid getting fleeced. It is a short walk from the wharf to the Vivaldi home, not too long even for the porter. Annina, holding on tight to her sister's hand as they follow the priest, gazes wide-eyed around her. It is so hectic on the quay she is afraid they will lose sight of Antonio; surrounded on all sides by weird new sights and sounds and smells, she cannot catch breath until they turn off left into a quiet street, leaving the hustle and bustle behind them.

It is an emotional family reunion. The Vivaldi household has been prepared for Antonio to arrive today or tomorrow, but his sudden appearance on the doorstep still takes everyone by surprise. *Mamma* Camilla makes no attempt to curb her tears and only very reluctantly allows him to escape from her arms. She has grown older, thinks the priest. The rest of the family embrace him one by one and just as warmly. He then introduces them to Paolina and Anna, and the two are at once accepted into the bosom of the family. Giambattista opens a bottle of wine and pours everyone a glass. This is a day of celebration! Paolina and Annina watch quietly from where they sit together at a corner of the huge dining table. Antonio is the centre of attention, revelling in answering all the questions fired at him. His father uncorks a second bottle and tops everybody up.

Antonio basks in it all. A real homecoming; the warmth of the fire, his family around him, the enticing aroma of his mother's casserole and of course all this surfeit of attention.

Paolina gives Annina a smile and winks to reassure her that all will be well, although it is a while before Giambattista Vivaldi, as head of the family, remembers formally to offer his two guests lodging.

It is a bit of a squash, but for the moment the sisters have a roof over their heads.

Later in the evening, when they are lying side by side in bed, Paolina stares into the darkness. Anna has fallen asleep at once, exhausted from the travelling and all the new impressions filling her little head. Paolina knows they cannot stay here long; the house is just a bit too small to accommodate them. The welcome extended by these people has been genuinely warm. And yet some instinct tells her this atmosphere cannot last. Camilla's eyes upon her had been too sharp, too enquiring. But perhaps Paolina is mistaken, she reflects, maybe she is imagining things. In any case, she resolves tomorrow to discuss with Antonio what his plans might be.

Early next morning Paolina, weary from a poor night and having slipped out of bed carefully so as not to awaken Anna, lets herself into the priest's workroom. The white, plastered space in which she finds herself is not large; hardly to be compared with his chamber in the palace of Mantua. But it is practical. There is enough natural light, and the place is perfectly neat and tidy! The table is empty and only the shelves are laden with bundles of carefully stacked paper and some beautifully bound books. She touches nothing, deciding instead to go back outside and explore the neighbourhood.

Upon her return a good hour later, Paolina hears voices in

Giambattista's workroom. Father and son are deep in discussion. 'Ah, Paolina,' Antonio greets her with a wide smile. 'Did you sleep well?' Without awaiting her reply he continues, 'You're just in time; my father is asking me all kinds of extremely awkward questions.' Beneath his outspread hands lies the ledger in which Paolina has been meticulously recording all his financial business. He pushes it over to her side and gestures for her to approach the table.

'Is something wrong?' she asks shyly.

Giambattista throws his son a sceptical glance and proceeds to question Paolina, indicating those passages and abbreviations that are not clear to him. She supplies him with such swift and concise answers that he soon shuts the cash-book. 'My compliments,' declares Giambattista in admiration. 'A man may consider himself fortunate indeed to have at his side such a gifted woman.'

Antonio beams and Paolina feels herself blushing.

'Oh well, it's only my job,' she says lightly.

Giambattista looks at them both as if expecting some further elucidation, but when none is forthcoming he simply opens a drawer, stows away the ledger and turns the key in the lock.

This was what Paolina was dreading. Turning to Antonio, she asks quickly in a low voice if she may have a word with him in private.

His eyes darting to Giambattista, Antonio takes her arm. 'We'll be back in a moment, father,' he says, leading her outside.

'It is extremely kind of your parents to put us up,' begins Paolina, immediately they are out of sight, 'but I am afraid the house is too small for us all. I should like to come to a proper arrangement with you concerning the work I do, without stepping on your father's toes. To be honest, I'm afraid there's no room for me here!'

'Nonsense!' laughs Antonio. 'My father is getting on in life and is certainly not looking for extra work.'

'You think not?' Paolina's voice is laden with doubt. 'You saw how he locked away your ledger. He might be pleased enough with what I did in Mantua, but that's all past history now. He is master of the house here, and will be for some time by the look of things. The house is too small and Anna and I shall only be in your way. And even if the worst were to happen and the situation were to change in the near future, sooner or later we will be put out on the street. I can't let that happen. I'd rather we packed our bags and left now.'

'Come on, Paolina, don't be so melodramatic. We're friends! Do you think I'd really just let you leave? Give me a few days more to sort out my plans. Once everyone gets to know I'm no longer chained to the court at Mantua there's a good chance all kinds of offers will start coming my way. An opera in Verona, Ferrara or in Florence again, or Rome, or possibly even Vienna!'

'Don't you think your father will want to go with you?' she asks.

'No, of course not. My mother wouldn't let him! A short trip of a couple of weeks maybe, but whole months off and away somewhere? She'd kill the idea stone dead. And who would be there to support me then? You know I don't want to go anywhere without you. I've grown too attached to you, and you know yourself you have made yourself indispensable.'

Paolina stares at him, her face alight with joy. 'It is so sweet of you to say so.'

The couple walking arm-in-arm across the square in the lengthening shadow of San Zaccaria attracts no particular attention. They might just as well be brother and sister.

In the post is a letter from Vicenza requesting Antonio to put on *Armida al Campo d'Egitto* as the last performance of the season there. The opera was a success a couple of years previously in the *Teatro San Angelo*, and again in Mantua. For a while this remains the only commission that comes in; apparently the news has not filtered through to all the theatres that Antonio Vivaldi is available for work again. In principle this poses no problem; the years in Mantua have lined the coffers extremely generously.

Upon his return Antonio handed in the letter of recommendation from the Governor of Mantua to His Excellency Count Johann Baptist Colledo, Austrian ambassador in Venice. His reception at the embassy went off in a most convivial and relaxed manner but did not lead directly to any offer of work. Antonio watches impatiently for the post each morning, but it never contains anything much apart from routine orders for new compositions. Venice, meanwhile, remains his home port, and with this in mind Antonio has asked his father to keep an eye open for some roomier accommodation; a residence more fitting to the status of a well-known composer whose music is now played throughout all the courts of Europe. His father, practical and grounded as ever, sees no reason for expansion. 'What's wrong with this place?'

Antonio grasps the opportunity to discuss Paolina's situation. His father fully appreciates, of course, that there is more between this woman and his son than mere friendship. Paolina is an intelligent lady, and an attractive one. 'But, he warns, 'you must not forget that as long as you are a priest you must behave accordingly.'

Antonio is offended. 'Nothing has occurred of which I need be ashamed, or for which I need account to others.'

'Fine,' responds his father. 'But can't she live somewhere else? That would leave plenty of room in this house and save me from having to keep swatting all sorts of rumours. People ask questions, you know.'

'Maybe it's about time my other sisters found a husband and moved out. That would make some room in the house, too,' snaps Antonio. 'And what do you mean, rumours? Not a soul in Mantua questioned what Paolina did for me. She was simply accepted as my assistant.'

His father sees this conversation is leading nowhere, and even though he is in charge of the family finances it is Antonio who brings in the most income.

'Very well, we can look about quietly for a bigger place.

As long as it's not too dear! And as for Paolina; while you still live under my roof, I keep control of all the administration. I've always done so and I see no reason for things to change now. I like to keep an overview. It's fine by me that she keeps things up to date while you are away. She's proved herself more than capable of that. I am sure she can make herself useful in other ways, and don't forget she has a sister to watch over.'

So Giambattista has the last word. Antonio has to be satisfied with his father's agreement in principle to a larger house, although it will be a good year before the whole family moves to a spacious corner property on the *Ponte del Paradiso*, close to the enormous church of *San Maria Formosa*. The neighbourhood represents a clear step up in the world, but his father finds the rent of seventy ducats per month outrageously astronomical.

Paolina has been shrewd enough in her summing up of Giambattista, and so it comes as no great surprise to hear from Antonio that his father does not yet wish to relinquish any of his tasks. She contents herself with the fact that the domestic arrangements are going fairly smoothly and a larger house may even be on the horizon. For now she resigns herself to the situation. She can in any case concentrate her full attention upon Annina, who is transforming herself day by the day into 'Anna'. The child has so set her heart on becoming a famous singer that Antonio has made enquiries among his associates, hoping to engage a music teacher for her. He has lighted on Catherina, who is older, has her theatre career behind her and would welcome a little extra income. She agrees to give Anna singing lessons, but Paolina is beset by doubt as to the wisdom of devoting so much of the girl's education to singing. 'What do you think, Antonio, is she really talented enough to justify it?'

He finds it difficult to come up with an honest answer. Anna is obviously highly motivated and definitely has a feeling for music. But at such a young age there is simply no way of knowing how the voice will develop.

Anna has no such scruples and her self-confidence and the expression she puts into her music lessons prove enough to impress her new teacher. The child's little face is unblemished, and if only the pox passes her by she will turn into a lovely woman.

The audience in Vicenza adores Vivaldi's opera. Paolina has stayed at home as Giambattista expressed the desire to accompany Antonio; the trip is a short one and Paolina has no desire to play gooseberry. She has decided instead to spend her time fruitfully renewing her acquaintance with Venice, and has already discovered some bookshops. Intoxicated, she breathes in the scent of freshly tanned leather, hand-made paper and ink. Hours pass by unnoticed as she immerses herself in her own world, leafing through new publications by Racine and Corneille or a reprint of Art Poétique by Nicolas Boileau-Despréaux. Very occasionally she indulges herself and buys a copy of something, clasping it to her breast like priceless treasure as she runs home on winged feet. Then, in the privacy of her little room, she gently opens the new book and luxuriates in the pleasure of reading. Outside these precious hours she looks after Anna and helps Mamma Camilla in the house. It is an uneventful life, but she feels safe and both she and Anna are thriving. Anna has made friends with one of the girls next door. They go to school together and share their secrets.

Mamma Camilla gets on quite well with both sisters. Anna is a sweet-tempered and polite child, less common a phenomenon than it once was, as Camilla is fond of remarking. The older woman accepts Paolina as a good friend of her son, no more than that. Although Camilla asks herself increasingly what the true nature of their relationship might be. She has her suspicions, purely intuitive, and follows her feelings just as any other woman and mother does. The truth is that from the first moment she saw them together she has had her suspicions and these have only grown in the meantime. She tries to lure things out of Paolina with apparently innocent but carefully aimed questions. But she has met her match in the younger woman. Paolina is extremely chary of Camilla's cheerful, bantering tales of her own past; using her infallible instinct for any attempt to trap her into similar revelations, Paolina is always ready with a neutral, courteous reply. But Camilla is not to be put off. One day when everyone else is out and the two women are preparing beans together at the kitchen table, she catches the young woman completely unawares.

'Why don't you just admit outright that you and my Antonio are Anna's parents?'

The words hit Paolina like a thunderbolt. Her heart misses a beat. Somehow she manages to act as if nothing is wrong and continues mechanically in her task. Oh, my God! After a moment she looks up briefly at Camilla. 'What was that?' she asks. Her only chance of buying time is to feign ignorance. She feels the blood rising to her cheeks and does not dare to look Antonio's mother in the face.

'You can't fool me, child. I've had eight children myself, so I've an idea how a woman treats her own flesh and blood. Antonio is my firstborn and he was a delicate child. Only God knows how I prayed for him when he was little. He was so often ill. I've sat and nursed him in my arms many a long evening, afraid it was to be the last. To be honest, I never expected him to grow to manhood; such a pathetic wee creature he was. But then he suddenly picked up, got stronger, put on weight. Mother Maria! My prayers were answered! I remember as if it were yesterday the way he played with his brothers and sisters. He was always different, he must have been destined for what he is today. But you know what? That look he used to have in his eyes, the way he did things, I see it all again now in Anna! She might not have his red hair, but her eyes, her smile, the way she bites her lip while she's dreaming up a reply, even the way she wipes her nose – it's my little Antonio all over again. And don't you tell me it isn't!'

Paolina is beside herself. She stares blindly at the beans, lays her trembling hands in her lap. What can she say? All these long years she has carried her secret deep inside her and not a soul has ever guessed it. She knows she can't deny it now, not lie to

Camilla. But what should she do? Admit everything?

The emptiness, the shame, is awful. If she could only she could get up and run away! To flee! She bites her lip, fighting back the tears that threaten to overwhelm her. What should she do? What in GOD'S NAME should she do?

But it is *Mamma* Camilla who gets to her feet, comes round to Paolina's side of the table and gently holds her to her breast. She feels a shudder pass through the younger woman's body as the sobs begin. At first a single, silent shock, and then another, until the weeping overwhelms her, shaking her whole frame and purging her of all the years of silence.

'Hush, hush, my child,' whispers Camilla, aware of her own part in all this anguish. Stroking Paolina's hair, she rocks her back and forth in her arms until she feels the worst is over. As the sobbing subsides, Camilla releases Paolina from her arms, fetches a glass of water and offers her a handkerchief. She then brings a chair up close. Paolina blows her nose and takes a sip of water, still avoiding Camilla's eyes, afraid of a new fit of weeping.

'Don't tell anyone,' she whispers, hardly audible. 'Nobody! No one knows. Not Anna and not Antonio. Please, I beg of you, tell NO ONE!'

Camilla soothes her, promising faithfully to keep her secret. With one last sob, Paolina begins her story.

'It was my fault. It happened at Epiphany, eleven years ago. I had been employed for a couple of months in a good position; chambermaid with a well-to-do family. When I first bumped into Antonio that night at the masked ball I thought he was simply dressed up as a priest. How could I have known he really was one? Everyone was wandering about in the most outrageous disguises and I thought he had got stuck in his role. We got talking, and I found him fascinating. In any case, it was a wonderful evening and we had drunk a lot of wine. The attraction was mutual; at least, that was how it felt. Next morning I gave myself a really good douching. I thought that would do the trick, although I know better now. When I realised I was pregnant there was only one way open to me and that was to leave town. In the meanwhile I had discovered that your son was truly a priest and I did not want to disgrace him. But I couldn't disown the child, either. After all, she didn't ask to be conceived.'

Tears are coursing down Paolina's cheeks again and Camilla lays her hand softly on the young woman's shoulder.

'My first thought was to go home, but I had just run away from there to come to Venice. My father was a drunkard; the whole situation in the house was hideous. So I decided to go to my aunt, my mother's sister. I finally found out where she was, living in a derelict farmhouse just outside Ferrara. Luckily, she was kind. I was able to confide in her and I had Anna there. But it was impossible for me to remain there. You see, Anna was hardly a year old when my aunt contracted the pox and soon after died of it. My uncle begged me to stay, but before my poor aunt was properly buried he had proved that he couldn't keep his hands to himself. When I refused his advances he threw Anna and me out on the street. I had no money, nothing. So I had no option but to return to my father in Mantua. My mother had walked out on him by then and nobody knew where she'd gone. She had never cared about me, and I'd never missed her. Home was a worse nightmare than it had ever been. The house was a tip and the shop – my father is a wig-maker – was just as bad. Of course, my father was pretty taken aback to find me suddenly appearing on the doorstep with a baby in my arms. But I told him the whole story and he agreed to take me back if I looked after the household and my two brothers. For the sake of appearances we would stick to the story that Anna was my younger sister, and to this day even my brothers know no different. For years everything went okay. My father even stayed off the drink for a while. I don't know what made him start again. Anna was getting older, and I was worried because I didn't at all like the way my father looked at her. And I was right, because one fine day he nearly had his way with her. My father had been on the booze and I'd slipped out for a moment, leaving Anna alone at home with him. And, my God, I only just got back in time before he got his filthy drunken hands on her.'

The memory is enough to reduce Paolina to tears again and, for her part, Camilla can hardly bear to listen.

'Then your son Antonio appeared, completely out of the blue, and rescued us! I had met him earlier that year and we saw each other regularly at the market. But this dreadful day he brought help with him from the palace and they took Anna and me back with them. That's how we got away from that hellhole, never to return. Antonio and I became good friends, and not a day passes without my thanking him in my heart. But I should not like him or anyone else to learn of my secret, for I am sure it wouldn't do him any good in his position. And Anna doesn't know, either. Perhaps she sees me more as a mother than a sister, but it's better for her sake, too, that she does not know she is the daughter of a priest and a silly, unmarried mother.'

Paolina dries her tears and takes a deep breath, then lets it out in a sigh of relief. For the first time in her life she has been able truly to share her story with another human being. It feels as if a lead weight has slid from her shoulders. Raising her eyes, she finds she can now meet those of Camilla, and they are filled with compassion. 'My poor child,' whispers the older woman, shaking her head slowly. 'Come to me,' and she embraces Paolina as she would her own daughter.

'Your secret is safe with me, my child. No one shall ever hear from my lips the things you have told me. My God, I had no idea you had suffered so much.'

She holds Paolina close awhile, and then goes quietly to the stove to make cups of hot chocolate for them both. Setting the steaming beakers down on the table, she points at the piles of half-shelled beans. 'Shall we get this lot done before the hungry horde returns?'

Paolina nods, blowing her nose again. The two women finish their task in silence. Paolina has given Camilla plenty to think about for the time being. What saddens her most, now she knows she is Anna's grandmother, is that she may never let the child know how close she is.

After the opera performance in Vicenza all goes quiet. So, on his father's advice, Antonio accepts an invitation to provide two pieces of work for the *Teatro San Angelo*. He is not wild about this commission; as far as the second opera is concerned he's happy to write just the final act.

Modetto has already tested the waters regarding how interested the Vivaldis might be in reinvesting their impresario energies in the theatre. So far they've refused, especially in the light of *Teatro allo Moda*, a merciless satire on the world of Venetian theatre, published by an author who prefers to remain anonymous. Antonio is pretty superior about this defamation; it might have been funny, but for the fact that he himself appears on the first page in the caricature of 'Aldivi'. Nobleman Benedetto Marcello, co-owner of the *Teatro San Angelo*, is soon revealed to have written the comedy. Much later, his brother Allessandro Marcello will offer his apologies to the priest on his brother's behalf, only to have them airily waved aside with a smile. But deep in his heart Antonio is wounded at yet another blow to his pride. Is this the sort of humour that appeals to the people of Venice? What has Benedetto to offer apart from some slick penmanship, the gift inherited from his mother Paolina Capello, a real poetess? The man's scribbled down a couple of elementary musical exercises in his life, nothing more.

But the little volume of witticisms probably owes its huge success to Marcello's acute observation of the scenes described. Antonio's father has a good laugh at it, anyway, and so does Paolina. But then it is not their names that appear on the front page.

Later that spring the whole family is preparing to move house, when in the middle of everything a commission, albeit not a very challenging one, comes in at last from the mainland. The *scrittura* is for a *dramma pastorale* to be premiered on the birthday of the Habsburg empress. The request comes straight from the imperial governor in Milan, and very probably thanks to the letter of recommendation from *Langravio* Filippo! *La Silvia*, as the pastoral is to be entitled, provides a good excuse for escape from the Venetian summer. This time Paolina comes along with father and son, even though the stay in Milan will be a short one; not only because Giambattista has decided to pay a visit to family in Brescia on the way back, but also because the house on the *Ponte del Paradiso* will be ready a week later.

The new house is magnificent! The space, the light that pours in through the exquisitely designed gothic windows... and on a corner too! For the first time the Vivaldis enjoy the sheer pleasure of not being crammed in between other dwellings. No shouting and screeching of next-door children hammering up and down the stairs all day. But what nobody can get over is the light! Almost every room has its own window, an unimaginable luxury! It's agreed that Antonio will take a work-bedroom on the middle floor, where Paolina and Anna have their own large, shared space. Antonio stares ecstatically out through his huge window, straight into the eyes of Maria, Mother of God, a statue that for centuries has adorned the entrance to the *Calle del Paradiso*. He feels sure She will bring him luck and he makes the sign of the cross in gratitude.

 The house does not lie directly on the square, and in many ways this makes a quiet and welcome change. But on the other hand, one has to walk farther to fetch water and do the washing. This is the only adverse comment anyone can find to make about their new home and everyone seems happy. Before winter has time to arrive the house is fully furnished. Paolina has had a bookcase made of lovely warm, dark wood. By now she has accumulated a small library of books by various writers, mostly French poetry but also discourses on the Roman Empire and the ancient Greeks. In Antonio's room she has appropriated a lovely corner by the window where together they spend whole days and evenings in silence, she deep in her literature, he searching for new melodies.

 Most such evenings end with a tender goodnight kiss, after which Paolina withdraws to her own quarters to slip into bed beside the warmly curled up, sleeping Anna. But quite often she and Antonio begin talking only when the evening is far advanced. Perhaps she mentions something she has read, or he the idea for an opera. Or he has stumbled on some quite new musical device and wants to tell her in detail about the composition. They also share their thoughts about the future and Anna. In fact, they never seem to run out of things to say and it's often deep in the night before sleep overtakes them, ending their discussions.

Mamma Camilla does not break her promise, although she cannot help showing her affection for Anna. Paolina says nothing, but is deeply thankful to Antonio's mother.

The new theatre season dawns, this time with nothing on the programme by Antonio Vivaldi. His patience is being severely tested; it seems all the impressive commissions are passing him by, and he doesn't like it. Paolina takes this to be the reason for his increasing tetchiness as the winter nights draw in.

Giambattista is beginning to get slightly concerned, too, although there are no financial grounds for this. The lessons that Antonio gives to various students, in addition to the usual commissions, provide a decent income. But still...

The long wait is momentarily alleviated with a performance of Antonio's oratorio *L'adorazione delli tre re magi al bambino Gesù* at the Jesuit college of *San Fedele* in Milan. Vivaldi suspects he has been given this commission as a result of *La Silva*, and Giambattista is of the opinion that he has been far too hasty in accepting it, for the job will bring in neither much money nor esteem.

But Antonio is too restless to refuse and puts on a *splendido* oratorio. Great is his astonishment at the end of the performance to recognise among the Jesuits an old familiar face: *Maestro* Francesco Gasparini!

'Sublime work, Vivaldi,' is the old man's hearty greeting as he enfolds the priest in a warm hug. 'My thanks, good Gasparini, how nice to see you. Tell me, how are things with you?'

The two men have maintained a somewhat erratic correspondence, their last exchange of letters predating Antonio's departure from the court at Mantua. It is almost a decade since they last saw each other. Gasparini's hair has gone completely grey, but his curls are as wild as ever and his eyebrows just as bushy. His face has grown fuller, he seems to have put on weight generally, and yet he seems bursting with energy.

'You have developed, Vivaldi. That sounded a lot better than the last time I heard you play.'

'Thanks not least to you,' Antonio replies with candour.

'Rubbish,' Gasparini gruffly brushes aside his acknowledgement. 'I always said you had it in you. But tell me what you're up to. I hear you have left Mantua?'

'Yes, almost two years ago already,' says Vivaldi with a sigh.

'And what have you been up to since? Your contribution to a performance of *Tito Manlio* in Rome is still fresh in my memory. It's a pity you weren't there, it was extremely well received.'

'You heard it?'

'I did indeed. Excellent work. I had expected to hear more of you in Rome.'

'That was my wish too, but apparently I'm simply not well enough known there, or perhaps they don't like my work.'

'You have never actually been to the city, either, have you?'

Vivaldi shakes his head.

'But my dear friend, why don't you come? Pay us a visit as soon as you can. I have a wonderful villa. Well, a bit different from in Venice.' He bellows with laughter. 'Really a splendid place. It belongs to the palace of the Borghese family. Rich as Croesus! And I get on famously with the Princess Maria Livia Spinola Borghese – or better said, she with me!' He winks roguishly at Vivaldi, who can do nothing but return his smile.

'Look here,' continues Gasparini, producing a creased scrap of paper. It is the announcement for his opera *Astianatte*, due to be staged over the coming weeks in Milan. 'Look what it says,' he points his plump forefinger at the final lines of text. "Francesco Gasparini, *Maestro del principe Borghese*". How's that for a game of soldiers? Not bad, eh? Especially in view of the fact that I hardly do any composing for them. It's a strange life. I left Venice for a quieter time, do you remember? And what happens? I seem to have got busier than ever. But there you go. It's hard to say no as long as people are paying me well for my services. But enough talk. Make use of my invitation and I'll take pleasure in introducing you in Rome. As long as there's so much money floating about, there's work enough for all of us!'

The auditorium has emptied while they have been talking, and the lights are going out one by one.

'Come on, Vivaldi. Let's get a move on before they shut us in for the night! See if we can find a bottle of wine to open somewhere.'

'Ah, Rome,' sighs Paolina romantically. Antonio has returned later that evening to recount his meeting with Gasparini. He is somewhat under the influence, and not only of the ancient city. He recalls how years ago he suggested to his father that he should go to Rome, and ended up in Florence instead. But this personal invitation from Gasparini will sweep aside his father's objections. Paolina's face is flushed with excitement. Rome! She must make sure that, whatever happens, she goes with them this time!
"*Terrarum dea gentiumque, Roma – Cui par est nihil et nihil secundum*",' quotes Paolina by heart from Martialis, the poet of ancient times. 'Rome, goddess of lands and peoples – comparable to none and to whom nothing compares.'

'I think those days are long gone,' counters Antonio prosaically. 'Apparently there are cattle grazing on the *rostra* and more ruins than houses still standing.'

'I don't care!' laughs Paolina. 'I just want to see it.'

Because this trip is one made more or less on the off chance, the father does not feel inclined to accompany his son; he has enough other business to attend to. Giambattista does not want to admit the true reason for his withdrawal, his unwillingness to leave Venice for any prolonged period of time. Camilla has suffered a bad chill this winter and taken weeks to recover. The fever went down fast enough to avoid lasting damage; her husband nipped it in the bud, and *Mamma* Camilla is getting well again. But she is still a little tired and weak. For the first time in her life, she finds running the house too much for her.

Antonio's parents were both born in the same year, some sixty-seven years ago. Both are well enough schooled in life to know that it does not go on forever. How many members of their family, friends and neighbours have they not lost already? They are grateful to have reached their present age without too many problems. Neither mentions the word death, but after so many years at one another's side each knows exactly how the other feels, and Giambattista, decide without a murmur to stay near at hand.

For the first time he shows real enthusiasm for Paolina's presence among them. He knows she will care well for his son.

After a short of exchange of letters with Gasparini, who again confirms his pleasure at Antonio's anticipated visit, the priest replies that he expects to arrive in mid-May. A perfect month for travel, not too warm or dusty on the road and not too cold either! Paolina has arranged all their travel documents, packed their bags, and they are ready for off. Camilla is sufficiently recovered to assure Paolina that she need have no worries concerning Anna, and the child's beaming face confirms this. She is quite content to stay at home and be spoiled by 'Nonna', as Camilla has asked the child to call her. And Paolina is delighted to grant them all the obvious pleasure they find in each other's company.

The Holy City is still licking her wounds after the Spanish War of Succession. The absolute power once held by the Pope had been long on the wane, but the final blow came with both French and German authorities showing their disregard for the Holy See. The

Peace of Utrecht in 1713 has resulted in frontiers being redrawn all over Europe. The new arrangement seems to satisfy every country involved, but in reality Europe is a volcano waiting to erupt. Despite the practical impotence of the papal state, the Vatican remains at the centre of the political world stage and every country that counts is represented here. The first decade of the eighteenth century sees the shutting down, on the orders of the Pope, of all public theatres. Opera performances may now take place only behind the closed doors of palaces belonging to cardinals, princes and the exiled Queen Maria Casimira of Poland.

Once the theatres are granted reluctant permission to reopen to the public, impresarios pick up where they left off, performing music they were forced to abandon ten years before, and Scarlatti, Bononcini, Pollarolo and Gasparini come resoundingly back into fashion.

As far as Vivaldi is concerned, both theatres and music are relics of another age, as dim and dusty as the ruins of the *Forum Romanum*. Paolina is in her element here. Her hands glide tenderly over worn marble and mossy mosaic. She gazes mesmerised at the toppled columns and crumbling triumphal arch and between the cow-pats sees spread at her feet the great city in its heyday. Antonio cannot share her ecstasies; it is almost inconceivable to him how the heroes of his operas ever lived here. Rome is an extraordinary conglomeration of diverse architectural styles. Between the rubble of antiquity and mediaeval urban villas arise her great *palazzi*. Baroque fountains, opulent flights of steps, imposing churches, all add up to an explosive visual expression of counter-reformation support for the strength, and particularly the power, of the Catholic Church. Yet, despite her renewed fervour for building, Rome remains a pale shadow of her former self. At this moment she boasts only a tenth of the inhabitants that lived here during the days of the Empire. Great areas of the city lie derelict and empty, grazing ground for cattle and goats, the empire now only of snake and lizard. Nobody dares to set foot at night amongst the old walls of the city, for it is well known that every kind of ghost walks there!

The most impressive villas lie along the Tiber and in the northern quarter of the city, pleasantly situated beneath the spreading shade of ancient trees. Every courtyard and newly landscaped garden is enhanced with classical statuary excavated from the ruined city. Against the old city wall and half enveloped in verdant shadow, Antonio and Paolina find Gasparini's richly decorated residence. More a palace than a villa, the building is superb, and this time Antonio Vivaldi cannot suppress his admiration. The house of his dreams! Might his own then also come true? It is a reverie suddenly dissipated by the sound of Gasparini shouting a greeting as he lumbers down the stairs to meet them.

'Welcome, Vivaldi, welcome. Now, who is this you have brought with you?' The sight of Paolina makes his eyes widen but his bow to her is one of the greatest respect. Antonio introduces her as his friend and travelling companion and she is welcomed with equal warmth. Gasparini is soon full of talk concerning all the plans he has for them over the coming few days. There will be meetings, concerts. But on the agenda for this evening is a trip to the theatre!

After the performance, Antonio is introduced to the Marquis Federico Capranica, owner of the eponymous theatre. As they talk, and whilst Federico scrutinises this priest with his halo of auburn hair, Gasparini lavishes praise on Vivaldi's work. Frederico knows the name well enough and the timing just happens to be right, for he is looking for new talent. With an increasing surfeit of ageing composers in his theatre, he is keen to hear what Vivaldi might have to offer him. Gasparini has already reckoned on things developing in this direction and invites Capranica to his house five days later. 'Your Excellency may then make acquaintance at your leisure with the virtuoso talents of our Venetian violinist and composer.'

With an amiable nod of the head the marquis makes plain his pleasure in accepting this arrangement. What the great man does not yet know is that later in the week Gasparini will have his house full of aristocratic music lovers, potential patrons, and even a cardinal. Francesco has drawn up a programme which will offer Vivaldi a prime opportunity to display his art as a violinist, and will also allow several of Gasparini's own young pupil singers to appear in the spotlights. Nothing gives the venerable composer more pleasure than to offer 'his pupils' a little bunk up the ladder.

Paolina has agreed with Antonio that she will stay in the background as much as possible. It makes sense to her that Antonio gets all the space he needs, and anyway she has soon discovered that while men like to talk with one another about music, they enjoy flirting with her even more. And she finds it tedious to have to keep on explaining her 'business' relations with the priest.

There is time in the mornings for the couple to go out together. Antonio loves most of all the shady woodland of the great park to the north of the city. High on the hill is a plateau where he can walk quite a way without getting too short of breath. At some points this path offers a magnificent view over the Tiber and he can see miles along the ancient *Via Flaminia*, the highway which brought them to Rome. From the same vantage point Paolina can imagine Roman legions marching northwards, clouds of dust billowing behind them along the paved road.

One morning they drive to the Vatican where Antonio finds himself just one of a multitude of clergy, milling like ants around the vast square. Priests and monks, nuns and lay brothers, bishops and chaplains, ecclesiastics from every land assembled here at the fulcrum of the Catholic world. The only one to remain out of sight is the Pope and Antonio does not have the patience to wait for an appearance, any more than to stand in a long queue to view the famous frescoes by Michelangelo. Another time, maybe.

Their stay in Rome lasts a good month, during which time Vivaldi meets many new people and each time is astounded anew at how they know him by name and appreciate his work. Just a week before the couple are due to leave comes the good news. The Marquis Capranica wishes Vivaldi to produce an opera for the *Teatro Capranica* this coming *carnevale*.

Other, smaller commissions will undoubtedly follow, Gasparini assures Antonio. 'Why don't you come and live in Rome?' suggests Francesco. 'You can sit out the rest of your life here quite happily; opportunities aplenty!' With a laugh, Antonio thanks his old mentor, by now also a dear friend; once again he has been of inestimable help to his former pupil. 'I shall give it serious consideration,' promises Vivaldi.

Paolina warmly embraces the veteran composer. They have got to know each other well over these last few weeks and she has grown to like him very much. 'What a treasure!' she exclaims to Antonio later. 'So sweet, the way he helped you. He must be terribly fond of you.'

'*Ercole sul Termodonte?*' Giambattista repeats the title of the opera that Vivaldi plans to stage in Rome. 'That's an old one. If I remember rightly Antonio Sartori once set it to music. Couldn't they have come up with something new?'

Antonio is not so worried. At the end of the day, a good story is a good story. His challenge lies in the fact that this opera requires an all-male cast. There is no place for women in the theatres of the Holy City and it is *castrati* who take the soprano parts. This gives Antonio a chance to revisit his arias from another perspective.

Impresario Modetto has stopped by again, still looking for someone to fill the seats in his theatre. He is disappointed to hear that he too must do without the Vivaldis for the coming season. The news that Il *Prete Rosso* is to produce an opera for Rome has spread like wildfire and Vivaldi's reputation is still growing.

Giambattista finds himself on the horns of a hefty dilemma. The stories brought home with them by Antonio and Paolina have a certain irresistible charm. Camilla's health has improved to the extent that he could safely leave her alone. Recognising her husband's split loyalties, she encourages him to go with Antonio this time. Giambattista at first demurs, but it does not take much to convince him that his wife can manage without him for a little while. Camilla agrees to send for him the minute she feels the slightest chill coming on. Paolina arranges all the travel documents and, along with warm clothes, packs various remedies recommended by the chemist to keep the whole family fit and well throughout the winter. It is decided they will leave in mid-November. According to the latest forecasts, not much snow has fallen so far and the road to Rome is relatively passable. Antonio would rather arrive earlier than later, so that he has time to rehearse. His first Roman opera must not be a flop!

His first glimpse of Rome leaves Giambattista disappointed. His mental image of the city is most certainly not matched by what meets his eyes on arrival. Cloud hangs ominously low over the hills, and the city on the Tiber seems to glower darkly from beneath them. Only the multicoloured mantles worn by its many tourists lend colour to Rome.

Rehearsals go fairly well, despite the rigid attitude of the *primo uomo*. Vivaldi believes this artiste to have as wide a range of notes in his repertoire as the average *prima donna*, so the musical experience is not so dissimilar from what he is used to. But the atmosphere in the theatre is a great deal less buoyant without any women around.

Rome romps her way through the long December nights. Concerts, theatre and banquets stud the diaries of the rich and famous, and before spring comes to the city everyone who is anyone will have been introduced to one another. Vivaldi cannot quite put his finger on what marked the breakthrough, but since Gasparini's introductions, including a fine concert performance for the Borghese princess Maria Livia Spinola, he feels for the first time in his life treated as an equal by the *Veneti Nobili* present in Rome. He is received as guest of honour at an ambassadorial reception at the

Venetian embassy and introduced to friends and allies of the Republic. The occasion swell his pride and he disports himself like a prince amongst the nobility. The only moment of awkwardness comes when he is presented to a man who looks down haughtily upon him from a great height. This tall personage, his features dominated by an immense nose, gives his name as *Le Chevalier de Saint-Georges*. Vivaldi, who has managed nimbly to extricate himself from an entirely vacuous conversation with the cavalier, later the same evening, learns the identity of the man who has bored him so. He is James III, pretender to the throne of England and Scotland, who has lived for years in exile in Rome, hoping for a chance to fulfil his ambition of reigning over his homeland. Vivaldi, with a quick glance over his shoulder at this lanky, rather sad figure standing staring into space, quips within hearing of the ambassador, 'I don't think the English are missing out on much.' But His Excellency keeps a straight face; he's been around long enough to know better than to make jokes at his guests' expense.

The premier of *Ercole sul Termodonte* brings in the New Year with a bang. The musical style is new to Roman ears, but they must have been ready for it; night after night the theatre is sold out. Giambattista is enormously proud of his son, who plays his part with more and more gusto with each successive performance. Just as delighted at this result is the impresario, who, the moment the curtain falls on the last night, writes out a new commission for Vivaldi to stage next year.

Once *Ercole sul Termodonte* closes, father and son Vivaldi take the opportunity to attend a few other theatres in the city. But the only highlight for them is a performance of Francesco Gasparini's *Dorinda*, dedicated by the composer to his patron Princess Maria Borghese. The production takes place before a select audience in Gasparini's own huge house. Here Antonio makes his first real acquaintance with Cardinal Pietro Ottoboni, vice-chancellor of the Roman Catholic Church. Ottoboni, who also hails from Venice, is a great lover of music who pours all his income and subsidies into the weekly concerts at the church of *San Lorenzo*. The church stands right next door to his *Palazzo della Cancelleria*, which is constantly milling with musicians and singers, there for a short or longer stay.

Vivaldi hears from the cardinal that he has much enjoyed Antonio's opera and looks forward to next year's offering. The two men discover an instant rapport, and friendship quickly blossoms between them.

'So you are off back to our Venice?' enquires the cardinal. Nodding, Antonio sees Ottoboni's eyes light up. 'Well, that's going to work out very nicely,' he says, lowering his voice and drawing Antonio into a corner where they can speak in privacy. It appears that, as patron of French interests for the Holy See, Ottoboni has been privy to the news that France is about to dispatch a new ambassador to the Republic. 'This individual is a very good friend of mine and he will certainly consider it an honour to adopt you as imperial "house composer". I shall keep you informed!' promises the cardinal in conclusion.

The trip to Rome could not have ended on a happier note: homage, accolades, new work and fine prospects. But for Vivaldi it is the recognition accorded by him by his own embassy that really counts. Nothing can cloud Antonio's sunny outlook on the way home; not the endless rain, the constant drenching that leaves them all sneezing and shivering in their sodden clothes, not even the miserable bouncing against one another all the way in a lurching stage-coach.

'Carry on like that and I'll write an opera for you,' Vivaldi threatens Anna with a gust of laughter. This spring he has discovered for the first time in her voice all the ingredients needed to make a fine singer. And for a girl of thirteen she has good control, too. Anna has never for an instant abandoned her ambition. What began as a game now starts seriously to take shape. The priest uses his theatre contacts to find her occasional work with a choir so that she gets a sense of how things go. Despite his frequent warnings about the fierce competitiveness of the world she longs for, nothing deters Anna. On the contrary, she is convinced she already sings and acts better than many a *seconda donna*. it makes Vivaldi smile to hear her speaking like this. She has the right personality for it, in any case, but it takes more than that to play a leading role! Nevertheless, he has enough faith in her potential to devote more time to nurturing her talents by giving her lessons. Her reading improves and he introduces her to new music.

It warms Paolina's heart to see the deepening bond between father and daughter. Every now and then it occurs to her she might disclose her secret. Should she tell them?

But something always holds her back. What would be achieved?

Anna never asks about her father, the wig-maker. It seems that she has no desire to delve into such things and appears perfectly happy as she is. And so, still guarding her secret, Paolina watches with a smile as Antonio leads the girl in playing her violin. I'll let things be, she thinks. All is well.

Antonio has unexpectedly received a commission from the *Ospedale della Pietà*. It gives him great pleasure, not only in view of the honorarium he has secured with very little trouble, but more because for years he has not worked with the *Figlie di Coro*. He had never imagined he would hear again from the management; after all, it was he who ultimately turned his back on the *Pietà*. He is curious to know how things have gone with everyone since. Now that Vivaldi's reputation has grown so much beyond Venice, the *Congregazione* would like to have him back. But the management is realistic enough to understand that the honorarium due to the priest nowadays is not what it was ten years ago.

A creative solution is found in a sort of contract whereby Antonio delivers two *concerti* per month for himself to rehearse with the choir. Of course, these works may be written anywhere in the world, including Rome, so long as the *Pietà* does not have to pay the postage.

The management is prepared to offer Antonio one *sequin*

per *concerto*. Given Vivaldi's rate of productivity, this fee is quickly earned and gives him a vague sense of pleasurable satisfaction that he is at last being compensated for all the extra unpaid work he did for the *Pietà* years ago.

It's a joy to see everyone again even though his welcome is less exuberant than once it used to be. Perhaps Vivaldi has stayed away too long this time, for even Anna Maria fails to fly into his arms as of old. Her teenage years lie far behind her and at twenty-seven she has been appointed *Figlia Privilegiata*, so that she too may now give private lessons. The same light shines in her eyes but she is more poised. The unruly mass of hair that framed her adolescent face is now trained back as though to tame her own feminine spirit. Yet it is with the same rapt attention Vivaldi recalls from years ago that she watches everything he teaches and demonstrates, and when her turn comes to play there is the same grace and flair in her fingering and the movement of her bow. That she stands head and shoulders above her peers is plain and comes as no surprise to Vivaldi; it only confirms the predictions he made long ago.

As the summer nears its end a letter arrives for Antonio from Amsterdam. He recognises neither the handwriting nor the name of the sender, Michel-Charles Le Cène. Reading it, it becomes clear to him that the writer is the son-in-law of Estienne Roger, his Dutch publisher.

The letter is a sad one. It appears that Estienne died the previous summer, leaving his business in the hands of one of his daughters, Jeanne Roger; Vivaldi has had some correspondence with her over recent years, since Estienne's eyesight began to fail. A few lines on he reads that Jeanne too is dead, having passed away in December. The publishing firm was then apparently taken over by businessman Gerrit Drinkman. But this man was denied a long career as a publisher, for after a couple of months he also was dead. The widow Drinkman had then sold the publishing firm to Michel-Charles Le Cène, who had planned to run it with his wife, Françoise Roger. But God willed differently and Françoise had in the meanwhile also abandoned this earthly life, leaving the letter-writer alone. Needless to say, he would now continue the business along the same lines as his father-in-law, and he hoped the honourable Don Vivaldi would continue to place his trust and his business with him.

Vivaldi carefully folds away the letter full of tragic obituaries. He is sorry to hear of the death of Estienne. It seems odd he had never mentioned his son-in-law, either verbally or by letter, but Estienne must have had his own reasons for this. With a sombre sigh Antonio lays the envelope upon the pile of manuscripts that form the basis for his next piece of work. This is far from finished and after today's letter he wonders whether his *Opus VIII* will ever see the light of day. The fact that he has never heard of Le Cène keeps nagging at him, and he decides to take his time in answering the letter.

His Excellency *Comte* Jacques-Vincent Languet de Gergy, new French ambassador to the Republic of Venice, has summoned Antonio Vivaldi to the embassy. The ambassador has still to make his first official appearance before the *Doge* and Senate, but in anticipation has begun furnishing his *palazzo* and meeting all kinds of people recommended to him. On the long list of names appears that of Vivaldi, also known as *Il Prete Rosso*, underlined twice. His good friend Cardinal Ottoboni has emphasised to him the extraordinary abilities of this priest as virtuoso violinist and composer. 'Innovative, energetic and full of surprises' is the description in the letter from Ottoboni, a lively enough pen-portrait to more than ignite the curiosity of *Comte* Languet de Gergy.

In the huge, echoing and still empty hall Antonio watches the Frenchman. His Excellency stands with eyes closed before the window, lapping up the last faint rays of autumn sunshine. Arrayed in a fantastic richly powdered wig and sumptuously embroidered silk jacket and breeches, and leaning on his gold engraved walking stick, the count is a statuesque personification of all the pomp and ceremony of the French court.

Vivaldi clears his throat quietly and waits for the ambassador to emerge from his reverie.

'Gorgeous, that light,' remarks Jacques-Vincent in soft, warm tones, 'just there, as it strokes the façades and roofs and is reflected in the windows and the water.' His hands follow his words, caressing like sunbeams the contours of Venice, almost feminine in his tenderness of expression. 'The Venetians are greatly privileged to live in such a place,' he adds with deference. '*Monseigneur* Vivaldi,' the ambassador raises his voice, looking for the first time directly at the priest, 'I have received extremely good references recommending you as composer of music for the embassy, should I so desire.'

De Gergy indicates the violin-case that a servant has taken from Vivaldi and set down nearby. 'To ask you to play for me would be to cast doubt upon the integrity of my references. But might I invite you to provide an interesting programme for myself and a few guests this coming Sunday; in the role, of course, of composer to the French ambassador? I am quite confident we shall arrive at an amicable arrangement qua conditions.'

Without awaiting an answer, Jacque-Vincent Languet de Gergy's gaze returns outside.

'Your most humble and devoted servant.' Vivaldi bids the count farewell and follows the servant to the secretary's office, where His Excellency's right-hand man makes him an offer so generous that the priest would not dream of disputing it.

Reclining voluptuously in the cushions of the homeward-bound gondola, Antonio reflects on the unprecedented ease with which he has signed the contract, and sends his mental compliments to the ambassador! Venice is indeed the most beautiful spot on earth, and above it is Vivaldi's star, still in the ascendant!

Along with his father and two good musician acquaintances, Vivaldi serves up a varied concert that proves nothing less than spellbinding to the ears of Languet de Gergy, his wife and their new friends. Indeed, the cardinal has overdone his praise not one iota, thinks Jacques-Vincent, returning his full attention to the bounding rhythms emanating from the redhaired priest.

Just as last year, father and son Vivaldi decide to set off in good time for Rome. Not only in case the winter weather turns bad and delays them, but also because Federico Capranica has asked no fewer than three times that they arrive for the beginning of December at the latest. This thanks to the increasing requests pouring in for private concerts to be given in the many *palazzi* of Rome. Antonio has received a similar summons from Cardinal Ottoboni, and this one he is clearly unable to turn down.

Paolina finds that the arranging of travel documents is becoming a less and less complicated procedure, as if the Senate is proud to allow 'her' Vivaldi to show the rest of the world what sort of music comes out of Venice. Camilla feels well enough to show her still hesitant husband the door. She is taking life more calmly these days, confining herself to keeping an eye on how her daughters and Paolina run the household. It took her a while to get used to this, and at first the girls could do nothing right. Good grief, how were these daughters of hers ever going to be able to look after a husband, let alone a family? But as time goes on she begins to see she was being unreasonable; they are all doing their utmost, after all. And the place is always clean, which is a lot more than may be said for every household in the neighbourhood!

Taking leave of Anna does not go well this time. She wants to come with Paolina and Vivaldi because she knows she will miss her singing exercises with the priest.

'Maybe next year,' Antonio promises. But she isn't persuaded, and marches off the quay in a huff without saying a proper goodbye. It is a dismal day and the boat passengers soon duck into the shelter of the cabin to warm themselves beside the glowing stove. 'What a joy it would be to be able to go all the way to Rome by boat,' mutters Giambattista later as, drenched in Padua rain, they try to find a seat in the unheated stage-coach. Via Ferrara and Bologna, the coach rattles endlessly on along the old Roman road, the *Via Aemilia* that later turns into the *Via Flaminia*. It is eleven days before Rome comes into view and an insipid sun offers the exhausted travellers a half-hearted welcome.

Federico Capranica grants Antonio just one and a half days to recover from the journey. A whole scheme has been drawn up for the Venetian priest, taking in rehearsals, invitations and performances. Naturally, *Il Celebre* Vivaldi does not have to accept every single invitation; people can come to the theatre. But still, Federico has marked with a star those names he considers most significant; all belong to the oldest families in Rome. According to Frederico, a small concert here and there will guarantee patronage and commissions.

Antonio informs Ottoboni that he is back in Rome. By return comes an invitation to come and dine at the *Palazzo della Cancelleria*, which Vivaldi accepts with alacrity. He holds the cardinal in high esteem, not only for his likeable character, but also for his great understanding of music and his ability to discuss it with anthusiasm.

There are no fewer than twenty people around the huge dining table. In one way, Antonio is disappointed, for he had naively hoped he would be pending this evening alone with the cardinal. On the other hand, this company of musicians and philanthropists soon proves diverse and colourful enough to provide an entertaining evening, and one upon which fine wine flows very freely indeed. It is the early hours of the morning before Vivaldi is deposited at the apartment rented by Capranica for his Venetian guests. Much against his will, the coachman helps the priest up the steps and bangs on the door. It is a long while before anyone answers and by the time they do, Antonio, supported by the sulky driver, has to all intents and purposes fallen asleep on his feet against the wall.

A drowsy Giambattista comes personally to the door, behind him Paolina carrying the candelabra. Shaking his head, the father tries to sling his son's arm about his neck, but Antonio is a dead weight. So Giambattista enlists the aid of the coachman and together they drag the insensible man inside and straight to Antonio's room on the same floor. A worried Paolina follows them and bends over Antonio as he lies on the bed. 'Nothing the matter with him, girl.' growls Giambattista, 'Too much to drink, that's all.' He manoeuvres the coachman out of the house and crawls back into bed. Paolina tries to undress the priest, but Antonio, completely lost to the world, puts up such a fight at every turn that in the end she decides just to loosen his collar and pull off his shoes. After making sure he's warm, she leaves the room, but still feels unnerved enough to leave the door open a chink.

The following morning Antonio amazes everyone by appearing halfway through breakfast and sitting down brightly at table. He looks tired and crumpled, but says he feels fine. His father is nonplussed, Paolina merely relieved.

'A very pleasant evening,' is Antonio's verdict, delivered as he dips bread into his coffee. 'Oh yes, and Ottoboni has invited me to play some of my work tomorrow evening at a private concert,' he continues, with a full mouth.

His father brings up the subject of the schedule. 'It's all getting very busy, son.' Antonio slurps his coffee. 'You're right, father, but who am I to refuse a *concerto* for the Pope?'

'What did you say?' Paolina busts in. Giambattista blinks. Antonio surveys them both archly, as if he is already attending daily audiences with the Holy Father. 'Is there something wrong?' he asks blandly.

This is all wonderful! What a golden opportunity, what a crowning achievement! He is eternally grateful to Ottoboni for laying on this small but oh so important concert for him. Ottoboni must have known what a favour he was doing him. 'Don't expect too much,' the cardinal had warned Vivaldi. 'The *Pontifex Maximus* is a music lover but he's no spring chicken, and he's none too fit these days. Confine the concert to a single piece.'

Antonio enjoys this trip to the Vatican. No joining long queues of pious pilgrims but instead a cordial welcome by the cardinal. He accompanies Ottoboni through the right-hand entrance in the imposing façade and enters the Papal complex. To the outsider this is a complete maze, but Pietro Ottoboni, at home here for more than thirty years, leads Antonio up and down staircases, and along endless corridors and galleries. Every wall is covered in frescoes or paintings and in the twilight the figures seem to come to life. Vivaldi asks the cardinal for leave to regain his breath before entering the presence of the Pontiff. His hand pressed against his chest, the priest tries to moderate his heart rate and regain his composure. 'An inconvenient condition,' he explains to the cardinal, who has stopped and is scrutinising his new friend. 'Another couple of seconds,' whispers Antonio. Concentrating all his attention on a fresco to calm himself, his eyes alight upon a warm-complexioned angel playing an antique violin. Just like Anna. He nods at the cardinal; he is ready now.

'Wait here,' Ottoboni instructs in a low voice, walking up to a door behind which, Antonio realises, the head of the church must be cloistered. Vivaldi feels the same tension in his abdomen that afflicts him before every performance; only this evening his audience is just one man. The cardinal knocks twice and opens the door. He steps quickly inside, the door is closed and all goes quiet. A theatre is always filled with clamour before a performance; at best a great buzz of excitement. Here there is dead silence. Antonio takes a step forward and has to resist the urge to press his ear against the door. Just as he is about to move again, the door swings open and a servant ushers him inside. Head high, Antonio Vivaldi enters the private quarters of Pope Innocentius XIII. The room is utterly different from anything the priest could have imagined. It is much smaller, for a start, and actually very simple. No canopied throne, no hall lit by glittering candelabra, and no dozen servants poised anxiously at the slightest raising of the Papal finger to do his bidding. The head of the Holy Roman Church is seated behind a large table. To his left sits Ottoboni, and there is no one else in sight but the man who admitted Antonio. Surrounding a candelabrum at the centre of the table are stacks of books and manuscripts. In the corner of the room stands a simple bed. The walls are lined by bookcases and hung with numerous small paintings. On the floor beside the bed lies a small mat, but otherwise the broad wooden planks are bare. In another corner smoke rises delicately from an incense burner, spreading much-needed perfume. For the smell generally pervading the place is awful, and not even the incense can disguise the stench of decay. It is the aura of mortal sickness, the same that hangs in the ward at the hospital of the *Incurabili* in Venice. Antonio stands eye to eye with the Holy Father and finds before him the pale and decrepit face of a friendly but feverish old man. Can this really be the Pope, and is the mighty Church of Rome truly directed from this sad, nondescript little cell?

But what is the protocol? Should he go to the other side of the table to offer his respects to the Pontiff? Antonio looks at the cardinal for guidance. Ottoboni gets to his feet and introduces Vivaldi to the Pope. The head of the church smiles congenially at the priest and extends his hand, embellished with its sumptuous papal ring. Vivaldi walks round the table, kneels respectfully and kisses the jewel. The priest receives a blessing and is disappointed to experience no special sensation of spiritual grace. Subdued, he gets to his feet and opens his violin-case. Whilst Ottoboni chats animatedly with Pope Innocentius XIII, Antonio swiftly tightens his bow and sets his instrument under his chin. His diffident, enquiring cough is answered with a confident nod from Ottoboni and, without further ado, he inundates the Pope's private rooms with music so charged with energy that even the spirits of the ancient Vatican must be roused from their lethargy. But Antonio's playing stops just short of that achievement, for Ottoboni soon signals that it is enough. The face of the old man at the table is aglow; his cheeks flushed with pleasure and emotion.

For a moment he has forgotten his pain. Slowly he claps his hands. 'Wonderful,' he says softly, directing his words straight at Vivaldi. 'I have never heard playing like it, certainly not from a priest.' He sighs. 'The mercy of God be upon you.' Coughing, the Pope raises a finger to his servant and the man steps forward to hand Vivaldi a purse. Bowing deeply, Antonio runs his fingers over the soft leather, trying to discern what sort of coins lie in the heavy pouch. Pope Innocentius XIII has meanwhile been seized by a violent fit of coughing and Ottoboni indicates to Antonio that they must leave. This they do rather hastily, for the coughing does not abate. Antonio makes the sign of the cross before the sick man, anxious to leave the Pope alone as quickly as possible out of respect for his vulnerable state. People capable of appreciating his music so intensely always evoke the deepest empathy in him.

Priest and cardinal retrace their steps in silence.

'That did him good,' pronounces Ottoboni at last.

'Is his condition serious?' asks Vivaldi sombrely.

The cardinal nods, putting his forefinger to his lips. 'Speak to no one of this,' he instructs Vivaldi in hushed tones. In reply the priest again makes a sign of the cross. This, he confides to the cardinal, has been one of the most remarkable meetings of his life.

But there is not long to reflect upon his encounter with the Pope, for a new season of rehearsals is underway. Vivaldi has produced just the second act of the first opera to go on this *carnevale*, entitled *La virtù trionfante dell'amore, e dell'odio, overo Il Tigrane*. All his attention is focused on the last performance of the season; it must be the highpoint of the year.

The libretto for *Il Giustino*, written fifty years before by the late Count Nicolò Beregan, has been set to music once already. Giovanni Legrenzi did so in 1683, and Antonio was just five years old when the curtain rose on *Il Giustino* at the Venice theatre *San Salvatore*. It was a major hit. Both Domenico Scarlatti and Tomaso Albinoni had since put on their own successful productions but, as usual, Vivaldi has chopped bits out of the plot, altered, amended and improved it. It is now, to all intents and purposes, a completely new story, one that takes place in Constantinople in the early years of the East-Roman Empire. With its classical elements of romance and rivalry, war and peace, and the ultimate triumph of true love, this is to be Antonio's new masterpiece.

The leading roles are to be taken by the same singers as last year; almost all, predictably enough, pupils of Francesco Gasparini. As always, Antonio has carefully apportioned the arias, yet this time not to the satisfaction of *castrato* Giovanni Ossi. The diminutive mezzo-soprano playing the role of Emperor Anastasio thinks he has been badly done by. Thus, as so often happens, the majority of rehearsal time is spent arguing over the length and number of arias and how and in which costume people will appear. This sort of bickering tests Antonio's patience to its utmost. Mostly he manages to contain himself, but on this occasion it all gets the better of him.

Giovanni Ossi is determined he needs an extra aria at the opening of the second act; why else is he onstage at that moment? As an extra, or to enhance the set maybe? Ossi even threatens to withdraw from the show, and only the pacifying presence of Frederico Capranica keeps the rehearsal on course. Although Vivaldi does have to compromise and promise to insert another aria. This sort of thing would never have happened had he had charge of the theatre. With gritted teeth, but nevertheless the ease and fluency of the *maestro*, Vivaldi sketches a new aria of ten lines for the 'emperor'. *Allora*, this'd better keep him happy!

It does. The entire production is a hit from beginning to end and Rome resounds with praise for the Venetian composer. His music is so different from what everyone is used to, and such a change for the better. From now on, everything put on in the theatres of Rome must measure up to the Venetian's 'Lombardy style'.

But the Roman public will have to wait for more; on the seventh of March the death is announced of Pope Innocentius XIII. The Vatican, along with the rest of the city, is now plunged into mourning, and all theatres are closed for a year.

With a shudder of sympathy, Antonio recalls the mild

features of the sick old man who listened with such intense pleasure to his all too short concert. Such is life. Antonio Vivaldi quickly concludes that Rome has little to offer him for the time being. The moment has come to turn for home again.

Actually, the death of the Pope suits Giambattista rather well. The closure of the theatres in Rome means that he and Antonio will not have to make the journey there again this winter. Once home, they find Camilla has been in bed for two weeks. Her symptoms are very vague and not terribly worrying. She feels chilly and fatigued the whole time. The only place she is comfortable is tucked up cosily in her own bed, with a freshly heated warming-pan slid between the sheets every hour or so. Giambattista is at first concerned, and then furious. 'Why didn't you let me know?' he roars at his wife.

Camilla responds that it is nothing serious and that she would only have upset him unnecessarily. But he will not be fooled, and refuses to stir from home for the foreseeable future. The Roman adventure has produced plenty of income, enough to enable him to relax over the coming year.

Paolina is delighted to see Anna again. In four months the younger girl has grown noticeably and made the transition from girlhood to young woman. Antonio is thrilled to hear the new strength in her voice; she is clearly on the way towards becoming a mezzo-soprano. He fishes out some arias written for Giovanni Ossi from the bundle of manuscripts brought back from Rome. He thinks Anna has a similar tone and range, although nothing like the power of the *castrato*. Anna greedily gathers up the new arias and excitedly embraces the challenge of learning them by heart.

The cancelled season in Rome gives Antonio's space and time to think about the future. He knows that his mother's failing health makes him unable any longer to persuade his father to accompany him on trips abroad. But he too has had enough of travelling for now. He appreciates home more than ever, working in his own room, surrounded by his own familiar things. Rome may be imposing, but she cannot touch Venice for sheer dynamism, or for loveliness as each change of light robes her in new splendour. The sounds and smells of her, mm! He shuts his eyes and sniffs the briny air interwoven with other unfamiliar, foreign scents. The smell of eastern spices escaping from the piles of bales and boxes on the quay; tar and sawdust from the *Arsenale*; freshly baked bread, fish, charcoal, fruit... and, well, even the stench of rubbish floating in the canals. Yes, this is home!

It is to be one of the most peaceful years in Vivaldi's life. The need he once felt to prove himself in respect of the *Veneti Nobili* is all but gone. Everyone has heard of his success in Rome, and of course Antonio is not backward in letting people know what a kind man the deceased Pope was, and how His Holiness appreciated the finest virtuoso violinist he had ever heard play. There is no end to the stream of commissions pouring in, and Antonio works calmly through them one by one. As the pressure on him eases, he also begins to invest more time in Anna. She has quickly absorbed the arias brought back from Rome and impresses Antonio with her interpretation of a role, bringing to it just the right element of drama. The more he thinks about it, the more Antonio believes she performs better than Ossi, for all his *prima donna* pretentiousness. He asks his father what he thinks of Anna.

'Splendid! Where does she get it from?' applauds Giambattista with enthusiasm. 'On you go with the next aria,' he prompts the girl eagerly.

'She undoubtedly has talent,' Antonio tells Paolina later. 'But if she wants to go on the stage she has to work on her technique and volume.'

Anna, however, can't wait to steal the show this very evening; she disputes Antonio's view that she needs more volume and reckons it's more a matter of presentation. She understands as well as anyone that she will never have the power and projection of a *castrato*, but how many vocalists are there who just stand there woodenly on stage bellowing like mythological monsters, without an iota of emotion?

Sometimes she honestly has to ask herself how many singers actually know what role they are meant to be playing. Or if they have even taken the trouble to read the libretto. True, there's often insufficient time for rehearsal, and singers are more than content if they feel some small affinity with the text. But some vocalists make a real mess of it. They perform exactly the same whatever role they're given, waving their arms about as if to make sure no one in the audience recognises a character from the story but only the presence onstage of 'Il Signolo, the great nightingale', or whatever ludicrous name they've dreamt up for themselves.

Oh, how much more magnificent would be a production in which everyone really lived his or her role! Anna knows precisely how she will achieve this and is desperate to show the public what she's made of. More and more small parts are coming her way, but she never gets a chance to stand in the footlights. As a member of the choir she always has to make do with the back of the stage. But each performance increases her strength and self-confidence, and she begins to resemble a fledgling eagle poised for its first flight.

Vivaldi has asked Tomaso Giovanni Albinoni to help Anna improve her singing technique. Antonio has never been impressed by the abilities as a composer of this far too self-effacing man. For a while, years ago, they had seemed rivals. But then Vivaldi gave good ear to the new style propagated by Albinoni and soon overtook him with his energy and the vitality of his own innovation. Before long Albinoni was trailing behind.

Antonio respects him more for his pedagogic talents as a singing teacher. For years Albinoni has had a music school, and Anna would be well placed there. There a time when prospective students had to audition for a place at Albinoni's academy, but those days are gone. Since the demise of the family business, in which Albinoni had been a stockholder, he can use every penny that comes in. Three years ago he lost his wife, the gifted soprano Margherita Raimondi, and was left with six hungry mouths to feed. Every new pupil is thus warmly welcomed to his classes, and he is soon delighted to discover Anna's above-average talent. Plenty of parents, convinced they have a child prodigy, send the child to him and he spends years giving them lessons, to absolutely no effect. What a waste of his time!

Tomaso Giovanni Albinoni, Zuane to his friends, hits it off with Anna straightaway. Her sparkling demeanour and unbridled dedication reminds him of his first, long ago encounter with his wife. Margherita was just fifteen, the same age as Anna is now, when Zuane heard her sing at the theatre of San Salvatore. It makes him feel old.

Is it the memory of his wife, and her talent? Or is Anna's mere presence enough to awaken his enthusiasm? She is a pretty girl and her physique betrays the full beauty of the woman she will soon become. She has the most wonderful eyes, superb lips and perfect teeth. Her skin is flatteringly light compared to that of Venetian women. I have a role for you, he decides, judiciously burying his daydream. At last, and sooner than she had expected, Anna finds herself in the theatre of San Moise, making her Venetian debut in Albinoni's opera 'Laodice'.

'She's still not ready for it,' is Antonio's critical verdict after the performance. Going by the bravos and loud applause, the audience disagrees. Anna looks stunning and has given her all. But nobody at the back of the hall has been able to hear her. Antonio decides not to share his opinion with Paolina, and congratulates Anna on her debut. She sits in her dressing-room, accepting gratitude and gifts as if to the manner born. The same young men who after any other performance can't wait to get back to the gaming tables, stand patiently in line to pay their respects to the captivating young singer. Anna lets them wait. As far as she is concerned, all of this is just the start.

The winter does its worst. A bitter wind rakes the streets clean, and one needs a very good reason to venture outdoors. Rain makes way for sleet that reduces visibility to nil. Everyone closes the shutters and stokes up the fire to keep out the cold and, even worse, damp, and social life comes to a virtual standstill. The bad weather also prevents the post from being delivered on time, which gives Vivaldi an opportunity to catch up with all outstanding commissions. In the absence of any plan for the coming year he has begun assembling work for his eighth *opus*. Two letters have come from Amsterdam begging him for new compositions. It seems Michel-Charles Le Cène is making a serious go of the publishing business, so Vivaldi decides to give him a chance.

Antonio discusses with his father some prospective pieces for inclusion in the dispatch, and makes a selection. His *concerto* 'La Primavera, Spring', written a couple of years before, always brings back sweet memories of Mantua and goes down well wherever he plays it.

He has meanwhile expanded this concert with three new *concerti*, 'L'Estade', 'L'Autunno' and 'L'Inverno'. People love the 'Four Seasons' and it forms a perfect basis for his next publication.

Vivaldi is composing regularly for the French ambassador. Languet de Gergy and his wife are both great fans of good music and need no excuse to listen to it. Thus, Antonio receives many requests to provide work for social occasions at the embassy, even if he has to compete for these with fellow 'house composer' Albinoni.

Up until now these pieces have been purely *concerti*, but Vivaldi has now received a commission to write a wedding serenade for the forthcoming marriage of the French King, Louis XV, to be played with great aplomb at the embassy. The fifteen-year-old king was originally to wed the Spanish *infanta*, but French regent Louis Henri de Bourbon found more political expedience in marrying the boy king to Maria, the twenty-two-year-old daughter of Polish sovereign in exile Stanislaw Leszczynski. The marriage took place in Fontainebleau on the fifth of September 1725, and a week later the happy event is to be celebrated in Venice. The ambassador regales the company with far too long a speech on the golden future of France, her king and the new queen, and the guests breathe a huge sigh of relief as His Excellency de Gergy at last announces 'La Gloria e Imeneo'. Don Vivaldi wastes not a second in starting up the orchestra to play his *serenata*.

To the great regret of many a Venetian, there will again be nothing by Vivaldi in the theatres this autumn. As usual, Modetto has sounded him out, and this time Antonio has not refused outright. 'I'll have a word with father about it,' he promises the impresario.

Anna has one bit part in an opera by Guiseppe Buina and another in the production of *Agide rè di Sparta* by Porta. Once more she wins great applause and another boost to her self-confidence. She reminds the priest of his promise to write an opera especially for her, but, without deflating her too badly, he tries to explain to Anna that he does not yet consider her ripe for a *prima donna* role. Unable to accept this, she does the rounds of all the theatres on the off chance of finding a role that suits her.

Most impresarios send her away empty-handed. 'Come back in a couple of years!' is the general response. She is too young.

But one man, Guido Nesario, is not so keen to send her packing. Instead he lets his glance wander lasciviously over the supple figure of the young singer. *Che donnina!* But he is soon jolted out of his mental seventh heaven when she says she lives with the Vivaldi family.

'Il Prete Rosso?' he ascertains. Anna nods. He is very sorry, but he has nothing for her, says Guido, staring regretfully after her at the loveliness of those perfectly formed buttocks. In retreat, they seem almost to be mocking him. But no one wants to burn their fingers on an underage singer from the Vivaldi household. It would cost Il Prete Rosso nothing to report you to the Inquisition, with all the consequences thereof!

Oh well, Guido commiserates with himself; there are plenty more shapely little singers in the world whom nobody concerns themselves about.

Antonio has some unfinished business. He could certainly perform again in Rome this season, but is this what he wants? His father will not be able to come. Paolina can of course organise all the practical side of things, but who will help him with preparations for auditions, rehearsals and copying music? Who will draw up final contracts for him? He knows his father is irreplaceable. And Antonio has plenty of work here for the moment; music for the Pietà and for the French, but now also for the Habsburg ambassador. He feels a great deal fitter without the stresses and strains of travelling, so why shouldn't he just stay put in Venice? He has noticed how his father postpones any discussion on the subject. Giambattista does not want to miss anything, but now that Camilla is becoming increasingly frail he wants to take no risks, either. For the moment his place is here in the lagoon.

'I'm not going anywhere, father,' Antonio finally announces, stepping into Giambattista's workroom. His father looks up at his son and lets the words sink in. Then he pushes back his chair, gets to his feet and gratefully embraces him.

'I can't leave her alone,' whispers the old man in apology, a tear trickling over his cheek.

'I can wait,' replies Antonio softly. 'We have plenty of time.'

Although she understands Antonio's decision, Paolina can't help being disappointed. She would have liked to see more of Rome, or other places familiar to her from her reading. And in private she is really beginning to wonder whether Antonio can envisage life without his father. They do almost everything together and the son relies heavily upon Giambattisita's opinion in everything. Antonio is nearly forty-eight years old and his father seventy! Is it not about time he stood on his own two feet?

She knows she can help Antonio adequately with his business affairs, but it is as if he never allows her entirely into his world. She can't quite put her finger on it, but there is always a trace of reserve. Maybe it's her fault. It's not always easy to uphold appearances for the outside world, to pretend she is simply the priest's assistant while in fact their relationship is so much deeper.

Paolina has tried to gauge if perhaps Antonio might be willing to leave the priesthood. But there is no question of it. He is *Il Prete Rosso*! It's part of his image, his trademark. He is afraid that by relinquishing his 'disguise' he might lose credibility.

Once again she wonders seriously whether this might not be the moment to reveal to him what they share. He has never asked her about it again. Does he suspect? No one in the house, apart from Camilla, knows her secret. Yet what sense would there be in telling him the truth now?

Anna has reached an age at which she begins to enquire about her mother. 'What sort of person was she? Did she love me? Why then did she leave?' Paolina tries her best to provide concise answers to her questions, and mostly these satisfy the impatient teenager. Anna makes no mention of her 'father'; it is as if he no longer exists for her. Paolina is surprised that, as an artiste, Anna uses his nickname of 'Giraud', even though she spells it in the Venetian manner 'Girò'. Anna knows this upsets Paolina but, self-willed as ever, she ignores the fact.

Having decided to remain in Venice, Antonio weighs up Modetto's proposal that he take over the theatre again. Giambattista has finally arrived at the conclusion that this would be a good idea. The theatre is just around the corner and he still has the energy to share the leadership with his son. For Camilla, there is the guarantee of the continuing presence at home of her husband and son, for the time being at least. Vivaldi goes off in search of a suitable libretto and finds himself fired with fresh enthusiasm. Each winding street, square and canal is soon buzzing with the news: *Il Prete Rosso* is back at the *Teatro San Angelo*!

In the far north there appears on the fourteenth of December 1725 the *Gazette d'Amsterdam* in which publisher Michel-Charles La Cène advertises *Il cimento dell'armonia e dell'inventione*, 'The Hazardous

Undertaking of Harmony and Imagination', otherwise known as *Opus VIII* of virtuoso violinist Don Antonio Vivaldi.

As sales get underway, La Cène cannot believe his luck. Orders pour in from all over Europe, so that he can barely print enough copies to keep up with demand. Antonio has as yet no idea of this. He stands poised on the threshold of a period of immense creativity during which he will produce ten new operas in the space of three years.

The *villeggiatura* have come round again, summer holidays for the *Veneti Nobili*, and this year Antonio Vivaldi, Paolina and Anna themselves depart in the wake of the aristocracy. Antonio has surprised Paolina with the news that they will be spending part of the summer on the mainland.

Paolina knows the priest well enough to understand that this trip will not be purely for pleasure. And, sure enough, it soon becomes clear that Vivaldi has been invited to the court of Filippo, Governor of Mantua, to give a *serenata* for His Excellency's birthday. Anna is keen to come along this time to find out how things are with 'Aunt Angelica'.

They are in no hurry and Antonio has rented a carriage for them alone from Padua, so they spread themselves out and travel in comfort. Prince Philip still reserves a special place in his heart for the redhaired priest. They correspond regularly, and with each of his letters Antonio encloses a new *cantata* for the prince.

His new gift is a *Serenata a Quattro voci*, and it is intended that this will be performed by two of Filippo's children, Josef and Theodora. They will be joined by the Duchess Margherita Pavesi Furlani, the prince's secret love, and Duchess Maria Caterina Capilupi Biondi. Quite some time is needed to rehearse the piece, and only eleven days after the birthday has gone by does Vivaldi deem it fit for an audience. The occasion is an informal one and Filippo is clearly moved.

As is the norm, Vivaldi receives a generous fee and the group remains three days as guests at court. Paolina and Anna have felt no need to go out into the city. It is pleasant enough to have a change from Venice and the stay at court provides a nice break, but a threat still hangs over them in Mantua.

The return journey goes more swiftly than the outgoing one, and in Padua they wait for Cardinal Pietro Ottoboni, who is coming for a long overdue visit to his beloved homeland. It has taken fourteen years for the Senate to grant him permission to return to the Republic. His appointment in 1712 as 'Protector of French interests at the Holy See' had breached the Republic's rigid rules of neutrality. But now that relations with France have improved, and it has become plain to the Senate that Ottoboni's appointment as vice-chancellor of the Roman Catholic Church is truly for life, the authority has finally accepted that Ottoboni poses no threat to the future of the Republic.

Cardinal Ottoboni and his entourage arrive late in the afternoon. A number of barges have already been awaiting him for some days, so the cardinal decides to embark straight away. The wind is in their favour and the outlook clear. They can be in Venice by this evening.

Vivaldi greets the cardinal warmly, and like old friends they step together into the first barge. Paolina and Anna follow, along with one of Ottoboni's servants. The vessel pushes off from the wharf and is carried on the current in the direction of the lagoon. The cardinal is longing to see La Serenissima again, and the two men spend the voyage exchanging the latest news out of Venice and Rome. Things have been dull in the Holy City, so much so that Ottoboni can't wait for the new theatre season. The new Pope is no great lover of music. On the contrary; he is an embittered man who lives by the rules and expects everyone else, and certainly the clergy, to do the same.

So the time aboard the ferry passes in pleasant conversation, and meanwhile the table has been laid in the saloon and set invitingly with open bottles of wine and dishes of cold chicken, fish and fruit.

'Dive in,' suggests Ottoboni congenially, tasting the red Cretan wine. Along with the meal goes plenty more enjoyable talk, with the cardinal glancing out through the window at regular intervals to check on their progress. He yearns so much to be reunited with his birthplace. Ottoboni has arranged this trip in meticulous detail and knows he is assured of a daily musical interlude. He cherishes the prospect of a performance at the *Ospedale della Pietà*, but even more the *serenata* to be given by Vivaldi at the French embassy in honour of the French king's birthday. Good company shortens a journey, and they are soon disembarking by the light of a full moon. They step down onto the *Molo* opposite the *Palazzo Ducale*, where their paths diverge.

A couple of days after the official grand entry into the Republic of the French ambassador – the man has been in Venice for years, but never before with Senate permission – comes the premiere of Vivaldi's opera *Dorilla in Tempe*. This marks the end of Ottoboni's visit; he would love to stay longer, but the Pope and the theatres of Rome await him. Priest and cardinal bid one another a fond farewell and, laden with music manuscripts, for Ottoboni has had several other composers hard at work for him too, the cardinal departs Venice.

The *Teatro San Angelo* is busy this season; every visitor from the mainland who has heard of Vivaldi grabs the chance to hear the priest with his own ears. Vivaldi has also received another commission from Luca Casimiro in Florence. He accepts with mixed feelings, knowing that this time he will have to fulfil his obligations without his father's support. Actually, he has no time to travel; he is far too busy here. But the temptation! The *Teatro della Pergola* has been suffering low box-office sales and Luca needs something to pull in an audience. Just now that means Vivaldi. The honour and the fee prove an offer too good to refuse, and Antonio says he will go.

The opera *Ipermestra* is based on a narrative by Salvi and is billed as a great triumph in prospect. Giambatttista has completed as many advance preparations as possible. The production indeed does prove a stupendous success, ensuring the survival of the Florentine theatre.

Antonio rushes back, afraid to get snowed in somewhere along the route, as happened twenty years ago. On the tenth of February comes the premiere of *Farnace*, with Anna in her first big role.

General Pompeo inflicts a defeat upon *Farnace*, King of Pontes, son and successor to Mithridates and great enemy of the Roman Empire. He naturally swears to avenge himself, and so begins a drama starring Berenice, Queen of Cappadocia, her daughter Tamiri, wife of Farnace, Pompeo, and Selinda, Farnace's sister. Suicide, revenge, seduction and betrayal are the ingredients of this rich spectacle, in which Anna takes the role of Tamiri. The well-known contralto, Maria Maddalena Pieri, who almost always takes masculine roles, is playing opposite Anna as Farnace. The contralto is short and stout and has thus earned the nickname *La Polpetta*, 'little meatball'. But she nevertheless moves with enormous and surprising agility across the stage. At forty-four she is the dowager of the company, and makes sure everyone knows it! Anna likes her anyway. *La Polpetta* brings life and character to her roles, a trait she immediately recognises also in Anna, and Anna mops up like a sponge every suggestion Maria has for her.

A terrible attack of nerves besets Anna in the days leading up to the opening. She even sleeps in the theatre. At home she mopes about like a bear with a sore head, completely immersed in her role. Paolina cannot understand it, but Antonio reassures her that it is quite normal behaviour.

'Now you've an idea how things go at rehearsals,' he laughs, making the sign of the cross in self-pity.

Vivaldi has no worries about Anna. She shows plenty of dedication and has learned her part well. A healthy dose of stagefright is quite admissible, and after all this is not the first time she has performed in public.

'Everything will be fine,' he promises Paolina, who is, perhaps, even more terrified than Anna.

And on the night everything is fine. The audience loves the drama, the music, and especially the performances of *La Polpetta* and Anna. The end of the premiere sees Anna drunk with happiness, completely overjoyed that it has gone so well. Not once has her voice faltered and neither has she missed a note. And you only have to listen to them to know how the public adores her! *Farnace* runs and runs for weeks, and Vivaldi decides on the last night to repeat the production the coming autumn.

It could not have been a lovelier start to spring. Only one thing dampens the success of Anna and *Farnace*, and that is the sad news from Rome of the death of Francesco Gasparini. Just last year he had been named *Maestro di cappella* of *San Giovanni in Laterano*, the cathedral of Rome. Giambattista is stunned. Francesco was a couple of years his junior and once more he is reminded of his own mortality. His mind full of dark thoughts, he opens the ledger to assure himself yet again that the family is financially safe for the foreseeable future.

The letter from Rome has quite a different effect upon Antonio. He re-reads it in silence, praying for the soul of his old mentor. Then, with a deep sigh, he puts away the death notice, never to look at it again. It is becoming more and more difficult for him to reconcile himself to the death of those around him. Each comes as a sort of sign from God, reminding him that with every heartbeat his own end approaches. He does not share the belief held by many that he will live on in his music. He barely recognises himself in his compositions when others play them, even when the violinist is Anna-Maria from the *Pietà*. Yes, even she, who plays with such technical perfection; it is her own heart and soul she puts into interpretation of his creation. It is not his pure work that issues from her instrument, but a translation, no more or less than that.

All things pass, including the triumphs of life. Tales are reaching Antonio's ears of other spells being cast over Venice; how the public is being charmed by music from a generation of contemporary composers such as Vinci, Porpora and Johann Adolf Hasse.

A new style and fresh sound, that begins to carry audiences along with it. Should Vivaldi go with the flow, or hold to his own direction? Given the positive outcome of the previous season, he decides on the latter course. Yet deep in his heart he knows perfectly well how capricious the public can be. Stupid people! Not one of them with a thought of their own in their head. It only takes ten loudmouths to shout 'This is great stuff' for the whole mob to traipse along behind like a flock of sheep. And back he comes to his old dilemma. Compose for the people or write works only for those capable of truly appreciating them?

About a year goes by, and Antonio is again confronted with death. On the night of the sixth of May *Mamma* Camilla peacefully breathes her last. She has kept to her bed for the past few months, tired out. Gradually her appetite has diminished and she has withdrawn into herself, as if finished with this world. Each day she has removed herself a tiny bit further from the family, and every member has sensed her unsaid farewell. Weeks ago she decided that she no longer wanted to see her grandchildren, Pietro and Daniele. She desires the two teenagers, sons of her daughter Cecilia Maria, to remember her as their kind and cheerful *nonna*. Camilla is conscious of the speed of her own decline. Her mind is still clear but she has no more physical strength for life. Antonio hates to see his mother like this, cannot bear to hear her speak to him as if already from the other side of the grave. He has to take good care of himself, she says, but would he please also keep an eye on his father? The poor man will find it difficult enough without her. Antonio feels all will be well. His father is good at looking after himself and of course he, Antonio, will care for him too.

Does he understand that Camilla still sees in him the tiny,

vulnerable child he once was? The little creature, whose life hung on a thread as he lay in her arms. How good God has been to her. Her son is now a great man, reasonably healthy and a success in the world. My Antonio!

'Take good care of Anna,' whispers the old woman, moistening her cracked lips with the tip of her tongue. 'Of course, mother,' replies Antonio. 'I always do. And she has Paolina too.'

His mother fixes him with a steady gaze, as if she has something more to say to him. With difficulty she raises a beaker to her dry lips, sips, returns it to the bedside table. 'Anna is your daughter,' she whispers hoarsely, hardly able to articulate the words. There is a moment of utter silence as Antonio stares at his mother. 'So. After all!' he manages at last, nodding.

'You knew?' she asks, amazement in her still bright eyes. The priest shrugs.

'I had an idea, but Paolina denied it.'

He does not understand how she could have hidden this from him.

'She has her reason for that,' murmurs Camilla.

'Does father know?' asks Antonio anxiously.

His mother shakes her head feebly. 'I swore to Paolina never to tell a soul. But I want to be sure that my family is safe when I'm gone. Promise me that you will do as I ask?' He feels the gentle pressure of her touch on his hand. Taking her fingers in both his warm hands, he kisses her softly.

'I promise, mother. Don't worry.'

A vague smile flits across her features before her eyes fall shut, and she sleeps. Antonio sees the quiet rise and fall of the bedclothes over her chest. He runs his hand over her grey hair, and silently leaves the room, her words still clamouring in his head. 'Anna is your daughter.'

For more than fifty years Giambattista and Camilla Vivaldi have shared their lives. Of course Giambattista can look after himself, but from one day to the next his life is radically altered. A vacuum has opened up inside him, and despite the presence of his children, neighbours, acquaintances and the many others who come to pay their last respects and offer their condolences at the funeral, he feels alone, terribly alone.

All that is left for him is to withdraw to his room, pour himself some wine and play on his cello melancholy fragments from long-forgotten songs from the hills of Brescia.

Antonio has already knocked several times on his door to ask if they might play something together. But Giambattista wants to work through his grief in privacy. His solitary music-making brings back memories of a youth spent with Camilla, and a sip or two of wine makes these reminiscences more beautiful than any reality.

Antonio quickly tries to banish any sadness at the loss of his mother. To watch his father moping like this is worse for him than missing her. But what worries him most is the secret that she revealed to him. Does Anna know the identity of her real father? And does she realise that Paolina is not her sister, but her mother? Why has Paolina never told her the truth?

He does not dare to ask Paolina, for in doing so he would betray the trust between his mother and her. And yet it saddens him to know that Paolina has hidden things from him. Does this mean that their relationship is less profound than he had thought it? He makes an effort to analyse the situation pragmatically. How would such knowledge change things? A priest with a bastard child? Such things are commonplace in Rome, and here in Venice too he knows of a couple of brother monks who maintain a whole family – Although it's true they are not also world-famous composers! For the time being he decides to say nothing and keep the secret to himself. And so everything stays just as it was before the deathbed confession.

His father lets it be known he has no energy to help his son in the theatre this year. Antonio understands entirely, and thinks he too will make a restful time of it. Modetto is naturally extremely disappointed, for the name Vivaldi is synonymous with cash. And Modetto is not alone in his sorrow, for Anna too sees her career go up in smoke. What is she to do with herself over the coming year? Antonio requests her kindly not to make such a fuss. He will see that she gets a chance to perform in a suitable production.

In the meanwhile, Antonio has been approached by the Senate to take part in a mission, the highlight of which will be a meeting with the Habsburg emperor. Publication has just taken place of Vivaldi's ninth *opus*, dedicated to Charles VI. The piece has apparently pleased the emperor, leading the Senate to determine that the composer must participate in the mission. The meeting is to take place in the port city of Trieste, its goal being to convince the emperor that the town is a magnet for smugglers. The waters of the Adriatic are seen by the Republic as her own terrain and the wealth of *La Serenissima* is founded largely on taxes on goods transported via Venice. Although this has been and remains a thorn in the flesh of many traders and skippers, Venice has been able to retain her monopoly on trade until Trieste was made a free port by imperial declaration in 1719.

The Senate has voiced careful concern over this decision, but such pleas seem to have fallen on deaf ears in the powerful neighbouring state. At first Venetian customs and excise patrol boats are able to keep control of trade with Trieste. But the vessels still being built, to an aging model, at the *Arsenale* are no match for the faster and more modern ships, coming out of Dutch and English yards. The supply of goods, and thus taxes upon them, is decreasing by the year, and the future of Venice is under threat. The Habsburg Empire is too strong for the ailing Republic, whose only hope lies in diplomacy.

Vivaldi has not the faintest idea what his role might be in the context of this mission, except perhaps to regale the Roman emperor with some music. As for the Grand Count of Austria, King of Germany, Hungary, Bohemia and Spain, Emperor of Rome, and many other titles besides, a musical interlude represents the zenith of his visit to the deadly dull port city of Trieste. The harbour lies in a landscape of bare, grey hills and this tedious, endless array of docks seems utterly unrelated to the rest of the Habsburg Empire. But the emperor has a grand plan. Trieste must become the gateway to Vienna; and Charles VI has set in motion a whole raft of measures to realise this. The mission on the part of the Venetians leaves him cold. Vienna will, naturally, study the proposals put forward by the Republic and, in its own good time, respond.

But the Grand Duke is glad to have the official part of the visit behind him and looks forward to the concert by Antonio Vivaldi. Something good comes out of Venice after all! His Highness has not yet made personal acquaintance with the composer, but he is familiar with his music. He has appreciated Vivaldi's dedication of *Opus IX* and he has listened with pleasure to earlier music by the master, although he finds it far too difficult to play. The ruler of the Habsburgs is himself a reasonably competent musician. After his accession in 1711 he fully restored to its former glory the *Hofmusikkapelle*. He has at his disposal a good hundred and thirty musicians, and it is not uncommon for Charles VI himself to conduct his orchestra from the harpsichord.

Theirs turns out to be a surprising encounter on both sides. Vivaldi has had no prior notion of the musical pretensions of his Royal Highness, nor how much the sovereign appreciates his music. At the end of the concert, Charles VI bombards the priest with all sorts of technical questions concerning runs, cadenzas and style. In the meanwhile, the two Venetian ambassadors, in their train two hundred fellow citizens, chat indifferently with the Austrians over subjects reserved for such occasions. The air is full of empty compliments and meaningless babble, whilst everybody's eyes are on the Emperor and the priest, deep in conversation in the shadow of the gallery. Now and then the Emperor is seen to laugh and gesture wildly with his arms as he extrapolates some point or another. No one can hear what is being said, but as long as Charles VI is smiling the Venetian ambassadors are happy. The Austrians start looking for their dinner, the schedule is running hopelessly late. But the Emperor is enjoying himself immensely and has completely lost track of time. At last the two men part company; not, however, before Vivaldi has promised his His Majesty a hand-written copy of his *Opus IX*. After all, anyone can buy a printed edition, and in any case, Charles has his objections to a number of sections. He has clearly indicated to Vivaldi what is to his taste and what he misses in the work, and Vivaldi has promised to send him a new copy at the first possible opportunity. Charles VI, though, is determined that Antonio shall deliver it to him personally in Vienna. And an invitation from the Emperor is not one to be refused.

Once homeward bound, the Venetian mission can only be judged to have been a success. At least, according to Vivaldi. The Senate will have to dream up a more fruitful plan for getting the economy back on its feet.

It is a good year before Giambattista regains his will to live, and then he spends more and more of his time with his few remaining friends. Whenever he returns home, it is to the imagined sound of Camilla's voice welcoming him across the threshold. The pain goes on and on. The house begins to get on his nerves and he has the urge to flee; just get as far away from here as possible. Does Antonio fancy another trip to Rome?

But time has not stood still, and Rome has become a closed chapter for Antonio. He understands from Cardinal Ottoboni that 'The theatre there is dominated by music from Naples.'

Antonio has another suggestion for his father. 'Why don't we go north instead?' he asks, pointing at the bundled stacks of manuscripts lying patiently waiting for a year now. 'I have a little parcel to deliver in Vienna,' he grins. 'If we go in that direction we should find a few addresses at which we are welcome.'

Over the years he has built up a solid group of clients, some but not all of whom have visited Venice. Invitations to play in palace and castle have also been accumulating, and until now the priest has held back on these. But now that Giambattista has itchy feet again, he is tempted to follow some up. The two men consider the practical aspects of their new travel plans and decide to set off in the autumn, returning in spring and thus avoiding the heat of summer. It is no difficult task to persuade Paolina to accompany them; she is more than ready for a break, and sets about preparations with verve and enthusiasm. Passports are her top priority, and then arranging leave for Giambattista, who is still a member of the orchestra of *San Marco*. Working from a list compiled by Antonio, she writes to counts, dukes and princes informing them that Don Antonio Vivaldi would like to pay them the honour of a visit. Very soon the replies start coming in, to the effect that the priest will be most welcome! Preparations take all summer, but by then Paolina has also drawn up a reasonably lean travel schedule. They persuade Anna to come along too. There will be plenty of work for her on the way, promises Antonio. She is not so sure.

Just as they are due to depart, Antonio's sees a house to let on the *Canal Grande*. It is not quite the palace of his dreams, but it does lie on the water, near the Rialto and a number of theatres. The rent is almost double that of their present accommodation. Antonio decides to say nothing to his father, and consults only Paolina. She loves the idea, so Vivaldi goes ahead and signs the contract without further ado. The house will be theirs at the beginning of May the next year. Paolina trims the travel schedule so as to be back in time to direct the removal. What a surprise that will be for father!

Well and truly ready at last, they leave for the mainland. They make a short and very practical stop at Treviso, where a greedy public is treated to a revised edition of Vivaldi's first opera, *Ottone in Villa*.

And then they are off again, on the road that takes them over the Alps and into the uncharted territory of Germania.

7

Vienna, November 1729

The massive stone walls of the city stand neglected and half-derelict, as if everyone has forgotten how faithfully they stood firm against the Turkish troops forty-five years ago. Only the oldest inhabitants can still recall the months-long siege of Vienna by Grand Vizier Kara Mustapha. The rapidly marched advance that announced the Grand Vizier's intention to stable his horses upon the grave of Saint Peter in Rome had caused Pope Innocentius XI the greatest consternation. Vienna was the last bastion of the Christian world against this furious horde. And what would be the result should the capital city of the Roman Emperor fall into the hands of Ottoman Empire troops? The Pope had finally managed to convince the King of Poland, Jan Sobieski, to come to the aid of his Christian neighbour. In September 1683, Kara Mustapha's army had suffered a thorough defeat. Then there followed a mad pursuit of the last remnants of the aggressor, that ceased only with the liquidation of the last Turk. The Christian soldiers celebrated their victory, and Vienna immediately began regeneration efforts.

The wealth and power of the Habsburg Empire has since attained a level at which any attack upon the capital is thought impossible. The threat nowadays comes from within. Her old walls are showing signs of fatigue, hairline cracks appearing in buttresses that, thanks to the zealous programme of rebuilding, now barely contain the city.

The *Hauptstrasse* is so busy that the stage-coach can only move at walking speed through the suburbs. From the bridge spanning the River Wien, Vivaldi has a good view over the city dominated by the *Steffl*, as the Viennese affectionately call the splendid dome of Saint

Stephen. Step by step the carriage makes its way towards the city gate of *Kärnthner Thorn*. Here the coachman turns left and drives on past the theatre. Vivaldi smiles. Now he feels at home, despite being unable to decipher a word of the German chatter all about him! The vehicle comes to a halt in the courtyard of the *Hofburg*, and Vivaldi and company are able at last to step down and stretch their stiff and aching limbs.

It has been a long journey, with many delays along the way. Snow alternating with rain rendered the roads very slippery. At one spot the highway had even been partially blocked by a landslide, a mass of mud and rubble making it almost impassable for the coach and horses. Grumbling incessantly to himself, the coachman had been forced to unharness the animals and walk them to where the surface was intact again. And then all the passengers had to follow suit, wading through the mud and waiting for the coach to be dismantled and transported piece by piece to firm ground before it could be reassembled. All in all a pretty time-consuming operation. It cost the company an entire day before, chilled to the bone and covered in slurry, they were able to resume their journey.

But this morning Vienna is in sight, and everyone has put on fresh clothes for their arrival. Antonio is looking forward to renewing his acquaintance with the Archduke of Austria and introducing him to his father, Paolina and Anna. A servant conducts them into a vast, unheated hall, filled with people patiently awaiting an audience. Subdued whispering; everyone is weighing up the others present, trying to guess what might be their reason for being here.

A good hour passes and the little group from Venice is getting fidgety. Anna sighs audibly and is visibly bored. Giambattista dozes. Paolina has a book with her, but can't concentrate on the contents. Everybody looks up expectantly at the sound of a door opening at the far end of the hall. Could this be the emperor?

Alas, no, it is the same old clerk who slouches past once more without a word. Now and then he addresses someone so discreetly that, try as they may, no one else can hear what is said. The ruler of the Habsburgs is clearly a very busy man. By the time three endless hours have crawled by, Venetian enthusiasm for this mission has seriously cooled. Antonio is tired of pacing up and down and has taken a seat next to his father. Anna hums scales to herself, and Paolina has finally got immersed in her book.

Antonio must have dropped off to sleep for a moment too, for he has not heard the approach of the servant now tapping him on the shoulder. 'Don Vivaldi?' enquires the man stiffly. Antonio gets to his feet and the man bows before him. The priest feels momentarily light-headed.

'A thousand apologies, Don Vivaldi, but *Herr Kapellmeister* is no longer able to receive you today. I shall show you and your company to your quarters.'

'*Herr Kapellmeister?*' responds the priest, outraged. 'I am here at the personal invitation of His Episcopal Highness Charles VII!'

Entirely unmoved, the manservant returns, '*Herr Fux* will receive you tomorrow morning. Would you kindly follow me!' It is as good as an order. Vivaldi and company find themselves humbly trailing behind the man to a side wing of the *Hofburg*, where the 'sisters' are given one guestroom and another is allocated to father and son. All but Antonio collapse gratefully upon their beds. A real bed, with clean sheets... a thing unheard of since their departure from Venice! Deeply disconcerted, Antonio stares of the window and notes the descending twilight. It will take more than clean sheets to calm his nerves. Why does the emperor not wish to see him? Did he take too long in responding to his invitation? Should he have come sooner? Had the monarch wished more promptly to take delivery by hand of the manuscript of *Opus IX*? The night is a long one for Antonio.

Only towards the end of the following morning are father and son Vivaldi shown into the presence of Johann Josef Fux, composer and choirmaster to Charles VI. About the same age as Giambattista,

Fux looks far less fit. Years of gout have taken their toll and the man suffers from pain in every joint, especially in winter-time. His mood is none the better for it either. Dead tired, the choirmaster sinks into a chair. He then informs the Vivaldis without digressing that the emperor will be absent for the next few days. 'Hunting in Hungary,' he adds with distaste; he evidently views such a pastime as utterly decadent. Antonio looks at his father, his disappointment evident. 'We received confirmation of the emperor's desire to see me,' insists the priest. It is by now difficult to hide his humiliation.

'Well, the emperor has decided otherwise. A not uncommon occurrence,' responds Fux, with a hint of displeasure. 'May I be of any further assistance to you?' The choirmaster is no great fan of Vivaldi's music; he considers it too frivolous.

'I should like personally to present your monarch with a copy of my *Opus IX* and to play for him a number of *concerti*. When do you expect His Highness to return?'

Fux sighs loudly and raises his eyes to the ceiling. 'It is difficult to say. If I were you, gentlemen, I should not waste my time waiting for the archduke. Naturally, I shall be more than happy to take possession of your *opus* on behalf of Charles VI.

At a sign from his father Antonio reluctantly relinquishes the manuscript.

'And of course you are extremely welcome to remain here for another few nights,' continues the choirmaster. 'What is your next destination?'

The sooner he can get out of here the better. 'Prague!' snaps Antonio, striding out of the room. Nodding in assent, Giambattista follows his son.

'What a joke!' snorts Antonio back in his room. Paolina and Anna have been waiting. 'Let's have another look at that letter,' he orders Paolina.

Opening the folder of correspondence, she takes from it the notepaper sporting the emblem of the Habsburg emperor. The letter has been composed by a secretary and clearly indicates that Vivaldi will be welcome at court. Now that he examines it more closely, however, Vivaldi sees it contains no further details and is not even signed by the emperor in person. Livid, he screws the sheet of paper into a ball and hurls it at the fire. 'Shall we begin packing?' asks Paolina, breaking the tense silence. She hates to see Antonio let down like this. He was looking forward so much to introducing her at court.

The whole affair has had a disastrous effect on Vivaldi's self-esteem. Is he not taken seriously? Is his music not up to standard, has he lost his touch? It is this last possibility that really concerns him. The notion that he might not be taken seriously as a composer he merely represses. He can only guess at the true reason for the emperor's absence.

The following morning the Venetians take the *Herrengasse* out of the city. As for the court, Antonio gives it not a backward glance; he has had his bellyful of Vienna. Paolina pats his knee encouragingly. 'Everything will be fine' she says, using Antonio's favourite refrain.

The journey is less than enjoyable. Antonio sits whingeing and whining day after day, poisoning the whole atmosphere in the carriage. Giambattista, sick and tired of bouncing over cobbles, announces that whatever else happens, once they reach Prague he will need a full ten days to recover before he travels a single mile further. Paolina has arranged that they shall first meet Antonio Denzio.

This many-faceted Venetian both sings and writes *libretti*, and for a couple of years has been impresario at the theatre owned by Franz Anton, *Reichsgraf* von Sporck. Paolina cherishes very high hopes for this encounter. Denzi, who about fourteen years previously played the role of Artabanus in Vivaldi's opera *La costanza trionfante degli amori e degli odii*, has written to say he is looking forward immensely to meeting the priest.

Her premonition proves correct. Antonio's face lights up at once upon seeing his fellow Venetian and the two men embrace like old friends. Denzio is full of his Prague experience, how he has taken over as impresario of Peruzzi, the operas he has staged since and the success they have bought him. Antonio hangs on his every word and Vienna seems forgotten. In Prague, Denzio is master of all he surveys; the establishment owned by *Reichsgraf* von Sporck is the only theatre in town. And the public here is showing more and more interest in Italian opera.

Following on the success of theatre productions at his summer palace, Von Sporck has decided there must be opera on offer at his city palace in Prague as well. Although the loss of his wife a couple of years ago has dampened the count's passion for music, impresario Denzio is still free to continue putting on productions. Work by Vivaldi has naturally been included in his programmes, but now he tests Antonio's reaction to a new idea. 'Is it not about time the grand master came and himself put on an opera in Prague?' The mere thought of it brings a smile to Vivaldi's lips. But first he would like to view the theatre and see for himself what sort of audience might attend, for the priest is not over-impressed by what he has seen of performances here so far. Hardly a premiere on offer, and a great deal of rehashed material played by second-rate artistes – although there is a big surprise in store when Margherita Gualandi turns out to be in town.

Vivaldi had entirely lost track of her, but rumours had reached him concerning a scandal in Naples a couple of years previously. 'Blessed is he who turns a deaf ear, priest,' she warns in her least sophisticated accent, pressing him close to her side. She joined Denzio's company the previous year, she tells him, and has since fallen madly in love with the tenor, Lorenzo Moretti. 'You'll not see me back in Italy for a while!' she winks.

On their second day in Prague, Denzio unexpectedly presents Antonio Vivaldi with a date for a concert to be given by himself. In ten days time virtually all the aristocracy of Prague will be back in the city. It is already mid-November, when the nobility gravitate back to town, leaving their estates in the hands of the tenants. Not everyone has heard the name Don Vivaldi, *Il Prete Rosso*, but after this concert it will never be forgotten. The music makes a deep and lasting impression on the assembled audience, so different is it from anything they are used to. Antonio Denzio, here a man of consequence, introduces Vivaldi to prince, count and squire. Commissions are agreed and invitations for new concerts received. It seems that Prague has more to offer Antonio and his father than they had ever dreamed possible. Apart from *concerti*, Vivaldi also performs a number of motets and cantatas in which Anna has a chance to shine. Such informal evenings give her an opportunity after the performance to bask in the compliments showered upon her by both young and old worshippers.

Not every name he is introduced to rings a bell with Antonio, but some he has apparently been corresponding with for years. Such clients are thrilled at last to be meeting the composer in person; his music is infinitely more magical when performed by the *Maestro* himself. Every conversation seems to culminate quite naturally in a new commission. But it is hard work; every day there are commissions to be drafted or lessons given, for many violinists long to learn some tricks of the trade from the *Maestro* himself, and the evenings are filled with performances and patient dialogue with endless admirers. As usual, Paolina stays out of the limelight, stepping forward as secretary to Don Vivaldi only in order to write out a request for work or set up an appointment. Keeping quietly in the background, she nevertheless enjoys each musical evening, occasionally by luck meeting someone with whom she can discuss literature and poetry.

These occasions are her only form of diversion in Prague, for the city on the River Moldau has little else to offer her. She would be hard put to it to explain her feeling, but Prague saddens her. Whether it is the people, or buildings like the brooding walls of the citadel of *Wisschrad*, or the domineering silhouette of *Hradschin* etched so sharply against the afternoon sky, she does not know. But she will be happy to leave this grey and sombre place. And the worst of it is that she has hardly been able even to find a decent bookshop in the city. In the handful of shabby little places she has stumbled upon, the shelves are filled mainly with volumes of local interest, hardly a work of French or Italian literature to be seen. She knows only a few words of German, and the local Czech dialect is utterly foreign to her ears. The couple of popular French novels pushed into her hands by bookshop owners she has already read. And it is just as difficult to come by some decent paper. Antonio has been overwhelmed with commissions and the stock of paper brought with them from Venice was soon exhausted. The priest wants to draft as much as possible here, both to save on postage and so that the client can pay in advance! At last, on Denzio's recommendation, she has found a retailer selling a reasonable selection of paper. Antonio will just have to make the best of it.

By the time they have been there a couple of weeks, Antonio Vivaldi has passed muster with almost the whole of Prague aristocracy. Nearly all the same faces turn up in the audience at every performance, no matter in whose residence a concert takes place. The priest befriends several of these individuals, and is permitted after a commission or two to add the title of house-composer to the growing list after his name. Often, such a distinction is celebrated with a chuckle and a clink of glasses, for the role of *Maestro di capella* is not usually of very great significance. The noblemen enjoy showing off the name Vivaldi as their 'own' composer without it costing them too much in reality. Antonio, on the other hand, has no qualms about brandishing his many titles whenever they might enhance his reputation. Thus, the priest grasps the chance, either out of opportunism or revenge, when the young man destined to become the son-in-law of Emperor Charles VI agrees, in a bout of drunken hilarity, to 'appoint' him his own *Maestro di capella di duca di Lorenza*.

Frans III Stefanus, Duke of Lorraine, has lived at court in Vienna since he was fifteen. With the death of his brother, who was to have married Maria Theresa, the emperor declared his wish that the younger take the place of his elder brother. The Duke of Lorraine has belonged to the Habsburg court ever since, and although it will be years before Frans can marry the emperor's daughter, the couple get along very well together.

This month the Duke of Lorraine is staying as a guest of his friend, Count Wrtby. Having thus put some distance between himself, the court in Vienna and his twelve-year-old intended bride, Frans feels free to bid farewell to his age of innocence. Next week *Il duca di Lorena* will be back in Vienna for his twenty-first birthday celebrations. Antonio would love to be a fly on the wall when old Fux is told that the new choirmaster to the emperor's prospective son-in-law is none other than Don Antonio Vivaldi!

Crocuses have spread their shining carpet of colour over the banks of the Moldau. Spring arrives, signalling nobility and landowners to depart once more for the country. With his father's help, Antonio has managed to complete all his work, and Denzio has promised to deliver the last of the commissions to clients. The impresario will miss Vivaldi. 'I'll send you a *scrittura*,' he vows, tears in his eyes, as they say their farewells.

'You know my price,' says the priest, with no expectations that Antonio Denzio will be able to raise the money. Prague is not Venice, after all!

At the end of April, Antonio and his party set foot on dry land once more in Venice. The homecoming is one of surprises for Giambattista, for everything is packed and ready for a move of which he is still ignorant. A couple of days later they take possession of the elegant new house, fittingly situated on the *Calle Sant'Antonio*, in the shadow of *Palazzo Bembo*.

'I'm never moving house again,' declares Antonio happily, leaning on the balustrade and gazing from the *piano nobile* out over the *Canal Grande*. To his right, the *Ponte di Rialto* unites the two halves of the city at its oldest and most central point. Vessels of every kind glide along before him, fully laden barges and gondolas carrying passengers. Afternoon sunshine softly strokes the façades of *palazzi* on the opposite side of the canal. Banners and multicoloured flags wave lazily in the soft breeze, giving the houses a stately air. What a view! No, he will never move again.

His two sisters, Margherita and Zanetta, have their own rooms at the back of the house. Father is regally installed at the front, and so is Anna. The two chambers next to the grand reception-room belong to Antonio and Paolina. Whilst furniture and belongings stand rather forlornly in the middle of the immense rooms, waiting to be unpacked, everyone blithely ignores the work to be done and instead enjoys watching the world from the windows. Giambattista tries his best to banish from his imaginings what this palace must cost in rent. He is too old now to worry about such things.

The Prague winter has been good for Vivaldi's reputation. Commissions keep on coming in, but the long-awaited *scrittura* for an opera in Vienna, Graz, or even Prague does not materialise. Antonio and Anna lose their patience; the call of the theatre is too strong. Anna is to fare better than Antonio. For even the doors of the *Teatro San Angelo*, which is nowadays generally considered the redhead priest's 'house theatre', remain closed to him. During Vivaldi's absence in Prague, theatre owners Benedetto Marcello and Bernardo Cappello have installed a new impresario, Fabrizio Brugnolo, a man who has never liked *Il Prete Rosso* and is determined to deprive the priest of earning a sequin more from *San Angelo*. The other theatres have had a similar attitude for years, and Antonio does not even bother approaching them. Giambattista suggests writing to venues beyond Venice.

Anna, meanwhile, wins a role as *seconda donna* in *Dalisa*, by Johann Adolf Hasse, playing next to the lauded mezzo-soprano Faustina Bordoni. Antonio attends a couple of performances of the opera at the *Teatro San Samuele*. Intrigued, he studies the reactions of the audience and attends closely to the music, which oozes Neapolitan style. The public goes wild, probably greatly helped by the performance of Faustina. Anna is a perfectly adequate *seconda donna* but definitely plays second fiddle to Faustina; the mezzo-

314

soprano wife of Johann Hasse has a much more powerful presence and voice. But Antonio is blind to none of his daughter's gifts. Now that he has time to listen properly, he finds her capable of truly moving him with her performance. Normally, his attention is divided. Directing a production demands too much concentration for him to respond emotionally. At the moments of most drama he is always a couple of notes ahead, like a helmsman who in navigating his ship through a storm must abandon the crew to their fate, their skill and the grace of God.

'You'd better watch out for the German,' warns Giambattista after a performance by Hasse. 'Just look at those folk, they're lapping it up. I'm old enough to know which way the wind's blowing. You're going to have to make a decision, son; either adjust your style or else give them something entirely new.'

Antonio shrugs nonchalantly. 'I think our first priority is finding a theatre, father.'

As if in answer to his prayers he is sent a complete surprise: a *scrittura* from Antonio Denzio. But the priest has his doubts. Denzio has made him a sound financial offer; that's not the problem. But Prague! Another excursion. Laying the proposition before his father, the priest discovers they share the same unease, but the older man also sees some advantages. 'Don't forget most commissions come from up north,' he reminds his son. 'They may amount to no more than bits and pieces, but at the end of the day they pay the rent.'

'Oh come on, father,' replies Antonio, irritated, 'Who's talking about the rent? We have enough money to live here for another hundred years.' Giambattista throws up his hands at ever having mentioned the matter. There are indeed plenty of funds, but to last a century? 'I should take Denzio up on his offer,' he insists. 'There's nothing for you to do here at present.'

'Don't you dread the journey?' asks Antonio.

'Well, if you don't mind, I thought I might stay here this time and use my time to correspond with various theatres. I'm too old to make another trek across the Alps.'

Antonio shakes his head vehemently. 'If you're not coming, I'm staying at home as well.'

'Why, in heaven's name?'

Antonio waves his hand as if to conjure a thousand reasons from his sleeve. 'Because...' he pauses, searching for words. 'Because what would be the point without you?' His father scratches behind his ear. 'Well, it's very nice of you to say so, son, but you are fifty-two years old now, and I think you're quite capable of putting on an opera without the aid of your father. What's more, you've got Paolina to support you. She can do everything.'

'She can't copy, or help with rehearsals. And who will keep the ballet, artistes and musicians in order?'

'Don't be so melodramatic, Antonio. Denzio will look after that side of things, and Paolina will organise your journey, the finances and the passports. Actually, in case you hadn't noticed, she's been doing so for years. So stop making such a fuss!'

Stroking his nose thoughtfully, Antonio watches his father sitting contentedly peeling an apple in front of the window.

'Camilla would have enjoyed all this,' remarks Giambattista between mouthfuls, peering down at a scene playing itself out in front of the house.

Antonio looks again at his father and sees a fragile old man blinking in the sunlight, enjoying his old age. No, it would not be fair to wrench him away from all of this, to take him off on an arduous journey. His father is right. He will go without him, Antonio resolves, however much he will miss him.

Denzio is thrilled to hear from Vivaldi that he accepts the *scrittura*. In advance of a libretto by his old friend Domenico Lalli, the priest sends off to Prague some music for the opera *Argippo* so that Denzio's musicians and artistes can make an initial study of it. The lead role is, of course, made for Anna Girò, who is currently putting on a dazzling performance in Prague in a rejuvenated version of *Farnace*. Audiences in Prague adore Vivaldi, and he learns to his considerable amazement that he can stand on his own two feet without his father around. What he does not so fully realise is how much credit is due to Paolina and her managerial finesse.

Giambattista is relieved to be staying in Venice this winter. He responds, on his son's behalf, to a great deal of correspondence, but also spends more time with his few remaining friends. For this he goes by water to the *Castello* district, for his cronies do not feel at home in the magnificence of the house adjacent to *Palazzo Bembo*. They do not for an instant begrudge him it, that goes without saying, but after visiting him and perching uneasily in the *piano nobile*, sipping wine from crystal glasses... well, once is enough. And, truth be told, Giambattista does not at all mind either. It is in *Castello* in the shadow of *San Martino* that he too really feels at home; here are his memories of childhood and growing up. And it is usually after dawn next day by the time the gondolier finally deposits him back outside the big house again, still very much the worse for wear. Having waited up all night for him, his daughters watch with relief as he crawls up from the landing-stage. Giambattista doesn't care. He has relived with his comrades the Venice of old, and, still half-drunk and drowning in melancholia, he plods upstairs, blubbering for Camilla.

The next day he has forgotten all about it.

Farnace goes on pulling in the crowds, for father has managed to arrange that this operatic runaway success be put on in Padua in May. Then comes summer, without any prospect of new work. Anna continues faithfully each day to run through her singing exercises. She wants to keep her voice in trim, even if there is little likelihood of her being offered a serious role for this year. Sometimes she wonders if it would not be better for her to present herself to some other impresarios. Away from Venice, for everyone here knows her as 'L'Annina del Prete Rosso', the priest's little darling, or so it is whispered. Ridiculous! But she has also found out for herself, meanwhile, how murderous is the competition. Female singers are ten a penny and some are even prepared to sing for nothing, just for the chance of standing onstage and perhaps being discovered. Every impresario has his own favourites, sometimes based on talent as a singer and sometimes simply on outer appearance, in the best instances a combination of the two. Anna can easily imagine how people take her to be Vivaldi's mistress; how else would she get to play *prima donna* in his operas? But it wounds her that such hearsay detracts from her being judged on her artistic capabilities. She learned long ago the folly of denying the rumours; it only confirms people's suspicions.

Perhaps if she lived independently, or tried her luck in another place? But what if such measures should fail? Run back with her tail between her legs? How keen would Vivaldi be then to welcome her back to his arms and straightaway offer her a new role? Might he not rather think that she had betrayed him?

Luckily for Anna she does not face an immediate decision, for two huge commissions come in for Antonio, one after another. The first is a request from Mantua for Vivaldi to act as impresario for the new season. The other is even better; the *Accademia Filarmonica* of Verona invites Don Vivaldi to provide the inaugural opera for its new *Teatro Filarmonico*. Fifteen years in the building, this magnificent edifice by architect Francesco da Bibiena is scheduled for opening with a fitting fanfare. A member of the *Accademia*, Scipione Maffei, writes the libretto *La Fida Ninfa* and sends it to Venice, where Antonio Vivaldi is soon trumpeting abroad how he is the *Accademia Filarmonica* composer of choice for this most prestigious occasion. So it comes as rather a blow to learn later that in fact the composer Orlandi had been selected and refused the commission. Nothing could be more debilitating for Vivaldi than this realisation that he is the second choice.

Late autumn sees Antonio, Anna and Paolina making a temporary move back to the court at Mantua. At the very last moment Giambattista decides to accompany the party. The journey, via Verona, is not too long, and he enjoyed his former stay in the city. But his biggest reason for coming along is the new theatre in

Verona. Giambattista has heard so much about the building that he just has to see it with his own eyes. Apparently the interior is a lavish tribute to baroque pomposity in which Bibiena has striven to incorporate the ultimate in acoustics and optics. From wherever you sit or stand in the opulent auditorium there is a perfect view of the vast stage, deeper and broader by far than in any of the old Venetian theatres. The décor is also designed by Francesco da Bibiena, to harmonise entirely with the rest of the building. Not much more is needed to lure the public away from everyday reality and into a fantastic other world. The enlarged podium allows dancers far more room for movement, and choreography is in the hands of no less a figure than Andrea Cattani, *ballerino della Maestà del rè di Polonia*. Giambattista is delighted to read further that the orchestra, with which he will again be playing, comprises 'i più insigni professori', in other words, only the most excellent professional musicians.

In sumptuous magnificence *La Fida Ninfa* matches the architecture of the theatre. Vivaldi may have been its second composer of choice, but the *Accademia* has no cause to regret having invited him. Not only do the *Veneti Nobili* present freely admit how impressed they are with their fellow citizen and composer, they are plain jealous of the ostentatious new theatre.

The success of *La Fida Ninfa* leads indirectly to Fabrizio Brugnolo, impresario of the *Teatro San Angelo*, entering into new negotiations with *Il Prete Rosso*. Performances over recent years have not done much for Fabrizio, and it is high time he had a success. The theatre is too small to pay the big stars, and one way or another the *San Angelo* has lost its place in the hearts of the people of Venice. Against his better judgement, but prepared to meet the priest halfway, Fabrizio offers him a new libretto. Vivaldi picks it up pretty lackadaisically; he has not forgotten how Fabrizio once showed him the door. And the new title, *Motezuma*, means nothing to him. The plot is written by Alvise Giusti, a pupil of Aposolo Zeno, basing his story on the capture of Mexico by Fernando Cortés, and Alvise admits in his foreword that he has not stuck too closely to historical fact. This does not much trouble Antonio, who has never yet made it his business to study Spain's past.

Whereas the real Montezuma paid with his life for the arrival of Cortés, Alvise Giusti rewrites history by allowing friendship to develop between their two peoples. Crowning this fictional triumph of chivalry over war is the marriage between Motezuma's daughter and Ramiro, brother of Cortés. Vivaldi opens the book and begins reading somewhat sceptically. But he is soon carried away by the story, and the same itch of inspiration comes to him that so often precedes good composition. It is all unfolding before him, the rich décor of the imperial palace, the exotic setting of a Mexican city. Here's something new for Venice to get its teeth into!

'Mauro will do the set and costumes,' Fabrizio informs him flatly, keeping a sharp eye on the priest's face.

Vivaldi does not flicker. Instead he lets a few minutes pass before laying the libretto back down in front of the theatre boss. 'Could turn into something,' he remarks blandly, picking at a fingernail. 'Of course, it's a bit risky trying to turn a foreign tale like that into a libretto. Hmm, I'm not sure I'd like my name associated with it.'

Fabrizio gapes at the book. Bloody hell, he thinks enraged, the man's playing games with me! Il *Prete Rosso* knows perfectly well how things stand here, business-wise and financially too. This theatre was his home from home for years! The impresario's mistrust of the priest is growing by the moment. The man's only out for money!

'Fine, I'll be off then,' Antonio breaks the silence.

'I take it you're not interested?' Fabrizio queries peevishly.

'Not without hearing all the conditions, and so far you haven't told me much. I am prepared to do my utmost to make your season a success, but you must understand I have my own decisions to make. There's a nice offer outstanding from Verona, for example,' bluffs the priest, 'and I can only be in one place at a time, can I not?'

Fabrizio swallows hard. 'What do you want to know?' he asks, admitting defeat.

With a triumphant smile Vivaldi sits down again and puts his cards on the table. His blood boiling, Fabrizio concedes that he has no choice but once again to line the coffers of the priest. A handshake seals their deal and like wildfire it spreads through town; *Il Prete Rosso* is back at *San Angelo*!

But not everyone greets the news with enthusiasm. The new generation of listeners knows the name Vivaldi from their parents, but his music does not hold the same appeal for them. Still, tickets for the opening night in November 1733 are quickly sold out, and no member of the audience is left unmoved by the Mexican adventure. The public is flocking back to *San Angelo* and Fabrizio Brugnolo can happily pay his bills again. *Motezuma* is followed by a revised edition of Antonio's *Dorilla in Tempé*, something he last put on at the same theatre eighteen years before.

Going through the score makes his toes curl. How could he ever have staged it in this state? He shakes his head, mortified at the arias and recitatives, and finally rewrites the whole lot, adding a couple of new arias from his Neapolitan colleagues to test public reaction.

Vivaldi soon realises that audiences respond best to a *dramma per musica* with reduced recitative and melodies that are more easy on the ear, and this convinces that him the standard of the average theatregoer is going downhill fast. Where, he wonders, will it all end?

The season is due to close with his opera *L'Olimpiade*. The narrative is based on a libretto by Pietro Metastasio and is not Antonio's own choice. But Fabrizio is determined to bring this librettist's work to *San Angelo*, believing it will raise the status of the theatre. Optimally adjusted to public taste, or at least the priest's perception of it, this opera too will prove successful. Antonio has applied his usual rigour to finding talent, and the full houses are thanks largely to his choice of cast. The *San Angelo* budget cannot meet the astronomical fees demanded by star *castrati* such as Farinelli. But Mariano Nicolini has shot from anonymity overnight to become the darling of the Venetian public. Having distinguished himself in Mantua two years ago in Vivaldi's *Semiramide*, Marianino, with his enormous stage presence and limpid voice, is about to grace the stage again in *L'Olimpiade*. It is a role that will establish his reputation and write his name for all time in the annals of world opera.

Vivaldi can look back upon a fine season. The same may not be said of Fabrizio, still chafing at the manner in which *Il Prete Rosso* has creamed off so much of the profit whilst, he feels, most of the work has fallen to himself as impresario. Blissfully unaware of his own overweening pride, he decides to go it alone next season.

Vivaldi could not care less. It was nice for old time's sake to put on a show at the *San Angelo*. But things felt different this time. The atmosphere was not the same with so many of the arrangements out of his control. He recalls with nostalgia the early years, when they would put the last of their capital into preparations for a new performance. How he and his father looked forward in trepidation to the first night and how their fears would be repaid a thousand-fold in the triumph of a great opening. The times when things went less well are, of course, long forgotten.

Yes, the *San Angelo* has seen better days. It is too small and poky, and the filthy interior reeks. The ceiling is blackened with the soot of years of lighted candelabra and the gilded angels now look more like flapping crows. Antonio cannot believe that this place once felt like home to him. Only this winter has it struck him for the first time how mediocre are the acoustics. It is with mixed feelings that the priest finally turns his back on the *San Angelo*. Ahead lies the pleasant prospect of directing a new opera at the flamboyant *Teatro Filarmonico*.

The *Accademia Filarmonica* of Verona has expressed the desire to appoint the priest as impresario for the coming season. The men of the *Accademia* are canny businessmen, but Antonio is not dissatisfied with his new contract. He is obliged to deliver two new productions for the coming winter in Verona, and has discussed several *libretti* with his father. For both productions they want a story that will hold an audience despite the absence of a Neapolitan *castrato* in the lead role. Giambattista is only too aware of the popularity of the modern music coming out of Naples, but he can't get used to it. And much the same may be said for his son. Yet to hang on to old traditions is tantamount to artistic suicide. Antonio knows he has to move with the times, while his whole being rebels against the idea of following the common trend in fashionable ditties. This runs so counter to his artistic conscience that he has to ask himself seriously for whom he will soon be composing. Older audiences will, of course, remain faithful to him, but youngsters no longer have the time or the inclination to sit through one of his works.

'Wrap it up in pretty paper,' suggests Giambattista.

Antonio looks baffled. 'How do you mean?'

'What I say. Package it in such a way that you arouse people's curiosity. So they get edgy when the ribbon doesn't come undone, and have to tear the paper off to get at the gift.'

Antonio scratches at his ear, gazing thoughtfully at his father. Slowly his meaning dawns on him, and a light comes to Antonio's eyes. He begins to laugh, Giambattista joins in, and they raise their glasses and drink to the future.

The two men work together over the coming days, combing through Giambattista's archives for a good idea for the libretto. The old man smiles at the sight of all the old documents he so meticulously assembled what seems like centuries ago. Every manuscript brings back memories, but he resolutely refuses to get distracted from the task in hand.

'*Tamerlano*', he whispers, blowing dust from the leaflet and opening it at the first page. 'That was a bloody good show.'

'It certainly was,' agrees Antonio. 'Gasparini! That would have been 1711 at, er... ah, yes, the *Teatro San Cassiano*.'

'Right,' nods Giambattista. 'Text by Agostino Piovene. That

might do for a start.' He adds a quick jibe for good measure. 'If Turks are good for anything, it's the theatre!'

Antonio takes his time to read carefully through Piovene's narrative. He makes a note here and there, and scribbles one or two amendments that enhance the drama of Bajazet, the defeated Turkish emperor who falls into the hands of Tartar ruler Tamerlano. The expressive role of Asteria, daughter of Bajazet is, of course, set aside for Anna. Bajazet, for whom the audience will immediately feel a surge of sympathy and who meets a sorry end, is to be played by *La Polpetta*, Maria Maddalena Pieri.

'Isn't she getting a bit long in the tooth for such a demanding role?' snipes Anna. 'She's well over fifty.'

Vivaldi refuses to dignify her remark by even a glance up from his work. Without looking at her, he replies, 'I have my reasons, and her voice is still very serviceable.' He has no wish to discuss the matter further. Of course, Pieri is a woman of a certain age and it is said her voice is not what it was a couple of years ago. But the public will never notice such a thing. Much more significant is the fact that *La Polpetta* remains the mistress of Luca Casimiro, otherwise known as the Marquis degli Albizzi, impresario of the *Teatro della Pergola* in Florence. Antonio knows this is a way of staying friends with Albizzi, and that has its uses. The role of Tamerlano's fiancée goes to a young and still unknown soprano, Margherita Giacomazzi. She auditioned a couple of weeks earlier with the priest and he knew straightaway he would be able to use her voice. Strong and clear as a bell, her sound will compete well with that of most *castrati*, and he takes sardonic pleasure in reworking the most popular aria and party-piece of famous *castrato* Farinelli in this *pasticcio*. For it is a *pasticcio*, a potpourri of Vivaldi's best work and that of other composers, that will form the basis for this opera. Once he has chosen the most important soloists, Antonio begins writing: short, incisive recitatives and dramatic arias. In the process the story begins to flow and his pen races from one page of manuscript to the next. Giambattista gazes dumbfounded at this show of speed and alacrity, only hoping he will be able to decipher the handwriting. For the faster Antonio composes, the more slovenly become his marks on the paper, and Giambattista's knows his eyesight is deteriorating. At this rate it will be a Herculean task to get all the parts copied out neatly.

The new opera surprises and makes a huge impression on the members of the *Accademica* and the public of Verona. Many young patricians had gone unwillingly to the opening of Il *Tamerlano*. After all, Vivaldi is a *vecchio*, an old man who writes music from another age. But because there is nothing else on the programme, the younger generation has gone along to the theatre anyway. As the curtain rises and the first allegro fills the hall, all the attention upstairs in the boisterous boxes is on the cards flitting across the table. But the young card players are soon distracted one by one from their game by the arias of Bajazet and Tamerlano. And as Princess Irene lets loose her aria *Qual guerrieri in camp armato* upon the unsuspecting public, the hall erupts. This they know! Catcalls, cheering and applause thunder about Vivaldi's ears, and it goes on so long, he nods to Giacomazzi to repeat the aria. How wonderful it is to be appreciated after all, thinks Antonio, letting the adulation and endless applause sink in, whilst he bows respectfully and the curtain falls.

Like a Roman centurion, Vivaldi makes his triumphant return to Venice. The season has been stupendous, much more financially rewarding than had been expected. It leaves Antonio with no great plans, although he's pretty sure he'll be back in the theatre again in the autumn. His father has had enough for the time being. Giambattista has a bad cold in the aftermath of Venice and stays in bed, assuring everyone that he is fine and will soon be up and about again. He does not let them see how tired he really is. But in spite of his reassuring words, the family is very concerned. He has no real appetite, and sleeps all day long. Finally Giambattista feels a little better, gets up, and gives himself a terrible shock by looking in the mirror for the first time for ages. He has clearly lost weight. His once round face is gaunt and drawn, and he grimaces at the old man staring back at him.

Antonio does not have to wait until autumn for a new commission. He is astonished, eleven days after his return from Verona, to receive an invitation from none other than Michele Grimani, owner of the flagship Venetian theatre *San Grisostomo* and the only slightly more humble *Teatro San Samuele*. Up until this moment the Grimanis have never deigned to give Vivaldi a second glance. The idea that the son of some yokel from Brescia might play in one of the patrician's theatres has been unthinkable. But the tide has turned. Not so much thanks to the name that Don Vivaldi has made, but more to the economic situation in which the Republic now finds itself. To the outsider, *La Serenissima* might appear at the height of her powers. Where else is *carnevale* celebrated with such verve and panache? Where else can be found such pomp and pageantry, more money changing hands each evening at the gaming tables? But this bejewelled smokescreen hides a Venice actually long past her zenith and fast declining towards a sad end. Already you can feel it in the theatres. Changing public taste and the massive sums of money paid to fashionable *castrati* threaten the future of the two grandest theatre houses. Verona has demonstrated to Michele Grimani the possibility of staging a successful production without big names such as Carestini, Caffarelli, Appiani and Monticelli, and the commensurate fees! The theatre boss has decided to approach Vivaldi for the annual 'Ascension Day opera' to be performed at the *Teatro San Samuele*.

'The gentlemen must indeed be desperate,' remarks Giambattista prosaically.

Antonio hardly knows how he should react to the letter landing in his lap so abruptly. For years they have ignored him, and now they find themselves in deep water and yell to him for help. He lets Grimani wait for a full reply, sending instead a polite acknowledgement and promising he will consider his proposal.

'Has Grimani an idea for the show?' Giambattista wants to know.

'Oh, that he has,' replies Antonio. '*Griselda*.'

'You're joking! That's a pretty tired old horse by now.'

'That, father, is exactly what I told him. But Grimani wants the story rewritten, brought bang up to date.'

'Mm, and have you thought what you're going to say to Signor Grimani?'

Antonio grins. 'Time's running out. Why don't we just wait and see just how desperate he can get? Once he's at the end of his tether we can dash to his rescue and cash in on it. And it'll be we who have the patricians by the balls for a change!'

Paolina puts her head round the door, surprised to see the two men so cheerful. She could not possibly appreciate quite how Giambattista's humiliation and anger has deepened over the years as, time and again, the *Veneti Nobili* snubbed his son.

When a fortnight later the contract is finally signed between the priest and a sour-faced Grimani, tears of happiness flow down Giambattista's cheeks. There is a just God after all!

Not long remains, but it's long enough for Vivaldi. He immediately allocates the leading roles to Anna and Margherita Giacomazzi. Given the time shortage, he incorporates into *Griselda* a couple of arias with which Giacomazzi won hearts in Verona. Grimani has dug up a young fellow called Carlo Goldoni to rewrite the text. According to Lalli's advice to Vivaldi, Goldoni has his uses but is still very inexperienced. Up until last year the fellow was working as a lawyer, but with little success. Having for some time cherished literary aspirations, he thus sought to practice his new art with a group of *Commedia dell'Arte* players. Last November, Goldini got the chance to write his first play, which when premiered at *San Samuele* surprised everyone, not least the author, by going down so well that Grimani offered him the stage again in January. *Rosimonda*, the second work from the pen of this aspiring playwright, apparently proved just as great a success as the first.

This vanquished the last of Grimani's doubts and, brimming with youthful self-confidence, Carlo Goldoni now knocks at Vivaldi's door. The thirty-year age difference between composer and young writer gives rise to a healthy dose of mistrust on both sides. Vivaldi is not familiar with the work of the lapsed lawyer, and for his part Goldoni cannot bring himself to appreciate the eternal recitatives he has heard in some of Vivaldi's operas. But as the meeting progresses they get over their initial unease and establish a sound working relationship. Goldoni soon learns respect for the energy and practical insight of the priest, and Vivaldi is impressed by the younger man's supple linguistic skills. Pooling their resources, the two swiftly come up with an opera that, at its Ascension Day performance, is received by the snob-ridden audience of *San Samuele* with its usual critical but overall enthusiasm. It is the first time in many seasons that Michele Grimani has closed with a viable opera.

The fact that someone such as Vivaldi has been responsible for this positive outcome is one he readily sidesteps. And, with all the opportunism of a patrician, he gives the priest a new *scrittura* for the coming autumn. This means another busy time ahead, for the exchange of correspondence with Marquis Luca Casimiro degli Albizzi has at last borne fruit and Vivaldi has been invited by the Florentine impresario to put on *Ginevra principessa di Scozia* as second opera of the season there.

Despite some inevitable wrangling with Albizzi, Vivaldi has managed to secure for Anna not only the lead role in *Ginevra* but also the place of *prima donna* in the first opera of the new season. It is *Cesare in Egitto*, commissioned from the priest a few weeks later. Vivaldi is much amused by the letter from the marquis, in which he elaborates upon how direly difficult it has been for him to persuade the *Accademia* that Signorina Girò is really right for this leading part.

"Whomsoever I speak to tells me the same thing; that she is a perfect actress, only no one can hear her. But enough of this;

I shall set aside my inhibitions and lend her my support," writes the impresario. Albizzo's main aim in all of this is to minimise the honorarium and thus increase his own share of the winnings. As an experienced impresario himself, Vivaldi is familiar with all the tricks and so takes the marquis' complaints with a large pinch of salt. The most he does in response is to remind the marquis subtly of his mistress.

'La Polpetta has triumphed in Verona, although her voice is not what it was in her younger days. Nevertheless, I feel she still has many years of stardom ahead!' he writes, hinting at the many other theatres with which he is currently in negotiations over future productions. Albizzi should be able to read between the lines and learn to keep his criticism to himself if he wants to see his beloved in one of Vivaldi's forthcoming productions. And, for the moment, that seems to be that.

Griselda has helped Vivaldi up another rung of the social ladder in Venice. His performance at San Samuele would seem to be the key to recognition for his whole body of work. For the first time for years invitations are coming in for concerti at the palazzi of the patricians, and even the Ospedale della Pietà once more seeks out the priest. Again, some time has passed since he did anything for the orphanage. The old arrangement whereby he was to deliver two monthly concerti has pretty well fallen by the wayside, mainly due to his being so busy with other work.

But now, in the light of his greatly enhanced reputation, the Congregazione finds the time right for a new approach. The idea circulating within the management committee is to reappoint Vivaldi as Maestro de'Concerti, not just to compose but also to teach. The priest is flattered, but not sure whether he should take up the offer. The modest treasury of the Pietà offers little chance of an honorarium commensurate with the status of Don Antonio Vivaldi. A hundred ducats per annum are all they can offer him. After much humming and hawing, Vivaldi accepts the position. As far as he is concerned it is charity work for the institute, and he considers the hundred ducats bare reimbursement for expenses.

The successes in Verona and San Samuele do not, however, lead to the huge commissions that Vivaldi had hoped for. Impresarios in the majority of cities serve up exactly what the public asks them for, and nowadays that is not Vivaldi. The fact that his letters meet with refusals makes him slightly nervous. What if no more scritture come his way? Antonio feels unwilling to worry his father with such questions, for the first autumn showers chasing across the lagoon have left the old man with another severe chill.

Indeed, Antonio's concerns over his father increase the nearer the new season approaches. Giambattista is obviously not well enough to travel to Florence. He lies in bed, comfortable enough in the care of his daughters. Paolina reads aloud to him a lot, and occasionally the old man asks for his violin to be retrieved from its place at the foot of his bed. But he rarely gets much farther than tuning up and playing a couple of slow tunes.

'I'll keep my fingers crossed for you all,' he promises with a smile as they are leaving. Antonio sends Anna and Paolina out of the room first, and then silently embraces his father. 'I'll be here waiting for you, son, don't you worry.'

Antonio swallows hard and nods dumbly.

'Off you go, my boy; they'll be downstairs wondering where you are.'

On his way out the priest turns and waves to his father, who raises a hand wearily in salute. Making his way downstairs, a grim-faced Vivaldi finds himself hoping against hope that he will see his father alive again.

A very cool reception awaits the Venetians in Florence. Marquis Albizzi has fully expected Vivaldi to have in prospect some new work for Maria Pieri, who, on her lover's advice, has accepted no other offer this season. It is a huge comedown for La Polpetta Maria to have to watch unemployed from the wings while Anna Girò gives

330

two consecutive dazzling performances as *prima donna*. Albizzi's initial reaction has been fury at Antonio informing him the theatres were showing a growing preference for young Neapolitan composers, and singers.

'You'll just have to try a bit harder, then,' was the impresario's vitriolic advice. But in subsequent discussions Albizzo has recognised, albeit unwillingly, that times are indeed changing. 'Is there any future for us at all?' asks the seventy-two-year-old.

Vivaldi shrugs. 'How goes it with ticket sales these days?' he asks in return.

'Not bad,' confesses Albizzo.

'Who's worrying about the future then?' retorts the priest with a good-humoured grin.

Immediately after the last night of *Ginevra*, Antonio, Paolina and Anna depart again for Venice. Not a word passes between them as the island comes into sight. How will they find Giambattista?

Father is up and about again. With the coming of spring, his spirits and health seem to have revived. But the winter has left its mark on him, and to the eyes of his returning family he looks far older than when they left a couple of months ago. The old man listens with interest as Anna relates her story of the two opera successes in Florence, and then discusses everything in detail later with his son.

Neither man alludes to the inevitable parting ahead. Both talk of the future as if life were eternal. But the long pauses between their conversations testify to their individual awareness of the true situation. Giambattista spends the afternoons in an easy chair set out for him in the shade at the front of the house, where he can greet every passer-by. He enjoys, as only an old man can, the busy activity and traffic of the street. The *Rialto* is still an important hub for trade and passage of goods, even if these are less exotic nowadays than when he first arrived in Venice as a ten-year-old with his mother. How things have changed! Giambattista sees few familiar faces now amongst the many hurrying past the house each day. Almost without him having noticed, the city has alienated itself from him. And yet he can look back upon a happy life. His mother would have been proud of him. Musing thus, Giambattista each day takes a little more leave of the world of the living. And one misty morning in May he decides never more to awaken.

Antonio's younger sister Zanetta comes, weeping, to rouse her brother. She does not have to explain the reason for her tears. Father! Leaping from bed, Antonio rushes to the old man's room and falls upon his knees at the bedside. 'Father!' he screams, panic-stricken. Giambattista's features look unnatural; his countenance is that of a dead man. The priest makes the sign of the cross and takes his father's hand, cold and stiff, in his own. With the utmost tenderness he strokes these fingers which for a lifetime gently encircled the neck of a violin, settled upon the bow; this hand that lovingly inscribed so many countless notes of music. The same fingers that were lifted against him in anger or admonishment when his father disagreed with some deed or decision of his. 'Oh father,' sobs Antonio, unable to comprehend this change. He feels himself fainting, the familiar iron band closing about his chest. He sinks, clasping his father to him as he loses consciousness.

Opening his eyes at last, it is Paolina's face he sees. Antonio is in his own bed and she is gazing compassionately down at him. 'How are you feeling?' He tries confusedly to wake from what seems a bad dream, struggles upright. 'Where is my father?' he asks hastily.

Looking into the shocked features with their red-rimmed eyes, Paolina answers softly, 'I am so sorry, my love. Your father is dead.'

The words hit him like a sledgehammer. Your father is dead! He falls back on the pillows, fighting for breath. So it is true. It is a fact! The vice-like grip about his chest is unendurable. Helplessly he stares at Paolina. 'What am I to do?' he gasps, completely overwhelmed.

She offers him a sip of water, stroking his face. 'Everything will be all right, my love, don't despair.' But that is exactly what he is feeling, despair! Where is he to go from here? His father has been his rock and compass. His very life!

The funeral takes place the next day. Paolina has arranged everything, despite her great anxiety over Antonio. For the priest has been prostrate since his father's death. He is a broken man, in no state whatsoever to make the voyage to the 'Island of the Dead' where the burial is to take place. Antonio keeps to his bed, sobbing inconsolably and refusing to speak to anyone. Paolina has asked Anna to remain at home and keep an eye on things. When Antonio is well enough, a memorial service will be held for Giambattista.

As his simple coffin is lowered into the grave beside Camilla, his grief-stricken son discovers there are no more tears to weep. He sits alone and glassy-eyed, staring into space and utterly isolated from the world around him. His mind, where there is always room for a song or tune, is empty. Filled with darkness deep as the grave wherein his father lies.

8

Venice, June 1736

A soft summer breeze steals through the open window, stirring the blank sheet of paper that has waited patiently all morning to be filled. But just as on previous days, Antonio picks it up and with a sigh returns it untouched to the pile. As if searching for inspiration that will not come, his absent minded gaze wanders outside again.

Although it is more than a month since his father's funeral, Vivaldi is still incapable of visiting the grave. He feels emotionally drained, and only Paolina's good care has prevented him from falling apart completely. The reality of Giambattista's death has not yet come home to Antonio, for how could his father have abandoned him so finally?

Paolina keeps a constant watch on the priest, bringing him regular meals and making sure he drinks enough. She tries to engage him in conversation, but it is as if he is in a trance, hardly conscious of what is going on around him. She does not force him in any way. She has discussed the situation with *abbate* Francesco and received his reassurance. He has seen such things before. Only her devotion, love and prayers will bring Vivaldi back to the real world.

And it seems Father Francesco was right. Bit by bit Vivaldi appears to be coming to himself again, although he has virtually no interest in anything going on beyond the four walls of the house. No one knows better than Paolina how devoted Giambattista and Antonio were to one another, but even she could not have suspected quite how close their bond was. She is happy with each sign Antonio shows of a return to normality, when he begins to want to eat again, and then takes a short walk. But she notes that he returns from such little outings without his old smile, re-entering the house silently and without his customary amusing anecdote for her. Antonio has always been ready to smile at the crowds of tourists, gawping as open-mouthed as half-dead fish on the stalls at the *Rialto* up at the ornate façades of *palazzi*, and so engrossed in such magnificence they all but promenade into the canal. Or the tableaux of builders he enjoyed a couple of months back, when Big-belly Beppo, his shirt just skimping his bulging pot, was balancing his wheelbarrow on the edge of the quay whilst his mate shovelled sand up rhythmically from a barge. The wheelbarrow was in fact long full, but Beppo's attention had been somewhat distracted by a deliciously done-up courtesan, with whom he was passing the time of day as she tripped past. The next shovel-full of sand proved the straw that broke the camel's back; the barrow overbalanced; Beppo lost control and the whole load tipped itself back into the barge. From under the heap, his foul-mouthed mate reappeared, hurling abuse, whilst, sniggering to herself, the lady disappeared around the corner. Or Antonio would describe the comedy of the many excited foreign traders, each bawling insistently in his own language, refusing to understand one another in their attempts to get the best price for their wares. Or weirdly attired figures selling relics from the Holy Land, always able to find some poor sucker keen to buy a finger-bone from however obscure a 'saint'. For Vivaldi, the street has always reflected the whole panoply of life, and he has revelled in its humour. No more, it seems.

Paolina does her best to involve him in everyday comings and goings. 'Write something,' she encourages. Completely devoid of motivation, he has nonetheless obediently gone and sat behind his desk these last few days. But his pen remains undisturbed and the paper as empty as his thoughts. Never more will someone cross the room to look over his shoulder, tell him truthfully what he thinks of the newly completed composition. Of course, there will always be plenty of people to tell him it is 'beautiful', or even 'exquisite'. But, however well meant, such remarks are of little value to Vivaldi. His father had but to hear a note or two and he knew if a piece was going to work or not. Moreover, he could explain exactly why not. Here a note too many, there one too sustained; timing very slightly out, or a miscalculated key. Antonio seriously doubts whether he will ever again be able to compose. He is deeply disinclined to accept critique from others. They offer it anyway, of course, but more from negative motives than in a creative spirit of objectivity. Exhausted, he stares back at the pile of blank paper to which he has just re-added this morning's empty page. The polished stone that has been warming in his hand he places carefully on top, so that the wind cannot scatter the white sheets all over the room.

Paolina's patience is beginning to wear thin. She starts to get really irritated with Antonio's sisters, Margherita Gabriela and Zanetta Anna, who are still living at home. Silent and withdrawn, the two sisters walk the corridors and rooms of the house dressed in sombre mourning like two dark ghosts themselves. Paolina seldom comes across them, and if she does meet them they look right through her. Things were different whilst Giambattista still lived, even though the many years of Paolina's presence in their home had hardly warmed the sisters to her, and they continued to treat her like an outsider. Antonio is now head of the household, and it would not be done to expel his sisters. Luckily, the house is big enough not to have to tread on each other's toes too much. But a week after the funeral Zanetta had seen fit to start clearing out her father's room, presumably with the intention of making it her own. Antonio had pounced on her, ordered her to leave the room immediately, and told her in no uncertain terms to show more respect for her father's memory. He had then locked the room and hidden the key.

The previous week he had let himself in again, hoping perhaps to find something there. But he was soon outside again, turning the key resolutely in the lock as if determined never again to enter.

Surreptitiously, Paolina has completed all her preparations. For the last couple of weeks Anna has been lodging with a friend and the plan is for her to stay away the coming week, too.

Paolina glances outside in time to see the yacht arriving. Going into the other room, she is stricken once again by the sight of Vivaldi, slumped and broken in his chair. Taking a deep breath she goes up to him, gently caresses his neck. 'Antonio,' she says softly. Slowly he raises his head. 'Come with me, we're going on a trip.' He blinks as if not comprehending her words.

'A trip?' he mumbles.

'A surprise! No questions, just come with me.'

But he is not that easily budged. 'A trip?' he repeats. She looks at him, her face alight with joy.

'Nothing could be further from my mind! Where in God's name are you thinking of dragging me off to? It's summer! Do you think I fancy swallowing a lung-full of dust and sweating like a pig in a stinking coach? Forget it.'

Paolina is simultaneously amazed and delighted. For the first time since Giambattista's death Antonio is behaving as of old. This kind of bloody-mindedness she can deal with! 'No dust, no sweat and we're not even going very far. Come on, I know you'll love it.' She takes him by the arm and feels him pull away.

'I don't want to go anywhere,' he insists in a low voice. 'I never want to go away again.' The note of hopelessness breaks her heart.

'Listen, if you carry on pining away like this I'll have to arrange another funeral in a fortnight, and that I do not plan to do! I've packed everything you'll need for our outing, so no more whingeing!' She drags him upright, and this time there are no protests.

A small yacht is lying moored in front of the house. The little vessel is clearly modelled on the fishing boats of the lagoon, but is more slimly built. The large-windowed saloon is richly adorned with engraved woodwork and gilt lions and offers more than enough room for two passengers. The sail, at half-mast, flaps idly in the breeze. Sunlight glitters upon the gilded ship, throwing its reflection up from the water and into the face of the approaching priest. Antonio, gazing silently upon the glistening scene, seems to absorb some of the glow. He may not be a born seaman, but he recognises beauty in the lovely lines of this little ship.

'Come along,' says Paolina for the umpteenth time, going to the edge of the quay. Tomaso, owner and skipper of Il Delfino, helps her aboard. Antonio hesitates once more before taking Tomaso's strong hand. But once the seaman has hold of him, he can no longer turn back. Tomaso leads him firmly to the stern of the vessel, where both passengers are soon safely ensconced in the saloon. The windows are all lowered to their full extent to keep the air cool. The interior fittings of the yacht are even more beautifully finished. Gorgeous gilt ornamentation, contrasting sumptuously with the crimson cushions into which Paolina sinks. All the carpentry is highly varnished to display the whimsical grain of its precious hardwood. Exquisitely embroidered drapery curtains the interior of the yacht off from the outside world, and a dainty, three-step ladder leads down into a sleeping cabin below the forward deck. Here, across the entire width of the ship, is a bed freshly made up with silk sheets! Antonio opens a cupboard door, only to find it filled with his own clothes. Paolina has done her work thoroughly as usual! Stowed away elsewhere is a full wine-rack, carefully designed to retain the bottles despite the ship's motion. His new environment appeals to Antonio and is pleasantly weakening his resistance. In the meantime Tomaso has cast loose and is punting the boat along the canal beneath the aloof gaze of palazzi. Paolina is overjoyed to see a smile appear on Antonio's lips. She knew this would work.

Once Il Delfino has passed the customs post and the Canal Grande has flowed into the Canale San Marco, Tomaso hoists full canvas and makes ready for full ahead. There is not enough wind to fill the sail, but no matter. They have all the time in the world.

It is low water and so Tomaso decides to sail south around the Isola di Santa Elena; the narrow gully between this tiny island

and Venice is becoming more and more shallow and Tomaso does not fancy sitting fast in the mud while the tide turns. Having rounded the island he changes tack, holding Il Delfino on a northerly course. Suddenly Vivaldi splutters and nearly chokes on his mouthful of wine. 'You're surely not taking me to San Michele?' he gasps, panic-stricken.

Paolina shakes her head, 'We will not visit your father's grave until you are ready. But perhaps it is time to try coming to terms with his death, Antonio.'

Seeing him shudder with renewed weeping, she instantly regrets her remark. Infinitely tenderly she draws him towards her and lays his head in her lap. Should they perhaps have stayed at home? She runs her fingers softly through his greying curls. Everyone may still call him Il Prete Rosso, but time and tide wait for no man.

A couple of hours later Antonio and Paolina arrive at the almost deserted island of Torcello. Neither have ever visited it before, but Paolina has always been fascinated by stories of this ghost city presided over by its glorious cathedral. Centuries ago, fleeing from Atilla and his horde, the people of the mainland had found safe haven on this sandy island and transformed it into the city of Torcello. It flourished for many years, but then the shallow creeks of the island began to silt up, and the city on the coast increasingly fell prey to any passing army. The freshwater marshes around Torcello offered a perfect breeding-ground for infestations of mosquitoes whose ambition seemed to be to claim as many of the population as possible by infecting them with malaria. A couple of hundred years ago, the desperate and dwindling population of Torcello migrated further into the lagoon to inhabit the islands of Rivoalto, much later to become Rialto, the heart of Venice.

Antonio is fascinated as Paolina relates this history. She points out to him the few remaining intact walls of long-gone palazzi, although Antonio finds it hard to imagine such lost grandeur. The early inhabitants had demolished their own past, taking with them to *Rivoalto* pretty well anything that might conceivably be used as building material.

Tomaso has made fast *Il Delfino* to the deserted quay and helped his two passengers disembark. The hottest part of the day is past, and it is also less humid. They wander at their ease along the overgrown path leading to the *campanile* of the old Byzantine cathedral of *Santa Maria Assunta*. The old *piazza* is barely discernible now amongst high grass and weeds. A narrow track leads to the entrance to *Santa Fosca*, where in the shade of the portico they discover at least a dozen sleeping cats, some of which open their eyes and whisk their tails in annoyance at being disturbed. The huge main door is locked, and there is no living soul to let them in. Following the gallery round to the front of the cathedral, they find a door standing wide open to the world. Once inside they are stopped in their tracks by the magnificence of the huge Byzantine mosaics covering a huge area of the walls. In silence they walk along the frieze depicting Bible stories from the New Testament; the Day of Judgement leaves nothing to the imagination. Further on, Antonio looks up, and suddenly there she is. High in the domed ceiling, breathtaking in mosaic: the Holy Virgin. 'Mother Maria', he mutters, falling spontaneously to his knees and crossing himself. Rays of late afternoon sunshine are dancing slowly across the inner surface of the cupola, so that it seems the Madonna herself is adrift in a haze of gold. With an expression of intense sorrow she stares ahead, showing the world the Son of God cradled in the crook of her arm, *Stabat Mater!*

The priest turns back to the scenes of the crucifixion. Now the pain of the mother passes through him like a sword. It is as if his own recent loss brings him up close to her agony, allows him to feel something of what she must have gone through. And he is consoled. His father did not suffer, after all; on the contrary, he lived a long and good life. Was it not about time he, as his son, realised this? How can he remain so full of self-pity? How can his misery be compared to that of Maria, Mother of Jesus? Paolina is right; life must go on. Ashamed, he bows his head before Maria in a long prayer of thanksgiving that she has opened his eyes.

The sun will be setting in less than an hour. Paolina and the priest sit side by side on a low wall, looking over the derelict marketplace. It is difficult for either to imagine this as the pulsing heart of a vibrant trading centre. Antonio gets to his feet and stretches. Paolina cannot help but notice the shine that has returned to his eyes, the healthy colour in his cheeks. 'Come on, Paolina, I'm starving! Let's see what Tomaso has ready for us.'

Hardly daring to believe her senses, Paolina jumps down to join him. 'Starving?' For weeks she has heard no such sentiment pass his lips. Hand in hand they walk back to the boat.

Tomaso has been frying fresh sardines, and Antonio cannot eat enough of them. After supper the two sit together in the saloon, the windows closed to keep out the mosquitoes. Just one small candle illuminates their private floating world, so that they can watch the lights of Venice glittering far off across the water. 'Strange, isn't it?' says Paolina. 'So near and yet so far away.'

Torcello is silent as the grave, and that night Antonio sleeps more soundly than ever in his life before.

The next morning they are greeted by the bleating of sheep, nosing inquisitively at the boat from the quayside. The weather is clear, and, if Tomaso's grin is anything to go by, the wind is in the right direction, too. He will not have to row today; this breeze will do all the work for him. Zigzagging her way between the creeks and gullies of the *Palude Maggiore*, Il Delfino picks her way through the great marshes. The extended reed-beds are paradise to a rich assortment of water birds, and herons arise screeching from their fishing-ground to glide low over the plumes of reeds and make a dignified descent somewhere further downstream. At last the little yacht emerges from the marshes, to find the waters of the lagoon stretching away ahead. Tomaso carefully sails the route indicated by poles standing up out of the water, for the lagoon's many fatal sandbanks are invisible from the poop deck. Past the islands of Mazzorbo and Burano scuds their little ship, and makes course south towards the narrow inlet between the long line of dunes that separates the lagoon from the Adriatic. A blue swell topped with silver foam mingles here with the green waters of the calm lagoon. Il Delfino is completely in her element, riding the waters as fearlessly as her namesake. Antonio enjoys the waves less. He likes being on board a boat, just as long as it doesn't rock about too much. Fortunately, the choppy conditions do not last long, and they are soon in the shelter of the Lido. Behind them pass fully laden merchant vessels, lying low in the water, and swift excise-and-customs boats. Now and then they see a returning fishing vessel, covered in scales. Navigating nimbly around a buoy, Tomaso brings them within sight of Punta di San Antonio, the sand dunes at the southern tip of Venice. Against the distant skyline they can make out the slightly tilted campanile of San Pietro di Castello cathedral. Letting down the sail, Tomaso brings his vessel round in a graceful swoop until she lies alongside, opposite the church of Santa Maria Elisabetta on the Lido. Among the houses surrounding the church is a trattoria, where Paolina and Antonio order lunch. From here it is just a short walk to the Adriatic coast. Neither has ever been on a beach before, and they cannot contain their glee at the tide rushing onto the shore as if to devour it. Down at the edge they can see children playing, offspring of the fisher folk who live in the shelter of the dunes, racing helter-skelter in and out of the water, splashing and shouting. Paolina and Antonio decide to wander along the waterline and, taking her cue from the children, Paolina soon kicks off her shoes to paddle through the foam. Antonio feels the wind blow through his hair as if for the first time. Licking the salt from his lips, he realises that he is breathing freely and without pain.

Reclining languidly against the warm hummock of sand at the base of a dune, they watch the white peaks of breakers shatter and leap free of the incoming tide. As wave after wave is thrown upon the shore, it seems to Vivaldi that the rhythm of the sea forms a melody. And suddenly, streaming as if a floodgate were opened, music fills his head again.

'I want to go home,' he announces abruptly. Paolina, lying back with her eyes closed and letting the sun warm her already wind-tanned face, turns to face him. 'What was that?' She surely did not hear aright.

'I want to go home. I am feeling a lot better and it's time I did something useful again.'

She is thrilled for him that he is so quickly recovered, but for herself she would very much have liked to sail around the lagoon for a few more days. And what awaits them back at home? Will he pick up his old life where he left off? There are no large commissions awaiting his attention, and Paolina very much doubts whether such will ever come in again. If the gossipmongers are to be believed, Vivaldi's operas have had their day. The modern public is interested only in modern music. Financially, the Vivaldi household is secure; from that point of view, Antonio need compose no more. But how would he take that? Paolina decides the less said the better on the subject, and stands up. Brushing back her hair, she helps him to his feet, and together they walk slowly back to the landing-stage.

Summer passes with not a *scrittura* in sight. It looks as though all the theatres have their seasons planned and there will be no opera by Vivaldi to be heard this year. Antonio is bad-tempered and feels his nose put badly out of joint. That his operas are no longer 'in' is perfectly plain to him, but he is equally determined not to adjust his manner of working to the new situation, let alone stop! He has already violated his own standards of quality quite far enough with the *pasticci* he has been producing over recent years. Enough is enough!

'Are there no other work opportunities?' asks Paolina. 'Could you not play in the orchestra of *San Marco*?'

'Pay's ludicrous,' snaps Vivaldi, with a surly shake of the head.

'Might we perhaps go elsewhere? Court employment, maybe?'

He shakes his head again, but sombrely this time. Mantua is an obvious possibility, but Prince Philip was recalled to Vienna last year and replaced by another governor, an amiable enough man, but unmusical. And anyway, an appointment in Italy would not be ideal, for 'modern music' has spread like a plague from Naples throughout the entire peninsula. Only the north offers any promise for the future.

But the music of Hasse, Leo and Vinci has by now also reached Austria and Bohemia... France might be a possibility. Or Russia, perhaps?

'Maybe we should accept the way things are,' ventures Paolina. 'If we take each day at a time, we can manage fine. I won't mind if we have to move to a smaller house.'

'Out of the question!' Antonio slams his fist down on the table, infuriated. 'I had to work for years to get this place. Now that I've got this far there will have to be a very good reason for me to give it up. There's plenty of money in the coffers, and I'm bound to get another commission sooner or later.' This is his last word on the matter.

Days go by without the post bringing any news. Again, the priest leafs disconsolately through the notebooks in which he keeps track of work delivered. There must be someone who could help him? His finger alights suddenly upon the name of Marquis Guido Bentivoglio d'Aragona, an old acquaintance from his Roman period. After taking over as head of the family, following the death of his elder brother, Marquis d'Aragona swapped Rome for Ferrara. Vivaldi has lost touch with him since, but recalls as if it were yesterday the marquis telling him that he would be glad to be his patron. Years have gone by since the priest sent him a concert for mandolin, d'Aragona's own instrument and one he plays quite well. A great deal of water has passed under the bridge since, of course, and the marquis will undoubtedly have forgotten his promise. But no risk, no gain! Antonio lifts the lid of his inkpot and in beautiful copperplate lettering inscribes a most courteous letter to Marquis

Guido Bentivoglio d'Aragona, inviting himself to organise the opera programme for the coming *carnevale* in Ferarra.

It takes less than a week for word to come back from Ferrara. Alight with anticipation, Vivaldi breaks open the seal and unfolds the letter, his glance racing over the contents. 'HA!'

'Paolina,' he screams, 'Paolina!'

White-faced, she rushes into the room. 'What is it?'

'I told you, didn't I? Take a look at this! Two operas for the *carnevale* in Ferrara.' He hands her the short but warmly worded letter, and she reads with a slowly dawning smile how the marquis will be delighted to make use of Vivaldi's services. And, in order to turn words into deeds, the impresario from Ferrara is on his way to Venice to discuss the plans with Vivaldi.

Abbate Bollani is a large, flabby character who spends the time he is kept waiting to meet Il *Prete Rosso* in ogling the room. He has settled, bloated as a toad, among the cushions of a chair, and has rudely refused Paolina's offer of refreshment. 'Don Vivaldi will be back at any moment from a rehearsal at the *Pietà*,' apologises Paolina, withdrawing and leaving the man from Ferrara to himself. She distinctly dislikes the lustful look in his eye.

'Esteemed friend,' Vivaldi welcomes Bollani. The abbot holds out his hand, but does not take the trouble to stand up. Vivaldi keeps a fixed smile, recognising at once that this man spells trouble.

'A good journey, I hope?' asks Antonio.

Bollani mops sweat from the hollow of his neck and waves away the polite enquiry. 'Let's get down to business,' he puffs. 'D'Aragona wants to hear your music. I don't know why, for it does nothing for me. But there you are; every man to his own taste. I might as well tell you right away, we have a limited budget and you will have to make do with an honorarium that undoubtedly falls far short of the preposterous sums you get offered here.'

Vivaldi continues to smile at the man opposite him, but his blood is boiling. Who does he think he is? Antonio has never heard

345

of the fellow until this moment and suspects him of being the type of impresario who does not let his business ineptitude get in the way of trying to make a profit on every contract. Antonio's brain is working overtime. His first priority is to get a piece of work staged in Ferrara. Once the audiences there have heard something, he will have them eating out of his hand. Now to find a way of stitching up this Bollani fellow.

'My esteemed Bollani. But of course I understand that you are working to a limited budget. Ferrara cannot be compared to a world-famous city such as Venice.' Bollani swallows and Antonio watches his eyes narrow venomously. 'My honorarium for an opera,' continues Antonio, 'is a hundred *zecchini*. I do not intend to barter with you over this. In appreciation of my friendship with the Marquis d'Aragona I shall refresh two of my favourite operas and ask six *zecchini* for each, the fee you would otherwise pay a copyist.'

For a moment Bollani is robbed of speech. He has heard how difficult it is to negotiate with Il *Prete Rosso*, and now he is being offered two operas on a plate.

'Which works do you have in mind, Vivaldi?'

'*Ginevra* and *l'Olimpiade*,' says the priest shortly.

Slowly Bollani nods his fat head.

'Have you engaged singers, orchestra and ballet?' asks Antonio.

'I have my eye on a number of people,' pants Bollani.

'Well now, to make sure these two pieces are perfectly staged I will select the singers myself. And you are in luck, for I know that signorina Anna Girò is available, and she has put on a dazzling performance in the leading role of both productions.'

'Signorina Girò, do you say? Eh, well, I'm not sure if I would agree to that. I prefer to keep the whole production under my own auspices, and my assistant Signor Lanzetti will preside personally over the auditions.'

This idea does not in the least appeal to Antonio. He might not know Daniele Lanzetto in person, but he has heard that he is an extremely mediocre tenor. This cockerel conducting the auditions? Over Antonio's dead body!

'You will appreciate that my magnanimous offer, whereby I more or less make you a present of two operas, involves you guaranteeing me that these works are flawlessly performed. You will appreciate, as a fellow professional, that I have to consider my good name.'

Bollani is sweating profusely, despite the coolness of the afternoon. 'All the more,' pursues Vivaldi, ladling it on, 'because the pressure of work and my commitments here will at first prevent me from attending.'

This last he has just dreamt up, realising as he talked that he did not at all fancy being cooped up with a bunch of amateurs for weeks on end in Ferrara.

'I am afraid that I cannot agree to these terms,' mumbles Bollani stolidly.

Vivaldi gets to his feet. 'That is a great pity. But let us remain friends. You see, I am so busy that this comes as no huge blow to me. My only regret is that my friendship with your marquis will be sorely tested, especially when I describe to His Excellency in my letter how I offered him two operas virtually for nothing. I can only hope he will not be too offended. But, no, I feel sure my honourable friend the marquis will respect the judgement exercised by his impresario. Bollani, it was a great pleasure meeting you.'

Bollani, however, does not leave his sofa. It is a couple of seconds before the implication behind Vivaldi's words actually gets though to him. A letter of that sort from Il *Prete Rosso* to the Marquis d'Aragona and he can say goodbye to his job as an impresario.

'It must be the damp,' gasps Bollani. 'I don't understand how you Venetians can live right on the water like this. I'm quite sure it softens the brain... my apologies Vivaldi, there has been a misunderstanding on my side.'

Good job the man has not lost all ability to examine his own conscience, thinks Antonio with relish. He knows the game is won. 'Fine,' says he aloud. 'Now let's get down to discussing an honorarium for the vocalists.'

Bollani is glad to get back to the mainland. Slippery as eels, those Venetians, he thinks, thankfully taking a seat in the coach. He has a notion that Il *Prete Rosso* has had him good and proper this time. But he is not finished with that wretched priest!

The scores of *L'Olimpiade* and *Ginevra* are unearthed and Antonio looks through them; not that he plans many alterations. The music looks fine to him, and he would be very surprised if anyone in Ferrara had ever attended a performance of either piece.

But things go differently than Antonio had expected. Once back in his home city, Bollani has written a letter to the priest that Vivaldi, upon receiving it, does not know whether to humour or treat with contempt. He re-reads the contents, then tosses the open letter onto the table. Is this Bollani's idea of revenge?

'What does he say?' asks Paolina, who has been watching closely whilst he read.

'According to Bollani, those holding the purse-strings do not wish to hear my *Ginevra*, but Hasse's *Demetrio* instead.'

'But that's impossible, you have a contract!'

'Oh yes, but they want me to re-work *Demetrio*, just as I was planning to do with *Ginevra*. It's all a ruse by that blasted Bollani. But what does it matter? We've enough time for rehearsals. And I'll have that thing by Hasse rewritten in no time, and in such a way that it becomes a Vivaldi opera, too.'

But *Abbate* Bollani apparently has one or two other surprises up his sleeve, for a second letter arrives, with the request that Vivaldi also exchange the second opera for a work by Hasse. What a nauseating little man, thinks Antonio with repulsion, pulling a face to match.

In the end it all takes much longer than he had meant, although there is no other work pending. He does, however, have cause to regret his decision to stay at home rather than travel personally to Ferrara, for this has provided Bollani with every chance to provoke him. The impresario shows a marked reluctance to refund the extra costs involved in buying and rewriting the Hasse scores. It takes a letter to the marquis and a message to

Anna, who is already busy rehearsing in Ferrara, to make clear to Bollani that he has a choice between paying up, or watching the singers suddenly go off 'sick'. Still huffing and puffing, he plumps for the former.

Antonio listens with difficulty to the excruciating report that Anna brings back of her experiences in Ferrara. A continually absent impresario Bollani, his tyrannical and completely tone-deaf assistant Lanzetti, who nonetheless keeps every singer in her place, a chaotic theatre, dreadful lighting and décor. Good grief! She's never seen anything like it. It's a wonder the public didn't walk out en masse.

'What a bunch of amateurs,' sighs Vivaldi. 'I'll write a letter to the Marquis d'Aragona and ask if I can take over as impresario next year. We'll show the poor folk of Ferrara what we mean by professional theatre!'

Paolina gives an acerbic smile. She hopes he intends to ask a better price for his work while he's about it. There has been little enough reward for all the time and trouble this winter. To her relief, the New Year brings with it the prospect of a new opera for Verona. It would seem that there, at least, they still know how to prize Vivaldi's work.

Antonio's self-respect is bolstered by the applause of an audience that includes the prospective king of Bavaria, a guest this evening at the theatre of Verona. *Catone in Utica* has proved an operatic success and, still fresh from the triumph, Antonio writes to the Marquis d'Aragona.

With a sinking heart, Guido Bentivoglio, Marquis d'Aragona, slits open Antonio's letter. In fact, he had hoped the close of *carnevale* would mark the end of his correspondence with the priest. He is fed up to the teeth with the perpetual complaints about Bollani and outstanding payments, and he had hoped everything was finally tied up. As usual, the letter opens with a flood of servile flattery, and it is a couple of lines before Vivaldi comes to his point: the arrangement of an entire theatre season for next year's *carnevale*. One would have thought the priest had had his fill of Ferrara, reflects the marquis. An ironic smile comes to his lips as he reads Vivaldi's emphatic description of his skill and experience as entrepreneur of whole productions, all, up until now, financed out of his own pocket. D'Aragona folds away the letter; he will reply to it later. He has serious doubts as to whether he should promote Vivaldi's interests, but on the other hand that damned Bollani has given him just as much grief, and surely there's no harm in teaching this clerical upstart a lesson.

Bollani is incensed. He has just heard that Vivaldi has been invited to lead the coming theatre season. 'How has he swung that one?' the abbot rages furiously at his assistant. The terrified Daniele Lanzetti, ears buzzing and feeling completely incapable of amending the situation, crumples.

'He has nothing to do with this place. This is OUR territory!'

Lanzetti holds his peace, afraid of saying a wrong word and thus unleashing the full fury of the man standing opposite him, foaming at the mouth. Bollani slumps down in a chair, grabs a bottle of wine, pours himself a huge glass and thumps the bottle back down on the table.

'Tell me, Lanzetti, how are we to keep that slimy priest outside the city walls?'

'The only person who can keep him out is the biggest man in the city, Cardinal Ruffo,' whines Lanzetti. Bollani stares glassily at him.

'Very good, Lanzetti, very good,' replies his employer slowly and thoughtfully. A cruel glint has come to his eyes.

Antonio Vivaldi has just put the final touches to a *concerto grosso* for the orchestra of the Amsterdamsche Shouwburg, to be performed in honour of its centenary on the seventeenth of January 1738.

He reads it through once more before Paolina packs it ready for the post. Antonio thinks back to his first meeting with Estienne Roger, the Amsterdam publisher. In the meantime his music has reached every corner of Europe, and Vivaldi wonders how much and how often people play his works. It is years since he had any contact with La Cène; for all he knows the man is long dead. Now and then he still receives a commission from the far north, such as this one for the theatre in Amsterdam, but such requests are fewer with each passing year.

Every commission is welcome, and Antonio is excited to see the enormous insignia of the Nuncio Apostolico, ambassador of the Vatican in Venice, in the sealing wax on the letter just delivered by messenger. Up until now Vivaldi has written nothing for the ambassador or for the cathedral of San Pietro di Castello. 'I have an immediate summons from the patriarch!' he calls out elatedly to Paolina. 'I hope they don't want anything from me at short notice, because we're on our way to Ferrara in a fortnight.' Paolina takes the paper from Vivaldi. It is brief; in the minimum of words Vivaldi is summoned to appear in person at the patriarchal palace on the island of San Pietro di Castello, at the farthermost point of Venice.

Giving back the letter, she sees it tremble slightly in her hand. Her intuition tells her there is something amiss here. But Vivaldi blithely pockets the letter, looks for his hat and throws his cloak about his shoulders. Paolina offers him a scarf. It is bitter outside and with Ferrara just a couple of weeks away he had better not catch cold.

The island with its cathedral and the palace of the patriarch seems to stand apart from Venice; a tiny fragment of land bearing the papal ambassador and patriarch, attached to the rest of Venice only by the fragile umbilical cord of a little wooden bridge. Venice has always maintained a singular relationship with the Pope. As long as there is no risk of harm to Venice's interests, Rome and the Republic walk hand in hand; but when the chips are down Venice comes first. Veneziani, poi Cristiani! In the past this has meant excommunication for the entire city, but no Venetian has ever bothered his head on that account. The gondola bounces softly against the quay next to the bridge. Vivaldi pays the gondolier, steps ashore and looks about him. Extraordinary that he's never been here before.

Everything is dead quiet. A single gull wings its way noiselessly over the great square, spread out like a blanket before the great cathedral. The doors of the palace straight ahead are closed, but through the windows, by the glimmering light of chandeliers, he can just discern the movement of silhouetted figures. The sudden tolling of the *campanile* bell breaks the silence, making Vivaldi start. Crossing the square, he bangs with the bronze knocker on the palace door. Almost directly the door is opened and the priest steps inside. To his astonishment, rather than being kept waiting he is ushered through immediately.

The *Nuncio Apostolico* looks severely down upon the priest kneeling before him in greeting. The papal ambassador is in no mood for formalities.

'I bear a message for you from His Eminence Tomaso Ruffo, Cardinal of Ferrara.'

Bemused, Vivaldi stares at the Nuncio.

'I must inform you that until further notice you are forbidden entry to the city of Ferrara.' Vivaldi cannot believe his ears. 'What is this, what are you telling me?' He feels his chest tightening painfully, so that he has to fight for air. 'There must be some mistake. I have to be in Ferrara in two weeks to lead the theatre, to do my work. This is surely a misunderstanding!'

The papal ambassador shakes his head forbiddingly.

'But why, in God's name, why? What reason is there?'

The Nuncio rubs his chin. 'His Eminence deeply disapproves of priests who no longer adhere to their devotions, who no longer take Mass, who concern themselves with public entertainment, who conduct relations with not just one, but several women. In short, priests who behave like out and out heretics.'

Outraged and incredulous Vivaldi listens to the list of

allegations. What sort of nonsense is this? He is almost sixty years old and in all his life no such imputations have ever been made against him. No one has ever so blackened his name. 'You must understand,' he begins calmly, 'an error has been made. Ill health prevents me from officiating at Mass. I received dispensation for this some twenty-five years ago. As for public entertainment, I am occupied solely with artistically responsible and religious works such as those I have been writing for nearly thirty years for the *Ospedale della Pietà*. And relations with women? Where on earth does such a ludicrous idea come from?'

Looking steadily at Vivaldi, the Nuncio draws a deep breath. He is perfectly familiar with the work of *Il Prete Rosso*. He has heard it everywhere, in the convents, at the *Pietà*, in *San Marco*. As far as he is aware, there has never been any scandal attached to this priest at the orphanage of the *Pietà*, nor are his relations with the Girò sisters tainted by anything other than common gossip. And how many priests are there whose main preoccupation is indeed earthly business, and who actually maintain a family into the bargain? The Nuncio knows, too, that no such attempt to thwart the priest's plans would stand a chance of succeeding here in Venice. But Ferrara is another kettle of fish. As part of the papal state, the church is the authority that carries weight there. The ambassador is merely the messenger of Ruffo, a cardinal infamous for toeing the conservative line. 'Your relationship with the Girò sisters is regarded as extremely suspect.'

A band of iron tightens around Vivaldi's ribcage. 'My relations with the Girò sisters? The younger, Signorina Anna Girò, is an extraordinarily competent singer, and for this reason, and this alone, plays the leading role in almost all my operas. Her elder sister Paolina is my secretary, and has for many years been responsible for arranging all my business affairs, especially when we are abroad. My poor state of health means I have to entrust many tasks to others. *Allora!* That is my relationship with these two ladies!'

The Nuncio spreads his hands. 'I am sorry, Don Vivaldi. As

I have told you, I am merely the bearer of a message. If you have business awaiting you in Ferrara I can only advise you to put the arguments you have just outlined to me before His Eminence Cardinal Ruffo himself.'

And with that the audience is over.

Shattered, his throat tight with unexpressed rage, Vivaldi re-crosses the square away from the palace. 'Bloody hell, not a gondola in sight!' The quay is deserted on both sides of the bridge. 'My God, have you no mercy?' It at once begins to rain, and Vivaldi clambers with difficulty, wheezing and gasping, over the wet planks of the bridge. Ahead he spies a couple of gondoliers sheltering under the bridge over the *Rio di Castello*. He hails one and is soon seated in the dry and on his way homewards. Now that he does not have to concentrate on walking, he can order his thoughts. What is the real reason behind the message from Cardinal Ruffo? How many commitments has he not already made? Who will fulfil his obligations to lead the theatres if he cannot be there? Ruffo, Ruffo. He does not even know the man. He must write directly to the Marquis d'Aragona; his patron will surely put in a good word for him. There must be some misunderstanding; there's no other explanation!

But Cardinal Ruffo is immovable. Marquis d'Aragona advises Vivaldi to place his productions in the hands of Picchi, another impresario in Ferrara.

'Another buffoon like Bollano, no doubt,' storms Vivaldi, reading the written proposal.

'Is there no other solution?' asks Paolina, worriedly scanning the financial details. All the contracts with the artistes, orchestra and the ballet are already signed. Antonio has asked the marquis to order that the productions be cancelled unless the cardinal reviews his decision. This form of 'circumstance beyond one's control' constitutes reason enough for dissolution of contracts, thus releasing Vivaldi from any financial responsibilities.

The cardinal, however, sees no reason to veto the planned productions. It is only Vivaldi who is not welcome.

'My God, what have I done to deserve this?' Antonio asks himself in despair. 'It is as if Ruffo is intent on crushing me completely. Oh, if only my father was here,' he moans. Paolina gives him a worried glance. 'If the operas can't go ahead, it looks as if you could be right. They are out to destroy you.' She lets him see the sum of all his contractual obligations. Vivaldi reels. It adds up to nearly his total capital!

'We cannot allow this to happen,' he says between clenched teeth.

'The operas have to go through, Antonio. Otherwise all has been for nothing,' wails Paolina in despair. 'Wait for the letter from Picchi. Perhaps he will be well disposed towards you. Think about offering him a decent salary. This must go ahead, cost what may!'

Picchi's letter is fortunately not long in coming, but it does not bring good tidings. The impresario is clearly at odds with the proposed honoraria; everything can be done for a third of the cost.

'Of course it can!' rages Vivaldi indignantly. 'If you scrape together all the market-stall holders between here and Ferrara and dump them on the stage. What is the brainless idiot thinking about? My God, what have I done to deserve this?'

Anna has been pondering long and hard the painful situation in which they find themselves, and she is more and more convinced Bollani is behind it. 'It would not surprise me if Picchi and Bollani are pals,' she remarks. 'And whose best interests would be served by you being banned from Ferrara? Who has no work at the moment? It's not the cardinal who has it in for us, but Bollani.'

Vivaldi lets her words sink in. He nods. 'You're right! To think I didn't realise it sooner. That is the only explanation.' He stares in front of him with his head in his hands. 'In that case, none of us are going to Ferrara. If those two are working hand in glove they will do everything they can to sabotage the whole business and line their own pockets. I'll let them hear nothing from me and then, just before *San Stefano*, inform Picchi they needn't expect any help from us. At the end of the day, the only person they have a contract with is myself, and it is they who have slammed the door in my face. Yes, that should put the cat nicely among the pigeons, because then Ferrara will have to do without any opera this *carnevale*.'

Anxious and puzzled as to the direction of Antonio's thought, Paolina catches hold of his arm. 'But our obligations, your money? We shall lose everything!' Antonio taps her hand to convey his confidence. 'Don't you worry. The feast of *San Stefano* will see the premier of *L'oracolo in Messenia*.'

He stands up and makes ready to leave the house.

'But where?' asks Paolina, lost.

'San Angelo!' he grandly declares. 'I am going to make Fabrizio Brugnolo an offer he cannot refuse.'

The impresario of the *Teatro San Angelo* listens with interest to the priest's story. 'A chance in a million!' Vivaldi praises his own proposal. 'Two operas, to start at *San Stefano*, with a brilliant cast, mesmerising dancers, and half the turnover for you!' But Fabrizio has dealt with Vivaldi before. The priest is a sharp customer, and one who never makes a deal to his own detriment.

'I have my programme complete,' the impresario tells him. 'And I can't disappoint people.'

'Look here, my esteemed friend. I don't have a lot of time and I'm not leaving here without a contract between us, the like of which you have not seen even in your dreams. I'll add a third opera, *Armida al campo d'Egitto*. It has been nothing less than a resounding success. I'll re-write the arias, trim the recitative, and you can bet your life it will raise the roof.'

Fabrizio scrutinises the priest, unable to divine what lies at the bottom of this extraordinary proposal. Half the turnover! Not the profits, this time, which depending on the costs can be pretty miserable, but TURNOVER! Vivaldi must be desperate; what's going on here? Fabrizio leans back in his chair and digs his finger in an ear.

'Sixty percent of the turnover, Vivaldi. Sixty percent, no less!' Antonio does the sum. It could work, just. If the audiences are big enough they will just cover their costs. Bitter, but relieved, Antonio shakes the hand of Fabrizio, who can hardly believe the turn of events. It is the most magnificent contract of his life.

'Shall we put everything down on paper right away, Vivaldi?' he agitates, in sudden terror that the priest will renege on their agreement.

'With pleasure,' beams Antonio.

The censor passes the libretto only on the twenty-seventh of December, the day after the feast of *San Stefano*. Three days later the *Teatro San Angelo* opens her doors and the auditorium slowly fills. After many a sleepless night, Paolina can at last breathe a sigh of relief, realising their costs will be covered. She watches with the deepest respect how Antonio night after night leads the orchestra as energetically as of old, as if triumphing over all adversity.

But once home, hidden from public gaze behind the shutters, he drops the charade. He is exhausted, tired through and through; and all too aware how close to the edge of the abyss he has been this time. He may have got away with it now, but he knows he can never again ask any favour of Fabrizio. Vivaldi has given away so much, cut his cloth so fine, the impresario will never agree to work with him again for less. His only source of satisfaction is that the theatre in Ferrara will lie dark and empty this winter.

With *carnevale* and its true-life drama behind them, Antonio and Paolina are determined to take life more quietly. The whole episode with Ferrara has cost Vivaldi a great deal of energy. In the end they have come out of it well, with all their costs covered. Yet Antonio has the strong impression that his name has been clouded, and he has bidden farewell to San Angelo.

But the urge to produce another opera is still there, and

357

growing because, apart from Verona and some small commissions, there has been no income over the past year. It is not clear what role has been played by the Ferrara fiasco in a decision on the part of the *Pietà* to release Don Vivaldi from his duties as *Maestro de'Concerti*. A couple of years previously Vivaldi had turned his nose up at the hundred ducats offered him for this post. Now every coin is welcome, for according to his updated ledger he is eating into his savings. This confirms his anxieties.

Gradually it has slipped into his consciousness, the fear that people will no longer ask him for work, his waning popularity. Worry gnaws away at him, but he keeps his inner state hidden as much as possible from the outside world, and in particular from Paolina. He has written anew to Verona, to Milan, Vicenza, Ravenna, even to Rome. But he receives in return only politely worded letters of rejection or no reply at all. Every invitation to play, whether at an embassy or a patrician's palace, is promptly accepted. Foreigners who come to his door are eagerly welcomed in, and allowed to leave only once the priest has found a chance to sell them one or more pieces of his work.

At least once a day Antonio pores over the ledger, examining and re-examining the figures. It becomes almost an obsession, and he gets increasingly restless if a couple of days pass by without anyone knocking at the door. Should they follow Paolina's suggestion and move to a smaller residence? If so, he would rather move far away from Venice, to some place where no one knows him. For what a laughing-stock he will be otherwise! How people will enjoy pointing him out, the flop of a composer who can no longer even pay his rent! He does the calculations and again banishes the idea of a move.

However hard Antonio tries to disguise his inner torment, Paolina sees it plainly. It troubles her that he refuses to talk things over; every time she asks how he is, he fobs her off with some evasive answer. She knows by now the folly of pursuing the matter. It only makes him angry.

Luigi Riggio Saladino Branciforti Colonna, Prince of Campoflorido, shows himself, as always, to be a generous host. His post of Spanish ambassador in Venice encourages him regularly to organise concerts for his diplomatic contacts. The prince has for many years been courting Signorina Girò, charmed not only by her voice but with her whole person. And this evening, too, his is among the loudest applause at the end of her *cantate*. Prince Campoflorido insists that she and her accompanist, the famous Antonio Vivaldi, stay awhile after the concert, and with the charm that is the sole preserve of Spanish ambassadors, introduces them as his friends. Anna and Vivaldi meet several persons new to them, and some introductions lead to a new commission or two.

His cousin Cardinal Alfonso is one of the guests to whom the prince introduces Vivaldi. 'It must have been a relief to you when Cardinal Ruffo retired,' remarks Alfonso affably.

'I beg your pardon? You are referring to the Cardinal of Ferrara?'

'I am indeed,' nods the cardinal. 'Were you not yet acquainted with the fact?'

Vivaldi shakes his head.

'My esteemed friend,' laughs the ambassador, 'is this not the moment to retry your luck in Ferrara?'

Antonio replies with another negative shake. 'No, thank you very kindly. That affair was far from good for me, both financially and in terms of my reputation.'

'Come, come,' chides the ambassador, 'are you not overreacting rather? You are a highly respected composer and a world-renowned violinist. Such a name is not so easily erased. No, Vivaldi, so far as I can judge, and many would agree with me, what we're talking about here is a simple case of envy and jealousy. You must not allow yourself to be brought down by it. Give it a second go.'

Antonio smiles faintly. I'm not making that mistake again, he thinks. But the Prince of Campoflorido will not let the subject drop, and a couple of weeks later invites the priest to come and talk again. Courteous as ever, the prince enquires how things are with Antonio.

'Has Don Vivaldi plans for the coming *carnevale*? None? What a shame. Do you know Geremia del Sette?' The ambassador pauses whilst Vivaldi tries to recall the name. 'A *soprano castrato* of unprecedented talent,' he adds.

'I'm sorry,' admits Antonio, drawing a blank.

'Would you be prepared to audition this protégé of mine?' asks the prince.

'Most certainly,' replies Vivaldi. 'It is the least I can do for Your Excellency.'

'Have you had any further thoughts concerning Ferrara?'

'I have, Your Excellency, and I am not sure whether I can expose myself to so great a risk again.'

The ambassador waves aside his words. 'Do not concern yourself about that, Don Vivaldi. I have fully acquainted the new cardinal with the facts, and he will not place the slightest obstacle in your path.'

The priest stares at the prince. The man clearly means every word he says. But dare he suggest such a thing to Paolina?

'I look forward to meeting your protégé, and once I have heard him shall suggest which libretto I think most suits him.'

With a smile meant to convey 'future assured', the ambassador thanks Vivaldi for his visit, and, to emphasise his sincerity, hands him a purse containing twenty-five ducats. The priest takes grateful possession of the money, and with it the knowledge that he must now fulfil the prince's request.

The castrato is not too bad, but Vivaldi is not over-impressed. Given the singer's voice and presentation, Antonio thinks Geremia del Sette best fitted for the role of the King of Persia in his opera *Siroe, re di Persia*. This work, set to music by Vivaldi about a decade previously, is now retrieved and spread before him for revision, as requested in a letter from the impresario of the theatre in Ancona. The man wants it ready for the summer season. The honorarium is meagre, but all that may be expected from a tiny venue whose productions Antonio suspects to be frequented only by drunken fishermen and sailors. He will send the music but will refrain from paying a personal visit.

In the meanwhile, Vivaldi has broached the subject of Ferrara with Paolina, and she does not think it a good idea. 'Will the ambassador cover us for all eventualities?' she asks.

'But what choice do we have, Paolina?' responds Antonio. 'I've no other work on the horizon.'

'It's just that... well, do we really absolutely have to accept this offer? All the little commissions are bringing in a reasonable income at the moment...'

Vivaldi looks glum. 'Yes, but for how long? The less people hear me the less they'll want a new *concerto* from me. And if things go on like that, in a year's time everyone will think I'm dead. Whoosh, vanished from the earth.'

'Nonsense. It's a safe bet your work will still be being played a hundred years from now. You mustn't be so pessimistic.'

'I'm not a pessimist, Paolina, I'm a realist. A hundred years, you say? Take a look at what's happened to the music of Monteverdi, of Peri and Camerata. Dead and buried, lost and gone.'

'Maybe you're right, but I don't want to risk the same thing happening to you again in Ferrara. Stay here; deliver the music and the cast like you did the first time, and leave the theatre to the people there.'

'So you agree I should do it?' he pursues.

'If you do it the way I have just outlined, you could try.' Uncertainty is uppermost in her reply.

Negotiations are soon underway, and the contracts signed. Vivaldi is to deliver two new operas, *Siroe, re di Persia* and a reworking of *Farnace*.

In the meantime, Antonio has also signed contracts with Pietro Mingotti, an adventurous Venetian who for a couple of years has been running the new theatre in Graz with his brother Angelo.

When more than a century previously Emperor Ferdinand moved his court to Vienna, Graz, situated on the eastern outskirts of the Alps, was to serve as centre of the Habsburg empire. About ten years ago the court orchestra of Vienna had performed one of Antonio's operas and awakened in the inhabitants of Graz a taste for Italian musical theatre. At first they were satisfied with touring opera companies who performed mostly in the open air. But three years ago Pietro deemed the time ripe for a proper theatre building, and ever since, three times a week, audiences in Graz have been enjoying the work of Italian composers. Mingotti has noted that 'old' masters such as Vivaldi go down best on this side of the Alps, and has thus made an approach to Il Prete Rosso. Vivaldi is honoured. After all the recent blows, it is good to hear that his work is still really valued. The two men quickly agree financial terms, and Vivaldi is commissioned to rework both L'adelaide and Rosmira for Mingotti. Antonio very much regrets that Anna is already booked for Ferrara, as Graz would have been a perfect springboard for her career in the north. Deep in his heart Vivaldi still remembers the humiliation of his first encounter with the Viennese court, a memory that remains despite the knowledge that his music continues to be appreciated in Bohemia and Saxony.

The speed with which he has reached agreement with Mingotti stands in sharp contrast to the Ferrara business.

At the beginning of January Antonio receives word that Siroe, re di Persia is not going well. The hall was full for the first night, but has emptied steadily evening by evening since. Is this revenge on the part of the people of Ferrara who, partly through Antonio's agency, had suffered darkened theatres the previous season? Or are the recitatives still too long for public taste? The situation escalates to the extent that the curtain has to come down prematurely on the production of Siroe, and the public is not interested in attending another single night of Farnace.

Everything may be reasonably well in order financially, but the same may not be said of Vivaldi's self-esteem. So his music is no longer good enough! He could not be more deeply wounded.

Grumpy and disillusioned, Anna returns from Ferrara, swearing never again to set foot in the bloody place. Never before has she been confronted with such a thankless public. All the blame for this she pours on the head of the leader of the orchestra, Pietro Antonio Beretta. Beretta might be *Maestro di cappella* of the cathedral of Ferrara but he is a useless harpsichordist. Apparently he has scrapped or simplified in the score all the most challenging harpsichord parts, which do indeed demand good command of technique, even from highly experienced musicians. It didn't help either that the hall was treated each night to Bollani and his constellation of hirelings greeting each aria and recitative with a loud chorus of booing. Vivaldi is finished once and for all with Ferrara, and immediately dispatches Anna to Graz, with a request to Piero Mingotti to give her the lead role in *Rosmira*.

A raw wind tugs at the shutters, and rain clatters on the streets and into the canals of *La Serenissima*. The gutters are overflowing, and it is difficult to discern where the quay drops into the depths of the canal. The city looks deserted, but the interiors of the gaming houses and great halls of the *palazzi* are teeming. The people in here seem just as oblivious to the filthy weather as to the parlous state of Venice herself. Money and family treasure changes hands at lightning speed across the tables, and everyone is in party mood. Why, precisely, is not clear even to the players themselves. But the inebriated need no reason for their excesses. It is *carnevale*! With their eyes fixed upon their assets, or on the softly heaving bosoms of the ever-present courtesans, nothing could be further from people's thoughts than the possibility that this city of pageantry, wealth and splendour might be sinking inexorably into the marshy depths of the lagoon.

Vivaldi gazes sombrely at the flames dancing in the hearth. It is as if he senses doom, the imminent downfall of his city, but in truth it is his own future that concerns him more than that of Venice. He has the distinct feeling that things are taking a turn for the worse. He is writing now only for the Pietà; it is all that is keeping him going. In stark contrast to the situation earlier in his career, he nowadays feels proud and honoured simply to be asked to write for the orphanage when it needs a new piece of music. As ever, the Pietà is the regular haunt of foreign kings and princes, and these are the occasions when his light can still shine. But such moments do not last long. Most evenings find him hugging the fireside until deep into the night, and drinking more wine than is good for him. Paolina often goes upstairs early, leaving him alone with his memories. By the time he stumbles away to find his bed at last, he has devised every kind of brilliant plan for the near future, only to awake late the next day having forgotten them completely.

News of the death of Benedetto Marcello later that year hits Antonio harder than he could ever have imagined. The *dilettante* Marcello, co-owner of the *Teatro San Angelo*, composer, and author of *Teatro allo Moda*, had always despised Vivaldi. But his passing signifies to Antonio the closure of yet another chapter in the musical life of Venice. It is with a bitter smile that he pours himself another glass of wine.

9

The new impresario of the *Teatro San Angelo*, Felici Dini, is not satisfied with ticket sales for *Feraspe*, an opera by Antonio Vivaldi, staged last November. Dini had allowed himself to be talked into staging the production by *Il Prete Rosso*, and offered the old man another chance only out of respect, because he had for so long kept the *San Angelo* alive and kicking. The public, however, had shown itself less susceptible and eventually simply stayed at home. Undeterred, Vivaldi resurrects his opera *Tito Manlio* and gets it straight past the censor. This will bring them back to the theatre in droves!

'I'm sorry, Don Vivaldi,' says Felici, having skimmed through the new manuscript. 'No one has more regard for yourself or your work than I do, but the public does not share my feeling.' He pushes the sheet music back across the table towards the priest, and looks into the eyes of an unhappy man.

'But what is wrong with the piece? Tell me, and I will make the necessary adjustments.' Vivaldi cannot hide his despair. Dini looks away, afraid of giving in again.

'It is not a question of re-writing; it is the whole tone, the style. People want something else. I really am most sorry. Perhaps next year?'

Infuriated, Vivaldi snatches up his score and walks out without saying goodbye. Dini sadly watches his retreat, a shadow of the man who for years filled halls night after night.

Outside, Vivaldi summons a gondolier. Just once he turns his head to stare up at the great façade that for so long was his second home. Then, in a sudden frenzy, he consigns his music violently to the water, and steps into the gondola. Seeing the state the priest is in, the gondolier wisely decides to hold his peace. Tito sinks slowly to the bottom of the canal, ink dissolving upwards in smoky spirals as it does so. Before Vivaldi reaches home, every note has mingled itself with the brackish waters of the lagoon.

The rejection by Felici marks the definitive moment of truth for Vivaldi: Venice has turned her back on Il Prete Rosso. There is no longer any future for him here as a musician. The last thing he wants is invitations coming in from patricians, all outdoing each other in the pleasant diversion of getting a once-famous virtuoso to play at their reception for the risible couple of coins they'd throw a street fiddler. Antonio has gone through the books once more with Paolina and the time has come for an urgent decision. Should he live to be as old as his father was when he died, their savings will not suffice. His sisters, neither with any real resources of her own, are entirely dependent upon Antonio's support. Fortunately, Anna has ample work, and is performing again this season at Pietro Mingotti's Theater am Tummelplatz in Graz. At least he does not have to worry about her.

They finally decide to cross the Alps, to where people still appreciate the Venetian composer. The very idea of ending up in a small labourer's cottage next to the Arsenale is one that Vivaldi will not countenance. It is all or nothing!

They plan is to travel via Graz to the Habsburg capital. Vivaldi has contacted Herr Selliers, manager at the public theatre in Vienna. A number of adaptations of Vivaldi operas have been performed there over recent years, well received by audiences. The manager confirms by letter that he is prepared to listen to Don Vivaldi's proposal, and Antonio takes this as boding well for the future. The theatre is situated, after all, right next door to the imperial palace. Who knows what might happen?

Vivaldi makes use of the spring to write his last pieces for the Pietà, whilst Paolina makes preparations for their coming journey. It is a long time since they made such a trip and she is surprised how excited she is at the prospect. How long they will be underway to their new home is unclear and, as long as there is also uncertainty concerning their final destination, she would rather travel light. She will miss her books. It may be a whole year before she sees her precious library again. She passes her finger lovingly over the soft, pigskin-covered volumes and decides to take just one more with her after all.

For the last time, Vivaldi relishes the experience of conducting the *Figlie di Coro* through a *serenata* for the Crown Prince of Saxony, Frederik Christian, son of August III. How many years have passed since Antonio played for this man's father? Vivaldi has very little contact these days with Johann Pisendel, who has by now risen to the dizzy heights of concert-master with the court orchestra of Dresden. The fact that seven years ago they appointed Johann Hasse *Hofkapellmeister* is a clear indication that the Germans have no real interest in Vivaldi. The exchange of greetings between himself and Prince Frederik is cool; Antonio can expect nothing more from Dresden. But, clearly ignorant of Vivaldi's feelings, Frederik Christian very much likes *Il coro delle muse*. In any case, it earns the priest fifteen ducats.

The management of the *Pietà* wakes up somewhat at the news that Antonio is deserting Venice for a while. He asks the *Congregazione* if it is interested in putting aside some new music for its own use and, after the usual round of negotiations, the *Pietà* takes twenty *concerti*. The twenty sequins will easily cover his coming travel expenses.

Vivaldi debates with himself which works he should take with him. The basis of most of his pieces he has stored safely in his head, so that he can write them out at will. In the end he chooses to pack only *L'oracolo*. He has instructed his sisters in the filing system used for his manuscripts, so that they know how to find and send on the right score should he request it. His father's room remains locked up. The rent is paid a year ahead, and the first days of May find them ready to depart.

It is with mixed emotions that Paolina and Antonio set sail for Trieste. From there they will go on via Laibach and Maridor to Graz.

In the churning wake of the ship, just now passing the Lido, distance grows between Antonio and his city of Venice. Seated on the rear deck, where he least feels the movement of the ship, he stares desolately at the *campanili* as they slowly disappear over the horizon. For the first time he is assailed by doubt as to why he is leaving, as if unconsciously he senses he might never see his birthplace again. Would Giambattista have decided differently? What would his father have done in his place?

Their stay in Graz is shorter than expected. He is met upon arrival at the *Theater am Tummelplatz* by a sombre Pietro Mingotti. The impresario assures Vivaldi he would like nothing better than to offer him a *scrittura*, but in all honestly cannot afford to. Expenditure for the new theatre has been crippling, and last season he filled fewer seats than the year before. Vivaldi soon sees he is wasting his time here, and decides to journey straight on to Vienna. Anna has already left. Mingotti gives Antonio a letter from her, in which she explains her plans. It seems she may have a chance of a role in Prague and does not want to miss it.

Antonio is completely thrown. The public must indeed be less and less interested in serious music, for why else would they abandon a brand-new theatre?

At best it is an ominous sign, and his concerns over the future are amplified. En route to the Habsburg capital, Paolina tries to lighten his mood. After all, Vienna has so much to offer him. Every jolt of the carriage increases his wish to believe her words, so that by the time they ride into the city on the Danube his tattered self-respect is intact again and his spirits high.

Once installed in their lodgings on the corner of the new market, Vivaldi takes a stroll to the *Kärntnertortheater*. He is looking for Jozef Selliers, the intendant with whom he has corresponded. It takes a while to track him down, and when he does Vivaldi finds the manager busily talking with a man he introduces to Vivaldi as *Herr* Holzbauer. Jozef Selliers takes Vivaldi aside, to continue their conversation on the other side of the hall. Ignaz Holzbauer must continue with his orchestral rehearsal.

'A try-out,' explains Jozef, indicating the stage. '*Hypermnestra*, an opera in three acts, sung entirely in German.'

Vivaldi stares at him, his eyes nearly popping out of his head. 'An opera in German?' he repeats. For the life of him, he cannot imagine trying to tone down that thumping German tongue and tame it into an aria.

'Not everyone in Vienna understands Italian,' Selliers expounds. 'It is not so long since the theatre offered audiences only Stranitzky's *Hanswurst* and, believe it not, that always drew a full house!'

Vivaldi laughs good-humouredly, but cannot think what in God's name the manager can mean. 'The public is beginning gradually to get used to Italian opera,' the man continues, 'but it seems a good idea to meet people halfway by giving them an opera in their own language.'

It sounds logical enough. But whether it can sound beautiful is another thing altogether. In any case, it restores Antonio's hope a little. As far as musical taste goes – if taste it is, for Vivaldi soon learns that *Hanswurst* is nothing more than the Austrian version of *Commedia dell'Arte* – Vienna has a great deal of catching up to do. This must work in his favour, and he feels lighter than he has for a long while; the more so once the contract with Selliers has been signed. The arrangement is that this autumn Antonio shall produce *L'oracolo in Messina*.

The moment their names are down on the contract Paolina feels the weight of the world slip from her shoulders. Antonio is recovering before her eyes. He is cheerfully humming to himself, and, best of all, is being sweet to her again.

Whilst he has been busy arranging his own work, she has been feasting her eyes on her new surroundings, taking herself into town each day. Their present rent is quite high, but the theatre manager has recommended *Frau Waller's Sattlerisch Haus*, just behind the theatre on the corner of *Kärntnerstrasse* and *Sattlergasse*. Frau Waller rents out several rooms to people temporarilly attached to the theatre. Jozef Selliers and she have for years had a good arrangement whereby, if people fail to pay their rent, the intendant simply docks it from their pay and reckons up with her later.

The apartment she gives Paolina and Antonio is simply furnished and not large, but satisfies them for the time being. The corner room gets plenty of natural light from two windows. Antonio moves the table, so creating a workplace for himself. They are at the front of the house, and the room can be quite noisy, for the *Kärntnerstrasse* is one of the busiest streets in Vienna.

The summer is spent in writing to inform all their old Bohemian friends and associates that Don Vivaldi will be residing until further notice in Vienna and wishes to put himself entirely at their service for the provision of a new composition or production.

The response is disappointing, but according to Paolina this is due entirely to the warm season. Most of the gentry and half the court are away in the country. The sultry days are best spent in the shadow of the willows on the Danube, so that often Antonio and Paolina take a carriage down to the riverbank and sit for hours in welcome coolness beside the water.

Antonio has his sights set energetically on autumn. His fervent hope is that Charles VI will put in an appearance at the opening of his first performance, for the Archduke of Austria is currently confined to his sickbed. Last week the regent caught a cold whilst hunting duck in the reed-beds of Lake Neusiedel. It has been bitterly cold recently; alternating storms of sleet and snow driven before a lacerating wind that has driven everybody off the streets. Inside the theatre it is not much better, but at least it's dry. Selliers considers it a waste of money to heat the place except for performances, so everyone is muffled up to the chin for rehearsals.

Only the members of the orchestra are left suffering terribly from cold, bare hands, as anybody can hear from their playing. Vivaldi for one, and it does not please him.

The sonorous tolling of bronze bells slowly penetrates the walls and resonates around the deep interior of the theatre. It's as if all the bells of Vienna are conspiring to ring in unison and drown out my music, ruminates Vivaldi irritably. Pausing to rub his hands and get the blood flowing again, he sees the steward storming into the auditorium. 'The emperor,' yells Selliers, with a wild look in his eyes. The entire orchestra and every artiste on the podium turn to stare at the manager. Antonio is by now looking straight into his face, distorted with weeping. 'The emperor is DEAD!' he stammers.

Slowly the full significance of his words dawns on Vivaldi and he begins to tremble. He sits down to relieve his quaking knees. 'My God,' he groans, making the sign of the cross. 'Why now? Why in heaven's name just at this moment?' He feels his stomach turn, and glances back at the manager. Every person in the hall knows the implications of his message. In accordance with tradition, all the theatres in the empire must be closed for the obligatory period of a year's mourning. Cursing and swearing, singers and orchestra alike abandon the stage for the auditorium. They want to see their money! Written into their contracts is a clause covering such an eventuality, entitling each to a third of the agreed honorarium.

After being paid, most pack their bags and are off at once to look for work in a theatre beyond the borders of the Habsburg empire.

Antonio is completely distraught. Where must he go now? Too numb to think things through clearly, he opts instead to seek out Paolina and tell her the bad news. The manager he leaves to himself, as sick at heart as Vivaldi himself.

The whole of Vienna is plunged into mourning and there is a general sense of unreality, as if their ruler cannot really be gone.

The emperor was as fit as a fiddle. Rumours do the rounds that he was poisoned, but by whom?

Maria Theresa, twenty-three-year-old daughter and heir to Charles VI, wastes no time in pronouncing herself Queen of Hungary and Bohemia and Archduchess of Austria; obviously, she cannot also assume the title of Head of the Holy Roman Empire. Vivaldi derives hope from this accession. Maria Theresa is, after all, married to Frans Stefan, former Duke of Lorraine, the same who, years ago in Prague, appointed Vivaldi his concert-master.

But there is no question at present of an audience at court. Not everyone in Europe is pleased to see Maria Theresa heading the Habsburg empire. The Prince-Elector of Bavaria, Charles Albert, considers himself the rightful heir to Charles VI and demands that, as highest descendant of the Habsburgs, he be directly given the title of Head of the Holy Roman Empire. Maria Theresa spits on her brother-in-law's claim. The Bavarian sovereign is married to her niece, but it does not look likely that a solution to this dispute will be found within the family. Charles Albert's claim receives the support of the French king; Spain and the Saxons swear allegiance to Bavaria. Vienna begins to tremble. Will the young queen be able to weather this political sparring match?

Out of the blue, Frederik II King of Prussia offers to 'come to her aid'.

If Maria Theresa is prepared to render up to him in return the wealthy province of Silesia, goes Frederik's grandiose proposal, he will ensure that Vienna remains free of Bavarian troops.

Maria Theresa is utterly isolated, for should she refuse his offer, Frederik II will have no option but to join the side of Bavaria, France, Spain and the Saxons. The new queen, however, is stalwart in her belief in the rectitude of her position, and resolutely refuses the proposal. A scant two months after the death of her father, Frederik II's Prussian troops march across the border, crushing Silesia underfoot.

Inexperienced and ill-prepared for statesmanship as she is, Maria Theresa soon discovers in what a deplorable condition her father has left the country. The army proves incapable of withstanding the Prussians. On the other side of the frontier, Bavarian troops are making ready for an assault upon Prague. By a stroke of good fortune, Anna has already left the city and, with some other singers, has arrived safe and sound in Vienna. Seeing no future here, Anna is now planning to move on. She and the rest of the group she performed with in Prague are travelling to northern Italy. If they are quick, they may still find roles for themselves there.

'Would it not be more sensible for you to come home, too?' Anna suggests to Paolina and Antonio. Like many others, she is convinced a war is looming. But Vivaldi sees things differently. Now that Frederik II has his province, things will calm down. 'When the theatres reopen next year, mine will be the first production! And what's more, there's a good chance I may be appointed *Kapellmeister* at court. No, Anna, we're staying put! And if by October next year you have no roles lined up for yourself, you can come back to Vienna. Be my *prima donna* again.'

Laughing, she embraces the priest. She has so much to thank him for. She has been able to build a good name for herself professionally, and nowadays it is she who often has the choice of roles offered her.

''Bye, sister,' says Paolina, kissing Anna on the cheek. She stands and watches as Anna runs down the stairs to join her waiting friends. Vivaldi waves to his daughter, but she is already gone. He shuts the door softly.

The last thing on Maria Theresa's mind is the court orchestra. She is seven months pregnant and her country is entering a state of war, when suddenly she is confronted with the death of her little one-year-old daughter.

Only the previous year she lost her eldest daughter, Maria Elisabeth, and events since have prevented her even from mourning this loss. Yet, despite pregnancy and grief, her energy seems unabated and she remains capable of motivating all around her.

Not only does she preside in the private sphere in her role of mother, it is evident to all across the land that she can stand her ground against the opposition, however powerfull.

On a chilly morning in March 1741, bells ring out again over Vienna, and the cannons roar from her bastions. For a moment people stop what they are doing, shocked into thinking the city must be under siege. But soon the news spreads: their queen has given birth to a son! Every inhabitant of the empire sees this as a good omen, and the future suddenly looks less bleak. Vivaldi does not share in the positive mood. He has no work, and that makes him restless. He has found out from Jozef Selliers which aristocrats hold the main posts at court and who might put in a good word for him in the near future. But even the old patrons of the arts are distracted by more serious business at present. Every now and then he finds a chance to sell some music. But unless people have the very best reasons for being in the city, most are staying away.

In June comes the long-delayed advance by joint Bavarian and French forces. The Austrian soldiers fight valiantly for their fatherland, but in vain. Each day more territory slips away from beneath their feet. In Vienna there is a rising sense of panic. Some citizens prefer not to await coming events, pack up their belongings and leave for quieter destinations. Jozef Selliers is convinced that October will see the reopening of his theatre and all will be well. Paolina is not so sure, and Vivaldi will not even entertain the idea of his opera being further postponed. He has his worries, of course, but what can he do? He feels his back against the wall. Wine no longer offers him a way out of his troubles. On the contrary, waking up with a crashing headache each day merely increases his sense of paralysis. Even a stroll with Paolina along the banks of the Danube has lost its appeal for him. Watching his depression deepen, she despairs. Then comes a day when he will not get out of bed. This is too much! 'Come on, Antonio,' she shouts angrily at him. 'You've been poisoning the atmosphere around here for days with your misery. If you don't pull yourself together, I'm going home!'

He stares helplessly at her. 'I feel unwell,' he mutters.

'Go a bit easier on the drink, then. I'm sorry, but I've no sympathy with you. If you're not happy here either, then let's go back to Venice.'

She pulls the sheets off him, throws his clothes in a heap on the bed, retreats to the doorway and stands there with her arms folded. Vivaldi gives a deep sigh and reaches for his clothing. Suddenly he is racked by sobs, and it is Paolina's turn to doubt herself. She goes back to the bed as he falls back upon the pillows, weeping piteously. Now that she is closer, she can see the spots of high colour on his cheeks. Laying her hand on his forehead, she murmurs, 'You have a fever.' She draws up the bedclothes once more, telling him. 'Stay where you are for now. We'll see about everything tomorrow.'

Nodding meekly as a small boy, he pulls the sheet up to his chin.

He has a restless night, and the next day his temperature seems higher than ever. Determined to take no risks, Paolina calls a doctor, who does not arrive until late in the afternoon. He sets his bag down wordlessly, and then asks Antonio how he feels and whether he has any pain. Antonio points to his head, chest and stomach. With a grave expression, the physician feels Antonio's brow, taps even more earnestly upon his chest and presses a finger twice into his abdomen, making the priest wince.

'We'll let some blood,' announces the doctor, as if he has found the definitive cure. From his bag he brings forth a knife and wipes it clean on his handkerchief. 'Have you a bowl for me?' he enquires of Paolina, without looking up. She runs off to fetch one, whilst the doctor makes an incision in an artery that is just visible through the skin of Antonio's naked forearm. Wending its way like a spring stream, blood trickles into the bowl. When the receptacle is half full the physician examines it with satisfaction, tears a piece of paper from his scruffy notebook, and lays this on the wound. He bends Antonio's arm up at the elbow to put pressure on the artery and so stop the bleeding. 'Fine. I'll come back tomorrow.'

But the fever fails to abate, and the following day the doctor repeats the same ritual. Vivaldi is feeling much weaker, whilst the pain in his stomach is worsening. On the third day there is still no improvement. The abdominal discomfort has by now given way to a sensation as of a red-hot poker being rotated in there. Antonio rubs his belly endlessly to try to soothe it, but to no avail.

Paolina tried giving him some porridge this morning, but it tasted foul. Even wine is bitter on his tongue, and does not bring the fever down. The room feels close, and sweat pours from his forehead. Street noise, the clamour of children, the clatter of horses' shod hooves on the cobbles, the scream of tradesman and pedlar, and the high shriek of the swallows, all the sounds of the outside world seem to be melting into an incomprehensible din. Time was when he could always focus upon one source of sound. Oh, dear, he thinks, I must be getting old! Opening his eyes, he finds the room, everything, revolving about him. He takes a deep breath, trying to counteract the nausea welling up inside him. But he can do nothing to prevent it, and a second later is vomiting into the chamber-pot that Paolina has just managed to put in front of him. The next wave brings up his breakfast. In disgust he coughs, spitting away the thick slime accumulating in his mouth. The vomit is stained red with wine. Paolina stares distastefully at the contents of the pot and blanches. That's not wine; it is BLOOD!

She crosses herself and murmurs a silent, fervent prayer for him. It cannot be true! She fears the worst, and does not know what more she can do for him. She hides her terror from him, but cannot shield herself from rising panic. She is not prepared for the end to come so soon, but neither does she dare to leave him to go and fetch a priest. My God, what shall I do? She screams inwardly for help. But knows there is no one to hear her plea.

Vivaldi falls back, defeated, on the pillows. Every move he makes is agony and his breath is coming in short, irregular gasps.

With her handkerchief she again dabs his face dry. It is taking all her self-control to hold back the tears. He needs me now, she tells herself urgently and repeatedly; he needs me, I must be strong for him! Taking his hand, she strokes it tenderly.

But Antonio seems to have slipped into another world, somewhere where her words and gestures no longer reach him. He is trying to shut himself off from all external noise, to make room in his head for his own music. Soon he can hear it, echoing back to him from the past as powerfully as ever, sending its pulses of energy into every fibre of his being. He opens his eyes and is relieved to see Paolina beside him. He does not want to be alone now; he does not want to be without her! He regrets having been so irritable with her. She is right; perhaps they had better go home. Exhausted, he closes his eyes again. In mounting dread, Paolina prays, 'Mother Maria, is there is no way of saving him?' The door opens suddenly, and his father enters. At ease and smiling, Giambattista walks up to the bed.

'FATHER! How happy I am to see you again! You are not a moment too soon, for I am just putting the finishing touches to a new opera, written specially for Maria Theresa. This work will be the best I have ever produced, father. The most scintillating arias and the most exquisite ballet. Ah, I see it all before me, I feel the wonder already...'

Giambattista sits down beside him and puts his arm protectively about Antonio's shoulders.

'All is well, my son. All is well.'

10

Paolina sits numbly on the empty bed, her hands in her lap. She has packed up all her own things, and those of Antonio, and must now wait for the intendant to come and help her carry the baggage down the stairs. Herr Selliers has promised too to walk with her to the halt where she has to catch the post-coach for Italy. It all feels like a dream, a dreadful, unending nightmare.

The doctor came back, certified Don Vivaldi dead and arranged for the body to be removed. The same day, a small service took place in the cathedral of Sint Stefan. Events moved so fast that it feels as if nothing has happened, as if time has simply closed over yesterday. Only Jozef Selliers took the trouble to attend the service. No other soul came to pay their last respects. The burial took place on consecrated ground, just outside the perimeter of the city. Before she knew it, everything was all over. In a daze she walked back from the graveyard. Back upstairs in their apartment once more, she buried her head in the pillow where just this morning he had lain, and gave vent to her anguish.

And now there is the return to her senses, the contemplation of what must be done. She counts up her resources and discovers that, once the doctor and the funeral have been paid for, she has insufficient funds for her journey back. Her only hope is that she gets back some rent money, for Antonio has paid a year in advance.

But the widow is as hard as nails. 'Paid is paid,' she growls at Paolina, slamming the door in her face. Dismayed, Paolina walks a couple of streets to where she has noticed a pawnbroker's shop, and offers him all the jewels Antonio has given her through the years. Knowing what they are worth, she is appalled at the paltry sum the man gives her, but what choice has she? The pawnbroker knows very well that his clients all have their backs against the wall, and she is no different. With a greedy and practised gesture he sweeps towards him across the counter all her jewellery, except for one ring which she manages to snatch back from the pile.

There is still a reasonable amount of money in her bank account in Venice. She will need it, for she now realises that Antonio has died intestate, and she has no claim whatsoever upon the priest's property.

Rather, she will be thrown back upon the goodwill of the Vivaldi family, a less than enticing prospect. Before leaving Vienna, Paolina writes a note to Anna, conveying the terrible news but asking her explicitly to withhold it from everyone else, including the Vivaldi sisters.

The coach passes through the *Kärntnertor* at a trot. To the left, in the shadow of the *Karlskirche*, lies the burial-ground where she must leave Antonio. She cannot believe it. It is unbearable. Her heart contracts painfully in silent resistance to the truth. She bites her lip until the blood flows. She cannot drag her gaze away from the newly piled plot of earth and, leaning from the open carriage window, waves, weeping, until the graveyard disappears from view. '*Adieu mon chèr, adieu.*'

Her suspicions have been well founded. The moment that Paolina tells his sisters of Vivaldi's death they turn their backs on her, afraid she will try to make off with his money. Antonio's brother Francesco Vivaldi, who is still living in Venice, allows himself to fall entirely under the influence of his avaricious sisters. As *pater familias*, he says, he will need all his deceased brother's resources in order to take care of them.

The next day Paolina and Anna find themselves put out on the street with their few personal belongings, and the same day the house is emptied and sealed. Paolina knows she has not a foot to stand on, and her dearest wish is to avoid a scene. This is the price she must pay for the anonymous love of Antonio Vivaldi. Her head held high and arm-in-arm with Anna, Paolina turns and walks away from the house without a backward glance.

Leafing through her diary, she plays now and then with the idea of committing to paper the story of her life with Antonio. But just as fleetingly she lets the thought go again. The fame of Il *Prete Rosso* fades more quickly than she could ever have imagined. If she should tell all, Anna would come to know her true parentage. And what effect would such revelations have upon the good name of the priest? With a shudder she recalls the terrible events of Ferrara. No, never shall she disclose the secret of Antonio Vivaldi.

Epilogue

La Vivaldi, as Anna Girò is today also known in Venice, enjoys many more years of stage success. Paolina lived just long enough to see the wedding between Anna and Count Antonio Maria Zanardi Landi. She knew her daughter would be in good hands.

The pregnancy was complicated and labour has gone on far too long. A baby boy, too weak to survive, dies minutes after birth. His tiny lifeless body lies next to the bed in the crib that for months has awaited him. Against the spotless white linen shroud in which he has been wrapped, flames his red halo of hair. Precisely two years after her marriage, Anna is to follow her mother to the grave. Unable to recover from the delivery, the singer develops a hallucinating fever that lasts days and will not subside. At last, her breath fails and she succumbs.

In 1765 Empress Maria Theresa, her hold on power now firmly established, appoints Duke Giacomo Durazzo as her ambassador in Venice. This avid music collector now grasps the chance to get his hands on an enormous library of works by Antonio Vivaldi. The name is one he remembers only vaguely, but precisely because the composer is largely unknown he can buy the works very cheaply. A bargain!

Durazzo passes the final years of his life in his birthplace, Genoa, and during his time there more or less sorts and bundles all the works by the Venetian composer. Up until Durazzo's death, however, not a note of it is played; the manuscripts simply lie stored meticulously in his library.

His heir, the Marquis Durazzo, later donates half the collection to the monastery of *San Martino* in Monferrato. It is thanks to Professor Alberto Gentili of the National Library of Turin that, in 1930, the collection is ultimately reassembled in its entirety. During a specially organised 'Vivaldi Week', held in Sienna in 1939, a selection of Don Vivaldi's music is brought back to life after nearly two hundred years in obscurity.

Alberto Gentili, however, is not to witness this festive resurrection. New anti-Semitic laws, introduced by Mussolini the previous year, have by now excluded and closed the Jews off from the rest of society.